Knight of The Dove

By William A. Kooiker

Knight Of The Dove

Published by
Kerlak Enterprises, Inc.
Kerlak Publishing
Memphis, TN
www.kerlak.com

ISBN: 0-9788777-6-4
ISBN 13: 978-0-9788777-6-7
Library of Congress Control Number: 2007941728
First Printing: 2007

Special thanks to everyone at Kerlak Publishing for all the encouragement and assistance.

This book is printed on acid free paper.

Printed in the United States of America

To Mom and Dad.

Acknowledgements

As always, my wife, Heather, deserves my endless appreciation for her ceaseless encouragement, as well as my daughter, Aubrie, for making each day of my life a little brighter. I also want to thank Carol and Pip for always being there. Additional gratitude goes to the following people: Rick and Tracey Ridpath, Kevin Carlson, Brian G. Murray, and everyone at Tussing who makes me feel at home each and every day. Finally, a special thanks to Allan Gilbreath for his wonderful assistance in putting this project together.

Contents

A Dove Before Dawn

The vultures circling the sky instantly told the rider something had gone terribly wrong. He pulled his aging mare to a halt and gazed at the foul beasts above, filtering the evening sun with their black squalor. There were many; almost two dozen. The man scowled and urged his mount ahead, gingerly leading it past the boughs of adjacent trees and into the clearing beyond. At his arrival, a handful of vultures took to the air, squawking angrily at his intrusion.

A gruesome scene, but the rider showed no surprise. He had seen it before. The massacre of these wagons was no different than others he'd come across recently. Taking a sip from his waterskin, he cursed the dead travelers for their stupidity. Passing caravans were not safe on the Border Road, and that fact had become increasingly more evident in the past few months. The narrow dirt pass weaved directly between two intense rivaling kingdoms, and anyone upon it was considered fair game. Roradith, the kingdom to the east, demonstrated an aggressive stance, and used their black-walled border fortress, Erdoth, as a vessel to raid every convoy which came along, regardless of its destination. A harsh cruelty of war, though not one of necessity.

Directing his mount past the loose debris, the rider absorbed every detail. Both wagons had been damaged and overturned, and all goods of value stolen. Three caravan guards lay in awkward angles over the dark stained dirt, their pathetic armor shredded and torn. A young man in his teens leaned against a wagon, his body pierced with arrows. Near him rested an older man, the boy's father perhaps, with a massive hole in his back, the edges crusted thick with dried blood. Various other bodies lay strew about the area as well. One woman lay motionless on her back, her lifeless eyes gazing upwards to the sky. The rider didn't want to dwell on what they had done to her.

1

Warily, the man inspected the scene. Judging by the freshness of the corpses, this butchery happened no more than a day ago, yet he had no need to feel anxious or fearful. The men who'd done this heinous act were long gone, and though most items of worth had departed with them, the rider sought anything salvageable.

After several minutes, his patience proved rewarding. A rusted pickaxe lay harmless in the dirt, its handle unbroken. He gazed at the tool from his mount and gave the faintest smirk. With a little work he could make the blade good as new.

Leaping off his mare, he knelt down and grasped the pickaxe, turning it over in his hands. Satisfied, he hooked the object to his belt and had nearly returned to his horse when something caught his eye. An overturned crate, half-hidden amid the wreckage, had a peculiar, snake-like object coming from beneath it. Squinting against the low-hanging sun, he moved carefully toward the modest looking container. Drawing near, he realized it was a leg, small and motionless. A hint of sorrow took him. Even the children are not spared, he reflected with a dour shake of his head.

Lifting the crate from the lifeless body, he was momentarily taken aback. A small girl, no more than six winters, lay on her stomach, her tresses matted across her face. But what struck the man was the color of her hair. The chin-length locks were *white!* Not a light blonde, but sheer white, like the wool of sheep. The man had never seen anything like it, and strangely, her loss saddened him greater. He wondered how much brutality the young girl suffered before her death. Gritting his teeth, he forced the mournful thought from his mind, yet as he continued to gaze upon the small body, something else occurred to him.

Where were her wounds?

The child's purple gown was muddy and stained, but it shown no evidence of harm, nor did the body it covered. The man knelt and gently turned the girl over. Her front side appeared the same, utterly untouched. Quickly, he thrust two fingers against the side of her neck, feeling for a pulse. Gods, she was alive! How had they missed her? The Roradith warriors never left survivors.

Had she fainted and then the crate fallen atop her, hiding her from view? Even so, the black army was always thorough and systematic in their destruction. It seemed impossible that a small girl could have escaped.

The man drew away the tangled ivory hair that covered her face. Innocent features gripped him, her closed eyelids giving the girl a calm, serene look. Still, something else dwelled within her; something the man couldn't place; yet it made her appear strong and defiant. He was immediately drawn to her.

Abruptly, the girl stirred and softly moaned, "Father?"

"Your father is dead, child." the man answered. But if she had heard him, she gave no response.

Placing his arms beneath her petite body, he hoisted the girl upon his shoulder and silently turned back toward his horse.

Twenty years later

"We are ready, Captain. The troop is eager to be off."

Amaria nodded. "Where is Royce?"

"On his way," the foot soldier stated, his spear at his side. "He should arrive shortly to see you."

"Very well. Get the men in formation. We depart as soon as I see Royce off."

The soldier bowed low. "Yes, Captain."

Amaria watched the lieutenant hurry away toward the soldiers awaiting him. Over the past day, she'd discovered she was just as eager to proceed as her men. For many years she had waited to undertake this particular march, and the sudden reality of it was difficult to fathom.

Glancing down at her platemail, the woman adjusted her pauldrons. The silver armor had been specifically fitted for her elegant, yet durable physique. She was beauty, grace, and power rolled into one; or at least, that was what her husband flattered her with at every opportunity. Hanging atop her platemail, from the front side of her shoulders down to her knees, a sturdy crimson cloth gently flapped, a magnificent looking white dove embroidered at the breast. Draped across her back was a flowing red mantle, also imprinted with the same exquisite dove symbol.

With a patient sigh, the woman took a moment to breathe the morning air. A soft mist hung languidly over the regiment of soldiers, bestowing them a sense of newness. The men had been awake for only an hour, but all were in high spirits, and hope laid firmly in their minds.

The sounds of hooves on cobble jerked her attention from the placidity of her surroundings. Two men, both atop strong russet geldings, approached her.

One of the men swung down from his horse and immediately greeted Amaria with a jovial grin. "Ah, there be my beautiful wife! It is a fine morning, is it not, milady."

Amaria couldn't help but smile. Royce had that affect on her. A tall, muscular rake with jet-black hair curled inward at the temples, his clean-shaven smile seemed ever present and there was nary a time his humor didn't sit upon the tip of his tongue. In sturdy leather garments, Royce ambled toward his wife and fell overdramatically to one knee.

"I am at your service, o' Knight of the Dove. Command me."

Amaria stifled a laugh. "Get up, Royce. Are you drunk?"

Royce stood at once, "Is that an invitation?"

Shaking her head, Amaria wiped a strand of ivory white hair from her face. "Hardly. How are your preparations?"

Royce gestured behind himself to the other man, still atop his mount. "As always, Jorg and I are always ready at a moments notice."

Amaria scrutinized Jorg with piercing emerald eyes. He was a thin, wiry fellow with a jagged scar over his left brow and a perpetual twist to his mouth. He'd aided Royce on several ventures previous, and had proven himself a capable and trusted companion. Still, Amaria felt uneasy, for she could never relax when Royce put himself in danger. Gazing at her husband, she pleaded, "Must you be the one to scout? Erdoth Fortress is a dangerous place."

Her husband could only nod, his expression a mixture of confidence and sympathy. He understood her concerns all too well, for he endured identical feelings each time she went to battle. "That is why you send the best, milady."

Amaria nodded submissively. "Yes, I know. But promise me that I will see you at the encampment."

"I promise." Royce tenderly kissed her on the lips. "I am already looking forward to it." Swinging on his heel, he returned to his horse and motioned to Jorg. "Come my friend, we must be leaving." Turning back to his wife, he called, "I will see you at noon in two days, my sweet Amaria!" With those words, the two horses pounded off, leaving a pocket of dust and a wistful Amaria watching them until they disappeared.

Drawing her attention from her husband, she turned to the line of men awaiting her. One hundred and fifty soldiers, mostly footmen with a handful of elite on horses, awaited her. She ambled near the face of the procession, her visage grim and resolute. Whatever qualms the troop had over their superior officer being a woman had been quelled years ago. It was well understood that she could best three or four of them at a time if forced to. Indeed, right from the onset of her time in the military, eight years ago, her battle-prowess had been proven extraordinary. Some even whispered that she had magical talents; though no proof of such a claim existed. Her colorless hair had granted her the title of "Knight of the Dove," but many called her the "Dove of the Gods." It was an identity she accepted with no objection.

Taking a lead position before the regiment, she mounted her white stallion and motioned her lieutenants into action. The column of soldiers commenced a gradual march that would last for two days.

When the door banged, Meran nearly dropped his book in shock. There hadn't been a visitor at his cottage for over a year, and certainly not one past nightfall. Carefully placing the tome down upon the desk, he reached for his cane, and amid a chorus of grunts, pushed himself up from the chair. His joints ached with age, and his steps to the door were slow and deliberate. Draped from a clasp on the adjacent wall, a rusted sword waited for him. Snatching the weapon with his free hand, he examined the chain lock that would only allow the door to open a half-foot. After he insured it was properly fastened and felt content with his safety, he cracked the portal open.

"Meran, you old fool! Let me in!"

A wide smile crossed the old man's face as he quickly undid the chain and threw open the door. Amaria, in full regalia, stepped into the entryway and embraced him warmly.

"Careful, child," Meran grumbled within her strong grasp, "these bones are not as sturdy as they once were." Following one final squeeze, Amaria released her grip and grinned devilishly. Meran, taking several large breaths, stepped back and looked her over, taking in every detail; her face, her hair, her armor. "So," he muttered with feigned self-pity, "the old man gets a visit."

Amaria laughed. "And why not? You saved my life once."

"No, child. The gods saved your life. I merely found you."

The woman shrugged. "Regardless, you are the reason I have become what I am." In some small sense, her words spoke truth. As soon as Meran had discovered Amaria in that fateful clearing on the Border Pass twenty years earlier, he had fathered her. Not long after, he began to witness the girl's extraordinary abilities, including a couple of phenomenons he could never hope to explain. When she turned sixteen, he made the arduous decision to part with his adopted daughter and take her to the city of Dhorn-Dyas where she could train to become part of the Illidor military. She still visited him on occasion, and sometimes Meran wondered if those brief visits were the only thing that kept him alive.

"You look as immaculate as ever, child." The old man stated simply, gazing at her unblemished face.

"I wish I could say the same for you." Amaria's humor had left her voice, for Meran's bearing no longer resembled the broad and vigorous man she recalled from her childhood, but rather that of a weak and wilted elder. His once thick hair was nothing more than thin silver wisps that fell to his shoulders, and countless wrinkles lined his face. "Father, you cannot live here any longer. Your body weakens. Even you must admit that. Let me bring you back to Dhorn-Dyas where someone can care for you."

Meran shook his head. "I have lived in this house for forty years. Age will not force me to leave. I shall die here happy and content." The old man turned away and quickly changed the subject. "Are you thirsty? I have no ale, but there is fine ginger mead I can offer."

Amaria declined with a wave of her hand while she found her way inside, taking a seat on a padded wooden divan. The interior of Meran's home was dark, but warm and cozy. Only a single lighted candle atop the desk added to the light given by the fireplace. When the old man finished pouring himself a glass, he gingerly eased his way back into his rocker. The candle flickered next to him and cast a bizarre glimmer of shadow about the room.

"So," Meran asked after a hearty gulp, "what brings you my way?"

"I have brought a contingent of men," Amaria stated as she leaned back with arms folded. To Meran, her emerald eyes seemed to sparkle in the firelight. "Our campsite is but a half-hour southwest from here. We have come to conquer Erdoth Fortress."

The comment caused Meran to raise an eyebrow. "Truly? How many men do you have?"

"One hundred and fifty."

The old man nearly choked on his drink. "One hundred and fifty? Have you lost your mind? You will be routed!"

"A second regiment, with an additional four hundred men and siege equipment is to meet us in two days. They come from the northern road. Together, we will empty those black walls."

Meran stroked his delicate, gray facial hair. A look of contemplation draped his features. Eventually he spoke, his voice soft and poignant. "And thus, the Knight of the Dove finally seeks her vengeance for a deed long past." He sighed deeply. "The destruction of Erdoth will not bring back your family."

The woman shot to her feet, her fists clenched. "Do not involve my family in this, Meran! It is a military operation. I have been given orders from Ser Darus himself to lead an army to overthrow Erdoth Fortress. It has been a thorn in the side of

Illidor for years!"

"Really?" Meran lowered his cup, placing it next to his book. "I've not seen an army come from that stronghold in ten years. Even their garrison dwindles. I would be surprised if three hundred men manned those ancient black walls now. The war has passed this area by, child."

"War passes nothing by, Father. When we stand over the fallen forces of Erdoth, it will be a victory."

Meran drew aging hazel eyes to the fire. The radiance of the flames prominently displayed the ever-deepening creases above his cheekbone. "Whose victory, child? Illidor's, or your own?"

The two horses twisted their way through the underbrush as hanging branches and leaves lapped across their faces. With silent stealth, Royce led the way, directing his gelding over dried pine needles and coiled flora. Jorg followed closely behind, his deep-set eyes constantly darting back and forth into the dark places between trees. The forest granted many obstacles to travel through, but it also provided excellent cover for the two men as they mapped the area and marked the defenses surrounding Erdoth Fortress.

From the west, a single wide road, cutting through the expanse of trees, led to the black-walled stronghold, and the woods proved to be an effective natural defense. A large army could not pass through the dense forest, and thus their approach along the road was easily spotted. Also, the wood almost single-handedly eliminated the possibility of Erdoth getting flanked from opposite sides.

Even so, Royce had been surprised at the lack of defensive measures taken. He concluded that Erdoth expected no offensives in the near future, and the notion made him smile, for Amaria would lead no common siege. Slinking along the shadows of the undergrowth, he counted only two guardposts along the road, both of them manned by a single soldier. They spotted two additional patrols, which they easily avoided by simply hiding away. Amaria had instructed them not to engage the enemy, and Royce always took her words to heart.

It was early evening, and the slanted rays of sunlight had difficulty penetrating the thick shield of vegetation. Royce took a moment to scan the area, absorbing every detail. He would enjoy planning a scheme of attack with Amaria. The fortress should prove a great challenge, but the satisfaction always matched the severity of the trial.

"Let us move closer to the walls, Jorg. I wish to see the balustrades," Royce directed.

Jorg grunted a response and steered his gelding behind Royce's lead. After twenty minutes of maneuvering through the flora they began to notice the tall black barrier slowly rise above them. Both men felt a sense of unnatural foreboding, and even the jacket of trees could not hold back the menacing gloom that emanated from the dark spectacle. The walls rose from the ground like a giant vertebral pillar holding the earth together, and for long moments, both men only stared at the monstrous barricade.

In time, Jorg found words. Clearing his throat, he whispered, "Let us make this quick. We have already gained enough information, and we place ourselves in needless danger."

Royce nodded. "Agreed, friend. We've seen enough."

Abruptly, a twig snapped near them. The two scouts swung their heads in time to see a dozen soldiers emerge from behind a thicket of bramble. On the opposite end, another dozen appeared, surrounding them. In their shock, both men nearly froze. Royce threw a glance at Jorg, silently asking; *How did we not notice them?* Jorg gave him no response.

One soldier wearing an open-faced helm coupled with black plate, and carrying a sword, stepped forward and announced, "Halt! You tread on restricted land. Step down from your mounts and be forthwith with your identities!"

"Please forgive us, sir," Royce implored with a humbled voice. "We are mere travelers that have become lost in these woods. Perchance you can direct us to the nearest road?" He flashed a charming smile.

Several men drew bows as the same soldier spoke again, his manner gruff and uncompromising. "You have been instructed to dismount."

Royce glanced at Jorg, speaking with his eyes, and then dropped his feet to the ground. "I have my papers of identity right here." He fumbled in his pockets as he neared the lead soldier. In one sudden movement, Royce's blade was freed from its hardened leather scabbard. Once he drew his weapon, he'd surrendered his life, but it mattered little, for he was dead already. The black army left no survivors, and he only hoped to distract them long enough to allow Jorg to escape. With startling boldness, he drove the weapon into the unprotected abdomen of the astonished soldier.

Because his attention focused on his enemies, Royce didn't see Jorg's gelding turn sharply and sprint into the woods. He also never saw the arrow slice the air and pierce through the back of Jorg's neck, dropping the man instantly.

Royce had cut down a second foe when an arrow planted itself into his back. He felt the pain, but he fought on, ducking the stab of an opponent's spear and lifting his own sword into the man's shoulder. His enemy lurched backwards, but another came at him from his flank, sending a blade into Royce's thigh. The scout screamed aloud and whirled his sword at the attackers head, hoping to decapitate him. Unfortunately, the man had already backed away. Royce pursued him when something extraordinarily hard slammed across his head.

His world swam for several seconds before fading into blackness.

Royce awoke, discovering himself supported by two men. His head pounded in agony, but he managed to lift it enough to view his surroundings. He was in a large hall surrounded by several black armored soldiers. Bright braziers covered the walls, and the light hurt his aching eyes. Directly in front of him, on a greystone throne, sat a particularly imposing figure dressed in the same black armor, but wearing a closed helm that had several spikes jutting upward and to the sides. Alongside him, standing at his right hand, lingered a smaller man, stooped in stature and wearing a hooded black robe.

"It is good to see you awake," the man on the throne stated. His voice was sepulchral, like the wind upon dead leaves. "You almost missed your sentence."

Royce coughed but said nothing. *By the gods, his head hurt!*

"Welcome, I am Harash, Lord of Erdoth," the figure continued. He pointed to the man next to him. "This is Vairees, my advisor. Now, if you would be so kind as to introduce yourself and inform us who you work for. Perhaps, I may spare you."

"I'll say nothing," Royce muttered, shaking the cobwebs from his throbbing temples.

With the barest tilt of his helm, Harash proffered, "Is that so? I would ask your companion, but—" a body was thrown to the floor in front of Royce. Jorg's body, his throat opened like a ripe fruit. "He seems speechless at moment." A chuckle escaped the man's headgear.

"Jorg!" Royce yelled, forgetting the pain in his head. "You godsbedamned bastard! Amaria Eversvale will tear out your heart!" Royce regretted the words the instant he said them. Silently, he scolded himself for his impetuous outburst.

Although his face could not be seen behind his helmet, Harash seemed to be smiling. "Well, that was easier than expected. Amaria Eversvale." Harash lifted an arm and rested his chin inside his palm. "'The Knight of the Dove.' Yes, I have heard of her. So that is who sent you. How interesting."

Royce said nothing more. He closed his eyes and lowered his head in apathy. He had failed his love.

Harash seemed to contemplate the situation. For several seconds, only silence pervaded. Then he stood and pointed a gauntleted finger to the lifeless body of Jorg. "Tie the dead one to a horse and send him back where he came from."

"What of the other one, lord?" Vairees, the man in the black robes, asked.

The armored lord stepped down from the dais and stood mere inches from the limp Royce. "Cut off his hand, the one with the rings, and send it along with the other man. Then hang him at the front walls."

Royce's eyes opened like saucers. "What? You . . ." His words were cut off by the fist that hammered into his check. Pain coursed through him as he sagged within the arms of the two men that held him. His lip had been split open and he tasted the torrent of blood which came forth. With no hesitation, his two retainers placed his arm on a thick wooden stand that seemed far too convenient to be present.

Things suddenly moved too fast. An oversized, shirtless man entered the hall holding an axe. Royce could only manage a whimper as the man advanced, his menacing axe blade glinting in the light of the braziers. Then he stood next to him. Royce tried to struggle, but his body would not respond. He forced his head upward, and stared into eyes as impassive as stone.

Royce garnered only a baleful smile before the axe was lifted high in the air.

The disk of light, in its full luster, shone powerfully in the star laden sky. Amaria lay upon her bedroll and had nearly fallen asleep when an officer woke her with urgent words.

"Captain! A horse approaches!"

In mere moments she stood on her feet. "A horse? Take me to it."

"This way, Captain." Amaria, wearing loose fitting cloth garments, followed the officer to the edge of camp where a handful of additional soldiers gazed into the night. She stepped alongside them and followed their line of vision. A horse trotted gradually toward them. They could hear its heavy panting, and it was obvious that the animal had run a great distance.

"Stay here," Amaria ordered the men. "Rhen, with me." The officer nodded and followed on Amaria's heels as she approached the exhausted beast. When she noticed a man on its back, she ran. The body had been tied firmly to the horse, each arm and leg bound with rope wrapped around the animal's underside. Amaria's heart dropped to her stomach, and without hesitation she moved to identify the body.

It was Jorg. The man was clearly dead, his neck twisted and disfigured. At first, Amaria breathed a sigh of relief. It wasn't

Royce. But then a different dread consumed her. The two men never separated when scouting. What then, pray tell, had happened to Royce?

"Look," Rhen pointed, "there is a leather bag knotted around his arm." The officer withdrew a dagger and sliced through the thin cord holding the bag to Jorg's corpse.

Amaria took the container from Rhen and proceeded to untie it. Reaching inside, the woman grasped a strange object. It felt spongy and mawkish in her fingers, and as she withdrew it, she understood why. A cry of shock escaped her, and with equal mixtures of astonishment and revulsion, she dropped the ghastly object to the ground.

"Hells!" cried Rhen. "What is it?"

Amaria could only stare. Bile formed in her throat, and it was all she could do to keep from vomiting. Turning her head, she looked away and somehow managed to form words. "It is a hand," she croaked. "Royce's hand."

"Royce's?" Rhen shook his head aggressively in disbelief. "How can you be sure?"

"The rings. Those are his," she paused, then added, "and *our* wedding ring."

Rhen couldn't take his eyes off the abhorrent image before him. With a quivering mouth he spoke slowly, each word emphasized, "By the seven hells!"

Amaria turned on her heel. "There is nothing more I need to see." Her emotions were spinning out of control, and she couldn't think straight. Without another word, she walked away. Rhen did nothing to stop her, just as he shouldn't have. He was smart enough to understand he could never quell the pain and shock she felt.

Soon after, she strolled near her bedroll, left alone to her ailing thoughts. No one had consoled her. It was all like some horrifying dream, and yet questions lingered in her mind. Was Royce still alive? Could she save him? Anger rose within her, and her path became clear.

Digging in her rucksack, she withdrew a small piece of parchment and a quill pen. The woman inked the paper intently, her wording lucid and meticulous. When Amaria finished, she rerolled the parchment and sealed it shut. Then, with ultimate precision, she began to don her armor. The thick steel felt empowering on her body, and her nerves began to tingle in anticipation. As she finished, she slung her quiver of arrows over her shoulder and did the same with her bow. Lastly, she tied her sword belt around her slim waist and mounted her white stallion.

Amaria took one final look around the encampment. A few men watched her, but none moved. They probably think I am merely riding off to remedy my aggrieved emotions, she mused. It didn't matter. Nothing mattered except the fury that burned inside.

Urging her stallion hard, she was soon sprinting past a thicket of trees and into an open plain. The darkness of night fed her; fueled her. She covered ground at breakneck speed, the sounds of the world around her, wind and wildlife, falling upon deaf ears. Her thoughts centered upon what lie ahead. In time, she came to a winding brook, and she followed the path of the trickling water until it emerged upon her destination; a small grove. She could just barely see the little cottage hidden within the copse of scratchwoods. Nearing the front door, she dismounted and banged her fist upon it as she had done only a day earlier.

Several minutes passed before she heard the scuffling of feet and the shifting glow of a lantern from within. The door creaked open and pensive eyes peered out. "Damn you, Amaria! Must you never visit me during the day? It is the middle of the night!" When she heard the latch come loose, she roughly pushed her way inside.

"Let me do the talking, Father. I have little time."

The irritation on Meran's face vanished. His visage turned serious as he looked upon Amaria, for her expression was one the old man had never seen before. A coldness had overtaken her. "What is it, child?"

"Erdoth has claimed Royce." Her voice was strangely unemotional.

Meran's eyes widened. "What? How has this happened?"

"I sent Royce ahead to scout the fortress. Only his severed hand returned, still wearing the rings he wore."

The old man breathed deep before making a slow path to his chair. He sat with his eyes fixed on the floor and his head shaking sadly. "That is terrible news, child. I am sorry." He had met Royce on two separate occasions, and like most people, had instantly taken a liking to the man's charm and humor.

Amaria had not moved from her place in the entryway. "I am going to Erdoth tonight."

Meran looked up and gazed into her malachite eyes; eyes aloof and distant. "Alone? You will never survive!"

"I do not plan to." Amaria paused momentarily, finding the correct words. "Father, I have come here for two reasons. The first is to say goodbye. The second is to hear from you a promise."

The old man had only half-heard her last statement. He was still absorbing her intentions with repudiation. "Amaria, do not do this," he pleaded. Tears began to descend his somber face. "Are you so ready to forfeit your life?"

Lifting her palm, Amaria said, "It is too late for persuasion. My mind is set." The woman stepped toward her adopted father. "I want you to move to Dhorn-Dyas, to live out the rest of your life in comfort. It is my dying wish." Plunging her hand into the pack hanging at her waist, she pulled out the rolled document and held it before him. "I have written a request that you be allowed to take residence in my quarters. My home is secure, and you will be well cared for."

"Too many reminders." Meran could barely choke the words out. He ran a trembling hand through thinning hair. "It will be a solemn existence."

For the briefest of moments, warmth shone from Amaria, and she placed an arm around the old man's shoulder, squeezing lightly. "It will make your daughter happy. That alone should give you peace." Then, quickly as it had come, the tenderness was gone. She withdrew her arm and straightened her posture. "There is no time to argue this matter. Will you give me your oath, or will you deny your own daughter's final request?"

Meran buried his head in his hands. "Revenge is a useless deed. You will gain no fulfillment."

She dropped the parchment in his lap and moved to the door. "I am beyond such advice, Father. Will you move to Dhorn-Dyas?"

"I promise, child. But I will never rest easy."

The seneschal stood at the entrance to Lord Harash's personal chamber. His cloth garments were spotless, and not a wrinkle could be found in the matted fabric. When Harash turned to view him, the servant dropped to a knee and lowered his head.

"What is it?" Harash asked impatiently. Not wearing his armor, the lord dressed himself in a simple leather jerkin with long pants. His face bore uneven facial hair and a copious brow hung over dark eyes. Long brown hair fell in knotted strands over his face, but the skin beneath was white and pallid. His bare arms displayed thick cords of muscle.

"Milord, a rider approaches from the west road."

Harash raised an eyebrow. "A rider? For what purpose?"

The seneschal twiddled his thumbs nervously. "War, milord. It is a woman. She has already killed four men stationed along the pass. A fifth escaped to warn us."

Harash's jaw nearly dropped to the paneled wooden floor. *The Knight of the Dove! Alone!* The Lord of Erdoth Fortress stared at his servant for a full minute, his mind spinning in deliberation. Abruptly, he turned from the seneschal and ambled to a chestnut armoire. "Prepare the defenses. All of them," he spoke as he withdrew his black platemail. "Oh, and have the fifth soldier executed for fleeing from a woman."

The full moon shown absolute in its brilliance. Glowing shafts of silver bathed the shadows below, lighting up the nighttime world. Had Amaria taken the time, she would have reveled in the serenity. However, the grimness of her deeds had taken the forefront of her mind.

The tall gates of Erdoth loomed just ahead, and she could already hear the high-pitched whistle of arrows as they rained from the parapets. Though still upon her stallion, she slung her bow in hand and fired one arrow after another toward the archers above. Even in the dimly lit night, she saw two bodies fall and land motionless onto the unforgiving earth. Still, more arrows cascaded around her, but in fewer number, and the five guards standing before the lowered portcullis drew her attention. She shot down three of them before they had time to react. The last two took cover behind trees until she'd gotten close enough to combat.

Leaping from her white horse, Amaria tossed her bow aside and unleashed her sword. She felled one guard immediately, but the last managed to parry her twice with his halberd before her shining blade sliced him cleanly from shoulder to hip. As she pulled the weapon loose, an arrow bounced harmlessly off the pauldron protecting her shoulder. She looked skyward to count the archers still firing at her.

Then she saw him.

From a rope, ten feet in the air, dangled a familiar looking body. Amaria went numb with fear. Let it not be him! Oh gods, please! Overcome with tension, she pulled a dagger from her boot and flung it in the air. The small blade cut the rope cleanly, and the limp form crashed roughly to the ground, becoming still in a graceless angle. She fell upon the body, quickly turning the neck to discern the figure's identity.

Sorrow took her. It was Royce. A stump resided where his left hand should have been, and his face was mangled, evidence that he was badly beaten before his hanging. She lifted his body up, cradling him as a mother would a babe. *Gods, no!* She pressed her face into the crown of his head, letting her tears dampen his already brittle hair. As she mourned, an arrow hit the ground not two feet away, pitching loose dirt against her body.

The flames of anger consumed her. She drew within herself, to her inner core, basking in its rage. Then she called upon the forces that mortals feared. It started as a simple hum from her mouth, but quickly escalated into shouts. Although her words were indecipherable to any who listened, those same words carried more power than one could imagine. The woman didn't even understand their meaning, but they flowed from her mouth with ease. "Gods of the sky, the earth, far beneath. Wyur, Carodon, Hysth, Kazgoth, I call upon you!" Amaria took a moment to peer above. An hour, perhaps two, before dawn returned the colors of the world. Balling her fists, she screamed, "Before the crest of the sun rises, grant me the deaths of those responsible! Let their bodies rot while darkness still rules the sky! Grant me power. Give me reprisal for this injustice!"

Amaria sensed it, felt the energy flicker, then set wholly ablaze. She had always been a highly skilled warrior, but the force she suddenly endured only multiplied her talents. In no way could she understand what was happening to her, but she had no desire to understand. She was overcome, she was powerful; she was death.

Stepping up to the barred portcullis, she calmly placed her hand upon it. The solid iron bars shattered apart, creating a space for her to walk though. Up ahead, the courtyard became a flurry of activity as the black armored army witnessed the miraculous act. The legion of troops rushed her as she stepped inside.

Again she raised her hand, and a column of fire erupted from her palm. A dozen soldiers were consumed by flames, their screams horrific as their bodies burned to ashes. But she had no time to revel in the victory, for other soldiers were upon her. They fanned out, surrounding the woman, and Amaria's blade flashed as she swung it in resistance. The ring of opponents collapsed as she went at them fearlessly. Feigning her body to the left, she rolled right and plunged her weapon into the abdomen of a surprised foe, then did likewise to a second after ducking a spear thrust. She was a whirling menace, the speed of her attacks supernatural.

Three more succumbed to her aggression before an opponents' sword slipped past her defense and thrust its way into the unprotected flesh beneath her ribcage. She punished the offender by severing his head. Though her wound wasn't fatal, it should have brought her immense pain; yet she felt nothing. Adrenaline and vigor governed her nerves.

Vaguely, as if far in the distance, Amaria could hear the shouts and curses of soldiers as they bellowed commands back and forth, but she paid no heed. Her focus was unreserved. She spun back and forth, delivering blow after blow to anyone near her, and the number of bodies at her feet amplified with each passing moment. Her sword was covered in the blood of her enemies. Yet, as the deaths increased, so did her wounds. An arrow had lodged itself in the backside of her upper calf, shifting painfully with each of her rapid movements, and though her armor was strong, it could not completely protect her from the powerful blows of her adversaries. Various gashes and bruises had been acquired, many along her arms and shoulders. Still, she fought on.

As Amaria pulled her sword free from the opened skull of a dead soldier, she suddenly realized that the attack had been broken off. What remained of the opposition had retreated inside the fortress. Others were actually fleeing, exiting the confines of the stronghold through the shattered portcullis. No more archers lined the ramparts, and Amaria was given a moment to gather herself. The courtyard looked like the site of a mass execution, and every corpse bore black platemail. She wondered how much time had passed during her hypnotic rampage. Taking advantage of the moment of clarity, she gathered two daggers lying loose on the bloodied ground, and also a bow and a quiver of arrows. Then she started for the gates which led into the interior of the fortress. Her limp was plainly visible, but Amaria didn't notice.

The gates lie open, like a black mouth enticing her closer; ready to swallow her wholly into some pungent hell. She embraced the feeling and stepped within the blackness.

The interior was cold and dim; the floor, walls, and ceiling; all stone, dreary and unwelcoming. Amaria didn't pause to take in her surroundings. She strode ahead with fortitude, and the four sentries that met her at the entrance were butchered mercilessly for their audacity to stand in her way.

Amaria roamed several twisting corridors and then climbed the first set of stairs she came upon. The woman had no particular destination in mind. Her only goal was to seek the one who murdered Royce. The second level proved very similar to the first. The soldiers foolish enough to confront her died swift deaths, and soon the passages became empty. The only sound was the resonance of her own boots upon the stone, echoing down the wide halls. She was alone.

Amaria ascended yet another flight of stairs, and discovered that two great double doors of solid oak barred her path. She took the iron handle and turned it clockwise. The bolt withdrew with a *click*, and the great doors swung open. Without even a moment's hesitation, she entered.

The chamber was a large sanctuary, with a makeshift throne placed in the center. Along the walls, at perfectly spaced intervals, burned braziers that lighted the area far brighter than any other room she had encountered within the stronghold.

"So, this is the legendary 'Knight of the Dove.'" A fully armored figure lounged upon the gray throne. Next to him, at his right hand, stood a rodent-like man in dark robes. The figure upon the throne spoke with full amusement. "I must admit, you are not looking well. And yet, I find that even in your current state, the myths speak truth, indeed you are stunningly beautiful."

The man's words caused Amaria to finally take a personal inspection of her condition; her face framed by a wild mess of hair and the rest of her covered with wounds. Though only two thin cuts lined her cheekbone, the rest of her body had fared much worse. She bled from several injuries, including an especially nasty lesion just below her collarbone where even her breastplate had been pierced. She understood that soon she would collapse from her blood loss, but she didn't have time to dwell on the fact. Her green eyes stared hatefully at the two men before her.

"That was an impressive display," the armored man said, referring to the battle in the courtyard. "Rarely do I get to observe such fine swordsmanship. Shall we make proper introductions? I am Harash, Lord of Erdoth." He stood from the throne and bowed low.

Amaria took one step forward. "You have murdered my family, and my husband." Her voice was bitter and acrid. "Your name means nothing to me. I have come to serve my vengeance. I have come to see you die."

Harash seemed taken aback. "Vengeance? Perhaps you are mistaken. I know nothing of your family, or this husband you speak of."

"My husband was hanging at your front walls!" Amaria spat.

Harash's voice feigned regret. "Oh my, *that* was your husband? How unfortunate. Had I known, I would never have done such a thing. Let me offer an apology." A bolt of searing light burst from the fingers of the small man standing next to Harash. Amaria had no time to react, and the radiant missile smashed into her torso. She was thrown backwards into the wall, the air knocked out of her lungs. Her sword escaped her grip and clattered to the ground several feet away. Harash released deep laughter and plodded his way toward the gasping woman, the robed man following behind. His voice mocked her. "So foolish. You will suffer for the deaths of my men."

Amaria groaned as she sat up and leaned against the wall. She guessed several ribs had broken, and for the first time since she had entered Erdoth, she suffered pain. Her eyes blurred momentarily, and it took great effort to shake the dizziness from her head. Was it over? Had the war she waged come to an end? She had already killed many. But, then she envisioned Royce swinging from the rope along those coal-black walls, his face distended and misshapen from the beatings. Her anger surged, and she was fueled once again by its embers. Looking upon Harash, she pictured him without his helmet, his eyes pleading for the mercy she would never deliver.

Her task was not yet complete.

Harash halted a few feet away from the downed woman. "Your husband was no man. He whimpered like the weakest of women." Turning to his robed companion, he stated simply, "Burn her."

The spindly man commenced a hypnotic dance, interweaving his arms and legs in an elegant motion as he softly muttered verbal chants. Had it not been intended to do her harm, Amaria mused, the motions would have been beautifully picturesque. As it was, his scrawny hands began to radiate and she knew she had little time for recourse.

Amaria's sword was out of her immediate reach, but she still had the daggers she'd procured from the courtyard massacre. With blinding speed, she seized one from her boot and flung the object at the wizard.

The robed seer's voice arrested in mid-speech, and his hands went instantly to his neck where the small leather handle of the dagger protruded from his throat. A deluge of blood poured down onto his robes, turning them red. With a single twitch of his eyes, he collapsed, dead.

Amaria hadn't watched the gruesome death, for after throwing the dagger, she had rolled to her left, retrieving her sword and swinging for Harash's skull. His blade intercepted the arching path of her own, and the two combatants commenced the solemn dance of war.

Amaria was surprised at the lord's battle prowess and the two parried relentlessly. Only her desire for vengeance kept her going, and their duel spilled from the large sanctuary into a small corridor. At one point, Harash slammed his heavy gauntlet into Amaria's jaw, and as she reeled, he lashed his sword across her shoulder, tearing plate, skin, and tissue. The woman shrieked in pain and stumbled, tripping and falling on the stone floor. Her blood poured a quick decent over her silver armor.

Harash laughed bullishly. "You are weak! I expected more!" With a cry, he brought his blade in low, intending to split the woman's head in two.

Before the weapon made contact, Amaria swayed to her right. The slashing blade just missed, and Amaria spun her head around with her arms, and sword, following. The whirling blade sliced Harash's breastplate, partially caving the thick steel inward. She heard the man grunt as he bent over, and Amaria pulled back her weapon, poised for a second blow. In desperation, Harash leaned in and pushed her away.

The Lord of Erdoth Fortress stepped back to put space

between them. "How do you still fight?" he yelled at her, clutching his side.

Amaria said nothing. The woman moved forward relentlessly, and again their steel embraced.

The sharp ring of colliding swords bounded off the walls as they scuffled, but Harash suddenly found it difficult to stand his ground against the unremitting charge of Amaria. He backpedaled, slipping through a portico that led to a terrace overlooking the courtyard. The stench of death invaded the nostrils of both warriors, but they had no time to notice.

Amaria pressed Harash, taxing the lord's defenses. The balcony was not large, and Harash had no room to flee. With his back against the railing, Amaria thrust her blade at his throat. As Harash lifted his own weapon to parry, she spun her sword and caught her foe on the hands.

The blade bit deep into Harash's wrists, and he lost hold of his weapon. The steel blade fell over the railing, dropping lazily to the ground far below.

With a triumphant smile, Amaria's placed the point of her sword at Harash's throat. "You are beaten. Remove your helmet so I may see your face," she ordered.

Harash fell to his knees. He shook visibly as he lifted the spiked helm from his head. His dark eyes gave way to untainted fear. "Please! I yield!"

"You murdered my family and my husband." Her tone was remorseless. "For that, your punishment is death."

"No!" Harash cried. "I beg you! Spare me! I—"

Amaria's stroke nearly carved his head in two. As she pulled free her weapon, the lifeless body slumped to the ground, crimson fluids expanding beneath.

With that final death, Amaria's task was complete.

As she stared upon the corpse of her last kill, the pain returned all at once. All her power, her anger, her rage; vanished, and she was as vulnerable as a newborn. Exhaling, she dropped her sword. The blade clanged upon the delicate tiles of the balcony while she sat down, her back against the terrace railing. She had accomplished what she came to do. She had slain the entire fortress.

And yet, Meran had been correct, there was only emptiness within her. All became clear, and she realized what she had done. She had failed.

Looking out upon the courtyard, she gazed upon the carnage she had wrought. She betrayed her honor. Her murderous wrath wasn't delivered in defense, nor for the Illidor cause. It had served no purpose but to feed the dark gods with her anger and hatred.

Tilting her head, she viewed her wounds. They were grievous, and she didn't know if she would survive. She no longer cared. Dawn had arrived, and she watched while the sun poked its fiery crest over the horizon. She soaked in its first rays.

As Amaria closed her eyes and allowed herself sleep, she wondered if there would be a chance for her redemption.

Prelude

A tortured soul.

Amaria Eversvale, the *Knight of the Dove*, so called because of the vivid locks of ivory that tapered down her face and the majestic beauty she possessed, knew agony. Like an unyielding decent, she had fallen to its lure, succumbed to its misery.

Once a proud soldier of the Illidor army, her rare gift with a blade was often rumored god-given. Those were joyful times. She had wed the man she loved, and through her magnificent war prowess, many a victory had been scored beneath the crimson Illidor banner. Her triumphs reaped great prestige and honor.

Yet, like the churning tides of the sea, tragedy beset triumph.

So was the case of Amaria Eversvale. It was a gruesome misfortune, her husband beaten and murdered by soldiers from the rivaling Erdoth Fortress, the very same stronghold, ironically, that had ordered the deaths of her real parents so many years before. The madness that consumed her was extraordinary. In her rage, she swore to avenge her husband's death, and that very night rode to Erdoth alone, blood and fury in her eyes.

When dawn arrived, nearly two hundred soldiers lay scattered about the fortress, a veritable graveyard of warriors, all slain by her hand. To harvest her vengeance, she had called upon the dark gods for unnatural strength, forbidden power. Such gods, ever searching for potential profit, had happily obliged, and it was these aberrant abilities through which she routed Erdoth.

And so, on that day, Amaria Eversvale attained justice for her husband, but achieved no peace in her victory, for honor is never attained in madness.

Erdoth's destruction had come with a price, resulting in a miraculous, yet horrific act that would destroy who she was, and leave in its wake a haunted figure consumed with remorse.

Prologue

"Is that spot sufficient, milord?" The man reached upwards, his finger pointing toward a ridge that jetted from the face of the mountain.

Jonathon Barrowswynd inspected the overhanging piece of land for a moment before nodding his approval. "That will do," he said, pulling his cloak tighter around his body to stave off the biting wind. With winter still two months away, the air had grown far colder than expected, and he yearned for the woolen coat he had neglected to bring along. All day, overcast skies had prevented the sun from sending any warmth down upon the mountainside, and Jonathon aggressively rubbed his hands together as he made careful steps up the steep slope that rose before him. In the distance, he could see many peaks rise far higher than the one they were currently treading, and it gave him perspective of just how little distance they had traveled, even after a full day of hiking.

With chilled limbs and face stinging, the ascent was proving far more arduous than he would have preferred. The dismal thought made him doubly thankful that he had hired a guide down in Yhull to lead the way. The small mining settlement sat at the base of the great mountain range known as Urak's Edge, and several of the inhabitants were well versed in the localized area of the rocky landscape. Being Jonathon's first foray up the mountains, and considering the dangerous wildlife that almost certainly lurked among the crags, finding an escort was a necessary move. The nobleman wasn't about to die screaming for mercy whilst some wild beast tore him to shreds.

Unfortunately, hiring an escort hadn't been easy. Jonathon was hesitant to divulge his true intentions, and most prospective guides were dubious about leading a stranger up Urak's Edge without knowing the purpose. But, like so many others,

Jonathon had placated one of them with plenty of coin. *Money is the ultimate persuader,* he mused grimly.

Loose pebble shifted underfoot, causing Jonathon to stumble and land hard on his right knee. The fall was painful, and he cursed angrily as he tried to right himself. His guide, and man named Peran, hurried down to him.

"Are you alright, milord?" Peran fervently brushed off the nobleman's cloak and helped him stand.

"I am fine," Jonathon answered, pulling up his pant leg to view the injury. His knee was skinned and bleeding, but Jonathon merely shrugged and pulled the cloth back over the wound. After he was finished today, a simple scraped knee would mean nothing. "Let us continue. I wish to arrive at our destination before dark."

"Of course, milord," Peran replied, returning to his lead position. Once again, the pair moved over the rutted ground of the mountain. Jonathon limped slightly, but paid little heed to the hindrance, keeping his thoughts squarely on what lie ahead.

Reaching to his waist, the nobleman pulled loose his waterskin and drank deeply. The hazy sky gradually turned grey, and Jonathon realized that darkness would envelop them within a couple of hours. In the fore, the nobleman could see Peran warily scanning his surroundings for danger. Although the stealthy man seemed at home in the roughly hewn environment of the mountains, he didn't appear particularly pleased with the current predicament. For a several seconds, he swiveled his head nervously in all directions.

Suddenly, the man froze. With head crooked, Peran stood motionless for nearly a minute.

"What is it?" Jonathon asked.

Peran looked back at him and brought his finger to his lips, then silently scooted down to where Jonathon stood. Leaning close to the nobleman's ear, he whispered, "Lyzcan. Not far off."

Jonathon's stomach rose to his throat. Lyzcan! Now *that* was an unpleasant surprise! A lyzcan was a gigantic reptile, rare enough that some still claimed it mere legend, despite all the concrete proof of its existence. Though shaped similar to a lizard, the lyzcan was the size of a small horse, and known to attack humans if presented the opportunity. Their chitinous skin, lightning fast speed, and razor sharp teeth made them a formidable foe and killable by only the most skilled warrior or hunter. Stammering fretfully, Jonathon managed to mouth, "What do we do?"

"We wait." Peran gazed off into the trees. "Lyzcans do not linger in one place for long. If it stays unaware to our presence, we are safe."

"How close?"

The guide gave him a careful look. "Very close."

"Can it smell us?"

Peran shook his head. "They smell poorly. They notice movement and noise." Unhooking a handaxe from his belt, Peran placed his free hand upon Jonathon's shoulder and pushed him down upon the stone. "No more talk. Sit still and wait."

For a half-hour they sat against a rocky crevice, anxiously waiting. At any moment, Jonathon expected the lyzcan to scurry into view and devour the both of them with utter ruthlessness. He had no weapons upon him, and he presumed that Peran's hatchet would cause as much damage on a lyzcan as wielding a blade of grass. Yet, despite the danger, Peran seemed a solid mixture of composure and attentiveness. Jonathan took a moment to gaze at his companion. The man was severely balding, but the raven-like hair that grew along the sides and back of his head fell freely to the base of his muscular neck. His facial hair was matted and uneven, his brows dark. Breathing calmly, the man turned to Jonathon and gave him an encouraging nod.

For a brief moment, the nobleman felt a pang of regret. His guide was protecting him, and Jonathon realized the futility of it. *How much I will let this man down!*, he thought.

Without forewarning, Peran leapt to his feet and turned to Jonathon. "Remain here. I will return in a moment."

He disappeared behind a thicket of trees, and for several minutes the nobleman heard nothing. The stillness was broken by the sudden fluttering of wings as a bluebird darted through the trees, nearly causing Jonathon to jump out of his skin in startlement. After cursing the innocent bird to eternal damnation several times over, Peran reappeared, a faint grin across his lips.

"All is clear, milord."

Gingerly, Jonathon rose to his feet. "How did you know the lyzcan was near?"

The guide shrugged. "I could hear it." No further explanation followed, and Peran recommenced his climb up the cliffside.

Jonathon shook his head a moment before falling into step behind his escort. Daylight was vanishing quickly and both men upped their pace. After a full day of trudging uphill through the mountains, Jonathon had grown tired, but Peran assured him they were very close to their destination.

Good to his word, the nobleman suddenly found himself standing upon a grassy plateau that ended in a straight drop-off. Even in the fading light, the view was spectacular. The world extended before them, stretching for miles on end. Far below rested the valley, and Yhull was a mere speck of dust in the expanse of land shadowed by the vast mountains of Urak's Edge.

Peran removed the leather pack from his shoulders and opened it. After some digging, he pulled free two apples and some dried, salted beef. With a hint of sarcasm, he inquired, "Care to dine, milord?"

"Nothing would make me happier. I starve." Jonathon, though not overweight, was not conditioned for such an extensive trek. His days as a nobleman, traipsing though the courts and palaces in his tailored garments, making pointless small talk with others of high esteem, did nothing to prepare him for a day's worth of hiking. Sore joints and aching muscles proved that. Sitting in the grass next to Peran, he groaned in relief.

The guide smiled, declaring, "Very good," and began dealing out the food. With a small knife, he sliced the two apples into bite-sized portions, placing the morsels on two thin wooden slabs that were obviously designed to function as makeshift plates. He then dealt out the salted beef, giving his charge a larger quantity.

"No, no." Jonathon waved a refusing hand. "Up here, you are

an equal. We split the food evenly."

Peran nodded politely and took an extra piece. "As you wish, milord."

"I placed a bottle of wine in that bag," the nobleman added. "Vintage stuff. Let us enjoy it!"

The guide frowned. "Milord? I saw them, but I figured you were saving them for a better occasion."

Jonathon wiped cold sweat from his jawline and ran a hand through his thick auburn hair. "There is no better occasion, my friend. Pull the stopper and let us drink."

Complying without argument, the guide offered the bottle to Jonathon, who took it and drank greedily. When he lowered the drink, he sighed contentedly, small red droplets falling from his clean-shaven chin. "Here, taste."

Peran grasped the glass bottle and took one swig. His eyes lit up. "That is marvelous, milord!"

Jonathon laughed, surprising himself. *When was the last time I did that?*, he wondered. After the last couple weeks, he had almost forgotten what it was like to truly submit to laughter, not when guilt had consumed him so. Turning to Peran, he said, "Yes, my friend, what you drink is as good a wine as you shall likely come across in your lifetime," he stopped a moment, contemplating his words, then added, "and none more expensive. Brought across the Great Sea from Gymon. A bit better than the slog you drink down in Yhull, I reckon."

"Yes, milord, far better. I must admit, I am anxious to see what has made you come up this way."

The smile vanished from Jonathon's face. "I fear I may disappoint you."

Peran had no answer to the nobleman's vague response, and for some time they sat and idly talked, devouring their own share of the food. As the meal come nearer to an end, Jonathon's unease grew more prominent. He began to closely observe the details around him, listening to the occasional bird chirping, or gazing at the greenery that struggled to survive in the cold, unfertile climate. Then he ceased using his eyes, and began to let his mind wander, recalling the thirty-seven winters of his life. He reminisced over his childhood in the large Barrowswynd estates that remained his home today. He remembered the first time he had seen his future wife, her deep blue eyes throwing glances at him from across the dining hall, then quickly looking away in embarrassment when he returned her stares. And his children. *Gods, his children!* He reflected on their young innocence and the overzealous manner in which they hugged him when he returned home each day from his time at the courts. Both Tanya and Erik were, in their own way, spitting images of their mom; Tanya with her sincere smile and tender listening ears, Erik with his thoughtful manner, always seeing what lay past the surface. They would grow to be upright, honorable people. For that, he was certain, and a mental pain gripped him fiercely.

How has it come to this?

They would never understand, never realize that this choice was not his own. He could never explain that circumstances had overcome him, controlled him. His hand had been forced, and there was no way to turn back the sands of time and prevent what was about to happen.

Finishing his last bite, Jonathon stood. His legs were wobbly, not from pain, but from a numbness that began to ensorcel his body. Looking at his guide, the nobleman asked, "Will you be safe up here, tonight?"

Peran raised an eyebrow. "Indeed. One night is not a concern. I have blankets for both of us, and I can gather breakfast in the morning. As long as a predator doesn't catch our scent."

Jonathon nodded absently and turned toward the lip of the plateau. He began making slow, unsteady steps.

"Careful, milord," Peran called behind him. "Do not get too near the edge."

"Worry not. I am fine," Jonathon answered, continuing to the very brink of the rim and only stopping when the tips of his feet brushed the drop-off. The sky had entirely succumbed to night, and the nobleman could see only blackness below him, like a swirling void waiting to draw him near. His breaths were shallow, his legs shaky. *What choice have I?*, he asked, only to himself. His body began to rock ever so gently.

"Milord!" Peran ardently shouted from behind.

The guide's frantic call fell deaf upon Jonathon, for his senses had failed him, shutting down just as he took one final step. His body fell forward, and the black void took him.

PART I

The Freecity of Valgamin

One

Amaria Eversvale gazed ahead at the stone walled city and sighed. Six months of travel had led her to this place; the very end of her exile.

Valgamin was the last populated city before the earth gave way to the mountains of Urak's Edge, or more commonly called, the World's Edge. The giant column of peaks, crags, and rocks was named so because beyond lie nothing but a drab, misty fog; a conundrum to every living soul. Those who had successfully journeyed through the mountains and witnessed the mist proclaimed that the grey film lingered so thick, one couldn't see one's own hands within it. Of course, it was also said that those who entered the void never returned. Amaria doubted the veracity of such tales, but found them intriguing all the same.

As she finished considering the idea of scaling Urak's Edge, her mind returned to its dark shell, the prison of her memories. Such a prison had plagued her relentlessly since the tragic events which changed her life forever. The turning point of her existence had happened a half-year ago, but the visions of that night haunted her as clearly now as ever before.

It was the day she butchered Erdoth Fortress single-handedly.

She had expected to die that day. Her wounds, grievous after such a great battle, had brought her close to death. Yet, she awakened a day later, her fatal wounds strangely healed. She would live; but for what purpose? A depression consumed her, for though her physical state wholly mended, she could never restore the stain upon her soul. And worse, by calling to the dark gods, she had opened herself to their whispers, their temptations. Though try she did, she couldn't close the conduit they now used to snake their way into her psyche. She could deny them, but they were constantly there, goading her subconsciously, luring her with sinister promises.

For her failure, Amaria had banished herself, leaving her kingdom and army behind. After looting the fortress of every coin she could locate, she rode east with no goal, no destination in mind. Unfortunately, rumors seemed to ride the wind faster than she could ride the ground, for everywhere she went, her destruction of Erdoth was already known, and she was celebrated as a hero. For the Knight of the Dove, such praise was bittersweet.

And now, at last, she approached the Freecity of Valgamin, the last city in line as she pursued her redemption. Valgamin, a community built by freelancers and mercenaries, lacked the grandeur of the great municipalities of the western kingdoms. It was built on the principals of practicality, not splendor. Perhaps, she pondered, it would be the perfect place to liberate her dismal existence.

Making a concerted effort to pull her mind from such unpleasant musings, Amaria inspected the walls of the city before her, walls that appeared to have been constructed only recently. On poles, rising up from ramparts above, were several banners shifting lazily in the breeze. Each banner presented the emblem of Valgamin; a plain white sword atop a russet backdrop. Guards peered down from the battlements as she reached the main western gate, and she waited behind two merchant wagons and a company of riders before her turn had come. A sentry approached her white stallion. The man wore simple chain and plate, a spear in his right hand.

"Milady!" the footman said, suddenly taken aback by her ivory white hair. It was a reaction she had grown so accustomed to that she rarely noticed the trifling responses. As the man stared at the tresses that fell past her elegant shoulders, he managed to utter, "Your name, please."

"Amaria Eversvale," she stated.

The guard's eyes opened like saucers. "Amaria Eversvale? You . . . you are the *Knight of the Dove!*" He viewed her silver platemail, examining the azure cloth banner that covered the top, from her front shoulders down to her thighs; a beautifully fashioned dove embroidered at her breast. Down her back was draped a cloak of identical color, complete with the same dove symbol. Once, she had worn a cloak of red, but had since abandoned her old standard following the failure at Erdoth Fortress. She believed she had disgraced the crimson mantle, and had changed to blue in an effort to leave her sorrows behind. Coupling her attire with her stunning, almost unnatural beauty, complete with stark white hair, there was no denying his claim. It took several moments for the man to speak, and when he did, it was through strenuous, insecure stutterings. "It is an honor. I . . . I have heard of your assault on Erdorth Fortress."

Amaria did not smile at the boyish compliment. "So has the rest of the world, it seems." When the guard did not respond, she furthered, "Am I free to pass?"

The man nodded emphatically. "Of course, milady. Enjoy your stay."

Amaria steered her mount forward, then abruptly stopped. Turning incisive emerald eyes back to the guard, she asked, "Have you a recommendation for a decent inn? One that will not run me dry, perhaps."

Thinking for a moment, the guard answered, "The Cardinal and the Jay. It is slightly off the beaten path, but a fine establishment indeed, and it shan't be overcrowded."

"And where shall I find this place?"

The man commenced an elaborate lecture concerning the correct directions, but Amaria quickly conceded in her effort to mentally follow them, deciding it was far easier to simply ask someone inside the city. She offered her thanks to the man and entered the Freecity of Valgamin, called 'the last refuge' by the locals. The large community sat upon unclaimed territory, which meant there was no overruling king to enforce laws upon the populace. Fugitives and renegades, whom had been banished from their own lands, had originally founded it, but word spread quickly and the area became a hotbed for individuals or families that fled unfortunate circumstances and were looking for a new lease on life, or perhaps to continue past transgressions unhampered. To keep some semblance of order to the increasing flow of colonization, a ruling council of five was hastily established, and that extended into the formation of a sizeable city guard to patrol the ever precarious citizens.

Leading her stallion beyond the stone walls, Amaria casually viewed the teeming streets and diverse buildings that bordered the avenues. It was apparent that there had been little or no schematic planning in the layout. The narrow roads, only seven to ten feet wide, twisted aimlessly, showing no cohesiveness or pattern. The city must have expanded extremely fast, for there were several instances of fine, well-maintained establishments neighbored directly by buildings that appeared terribly neglected, or deserted altogether. Such rapid growth had obviously given the contractors and builders no time to establish regional zoning districts. The whole area seemed a mass cluster of unrestrained energy and confusion, with only the city guard to combat the chaos.

Amaria selected a street at random, riding slowly as she absorbed every detail of the city that sprawled before her. Businesses pressed tight against the tapered roads, vying to win prospective customers from their competition. The stench was similar to any other city she had encountered, animal dung and garbage mingled with the sweeter aromas of a passing woman's perfume or nearby cooking from a bakery or residence. A passing waft of fresh bread caused her stomach to growl, and her hunger grew rapidly.

Squinting in the bright afternoon sun, she curiously viewed the bustling crowds. Most traffic was on foot, and the sheer variety of inhabitants was stunning; artisans, soldiers, merchants, beggars, housewives, mercenaries, laborers, nobles; none seemingly identical in skin color or attire worn. Indeed, Valgamin was proving to be the world's centerpiece of diversity. Choosing someone to ask directions to *The Cardinal and the Jay*, or any inn for that matter, would not prove difficult.

After two futile queries, the third person, a young male laborer obviously taken by Amaria's appearance, pointed her in the right direction. A subsequent follow-up to a city guardsman found her gazing upon the building that called itself *The Cardinal and the Jay*. The structure was nondescript; a two-story, timber post-and-beam building with no ornamentation to speak of, save for the sign that hung below the awning on hinges. Upon the slab of wood revealed a remarkably well-done painting of a nested red cardinal gazing upward at a blue jay in flight, an egg gripped within the fleeing bird's small beak. The hinges groaned as the sign swung lightly in the cool breeze.

Flanking the establishment on the right was the hostel's stable, an open-faced canopy that had room for four, perhaps five, animals. Currently, only one stall was filled, and its occupant appeared to be a donkey.

A stable boy hustled to Amaria as she dismounted. After removing her saddlebags, she handed over the reins and said sternly, "Guard him with your life, boy. Not only is he worth plenty of coin, but I have a personal attachment to him. I'll see that you are well rewarded if he is properly cared for."

The boy was taken aback by Amaria's gruff words, which completely contradicted her physical elegance. He stared open-eyed for several seconds before nodding and stammering, "Yes, milady."

As he turned to lead the horse to the stable, Amaria seized his arm. Her grip was uncommonly strong, and the boy slightly cowered, thinking she was to berate him. Reaching into her belt pouch, Amaria pulled free two gold scepters and placed the coins in the servant's hand.

The boy's jaw dropped, and Amaria grinned inwardly. No doubt the value was more than the lad would likely make in a full month's worth of labor. If nothing else, that should keep him faithful. The servant gave an excessive display of appreciation before taking the great horse into the stable.

Amaria entered the inn, and immediately allowed herself time to adjust to the darkened interior. The anteroom was small but serviceable, a single door positioned on the left that probably led to the dining room. To her right was pitched a steep flight of stairs. The innkeeper leaned against the counter, but quickly righted himself upon seeing Amaria.

"Welcome to the Jay, milady. How can I assist you?" The man spoke in the common tongue, but with a heavy accent. He was small shouldered, but his belly pushed the limits of the tight fitting cloth tunic he wore. His face appeared aged, complemented by creases around the cheekbone and thinning locks of grey. When he smiled, however, Amaria saw honesty in the man.

She stepped to the counter and said, "I have been told that you run an upright establishment."

The man beamed proudly. "You have been told correctly, milady."

"Do your rooms have clean tubs?"

"As clean as is humanly possible." The innkeeper motioned toward a female servant that had just descended the stairs. The servant, a girl no more than sixteen winters, displayed red-hair and pale skin, complete with thick freckles across her nose and cheeks. "Janea cleans them thoroughly everyday."

Satisfied, Amaria reached into her belt purse. "Very well, I shall take a room."

The innkeeper withdrew a crumpled piece of yellowed parchment and began to scrawl upon it with a quelled pen. "And your name?"

"Amaria Eversvale."

She waited for the common reaction she received every time she divulged her identity, but to her surprise, the innkeeper did nothing. "For how long will you be needin' the room, Mistress Eversvale?"

"I cannot say for certain," she answered. "May I pay for two nights, and should I require the room longer, continue payments?"

"Of course." The innkeeper paused to write something down, then announced, "That will be two crowns, milady. Janea will show you to your room."

Amaria paid the correct amount and took a key from the innkeeper. "May I have a bath drawn? I have ridden since dawn and would like nothing more than to relax in some warm water."

"Janea will see to it, Mistress Eversvale. Should you need anything else, she will help. Or, you may ask me anytime."

Amaria followed the servant up the flight of stairs. When she arrived at her chamber, she viewed it indifferently. It was not a suite by any stretch, but it was large enough to hold a small tub in one corner, a straw cot in another, and a cheaply made desk and chair. The single window allowed light to stream through, and a sconce hung upon one wall. In the center of the room, a tiny circular rush covered the hardwood floor.

Amaria set to unloading her belongings upon the desk, and then began removing her armor and clothes while Janea, down in the kitchen, set the water for her bath. When the water grew warm enough and was placed within the drum, Amaria, the firm and splendid magnificence of her physique completely unveiled, wasted no time easing her body within. She was tall for a woman, but not overly so, and she closed her eyes while the water massaged her, thinking of little else. After several minutes Janea returned from a separate errand, a towel over her shoulder. With nothing better to do at the moment, and hoping for a minimal tip, the girl positioned herself behind Amaria and began to quietly wash the woman's hair, wiping the pure ivory strands free of the dust that had conspired to cake the woman's head.

Only the soothing sounds of sloshing water were heard until Janea spoke with a quiet voice, "I have never seen hair like yours, Mistress. It is beautiful."

Wrenched from her mindless trance, Amaria opened her eyes. The innocence of the girl was a welcome diversion from the tormented world she lived within. "Sometimes I wonder if it is a blessing, or a curse," she responded.

Janea appeared unable to fathom such a statement. "I would give anything to have hair like that."

"Would you?" Amaria strained her neck enough to view the servant behind her. The girl's hair was loose and fell in ringlets down the front of freckled shoulders. "It seems to me that your own hair has a unique quality of its own. I am sure you have no trouble with the young lads. I would keep it if I were you."

The girl blushed and giggled, obviously pleased and flattered by the comment. She fixed her vision upon Amaria's armor. "Are you truly a warrior?"

Amaria could hear the admiration in the child's voice, and she wondered just how little the girl really understood of battle. In a serious tone, she said, "I am. But understand that war is not all glory and triumph as the bards sing of it. Again, I often wonder if it is a curse and not a blessing. Taking lives has a deeper impact than any physical wound suffered. Many men, some honorable husbands and fathers, have been killed by my hand. That knowledge never goes away."

Janea had not expected Amaria's answer, and the girl went deathly silent. When Amaria finished bathing, Janea handed her the towel and began emptying the drum. Amaria dried her herself fully, and then slid into a high-strapped chemise.

"I wish to take a brief nap before I explore the city tonight. Can you wake me in an hour, Janea?"

The servant was unused to clients calling her by name, and it delighted her. "Of course, Mistress. Is there anything else you would like?"

Amaria shook her head. "That will do." She handed Janea a silver crown. The girl took the coin and whisked from the room with a smile across her face. Amaria watched her leave, then laid back upon the cot with her eyes staring up at the ceiling. Within seconds, sleep had taken her.

It was nearly dusk by the time Amaria departed her room. Although the daily retinue of commercial traffic had halted, she discovered that night life in Valgamin was nearly as active. Brothels seemed as frequent as taverns, and freebooters lined the streets mixed with the occasional whore. City watchmen seemed content to let festivities continue unimpeded as long as the damage was kept to a minimum and the safety of the people upheld. Amaria took in every detail, learning everything she could about Valgamin. Most of what she absorbed was useless knowledge, but one never knew when the slightest tidbit could turn into an extraordinary opportunity or stroke of fortune.

She wasn't wearing her armor on this night, choosing the comfort of a loose fitting white shirt and beryl sarong that stopped below the knees. The outfit did her body little justice, but she was not out to impress anyone this night. In fact, it was rare for her to wear anything revealing. Only when she felt visual persuasion would improve an act of delegation did she stoop to such a recourse. For what it was worth, her body needed little additional aid to garner attention.

Although she left her armor in her room, her sword belt remained around her waist. It was the first rule of a soldier - always carry an instrument of defense.

Amaria selected a tavern called Merton's Well. There was nothing about the establishment that stood out from the others, but she was tired of walking about, and Merton's Well was the next tavern in what seemed an endless line. Like most watering holes, the interior was poorly lighted. Two oil lamps hung from opposite ends of the room, and only one table, obviously meant for nobles and others of high esteem, held a candle. The bar was on the right side, as were the eating tables. On the left were the gaming tables, and two separate groups of sharpers played what looked to be some form of dice. At regular intervals, the men would explode into hoots and howls.

Scanning the throng of patrons, she spotted a table that held a single man drinking quietly amid the clatter around him. His plate was empty, and he seemed content to converse solely with the ale that he carried to his lips. Having spent entirely too much time alone during the duration of her travels east, she decided a little conversation would do good to keep her from her self-loathing thoughts.

Amaria approached the table and asked casually, "May I sit here?" Her mannerisms and half-smile gave the impression that she was not interested in anything more than a bit of friendly company.

The man looked up from his drink and calmly viewed her. Shrugging, he pointed to the chair across the rounded table. Amaria lowered herself, studying the man as she did so. He was bronzed-skinned, with black hair pulled behind his head in a clasp. His mustache faded within his chin hair, twisted tight into two separate braids an inch long. Dark hazel eyes, incisive and piercing, exuded no notions of ill intent and Amaria felt comfortable under their scrutiny.

"It seems you are being unsociable this night," Amaria joked, as she motioned to a serving girl.

The man leaned back in his chair and lifted his hand to caress the braids under his chin. He looked to be no more than thirty-five winters old. Tilting his head ever so slightly, he said, "The common raffle can grow wearisome."

Amaria chuckled, "Just so. We have all fallen pray to its wrath before, yes?" The waitress appeared and Amaria ordered her meal before restoring her attention on the man across from her. "What is your name?"

The man studied her. "I do not often give my name to strangers I have just met."

Amaria lifted her shoulders apathetically and held her palm upward. "So be it. I shan't force you. I only felt a little conversation could do me good."

Nodding, the man said, "It can probably do us both some good. In truth, I have no real reason to hide my identity, and you do not strike me as someone who intends me harm. I am Ornan Parémar."

"Parémar? That sounds Radamash?" Although Amaria was no paragon of geography, she had studied enough for strategic military purposes to know that Radam was the largest and most prominent kingdom in the far south. She was also practiced in various dialects that had mingled near her home kingdom of Illidor. Ornan   though he was speaking common   had a heavy sweep to his speech that was very similar to Radamash, the language of Radam. The name Parémar was also a Radam surname.

Ornan nodded, "Not just Radamash, shera, but the very heart itself. I grew up in the capital city, Kadar."

Amaria knew nothing of the word 'shera,' but from context she guessed it meant the same as 'mistress,' or 'milady.' Placing her elbows on the table, she asked, "And what has brought you this far to the northeast? Kadar is a long journey from here."

The man took a sip from his mug, and then ran a wrist across his lips. Amaria noticed that his ordinary leather garments were clean, but deeply stained, as if he owned few outfits and wore the same ones often. "Like every other ambitious nation, Kadar wished to take advantage of the obvious financial opportunities Valgamin presented. Several primary merchant guilds collaborated to put together a massive caravan full of expensive goods. The merchandise was exquisite and certain to reap massive profits in such an emergent setting." Ornan paused, biting his lip for a moment, "I am a simple, common laborer. Yet I can defend myself if need be. Fortunately, I was exactly what the caravan needed; a body to help with the menial work, and act as guard during the long, often arduous trek. I made a good bit of coin."

"So the caravan made it to Valgamin safely, then?"

"We did, and with little trouble save for the land itself. The convoy was large enough that most bandit gangs were outnumbered or simply too intimidated to accost us. After we arrived, things went quite smoothly. True to the plan, the merchants scored big, and their earnings made rich men even richer." Ornan slowly shook his head, a smug look across his features. "I was to return with them, but a local warehouse owner offered me a fine position. I now whittle away the days loading and unloading cargo at Jericho's Warehouse. It is painstaking work, but I make a good sum. I plan to return to Kadar someday, perhaps when another convoy arrives. Of course, that could be two weeks from now, or two years."

Amaria's food arrived, and her hunger forced her to attack the plate unabashed. The meal was nothing to be envious of, but she starved and anything sufficed. Between mouthfuls, she commented, "Your family must miss you." She suddenly thought of Meran, her adopted father who had raised her after the rest of her biological family had been murdered, when she was but six winters old. Picturing the old man's face aggrieved her. He had warned her, *pleaded* with her, not to attack Erdoth Fortress on that fateful night, but she had ignored his cautions. Her regret slowly consumed her conscious. How much blood she had spilt that night! And for what? Suddenly, she longed for Meran, to cry like a small child upon his aged shoulder.

"I have no family, shera," Ornan answered. "My mother and

father both died when I was very young. Mother from sickness, father from grief. I was an only child, orphaned at the age of seven. I had little choice but to develop very good thieving skills to survive. At twelve I began honest work to earn my keep. I taught myself to use whatever makeshift weapon was available if certain situations arose." He emptied the bottom contents of his drink, exhaled deeply, then banged his glass down upon the chipped wood of the table. "I loved once, but even the prettiest flowers wither, as did my affection for her. It has been many years since I have seen my first love. Still, there are old friends I miss. As the saying goes: time dictates life. I will see them when I see them."

Amaria sipped an especially poor tasting ale. Making a concerted effort not to grimace, she lowered her mug and resumed the meal, which had shown itself to be less disagreeable to her tastes. She hesitated long enough to comment, "I admire your outlook on life."

"What choice have I? Dwelling on negatives changes nothing."

The woman froze; her fork halfway to her mouth. She lowered the utensil and gave the man a piercing look, as if boring a hole through his head. To his credit, he stared back coolly. "Why do I have a sudden feeling that perhaps our meeting is no coincidence? Those words you just spoke of," she hesitated, trying to articulate exactly what she meant to say. "They seem meant for me alone."

Ornan wrinkled his forehead. "That is difficult to respond to, shera. You have yet to tell me your own name or your tale. I assume you are not some whore cajoling me for a few coppers."

What followed was not planned, nor considered. Amaria had only intended to reveal minor details of her past, but as she proceeded to speak, she inexplicably found herself opening like a fountain, telling everything from how her parents were killed, all the way through to her bargain with the dark gods and subsequent assault on Erdoth Fortress. It had been many, many months since she had spoken candidly with anyone, and in some strange way, Ornan pulled deep-rooted sentiments from her. He listened quietly as she described her late husband, Royce. The woman was not prone to emotion, but she fought hard to hold back the tears that welled in her eyes while she reminisced over the life she had once known, and then cast away. Gods, it was surreal! Why was she speaking so openly, when all her life she had been so private? The only part of her tale which she intentionally left out, was her concern over the mental channel that remained open, allowing herself to be subconsciously exposed to the ceaseless murmurs of the dark gods.

When she finished, the man from Radam slowly stroked his goatee. "Amaria Eversvale," he mused aloud. "I cannot place myself in your boots, but it seems to me that if you desire to continue east, you have run out of space. Only the mountains remain. Perhaps it is time to face that which you flee from."

"And what am I fleeing from?" Amaria asked, interested.

Ornan lifted his eyebrows as if the answer were obvious to everyone except her. "What indeed?" He leaned forward, looking hard into Amaria. "If your story is true, shera, then you have obviously been gifted great talents. You are young, beautiful, intelligent, and no doubt can handle a sword. Yet, you have faults, as do all of us. You are not so different."

Amaria brushed white hair from her face. "And what are your faults, Ornan Parémar?"

"Too many to name, shera." Ornan smiled, displaying teeth that were slightly gaped but not damaged. His words held no admonishment, but were rather sad and solemn. "But, I have yet to ravage a fortress and avenge my family, as you have." He paused, letting Amaria reflect on the life-shattering consequences of her overzealous desire to destroy Erdoth. When he spoke again, he did so with a touch of encouragement. "You must already know that your ride east will not make your past deeds vanish, so why not turn and face what you have done. Better yourself, rather than tear yourself further apart."

Silence ensued for long moments; while Amaria reflected on the unexpected wisdom of a man she had only met an hour before. Ultimately, she remarked, "You speak as if you have some experience on the matter of regret."

"We all have made choices we regret, shera."

Amaria's mind reeled as she attempted to assemble the reasons why, or how, this chance meeting had come about. She had always been aware of the battle between the gods of light and the gods of darkness. In Illidor, she had supported the local temples that housed the priests who dedicated their lives to the worship of the good deities. Occasionally, she would even pray at these temples. Still, she never truly considered what impact such actions might have on her life. She had difficulty fathoming how a meeting, such as the one she now held with Ornan, could actually have been orchestrated by a higher power. It almost seemed silly. Yet, as she considered Ornan's wisdom, there appeared to be few other explanations, save for incredible luck.

"Sometimes," Amaria said, unsure exactly why, "I feel like I have little control over myself, as if the gods intentionally tempt me into brazen actions."

It was Ornan's turn to be silent for several seconds. Eventually he shook his head and proffered, "Perhaps. Perhaps not. You exude a strange aura, shera. Of that, I've no doubt. But I am no *qearza*." When he noticed the confused expression upon Amaria's face, he corrected himself, choosing the simplest interpretation of the Radam word. "Holy man. My advice cannot extend to such themes."

Just then, one of the groups at the gaming tables erupted into a torrent of angry shouts. A chair toppled over, and two men appeared to have withdrawn daggers while hurling curses and threats. Quickly, the remaining gamblers intervened before the combatants could cause physical harm to one another or themselves, and after several tense moments, the game had resumed as if the spout had never taken place.

Pulling her attention away from the short-lived entertainment, Amaria abruptly felt the pangs of fatigue. She realized that a good night's sleep was her next priority. Politely, she said, "I have enjoyed our conversation. But I believe it is time for me to retreat to my room."

Ornan tilted his head slightly. "As have I, shera. I hope it will not be our last."

As she stood from her chair, the woman recognized that she felt a strange kinship to the man, and she offered, "I know where you work. I will seek you out in the following days."

"I would very much like that, shera. Good night to you."

Amaria paid for her meal and then exited the tavern. She quickly determined that it was nearing midnight, and she walked at a brisk pace, still thinking of the words Ornan had offered her. The swarm of people had begun to thin out, though there remained enough commotion to cause her irritation. Only a few stars showed in the sky, and the moon was but a sliver in the black mass. Amaria noticed that the clouds had thickened since earlier in the day.

She had covered half the distance to the Jay when a voice called to her from behind. "Milady! Do you know how to use that?"

Swinging her shoulders, Amaria witnessed three men hurrying across the street toward her. All three of them were armed with short blades, though none wore armor. Their clothes were made of tattered cloth, tunics over torn trousers. Amaria had an inkling of what their intentions might be.

Reaching her, the man in the center spoke aloud. He was a heavyset lad with thick curly hair that grew straight upwards in a ragged fashion. "Such a pretty lass to carry a sword. Now what would you be needin' that fer?"

Amaria rolled her eyes. When she spoke, her voice was layered with annoyance. "Gentlemen, I haven't the time for this. If it is all the same to you, I wish to be on my way."

The man on her left, a wiry fellow sporting several missing teeth, gawked at her vain appeal. The center man, whom Amaria guessed was the leader, hushed his friend and replaced his attentions upon the prize. "But we have only just met. Fer three days we 'ave not had the companionship of a pretty lass like yourself. Why not make this easy? Sure'd be a shame if we was forced to "

His words were cut short by the boot that found itself in his gut. Amaria's kick was lightning fast, and as the man keeled over in pain, she secured the rusted blade from his hand and pushed him backwards hard. Unbalanced, the man fell to the ground, his head knocking against the stone beneath. His comrades, now in a frozen stupor, watched while she placed the man's own sword against his neck, the tip pressing the skin beneath his chin.

A fire surged through her, a burning desire to kill the man and slaughter the others. Surely they deserved to die! Their plans had been no less horrifying, and three deaths would mean nothing to her. The man below her coughed from pain as he continued to grip his stomach. Ultimately, he looked up at her, his visage the embodiment of shock and fear. "Please, milady! We wasn't going to do nothing to ya."

Amaria's face was stone as she fought an internal battle. How badly she wanted to see these men dead! Agonizing moments passed, but through sheer will, she managed to drop the weapon mere inches from the man's neck. Turning her back on the other two, she strode off into the night, not giving any of them another thought. Unsurprisingly, they let her go without another word.

Reaching The Cardinal and the Jay, she discovered that the innkeeper was still awake. He smiled from behind the counter as she entered. "Ah, Mistress Eversvale. Before you depart for your room, you must know that a message was delivered for you." He shuffled through some papers and pulled out a folded piece of parchment. She took the message from his hand and proceeded to remove the seal. The paper was crisp and quite thick, obviously of finer quality. Unfolding the note, she gazed cynically at the message. It was brief, scrawled neatly in black ink:

Mistress Eversvale, it has come to the attention of the city council that you are currently located in our fine city. It is with distinguished admiration from us that we are given the opportunity to house the legendary 'Knight of the Dove.' We would be more than honored if you would grant us your presence as guest of honor for a luncheon tomorrow at the council hall. Veran Marticis, Second Council Member of the Freecity of Valgamin.

Amaria looked up from the parchment, locking her sight upon the innkeeper. Her words were dry and steeped with irony,

"Apparently, the wind travels quickly in Valgamin."

Two

Amaria shimmered in full regalia. Wakening early that morning, she had painstakingly cleaned and polished her armor and sword, as well as thoroughly washed her mantle. She was to be the guest of honor, no doubt for her perceived victory of Erdoth Fortress, and as such, it was imperative that she look the part of what they expected; The Knight of the Dove in full glory. Now, standing amid her hosts, her silver plate shined with a luster that surpassed all the expensive finery worn by the council members and stewards within the large dining chamber. Their looks of puerile admiration and excitement told her that she had succeeded in her efforts.

Not that she was happy to be there. If she had been given a choice in the matter, she'd be eating lunch alone at some quiet tavern. But, Amaria was no fool. When needed, she could play the role of a dignified patrician easily enough, despite the fact that such cursory and superficial acts grated on her nerves. Turning down an invitation of honor to dine with the city council would be excessively impolite, and she had no desire to risk gaining enemies within a city she had just arrived in.

Inside the banquet hall stood four members of the Council seat of Valgamin, and a dozen or so stewards and magistrates. One of the council members, an older man with thinning, grey hair, bowed deeply and introduced himself as Veran Marticis, Second Council Member of Valgamin. He then continued introductions, following with the rest of the council and moving to the other nobles in attendance. Amaria greeted them all but made no effort to remember names of the secondary magistrates.

Servants pulled chairs from the room's only table, ushering men to a predetermined seating arrangement. When Amaria was led to her chair, she found herself placed inbetween the third and forth councilman, which was obviously the designated place for the guest of honor. The servant holding her chair smiled haplessly as Amaria lowered herself, then quickly departed with the other servants, momentarily leaving the assembly alone. Amaria took a moment to study her surroundings.

The dining hall, a prime example of the city's apathy toward excessive lavishness, displayed only two tapestries of average quality upon the walls. A suit of armor rested near the main entrance, while layered curtains draped the middle portion of the room's single window. Hanging from the ceiling was a twelve-pronged silver chandelier, bestowing ample light across the otherwise scantily adorned hall. The lone table was oblong, made of pressed and polished oak, sturdy but inexpensive. Amaria couldn't find a single stain or blemish upon the table's smooth surface, and she wondered how often such gatherings took place within the room. One chair, resting beside the second councilman, stood empty. She found that curious. Was the First Councilman detained by something else? Perhaps he was merely in travel somewhere, or had fallen under the weather.

The servants returned with a plethora of drinks and appetizers. Different wines and meads were placed at strategic locations about the table, while willing takers chose between small dishes of various spiced meats and fresh fruits. Amaria opted for a goblet of vintage Dy'rinth wine, finding its taste quite agreeable. The pear slices she chewed on were far sweeter then the pears back in Illidor, and she decided that the lack of opulent décor in no way hindered the quality of the meal itself.

In time, councilman Veran Marticis broke the roving small talk by directing his raised voice to Amaria. "So, tell us, Mistress Eversvale, why the famed Knight of the Dove has chosen to bestow her presence upon our insignificant city?" The man gazed upon her innocently, his question obviously meant as a complement.

Amaria lowered her glass and casually viewed the man. Veran, like the rest of the council members, wore a twin-breasted black doublet with identical silver buttons running down the front. The remaining men were dressed in fancy tunics of various colors, some supplementing their finery with feathered hats.

None of the men appeared wise in the ways of soldiery. Amaria felt as if she could say anything, and they would concur as if every opinion or theory she expressed was flawless. But, the better side of civility won over. Smiling, she said, "Had I an answer to give, I would do so willingly. What you know of my conquest on Erdoth is not the story in its entirety." She paused to pour herself more wine, and then concluded, "In a way I cannot express, that episode of my life has forced me to reexamine my future."

Veran waited for an elaboration, and when none was forthcoming, he hesitated. Such an elusive answer had rendered the man speechless. To his relived fortune, the servants reappeared, this time bearing the main course; a superb combination of seasoned boar and antelope. Amaria wasted no time delving into the tasteful delicacy, savoring every bite. She had little doubt that this was the best meal she had eaten since before the events at Erdoth Fortress. Over the past several months, she had grown so accustomed to the cheap, excessively bland meals of low class eateries and inns; she had nearly forgotten what good food tasted like. And this time she hadn't paid a single copper!

From the corner of her eye she noticed one of the stewards in attendance staring at her while she ate. When she made eye contact with the man, he simply nodded, smiled courteously, and then returned to his meal. This happened twice, and could have happened a third had Amaria elected to look his direction again. Still, she could feel the man watching her.

Seeking conversation to divert her thoughts, she turned to Veran and asked, "How do you maintain civility in a city such as this?"

Veran dotted his lips with a cloth napkin. "Well, due to the speed of Valgamin's expansion, and the," the older man paused, finding the correct words, "*boisterous nature* of many of our citizens, we found that a strong measure of public stability was the first step. The city watch does an admirable job of keeping us protected from the outside, all the while maintaining order within the streets. Due to their venerable diligence, the common crimes of other large cities, such as theft, rape, and murder, have been driven to a minimum."

"Three men attempted to accost me last night as I returned to my room from a tavern. I almost killed them, but instead chose the better path a valor, I suppose," Amaria said dryly.

The candid report immediately caused Veran to throw uncomfortable glances about the table. The Fourth Councilman, a man named Tyris Andor, stepped in and calmly responded, "I believe all of us can express our sincere apologies that such an event took place, and we are greatly relieved you are unharmed. Please understand, Mistress Eversvale, that any community with a sizeable population will still have its occasional drawbacks. However, know that occurrences such as the one you describe are rare, indeed. We have done everything in our power to eliminate these unpleasant, and unlawful, incidences, and justice is swift and unyielding. Murder and rape are both punishable by execution, and theft by dismemberment. Although we still have improvements to make in other areas of our growing society, such as effective districting and closely surveyed commerce, we feel that safety is the largest priority. The walls you saw as you entered the city have only been built in the last five years. One of many steps we have taken recently."

Amaria listened as she sipped her wine. Tyris was younger than Veran, perhaps in his early forties. His countenance was rigid, and his deep-set eyes flaunted a slyness that was absent from Veran's. Still, Amaria sensed no secret ambition concealed behind the man's words. "Have there been any outside threats?" she inquired.

"None that have caused us concern." Veran replied. "Yet, we take every threat seriously. The wealth that has begun exchanging hands here has caught the attention of surrounding kingdoms, among others."

Amaria had to admit that Valgamin would be an attractive proposition to a power hungry nation. She understood that often it is wise to assume everyone is an enemy, lest you become betrayed by a friend. No doubt this was the stance Valgamin had taken, trusting none beyond the walls of their remarkable city.

Once again, she was inexplicably drawn to the empty chair. She hadn't realized she was staring until Tyris brought it to her attention.

"Ah, yes," the Forth Councilman said, sadly. "I see you have noticed that we are missing a host. Though I am loath to speak of it, a baffling tragedy befell our First Councilman only a week ago."

A strange tension suddenly filled the room. Nervous looks were exchanged, and Amaria gazed from face to face, searching for clarification.

It was Veran who offered details, his voice solemn and uneasy. "To the puzzlement of everyone who knew him, our First Councilman, Jonathon Barrowswynd, climbed up a section of Urak's Edge, then threw himself off."

"He killed himself?" Amaria said, startled.

"As much as we can gather. He had hired a guide to lead him partway up the mountainside. The guide reported the incident after he returned to Yhull, the mining community at the base of Urak's Edge. He explained that Jonathon had never given reason why he wished to climb the mountain, but apparently the guide never expected him to jump off the edge. The news was a shock to all of us, and disturbing as well. Jonathon has left behind a loving wife and two children. We can think of no reasons or clues as to why he would have done this."

Amaria rubbed her chin, pondering the case. "How can you be sure he was not murdered by this 'guide'? It makes far more sense than the story you have given."

"Obviously, that was our first inclination." Veran slowly shook his head. He was unable to hide his distress over the strange event. "We summoned several priests to discern whether the man was speaking lies. But, he was clearly traumatized, and the priests found no hints of deception within the man's troubled words. It simply doesn't add up. Why would Jonathon go through all the work of traveling to Yhull, and then climb a mountain, just to kill himself? He could have accomplished the same feat by simply leaping from the window of this very building."

An awkward moment followed, then Tyris added, "As you can see, we are all very disturbed by what has taken place. Jonathon was a good man with plenty to live for. His death lays heavy on our hearts."

Amaria had little else to say on the matter, and the remainder of the meal was eaten in relative silence. As she finished up, she continued to sense the eyes of the steward who had been staring at her for much of the luncheon. It had taken all her self-control not to rebuke the man aloud for his irritating rudeness. But she held herself, and soon the council began to rise from their chairs, marshaling an end to the meal. The others rose with them, and Amaria spent a few minutes thanking the hosts and giving appreciation for their kind hospitality. Veran had even suggested that they house her in one of the extra rooms of the council hall, but she declined. Debts of any kind were not welcome, especially when those debts were owed to the council itself. Still, the council and magistrates openly admired her for attending, and most of the men in attendance praised her for battle prowess or her beauty. She countered their acclaim with an excess of courteous gratitude before excusing herself.

Departing the banquet chamber, she moved into the entrance foyer. The room was very similar to the dining hall, with little embellishment upon the drab stone walls. The whole of the city council building was nothing more than a three-storied keep with rounded turrets in each of the four corners. Yet, it was used for every administrative function. Each room, save the dining hall and lobby, was a "court" of some kind, and every judgment that pertained to the welfare of Valgamin was made within these rooms. The council, along with the secondary officers and magistrates, concluded criminal trials, taxes, military designs, land plotting; all this and more inside the stronghold.

A standing receptionist nodded to her as she approached the exit, and then someone called her from behind. She turned and realized it was the man who had been staring at her during the meal. He hustled to where she stood and spoke apologetically, "I am sorry to trouble you, Mistress Eversvale, but there is a matter I wish to speak to you about."

Amaria said nothing as she studied the man closely. He was no older than his late-thirties; square jawed with a short scar above his right eye. He bore a thick mane of long, straight auburn that dropped freely along the sides of his face, and a thin layer of hair over his lip and chin. Yet, it was his eyes which Amaria noticed most of all. They were an icy cobalt, sharp and piercing. The man was skilled at masking his thoughts, for she could read nothing from his expression.

When Amaria gave no immediate reply, the man continued, "I am Thavas Iimon, advisor and steward of the Third Councilman, Senastas Baranor."

Amaria had to think hard to remember the Third Councilman, as he had remained very quiet during the meal. He was young and obviously intelligent, for his manner spoke of a chap who understood the method of a wise leader; say very little, but soak up all that is said and done by others. In Amaria's experience, she knew that those kinds of men gained a great amount of trust from followers. They were also the most dangerous.

"What is it you have to say?" Amaria asked, still cynical of the man who had shown no reservations when he gaped at her during the luncheon.

Thavas, sporting a grey brooched tunic with silvered trim, pointed toward the exit. "Let us walk outside. The fresh air will be welcome." Amaria followed the steward beyond the portal of the council hall and into the light of day. Well into the afternoon, the great orb of light pulsated liberally down upon a populace that consumed the streets with industrious activity. A stone stairway led from the entrance of the keep down onto the road, and the two of them turned right, falling into step with the rest of the crowds. "What do you think of our city?" asked Thavas.

"It is a spectacle to be seen."

Thavas laughed. "Indeed. I have lived in many places during my lifetime, and none have the flair of individualism like Valgamin. You'll not find a place more accepting of outsiders, for in truth, *everyone* is an outsider."

They rounded a corner and Amaria could see a substantially sized temple standing several blocks in the distance. It was made of marble, or some kind of white stone, for it shined regally in the bright afternoon sun. Amaria stopped abruptly and faced Thavas. "I am assuming that you intended to say more than just your opinions of the city? If not, I shall be on my way."

Thavas halted as well. He returned Amaria's stare, seemingly unintimidated by her gruff bearing. "Oh yes, much more, in fact. But I am not the one to give you such details. I am here by orders of Councilman Baranor to see if you would be willing to grant him audience?"

"Grant him audience?" Amaria scoffed. "I just did! Is that not what our little meal was meant for?"

The steward held up his hands. "Let me explain. We have recently discovered something amiss in Valgamin. Something that is dangerous enough to put our wonderful city in peril."

Amaria shrugged. "So contact the city watch. It is their job to handle such matters."

"But that is the problem, Mistress. If we divulged our secret information, it would only make the situation worse. As it is right now, only Councilman Baranor knows. We have elected to keep our information a secret for two reasons: One, to keep the council from panicking. Two, the fewer that know of the threat, the easier it will be to seize it."

Amaria issued an exasperated breath. "Then tell me the problem. Be forthwith with your information or speak to someone else. I will not listen to your ramblings for mere amusement." Something about the man grated on her nerves, and his brusque manner gave her no remorse. She couldn't discern whether this was simply the way he normally conducted himself, or if he had saved this attitude for her benefit alone.

"Unfortunately," Thavas exclaimed, "I cannot. This is not the time, nor is it my place, to do so. Before your anger with me reaches its pinnacle, please listen to my offer."

"Go on."

"Councilman Baranor wishes to speak to you on a more private basis. He will fill you in on the situation. Grant him at least that, and afterwards, if you wish to take no part in his proposal, you may walk away."

Amaria absently fingered the hilt of her sword. In truth, she'd rather just walk away right then and there. But, looking into the steely eyes of Thavas, something intrigued her. She couldn't explain it, but she found her obstinacy giving way to curiosity. "And how exactly would Councilman Baranor like to meet me?"

Thavas smiled, as if victory had fallen into his grasp. "The arena will be having one of its better exhibitions tonight. It will begin at the ninth bell. He is hoping you might accompany him. I believe you will find it quite entertaining."

The Arena! More like a field of butchery, she thought repugnantly. Considered barbaric and abhorrent, killing for sport and entertainment had been outlawed in her home kingdom of Illidor, just as it was in many of the presiding monarchies and empires across the world. But, with the sundry makeup of Valgamin, somehow the inclusion of an arena seemed fitting. Perhaps the experience might broaden her understanding of the city. In resignation, she offered, "Send an escort to The Cardinal and Jay at the eighth bell. I will speak with Councilman Baranor, but I promise nothing else."

"Excellent! That is all I can ask." The man clasped his hands together. "Trust me, Mistress, you will find him quite an amiable man. Senastas might be young and quiet, but he is very intelligent and his love for Valgamin seems to have no bounds."

"That is truly wonderful." Shards of irony gripped her voice. "Until then, please allow me to be on my way."

"Of course, Mistress. I will send word to Senastas immediately." With those words, he spun on his heel and hustled away, leaving the woman alone.

Amaria watched him disappear amid the cluster of people before turning her gaze to the sky. It must be around the third bell, she guessed. That left five hours before her meeting with the councilman. Her eyes zeroed in upon the great temple for a second time. An urge welled within her, and she suffered a sudden need to visit the place of worship. Not since her days back in Dhorn-Dyas, the capital of Illidor, had she prayed to the gods of light. She was long overdue. Wiping a trickle of sweat from her brow, she took a step toward the temple, then stopped. Like the crashing of the surf upon the shore, an overwhelming feeling pressed her, and she felt unprepared to cope with her self-inflicted transgressions. Would the holy priests recognize her appalling spiritual wounds of the past? How would they view such sacrilege? Probably, she mulled, by casting me away in revulsion. She had no desire, or conviction, to face scrutiny of that manner. With a bitter frown and a doleful shake of her head, the woman turned away and commenced a sorrowful gait in the opposite direction.

Once again I flee from redemption, she mourned, only to herself.

*

The large wolf leapt forward, its gaping maw primed to tear out the man's throat. At the last moment, the blunt edge of a warhammer slammed forcefully across its head, snapping the animal's neck, and crushing its skull. The beast crumpled to the ground, its lifeless body resting awkwardly upon the dirt surface of the arena floor.

The victor looked up toward the crowd and raised his weapon in triumph. The mass of onlookers applauded and jeered while servants carried away the two unfortunate animals he had slain.

Amaria peered down upon the scene. To her surprise, the carnage had little effect on her. Her years of service in the Illidor army and the consequent bloodshed from her own hand had hardened her to the gruesomeness of war. Such sentiments were a normal result of a soldier's duties, but she found them disconcerting all the same.

The man with the warhammer still paraded about the arena, welcoming both the crowd's approval and disproval alike. Amaria knew the type of man; an untrained, undisciplined brawler. She had killed more than a few in her day. Sure, he could handle a weapon, but place him in a real war, with trained soldiers, and his uncontrolled style would be his demise in seconds.

The arena proved to be an impressive structure, though not as large as she had expected. About sixty feet from end to end, and thirty feet wide, the elliptical field was designed to support only one or two skirmishes at a time. Row after row of seating benches surrounded the open-aired stadium completely, and almost every space was filled, the moonlight spilling down upon their mottled faces with tender strokes of silver. On one end, a balcony had been built, obviously to stage nobles of importance, or perhaps the council members themselves. Surprisingly, she found herself sitting in the stands among the rest of the populace, next to her host, Senastas Baranor. To her displeasure, sitting on the other side of the councilman, was Thavas Iimon. She wondered if Senastas, by not sitting in the balcony, simply desired less attention or if he actually wasn't allowed up there on this night. Either way, she was happy to be sitting with the masses and not looking down from a veranda where everyone could witness her.

Senastas had shown himself as a bright, ponderous young man. Unlike many nobles she had met in her lifetime, he had thus far spoken very little about himself. Although their conversations hadn't touched upon the primary reason for their meeting, he had gone out of his way to ask Amaria her opinions on various topics, only occasionally commenting himself. His demeanor impressed her, for the man couldn't be beyond his twenties yet, and in his own way seemed wiser than most kings.

Thavas had yet to say a word, a fact for which she was thankful. Something still goaded her about the man. She couldn't place it, but she was far happier with his silence and hoped he would remain so.

"These matches have only been the preliminaries, to raise everyone's thirst for death, so to speak." Senastas added a touch of cynicism to his comment. Amaria wondered how much the young man really approved of what they were watching. "The main bouts will start soon," he added.

"How often do you attend these exhibitions?" Amaria inquired.

"Not often," he admitted. "This is the third time." He thoughtfully rubbed his cleanly shaven chin. "To be honest, there are times where I feel I haven't the stomach for it. As you can see, I am not made for the harshness of war, and will certainly never witness the front line of a battle. I find that seeing these little scuffles gives me a small understanding of just how brutal war can be."

Amaria viewed the councilman in earnest. A handsome rake, with cropped brown hair and eyes that exuded sincerity, Senastas had replaced his black doublet from the earlier luncheon for more comfortable garments; a loose fitting shirt of green and black, wide bottomed trousers tucked beneath buckled boots. Under his shirt, Amaria could see he was trim and fit, but his spotless hands displayed clear evidence that he had never seen a hard day's labor in all his youthful life. Amaria smiled as she spoke, "Some men are made for war, and some are not. Do not feel slighted, Councilman. Of all people, soldiers need leaders of wisdom the most."

Senastas smiled, but said nothing. A dualmaster walked to the center stage of the arena and presented the next match. Two men appeared from opposite sides. They did not appear to be the brash, low-born kind of man like that of the previous brawler, but rather looked to be nobles. They carried broad-bladed sabres at their sides, and only padded armor. The dualmaster called to the audience, "This next bout is a duel of skill!" He then went on to introduce their names and noted that the match was two out of three touches. Senastas seemed relieved that at least one match tonight would not end in death.

He seemed to enjoy watching the two men dance about the arena, their blades in perpetual motion. When the first noble scored a touch, Senastas cheered openly as the fighters returned to the center and the dualmaster started them again. To everyone's surprise, the second bladesman scored the last two touches for a win, and as the two competitors shook hands afterwards, the people applauded them with a plethora of shouts and whistles.

The next contest was announced as a battle to the death.

Three separate men made the slow walk into the confines of the arena, each of them carrying weapons of their choice. The crowd escalated in fervent excitement. Senastas quickly said, "Perhaps we should discuss the reason I have brought you here."

Amaria tilted her head in agreement as she observed the obvious discomfort in the councilman's face as he considered the ensuing battle. "Certainly."

The councilman seemed to briefly falter, as if troubled. He eyed her with somber intensity. "There is a concern which has been brought to my attention. It concerns an inhabitant of Valgamin."

"Go on," Amaria prodded.

"There is a man who lives a very solitary life within our walls. Most citizens are unaware of him, but he exists all the same. It took some brilliant investigating," he cast a glance at Thavas, "and a stroke of luck to locate him ourselves. His name is Ephram Yâramesh, and he is a manipulator of the arcane. We also have reason to belive he is the true cause of our First Councilman's suicide."

Amaria almost laughed aloud, but held herself out of respect for Senastas. "By the gods, a wizard! Why am I not surprised? It is always a wizard of some kind, yes?"

Senastas frowned. "There are others in the city that practice the arts of magic, and are no concern to the council. They have made themselves known from the very beginning, and allow us to monitor their livelihood with no reserve. This Ephram, however, has kept himself hidden, and had Thavas not come across some strong evidence of his presence, he would still be unknown to us."

"As Councilman Baranor expressed," added Thavas, speaking for the first time, "it was by a mere stroke of luck that I found such evidence. Two weeks ago, one of my servants spied a man prowling about the grounds of the council hall during the late hours. I happened to be in my study that night, and I was notified immediately. Obviously concerned, I went to investigate, and true enough, a robed man was standing in the shadows beneath the rear balcony. Unfortunately, it was very dark and I could see little of his appearance, but I watched him for nearly an hour as he stood inconspicuously. I couldn't begin to imagine what he was doing, but he exuded a peculiar vibe which bothered me to no end. In time, the figure departed, and from a distance I followed. I was stunned to find him enter the building of one of our local merchants. A bootmaker, actually."

Senastas jumped in, "Thavas turned the information over to me, and the next day I sent my investigators to question the bootmaker. He claimed to have no knowledge of any man living or using his shop and quarters. Obviously, we found that very odd. Either the bootmaker was feigning ignorance and was actually housing the man purposely, or he was completely unaware that a stranger was coming and going from his building. By then, my interest was peaked and I was not about to relinquish the investigation."

Down in the arena, one of the warriors had fallen. The two that remained circled each other warily, sizing up their foe. The crowd roared as the men once again collided and the fight resumed. Senastas peeled his eyes away from the action and fixed them on Amaria.

"I put my men to work, and for several days they searched records and spied upon the bootmaker's shop. Two full weeks had passed before new information came forthwith. Thavas' servants," the councilman threw a darting glance at his companion, "or thieving spies, actually, made another discovery. Sneaking into the bootmaker's store one night, they instigated a thorough search of the small complex and discovered a hidden entrance to a cavern within the cellar. How this wizard went unnoticed in and out of this man's house remains a mystery."

"Wizard's have ways of going unnoticed if they wish to," Amaria commented.

"Apparently so," Senastas glumly remarked. "It was then that I made a brash, and horrible, call of judgment. I hadn't enough knowledge of the situation yet to justify telling the rest of the council, but I felt the threat was dire enough that I needed to do something. By my order, I had Thavas send his two spies into the cavern itself in a dangerous attempt to gather more information about this mysterious figure. They returned triumphantly, bearing a document that revealed his identity and profession. Ephram Yâramesh, a sorcerer of some kind. Sadly, little else was revealed by the document, and so we ordered them back inside the cavern a second time." The councilman faltered. "They never returned."

Amaria kept quiet, responding only with her compelling green eyes. For a second, she allowed herself to glimpse the battle below. One combatant's torso was terribly bloodied, and he seemed unable to use his left arm. Still, he fought on, backing away in defense as his opponent rushed him again and again. It was only a matter of time before the wounded man succumbed, and true to form, the aggressor scored a fatal blow upon the wounded man's chest with a brutal thrust of his broadsword. The dying man sputtered before collapsing upon his stomach as the conqueror removed his blade. The onlookers erupted into a mixed chorus of stanch approval and angry jeers as the victor urged them on, taking the two dead bodies and stacking them under his feet while he raised his bloodstained sword high in the air.

Lost in his own thoughts, Senastas never appeared to notice the commotion around him. "Shortly after, I received a cryptic message. It was short, but poignant nonetheless. It simply said: '*I am not to be trifled with. Do not allow more than one councilman's death to be on your hands.*' and was signed: '*Ephram Yâramesh.*' That was the very same day Jonathon leapt from Urak's Edge. I have been a wracked with guilt ever since."

Amaria considered the story. A thought occurred to her. "How would this wizard know it was you who had sent the spies into his cavern?"

The councilman shrugged. "Perhaps he tortured them. I know not, and in truth, I do not wish to know."

"Torture," the woman consented, turning the tale over in her mind. More than anyone, she understood the burden of holding responsibility for the deaths of others. It was her own husband she had ordered, albeit hesitantly, to scout Erdoth Fortress, and the result was his own gruesome demise. Merely one of many things she regretted from those events that would plague her life ever after. Softening her voice, she said to Senastas, "I do not think you can blame yourself, and I speak honestly. You have an obligation to protect the citizens of Valgamin. Yes, you might have approached the situation differently, but you acted on what you believed was the best judgment at the time. I cannot imagine the other councilmen doing things differently."

Senastas shook his head. "Some would have," he muttered.

"So why tell me this? What have I to do with this wizard?"

The councilman wringed his hands together as he looked to his advisor. Several moments later, he focused on Amaria. "I must follow this through to the end. There is no question in my mind that Ephram is a dangerous man; too dangerous to be left alone to his whims. If he can force a man to willingly commit suicide, even a levelheaded noble with much to live for, than he is extremely dangerous and must be purged from our city. I still do not wish to make the rest of the council aware of this. Word would seep from their 'confidential' informants, and soon half the city would be up in arms. I can only imagine the consequence of that."

"The wizard would not be pleased," Amaria commented.

"No, he would not. I fear his anger would result in far more harm than I am willing to allow." The councilman fixed Amaria with hard eyes. "This, Mistress Eversvale, is where you can be of help. You can assist me in eliminating this man from Valgamin."

The woman furrowed her brow, circumspect in visage. "But I am no assassin, nor a thief to sneak unnoticed into a hidden cavern. I am a battlefield soldier."

"Our hope is that a fight will be unnecessary. With enough show of force, I believe he can be *persuaded* to leave on his own merit."

Amaria guffawed. "I am one woman."

"But you are the *Knight of the Dove!*" Senastas emphasized each word of her title with grandeur. "You have conquered a fortress single-handedly! Who better to confront a powerful wizard? Furthermore, you will not be alone. Thavas will go with you. Although he is merely an advisor and steward under my service, he is quite formidable in a fight. Together, the two of you should convince Ephram that he is no longer welcome in Valgamin."

"And what do I get out of this?" Amaria wondered aloud.

A flicker of delight passed through the councilman's expression as he sensed her coming acceptance. Smiling, he said, "Name it, and I will do everything I can to comply."

She sat thoughtful for several moments, eyes of jade gazing blindly at nothing. In truth, she didn't know what she wanted, but it never hurt to discover what was on the table. She wondered if a reward was truly necessary. Was the mission itself necessary? These were questions that needed time answering. "I will ponder your offer, as well as my compensation."

Senastas anxiously nodded, "You must decide quickly. I can wait no longer than two days. After that, I will have to proceed without you. I grow nervous with each passing day that this man infests our city."

Amaria ran a hand through her thick, ivory hair. "I will respond within two days time. I assume I can find you at the council hall?"

Senastas half grinned. "Almost always, milady. I will look forward to hearing from you."

"And remember, Mistress Eversvale," Thavas furthered, "I'll be there to accompany you."

The woman fixed the steward with a callous stare. "And understand this, Thavas Iimon, I don't trust you."

Standing from her chair, Amaria gave her farewells and walked off. As she left, her mind kept repeating the same phrase; *Why is it always a godsbedamned wizard?*

Three

A billowing cloud of dust, fashioned from a squall of roguish wind, carried across the graveled earth with whirlwind-like vehemence. Both arms wrapped around the large crate, Ornan could only shut his eyes to ward off the loose dirt until the wafting haze of grime had passed him by, leaving his skin one full shade of taupe thicker than before.

From a short distance, Amaria watched the man grunt as he heaved the crate onto a wagon before taking a moment to rest his limbs. Ornan was shirtless today, wearing only loose leggings that were cut off at the knees. Though his torso was somewhat swathed by the wind blown elements, she could see his trim, muscular frame expand and contract aggressively to his heavy breaths. Those crates were not small, and she guessed that the contents inside bore plenty of weight as well. Although his work could be considered proletarian, it was by no means menial.

Amaria approached him as he turned back toward Jericho's Warehouse, ready to gather another box. His hair had been pulled back and held by a clasp while his face had been layered by the same filth as the rest of his body. She called out to him, teasingly, "Radamite! A word with you!"

At first, Ornan appeared startled. When he recognized who called to him, his mouth swelled wide in delight. "Shera! It is wonderful to see you!" He stopped suddenly, fingering his tattered trousers. "Apologies for my lack of decency. Had I known you were to visit, I would have worn more suitable attire."

Amaria grinned. "You are forgiven."

The day was uncommonly hot, and Ornan wiped dirt and sweat from his face as he eyed Amaria. The woman was dressed for comfort; a thin cloth shirt and leggings, both of them white, matching hair that remained remarkably unblemished even in the sweltering heat and wind. Ornan wondered if it was even possible for her to look unattractive, regardless of the circumstances. Clearing his throat, he casually waved his hand to encompass the building and asked, "What brings you to Jericho's Warehouse? Not for the scenery, methinks."

"I am wondering if I could take a few moments to speak with you regarding a curiosity?"

Ornan raised an eyebrow. "A curiosity? Nothing draws a man more than the curious. Come with me."

The pair walked through the large opening that was the wagon entrance to the warehouse. Once inside, Ornan shouted over to a large, bald fellow with skin black as coal. "Baor! Fifteen minutes?"

Baor, who had been sifting through an open encase, paused only long enough to answer. "Of course."

When the two of them had found a quiet corner inside the building with a stone bench to sit upon, Ornan opened his waterskin and took several large swallows. The interior of the warehouse was well ventilated and cooler than the harsh scrutiny of the sun.

"Your taskmaster seemed overly responsive to your request," Amaria commented after Ornan lowered his drink.

"Yes, reliability has its rewards. In my life, I have discovered that the path to respectability comes from asking few favors and doing more than what is expected of you. I am not a vain man, shera, but I can truthfully say that I believe Baor would rather lose half his staff than give me away. There is something to be said for that."

Amaria nodded in concurrence. "Indeed. You would have made an excellent soldier."

"There are enough soldiers in this world, shera."

Bursting into laughter, Amaria slapped the bare shoulder of Ornan, throwing a spew of dust into the air. "Many men carry a sword, Ornan Parémar, but few are worthy of being called a soldier." It suddenly occurred to Amaria how much she was enjoying herself. For so long she had been miserable, wallowing in her own self-pity. It had made her perpetually irritable and generally unpleasant for most people. It wasn't her nature to be angry, but circumstances had altered her in a way she would always lament. Still, somehow, this man from Radam had brought out the 'old' Amaria, the woman that had been respected and followed. The same woman who had a husband and adopted father, an emotional foundation of her life. How she reveled life in those days!

And then she destroyed it all.

Her husband, Royce, was dead, killed by her own overzealous quest for vengeance. She didn't even know where her father was, or how he was faring. How could one recover from such a failure? What was it about this Radamite that gave her a sense of her former life? She hardly knew the man, yet he instantly put her at ease. It wasn't a romantic connection, but some kind of sibling kinship she felt.

As was so common over the last six months, Amaria had fallen within her inner thoughts, and it took a comment from Ornan to pull her free. "So, shera, what curiosity has brought you seeking my advice."

"Have you ever heard the name Ephram Yâramesh?"

Ornan thoughtfully pondered the question. "I do not believe so. Does he reside here in Valgamin?"

"So I am told. It seems that one of the council members, Senastas Baranor, is concerned that a wizard by such a name had become a threat to the city."

Upon hearing the word 'wizard,' Ornan visibly flinched. "It is ill-advised to trifle with those who have the power of the arcane, shera. They are strange and unpredictable. If this man does exist, it is no surprise I have never heard of him. Most wizards, so I am told, keep a low profile."

Amaria absently fingered the edge of the bench while she thought of her own experience in using the dark arts. "I have been asked by this particular councilman to enter the home of this wizard and confront him."

"Alone?"

"No. I have been offered the aid of one of the councilman's stewards. Supposedly, he can handle himself in a fight."

Ever so slightly, Ornan inclined his head. "I do not claim to have much knowledge in the arcane, shera, but I would assume that if one were to confront a wizard, there would be very little 'fighting' involved."

"I do not trust this steward. Something about him troubles me."

Ornan stared blindly at the floor, soaking up the woman's words. "You still have a choice, yes? You can refuse."

Amaria stood from the bench and paced before the Radamite. In her white clothes and stark bleach hair, she looked almost a spectre in the dank interior of the warehouse. "Only a week ago, the First Councilman committed suicide. Were you aware of this?"

"Ah, yes." The man gravely shook his head. "A tragedy. From what I hear, he was admired, even beyond the circle of nobles."

"This councilman I have spoken to believes that Ephram Yâramesh is the reason this man is dead. He insists that Valgamin would be placed in great peril if this wizard were to remain among the populace."

Ornan also rose from the bench and walked to a nearby drum of water. He splashed the fluid across his face several times. Small droplets ran along his chin and continued down his chest, leaving obvious trail lines amid his sullied torso. As he enjoyed the cooling effects, he called to Amaria, "What of this councilman? Is he a dubious man, like his steward, or can you trust him?"

Not desiring to yell their conversation back and forth for everyone in the building to hear, Amaria quickly stepped over to Ornan. Lowering her voice, she replied, "Senastas seems a good man. I saw no ill meaning in his words. I believe he is genuinely concerned."

"Then all you must do is choose."

Amaria scoffed loudly. "As if all choices were easy! In truth, I prefer not to get involved. I do not fear this wizard, but I am not eager to engage myself in situations which I know little about." She pulled her blade halfway out of its scabbard, gazing at the steel as it reflected the dull light surviving within the warehouse.

"It would not be easy to refuse this councilman, however. He is young, idealistic, and has placed everything on the hope of my acceptance. He refuses to involve the city watch for fear that public paranoia will ensue, which is understandable. But if I decline, who takes my place?" The woman lifted her shoulders, lowered her head, and rubbed the back of her neck. "I feel I have to accept."

Ornan said nothing immediately. He rubbed water over his arms, the wheels of thought revolving behind his eyes. After some time, he posed the question, "What troubles you about this steward? Do you think he will betray you?"

Amaria returned her weapon fully into its casing. "I don't know. I can't truly say." She flipped a loose strand of hair from her face. "A sense of unease, I suppose."

"Then I will go with you."

"What?" Amaria stared at the man, jaw open. "Absurd! You hardly know me! I go to face a wizard. This is no time for some false sense of grandeur."

"I will not go to face the wizard, shera. I go to keep watch on this steward."

Amaria turned and moved hastily to to exit of the warehouse. Ornan hurried to follow. "I will not let you go," she said to the man behind her. "We have only met twice. Why should I trust you any more?"

"You trusted me enough to reveal your story." Ornan grabbed her by the arm and spun her to face him. The woman scowled, but did nothing more. "You need someone on your side, shera. And," he stopped, searching for suitable words, "I could use the friendship. I often feel I live alone on an island."

Who would have thought, the man was lonely! The Knight of the Dove's appearance grew sharp, hard. "I cannot have another death on my conscious."

"I do not intend to die, shera."

Amaria furrowed her brow, the agony of a previous transgression saddling the delicate creases around her jaded eyes. "Intentions are like flowers, Ornan Parémar. They seem honorable and just, but eventually they choke on weeds of blackness. Such honor withers away and surrenders to the darkness that twists it into something far different, something never expected."

Ornan's features turned sad. "And when will you free yourself of that darkness?"

Amaria did not answer. She turned away, looking up into the cloudless scope, slowly veering her sight toward the sun. *Can I free myself from the darkness?*, she wondered. Her face absorbed the sunborne heat, and as she considered the warmth, she wondered if the fiery orb was a symbol of the tormented anguish that blazed at the very heart of her soul.

Four

The bootmaker, a squirrelly man named Dandren, wrung his hands irritably. "For the tenth time, there be no secret door down here!"

The other three people in attendance continued to inspect the small cellar, ignoring the complaints of the owner. Amaria had immediately ascertained that the small storage space was rarely used. One rickety shelf lined the wall opposite the stairway leading upward, and a few dusty baubles of little importance rested upon the cracked wood. Nothing else filled the damp space save for the four people standing upon the floorboards.

Although she had argued vehemently with Ornan, the Radamite had proved the more stubborn, insisting that he accompany her. Outwardly, she showed disapproval, but in truth, she was glad for his presence. She trusted Ornan, though she had no explanation why. He had the ability to ease her tensions, and indeed, few had such an effect upon her. Amaria threw a quick glace his way. Today, Ornan wore thick, studded leather garments. An unremarkable sword was gripped in his right hand, its hilt unadorned and dressed with notches and scrapes from past use. Despite its common look, the weapon was formidable, for the steel was sharp and well cared for. It was a stark contrast to her own sword, which was extravagantly garlanded. The handle was shaped into a dove at the pommel, and several golden inlaid designs adorned the hilt and blade. The only flaws were the scratches and scuffs of battle that could not be repaired.

Thavas had donned a sleeveless robe of the same color he always wore; grey with silver trim. Now that Amaria saw his bare arms for the first time, it was obvious that during the previous occasions the steward had intentionally downplayed his physical strength with long-sleeve garments. His arms were not massive, but they were muscular and well exercised. A sword belt was wrapped around his waist, but he seemed to be wearing no armor of any sort; a fact that Amaria found interesting. Additionally, he had shown much displeasure, as had the Councilman Baranor, when they learned that another man accompanied Amaria. Neither trusted the outsider. Once she had given them an ultimatum, however, they quickly consented.

Amaria, dressed in full gear, was running a hand along the wall, searching for any indicator of a hidden door.

"Here it is," Ornan shouted. The Radamite was sliding his sword along a crease in the floor. After making a full square, everyone could see the outline of a hatch well concealed in the far corner of the room.

"It cannot be!" the bootmaker shouted, utterly perplexed.

He was ignored, and the others looked on as Ornan worked to free the slab of timber. "There is no handle. I will have to jar it loose." He readied his sword and shoved the steel hard into the thin space between the wooden slab and the floor. With much effort, he successfully wedged the trapdoor open, while hinges squealed in protest.

All four people peered down into the square opening. It was pitch black, like a yawning mouth of still shadow. The bottom was invisible from their perspective, making the hole seem an endless chasm. Thin iron rungs had been fastened into the rock along one side of the gap, meant for climbing.

"It appears we have found what we are searching for," Amaria stated dryly.

The bootmaker was ranting incoherently, absolutely staggered at the reality that a trap door was hidden in his cellar. Unfortunately for the distressed man, the others paid him no heed.

Looking down the shaft, Thavas slowly shook his head. "I hear nothing. How far do you think it goes?"

"There is only one way to find out," Amaria announced. "Let's get the torches lighted and be done with this."

Ornan had offered to carry the small pack of supplies around his shoulders, and he quickly removed two torches that had been poking their way out the top. Minutes later, two sticks of flame threw dancing red light across the walls of the cellar. Ornan kept one, and Amaria handed the second to Thavas.

The steward hesitated, asking, "Why must I carry the other?"

"Because you are going down first," the woman said flatly. As Thavas took the torch, Amaria grasped his wrist tightly. Her eyes bore upon him, bitter and unsympathetic. "Do not question me again, Thavas Iimon."

The man held her stare for another second, giving no quarter. Then, saying nothing, he pulled away and began lowering himself into the black pit.

"Wait! What am I to do?" the bootmaker called.

Amaria placed a slender hand on his shoulder. "It is best if you pretend you never saw this, my friend. Do not board it up, though, until we have returned and given you permission. None of us would like to be trapped down below, and I'm certain it would make us very *angry*." The woman gave an especially hard emphasis on the last word, giving the bootmaker the impression that it might have been a threat more than advice. One look into his quivering lip assured Amaria that he would wait. She slipped down into the trapdoor, followed closely by Ornan, taking the rear guard.

The aperture proved far deeper than any of them could have imagined. Near ten minutes they descended, the air around them musty and damp. The size of the well never widened, and the closeness of the rock walls and the darkness that pressed against them gave each an unwilling sense of claustrophobia. At one point, Amaria muttered sardonically, "I do not believe this hole is a natural rock formation."

"But how could something this *long* have been cut so effectively? And the bootmaker never knew!" Ornan countered in disbelief.

"Who can say?" Amaria answered. "Perhaps the answer lies at the bottom."

They continued downward, and just as it seemed they were about to climb straight down into the bowels of the abyss, the walls suddenly opened and a great cleft exposed itself. A minute later they had reached the bottom, exhausted arms and all.

They stood at the base of a subterranean passage. Dark rock rose upward on their sides, flanking them, but ahead weaved a wide pathway that for all purposes looked like a naturally formed corridor. The ceiling was high above, past the weak light of the torches, and Amaria couldn't distinguish where the iron rungs disappeared into the small cavity that led back to the bookmaker's cellar.

The ground was uneven and jagged, but passable. Amaria motioned for Thavas to take the lead. The steward, timberstick in one hand and sword in the other, started a timid gait forward. He moved slowly, making certain of his footing as the darkness nibbled at the edges of the torchlight. While Ornan was busy keeping his vision firmly locked on Thavas, Amaria was immersed in her surroundings. She had served as a soldier for eight years, but never had she found herself in a predicament that forced her below the surface of the earth. Like most anyone, she had heard tales of adventurers who purposely sought out dungeons and underground caves in search of treasure and fame. Most stories were almost certainly false, but even for those that held a glimmer of truth, she deemed such acts as pure idiocy. Yet now, sauntering cautiously through the darkened, cavernous path, she understood the lure.

There was an air of mystery, of the unknown, that surrounded them. It excited her, and her sword arm tingled in anticipation of what lie ahead.

Further on, a faint glimmer of light began to show. The three proceeded cautiously, and the luminance increased as they drew closer. Amaria felt a tinge of anxiety, and the scrape of steel was heard as she instinctually slid free her own sword from its scabbard. Despite her vigilance, there appeared to be no obstacles or enemies lurking in the corners, and they moved along the passage completely unhindered. With each step taken, the air grew sultrier, and save for the dull tin clanging of Amaria's armor, silence rang true.

Rounding a corner of jutted granite, they discovered themselves at the entrance to a large subterranean cavern. A light, the same light that had led them there, filled the area enough to allow them ample range of vision. Looking about, Amaria could find no source for the illumination. It was as if the light was simply there, without cause or purpose. She knew that not to be true.

High above, formations of stalactites pointed downward menacingly, but underneath the ground had grown smoother, as if intentionally leveled for travel. In all, the opening was nearly two hundred feet across, and half that in width. Amaria admired the scene when a soft elbow brought her from her reverie. She turned and saw Ornan pointing toward the opposite end of the great orifice.

Several small tables and a desk were neatly organized. Upon the tables were strange mechanisms of various sorts, and loose parchment sprinkled both the tables and the desk. Many shelves circled the makeshift work area, crammed with books and more devices that Amaria had never seen before. The slightest tinge of pipe smoke wafted about the air, a warming sense that contradicted the remote depth of their location.

What truly commanded Amaria's attention was the figure sitting at the desk.

If ever there was someone that epitomized the banal assumption of what a wizard should look like, this man was it. He had a long, drooping white mane that fell past his shoulders, and identical hair grew from his upper lip, fading into a long beard that reached his chest. He sported the bushiest, most ruffled looking eyebrows Amaria had ever seen upon anyone. On his head was a black wide-brimmed hat with a rounded top, and he was dressed in heavy robes the color of ebon, with crimson trim. The long sleeves of his arms hung low beneath thin wrists. Motionless, the man appeared completely engrossed in a piece of paper held before him, when abruptly deviant eyes shot up, gazing across the cavern and directly at the three intruders.

"Ember and ash!" the man cackled in disgust, dropping his paper in a theatrical motion and standing from his chair. He was tall, well over six feet. "Agmon! Damn you! I should have expected you to show your miserable face around here sooner or later."

Amaria realized that the wizard was speaking to Thavas. She whirled her head to the steward, her glare harsh and scrutinizing. "You *know* this man?"

Thavas ignored her. He held a cautious stare directed at the robed man. "We are here to kill you, Ephram!"

An amused chuckle escaped the lips of the wizard. "No doubt you are." He viewed Thavas with a look that bordered pity. "You were lucky to survive the last time, Agmon. Are you so anxious to die by my hands?"

The wizard took several steps forward, slightly lifting the brim of his hat to regard the trio.

"And who have you brought with you? No, let me guess. Mere pawns that you have mislead in order that they unknowingly join your little agenda. A ragtag band if ever I saw one." Dark sockets halted as they fell upon Amaria, inspecting her thoroughly. Ephram smiled, causing the man to appear almost senile. "Though this one is a pretty lass. A bit too young for these old bones, mayhap, but I'm wiling to give it try."

"Thavas!" Amaria demanded, "What in the hells is going on here?" Confusion lined the woman's features, and a quick glace at Ornan informed her that he was in the same position.

"Thavas is your name now, is it?" Ephram interjected. He calmly scratched the white beard at the base of his chin. "Not a bad name. Definitely better than Agmon." Addressing Amaria, he said, "I believe introductions are in order. I am Ephram Yâramesh, sage and Arch-Priest of the Temple of Hysth, the great god known by many as the *Corrupter*, though we in his service prefer to call him the *Shaper*. May I know the names of those who are about to kill me?"

"You may not know "

"I am Amaria Eversvale," Amaria boldly announced, cutting off an infuriated Thavas, "known as the Knight of the Dove." She didn't know why she offered her identity, but she felt no regret. For some unexplainable reason, she held a cavalier, unconcerned manner over the present circumstances. Something was lacking inside her, but she couldn't put her finger on it. And then, like a brick against her head, she realized what was missing; her fears. She wasn't consumed by terror, as any normal person should when standing face-to-face with the Arch-Priest of Hysth, a powerful dark god. Her life-altering moment, her vengeful rage, had happened more than six months ago, and yet she was still discovering new effects. *What in the hells happened to me?*, she wondered darkly.

Ephram's eyes engulfed the woman, dissecting her fully. In time, he smirked as they widened in comprehension, "Of course, how ignorant of me. I had sensed the chaos in you, but I hadn't placed it together. Scorn me, so obvious it is! Unless I am mistaken, you have had dealings with my lord in the past, yes?"

"It is something I will regret for the rest of my life," Amaria spat.

Ephram lifted thin shoulders, his heavy robes rustling slightly. "Only time can make truth of that. There is great potential in you, Amaria Eversvale."

"Stop!" Thavas shouted. "She has come to aid me in defeating you, Ephram. She has no use for your subtle hints of recruitment."

"Bah! Your words carry no weight with me, Agmon." Ephram reached out a slender hand and spoke a short word under his breath. There was a momentary flash of light, and when it dissipated, the wizard held a long object in his hand. It was a finely crafted ironshod staff that glinted fiercely in the bizarre sourceless light of the chamber. The staff spiraled on one end and held a figurine of some type of beast, a monstrous representation of Hysth, Amaria presumed. Weapon in hand, the sage slurred, "You are nothing more than a myriad of deceitful lies. Does the woman even know that she is standing side by side with a minion of Wyur? Perhaps you should tell her the real reason why the good councilman killed himself."

Before any verbal response could be offered, Thavas rushed forward, his sword primed to strike. At least fifty feet of ground separated Thavas from his target, and as the man covered the gap with exceptional speed, Ephram raised his staff and mouthed a single syllable. The engraved beast at the end radiated for the briefest of moments, and then a luminous blinding light burst forth into the torso of a stunned Thavas. A wave of pure energy consumed him and his body was thrown violently backward, landing hard upon the stone ground.

Amaria wasted no time. Before the wizard could direct a second magical attack, she was on him, swinging her sword in an effort to decapitate the sage. Ephram swiftly brought his staff to meet her sword. Although the force of the collision was great, the ironshod pole held firm and deflected the blow. Undeterred, the woman continued, assiduously hacking away. The wizard was able to parry each maneuver, but the forceful attack caused him to step away. Amaria managed to drive her forearm into Ephram's chest. The surprised wizard grunted from the jolt, stumbling backward and tumbling to the ground.

The countless black and red folds of Ephram's robes lay in a muddled heap. Amaria was ready to pounce on her downed foe when a small pillar of fire rose from the ground before her. The blaze quickly spread, surrounding the wizard in a circle. The image was startling and Amaria hesitated, mesmerized by the ethereal flames. Ephram gradually stood, encircled by his corposant shield. The woman vaguely heard him intone words in a muffled cadence, then much louder cry, "Come forth!"

From seemingly nowhere, Amaria watched two dog-shaped beasts coalesce before her very eyes. Strangely, the animals were not of solid matter. They were ghost-like in appearance, sallow and translucent. Amaria watched the phantom-like beings curiously. They danced around her as if they were of solid matter; making the physical motion of barking, though no audible noise came forth. In a ghastly way, the sight was somehow sad and depressing. One suddenly leapt for her face. Instinctively, she brought up her arm, though she all but expected the spectral animal to pass undisruptive through her body.

It didn't. Transparent teeth bit into her forearm. Amaria didn't feel the sting of a normal puncture wound, but rather the sensation of being jabbed by a thousand frozen icicles. Her arm went bitterly cold, and she furiously shook to wrench her limb free from the jowls of the beastly phantasm. The animal released its hold and fell back, but in turn, the second attacked. Amaria's arm was half numb, but she managed to raise her weapon to the oncoming enemy. When her blade contacted the beast, to her delighted astonishment, it dissipated instantly into nothingness. The woman turned back to the other, and when it dived in, she sidestepped and sliced downward, her blade going through the backside of the apparition. Just like the first, it dissolved away as if it were never there.

Feeling a minor sense of triumph, Amaria blinked and turned just soon enough to see the silver glint of a staff as it bashed her temple. The woman's head and neck, followed shortly by the rest of her body, spun wildly and carried her to the serrated cavern floor. As she landed, she wondered for an instant how the wizard had managed such a strong blow from such a frail body.

Amaria lay still for a brief second. A warmness trickled down the left side of her face; her own blood. She had no time to consider the wound, for she knew the wizard would be upon her. Rolling to a knee, the woman caught the tail end of Ornan diving at Ephram, his own sword arching savagely.

Ephram stood, unconcerned, as his attacker veered toward him. Just when it seemed the wizard would be sliced in two, he raised his staff and caught the Radamite square in the jaw. A flash of wild electricity lit up the cavern, and when it dispelled, Ornan lay in a crumpled heap against the face of the distant wall.

Amaria was back on her feet and ready to take the offensive once more, but the wizard's words stopped her.

"Enough! Agmon!" Ephram called, his vision shifting beneath his thick brows to view the steward. Thavas was limping feebly toward Ephram, his face grimacing in pain while he tucked his left arm against his side, the way a man does when ribs are broken. The wizard bestowed an expression of compassionless pity as he watched his enemy struggle. "Wyur has no place in Valgamin. Your pathetic god is nothing more than loose pebble beneath Hysth's mighty feet. But," the old man sighed, "I am not without pity. Leave now; take whatever followers you have brought with you, and return to your pitiable little refuge up in the mountains. If you do this, I will let you live. Mind this, Agmon, I have already spared you once before. A second time is unheard of."

Thavas coughed hard, but his progress never halted. "How generous you are. You spare me, only to warp the minds of every soul in Valgamin as Hysth towers over the city like so many ravens. The *Corrupter* will not succeed!"

The old man rolled his eyes. "Spare me your righteous forgery, Agmon. You care nothing for the people. You only wish me dead to open the door for Wyur to move freely in the city. The dark gods only know how the city would fare under the *Deceiver's* foothold. Within a year, the populace would have all killed one another in their own fraudulent lies. No, Agmon, I do not think you have Valgamin's best interest at heart. Under Hysth, the *Shaper*, the city would grow strong and united!"

As the two rivals bickered, Amaria divided her attention between worrying for Ornan's condition and attempting to grasp some semblance of understanding over what was taking place. She now realized that Thavas was a servant of Wyur, the god of lies, commonly called the *Deceiver*. Somehow, she had gotten herself thrust into the middle of some feud between two evil factions. Though she wasn't pleased by her predicament, it certainly made for an interesting state of affairs. Hysth was an ages old god of darkness, one who had, if some of the theological scriptures were to be believed, caused war and chaos in the realms for several millennia. Wyur was an upstart deity, his inception to prominence starting sometime in the last two centuries. Both gods served darkness, both were narcissistic, and no doubt Hysth had no intention of giving ground to a newcomer, especially in a city ripe with impressionable souls, such as Valgamin.

Amaria quickly risked a glance at Ornan. The man lay motionless in an awkward angle, but she could see the subtle rise and fall of his chest, assuring her that for the moment, he lived. She returned her concentration upon the two enemies.

"If you will not leave," the arch-priest was saying, "then you give me no choice. I must kill you."

Thavas looked to Amaria. "Strike him down!" he pleaded. "You cannot fathom the power he holds. He must die!"

The decision was not an easy one, but she allowed herself to act on impulse. It is easier to eliminate the more powerful foe first, she surmised, and then worry about the other. Her blade whirled at the wizard.

Ephram flung his staff upward to deflect the killing blow. The two weapons slammed together, hurling the clatter of metal on metal bounding off the large walls. His defense successful, Ephram stepped backward, the countless fabrics of his robe tousling as he regarded the woman.

"It was a foolish choice, milady," he said poignantly, "but I'll not hold it against you. Wyur can deceive even the most astute minds. You have much promise, Knight of the Dove, and it does me no good to see you die. Our next meeting will be on far better terms."

The arch-priest muttered a word and waved his arm. The area around him grew thick with sudden mist. It seemed to emerge from nothing, but quickly overcame Ephram, then Amaria. The woman began lashing out with her blade as she realized what was happening, but she was not quick enough. Seconds later, when the ill-gotten mist vanished, Ephram Yâramesh was nowhere to be found. Amaria quickly scanned the room. The old man was gone, and the papers and books that lined the desk and shelves seemed to have vanished with him. She scowled, for there was no debating his immense power. Ornan was in the same place as before, still slouched gracelessly against the cavern wall. Thavas was also present. The servant of Wyur cursed angrily at his, or perhaps *her*, failure.

Our next meeting will be on far better terms, Ephram had said. What in the hells was that supposed to mean? Amaria didn't even want to consider the possibilities. She had no plans to see that crazed wizard ever gain. Drawing away from the cryptic words, Amaria ran to Ornan's side and inspected his body. The Radamite had suffered a sizable blow to his head, as evidenced by the swelling just below the crown of his skull. He also sported several bruises, most certainly from his impact against the wall.

Otherwise, he seemed fortunate to still be in one piece. His breathing was steady, and Amaria was certain he would live another day. Gripping her sword, she commenced a steady march to where Thavas stood.

The steward was checking his ribs when he suddenly felt the cold steel of Amaria's weapon pressed against his throat.

"You have some explaining to do, Thavas Iimon, or should I call you *Agmon!*"

Shortly after Ephram's departure, the supernatural radiance of the cavern had dispelled. The comely warmth of the grotto had been replaced by unrelenting gloom. Amaria had hastily retrieved the torches, but even with the timbersticks lighted, she felt as though she stood encapsulated by a fading glow that struggled to stave off eternal blackness.

Ornan had regained consciousness, but he was complaining of a massive headache and was lying on his back within the torchlight. Thavas was sitting next to the Ramamite, his arm still nursing his injured ribs, though his attention was on Amaria, who loomed over the steward like a panther toying with its prey. Her own sword was in her right hand, Thavas' sword in the other.

The steward looked up at her, cobalt eyes turning crimson in the flame of the torches. "I never lied to you, Amaria."

"You intentionally deceived me!" she spat, making every effort to hold back the anger that threatened to disembowel the steward where he sat. "Is Senastas a minion of Wyur as well?"

Thavas ran both hands through his long auburn hair. To his credit, he showed no fear sitting beneath the woman's furious scrutiny. "No. He knows nothing of my association with the *Deciever*. I spent half a year gaining his trust as a minor nobleman well schooled in the affairs of administration. In time, he hired me to act as one of his counselors."

Amaria offered a wicked smile. "I have a feeling that he will not be pleased when he discovers that his advisor is under the dominion of Wyur."

"No." The steward shook his head. "And you mustn't tell

him."

The woman balked. "Why not? Perhaps you haven't lied to me, but you have certainly lied to Senastas. Of course I will tell him. It is his right as a councilman to know. I shall enjoy watching you squirm as they dole out your sentence. You deserve the executioners axe for parading as a nobleman and acting as if you care for the city." Her expression darkened. "The wizard implied that you are the reason the councilman killed himself."

"He lies! In no way was I involved in his suicide. That has Ephram's mark all over it. I hold no power so strong as to cause a man to climb a mountain and jump off."

Amaria unlatched the straps of her cuirass, letting her torso breathe just a little beneath the armor. "Regardless, Senastas will have you at the gallows, and I'll not shed a tear."

"If you tell Senastas, then you will have no way of finding Ephram."

"I have no interest in meeting that wizard ever again." The woman cursed, casting a glance at the lounging Ornan before returning her brooding fury upon Thavas. "What madness led you to believe we could defeat him? He is the Arch-Priest of Hysth!"

Thavas lifted his hands, placing his palms open and pointed upward. "Yes, and you are the Knight of the Dove. Who else could defeat him?"

"Well, we shall never know," the woman stubbornly announced, "for I have no intention of facing him again."

"Do you not understand? You must face him. Through Ephram, the *Corrupter* will warp Valagmin. It will no longer be a free city, but one fashioned to serve the purposes of Hysth. The populace will not even be aware of who they serve, for it will be coated by good deeds and false promises. You cannot imagine what will happen."

Amaria began pacing. Her blue mantle shifted lightly while she moved back and forth in front of the seated steward. "Even if what you say is true, it could take years, decades perhaps, for such a transformation to take place. There are temples in Valgamin dedicated to the gods of light that will combat him every step of the way."

"Hysth will win," Thavas said frankly. "There is no unity in this city. He will unite them through treachery, then slowly turn them to the darkness." He paused, following the eyes of Amaria with his own. "You cannot turn me in, Amaria. I am the only one who can help you defeat Ephram."

A sour smile crossed Amaria's face. She didn't like what was happening. In simple terms, she wanted Thavas dead. She held nothing but untainted rage for the man who posed as a steward to the fine, young councilman, and then led her into a suicidal confrontation with the Arch-Priest of Hysth. He was a man that lived off his own deceptions, and she had no doubt that he would continue to mislead her if she followed him. And yet, regrettably, there was merit to what the man claimed. Ephram was indeed powerful, and there was no doubting his connection to Hysth, for the wizard had voluntarily offered the information. How much of a threat to Valgamin did Ephram pose? Was it substantial enough for her to get involved? And why should she care? After all, she wasn't planning on staying in Valgamin long enough to see the damning effects. Endless questions, never answers, she mused. Aloud, she said, "How can I willingly take sides with a minion of Wyur? If I defeat Ephram, that leaves the city open to the *Deciever*."

"My only interest is to see Hysth removed from Valgamin. But, you may deal with me as you see fit, *after* we defeat Ephram."

"*If* we defeat Ephram."

Thavas said nothing. He lowered his head and poked at his ribs. His exquisite robes had been sullied from the scuffle, and a series of thin scratches outlined his right cheek.

Several minutes passed, silence imbuing the trio. Deep in thought, Amaria probed the benefits and negatives of her available choices. When she finally did settle on a decision, she wasn't even sure what had caused her to do so. She placed the tip of her sword against the chest of Thavas and shot him an implacable stare. "You have a temporary pardon, Thavas. But keep this in mind; I trust you no more than that wizard. Any attempt of trickery, and I will leave your head several feet from your shoulders. Understood?"

Thavas nodded. "Quite clearly. Now, let us leave this Wyur forsaken hole."

Turning to view Ornan, she asked him, "Can you climb in your condition?"

The Ramadite grunted an affirmative, groggily sitting up and shaking the cobwebs from his head.

"I will have trouble climbing with my injury." Thavas pronounced.

"Do not think I am carrying you." Amaria lowered her hands and helped Ornan to his feet. The man still seemed a little woozy, and the long climb back into the cellar of the bootmaker's store worried her. Still, Ornan made no complaints as he declined to lean on her shoulder, preferring to walk on his own. Amaria turned back to Thavas. "You can stay behind if you wish."

Grunting, the steward rose to his feet, falling into step behind the others as they made their way back through the cavern darkness.

Five

As the sun greeted the sleeping city with its first rays of warmth, Amaria was already making her way through the streets of Valgamin. Much of the populace still slumbered, and only a few souls had filtered their way outside to supplement Amaria's early rise. A quiet, calm morning, she surrendered to the much-needed serenity.

Three days had passed since her skirmish with Ephram, and from that time until now, Amaria had simply rested, doing very little while she waited to hear from Thavas. The steward had parted ways with her shortly after the fight, saying he would contact her when the next tactic was arranged. Amaria suspected the man would simply flee once they returned to the surface, but the servant of Wyur proved relentless in his goal to bring down Ephram, for he took them directly to Senastas and described the confrontation, omitting only his association with the *Deceiver*. The councilman was relieved that everyone had survived, but he displayed obvious concern over Ephram's escape. After a lengthy discussion, Amaria and Ornan left the two men to their own designs.

Over the past two days, she had visited the Radamite twice. The swelling on Ornan's skull had come down, and his recovery was mostly complete. She wished she could say the same thing for herself. Though she bore no significant physical wounds, the conflict with Ephram continued to stab her mentally. She was filled with nagging questions, and no answers were forthcoming. Did assisting Thavas make her a servant of Wyur? At the time, it seemed her choice was limited to the lesser of two evils; either let the city fall into the grasp of Hysth, or help Thavas bring the arch-priest down. Still, how could she justify fighting alongside a man with palpable evil intent? And the most infuriating part was that she *knew* he would continue to mislead her, and thus far she had done nothing to stop it. The same question formed over and over: How dangerous was Thavas Iimon? There was no questioning the power of Ephram Yâramesh, for she had seen it first hand. Thavas, however, remained a complete mystery. He had shown very little battle prowess during the scuffle, but was he merely holding back his abilities purposely? She hadn't trusted him from the very first time they'd met, and it seemed that wasn't going to change any time soon.

Aimless in her tranquil walk, Amaria allowed the street to take her where it may. When the woman regained her senses, she discovered that she was standing directly in front of the great temple of the gods. Wide-eyed, she gaped shamelessly at the spectacle before her.

The structure was massive and absolutely stunning to look upon. No church in Dhorn-Dyas could compare. Built of white marble, it practically lit the street with its radiance as four towering spires rose toward the heavens, capping an enormous apse that most certainly held several chapels within. Regal looking buttresses arched alongside the building, filling the open spaces with majestic grandeur. Amaria could see no blemishes along the outer walls, and she wondered how recently construction of the church had been completed.

Standing in front of the temple, a cleric was busy tending to some early morning duties. The man had apparently taken notice of Amaria's admiration, for with white robes flowing, he quietly approached her.

His voice, soothing and gentle, came upon her, "You know, I see it many times a day. Yet every time I look upon it, I am humbled." The cleric turned wizened eyes to Amaria, but the woman took little notice. She was still silently captivated by the spectacle. The cleric continued, "Are you simply passing by, or have you come to speak with someone?"

Amaria looked away from the gleaming temple and onto the white robed stranger. The cleric sported hawkish features; a thin face with a pointed nose. He was perhaps in his forties, though his greying hair was still thick and his cleanly shaven face smooth and vital. Hazel eyes gently regarded Amaria. Those eyes should have comforted her, but instead, they rendered her self-coconscious.

Clearing her throat, Amaria searched for words, but only maganged to strain in puzzlement. "I . . . I am not sure."

The priest smiled warmly. "I can see that you have questions, whether you wish to ask them or not. There is nothing to fear, milady, for anything you say is kept in confidence. Come inside and I will attempt to satisfy your queries." He started for the temple doors, fully expecting Amaria to follow. Though she half expected to turn and flee, she found herself trailing the white robed priest as he entered the great temple.

If the exterior of the building was a spectacle, then the interior was utterly pristine in comparison. The two stood within a grand foyer, a large open space covered with divine murals, tapestries, stained glass windows, and several sculptures. In the heart of the cherubic beauty rested the colossal statue of a robed man, standing nearly forty feet in height. The arms were spread outward and the head tilted down. Strangely, no face adorned the stone skull, as if it had been forgotten or intentionally left out. Amaria stepped closer to the looming statue, straining her neck upward to study the piece. The cleric followed at her side.

"Who is this supposed to be?" Amaria asked.

"That is Aohed. The god of the gods. The *Creator*. The one who holds dominion over all others. This temple is dedicated to Aohed. It is the only temple in our world that is committed directly to the *Creator*."

"Why?"

The cleric ran a thin finger along the toes of the statue. "Aohed stands above the other gods of light, so few believe they can worship him directly. The other deities of good, all of them worthy of worship, often act as mediator for Aohed."

"How did this temple become the only church of Aohed?" Amaria quietly asked.

"Six years ago, the council commissioned a large sum of money to offer the ever increasing populace a primary place of worship. There are several gods of light to choose from, so the obvious choice was to dedicate the church to Aohed himself. It proved a wise selection, for citizens from varying domains of worship all feel comfortable giving their revere to Aohed, who looks after the other gods. And even Aohed has opened himself to our prayers."

"Why is there no face?"

"Because Aohed has many faces. Each god of light, from Eeios the *Sufferer*, to Narosor the *Warrior*; they all show an aspect of Aohed. His gifts are distributed through the other gods. Thus, one face would not do Aohed justice."

Amaria continued to stare at the stone figure. Something inside her wanted to desperately embrace the piety of Aohed, to openly receive the teachings that followed the path of light. The spiritual solidity would be welcome. At the same time, she wished to rebel against the perceived narcissism that the gods of light bestowed. She was torn, and her own self-doubt angered her.

The cleric watched Amaria closely. After a short time, he said, "Let us go to my study where I can hear your questions."

The woman nodded, letting her temper subside. They quickly exited the lobby, eventually coming to a small room. The cleric closed the door behind them and motioned for her to sit in a padded chair while he took a seat behind his desk. Amaria casually looked about the study. It was a humble room, presenting simple wooden furniture and a massive amount of books lining each wall. Candles lit the interior, giving it a brown tint and a warm, cozy feel. Papers lay sprawled atop the desk and many freshly written pen marks graced them. The priest gently cleared the area before him and let his bony elbows rest on the oak desk.

"I have just realized that I have not properly introduced myself," the cleric said. "I am Ishvar Aronis, cleric and servant of Aohed."

Amaria leaned forward. "It is an honor to meet you, your holiness, and I appreciate the time you have given me."

Ishvar modestly downplayed the complement. "A servant of Aohed is always willing to hear from those in need. You needn't be so formal, milady. You are not the first person to have sought my council."

"Apologies, your holiness, but I am unaccustomed to the ways of the church." In awkward nervousness, she absently tugged on the sleeves of her shirt.

A chuckle escaped Ishvar's lips. Soft eyes locked upon her, his face cool and sympathetic. "What questions have you, milady?"

Although Amaria had never prepared to meet a priest on this morning, there had been several questions bounding in her head following the conflict with Ephram, and this seemed the perfect time to seek answers. With a deep breath, she said, "Tell me about Hysth."

In an instant, Ishvar's pleasant features spoiled as a frown crossed his face and he appeared subversive, vision falling away from Amaria and onto the oaken desk. But, the change lasted only an instant, and he quickly composed himself, regaining his erudite bearing. "Hmm," the cleric said in contemplation, "the *Corrupter*. You would do well to avoid dealings with such an evil entity."

"I believe your words, holiness, but please elaborate. There are things I must know."

"What must you know?"

Amaria sighed in exasperation, "Anything you can tell me."

Ishvar did not answer immediately. He rubbed his hands together, pondering the woman's words. "Hysth is of the original four; ordained to godhood by Aohed himself. He is of the ancient world, many millennia before our own existed. It is written in the archaic scripts that Hysth was a creative god, full of imagination. He also had a sense of humor and entertained his godly brethren with laugher. For an indefinite period of time, Hysth flourished in paradise." The priest stopped a moment to collect his thoughts before continuing, "It was Carodon, the *Betrayer*, another of the original four, who conceived and then plotted to destroy Aohed and take his place as god of the gods. Through great persuasion, Carodon convinced Hysth to aid him in Aohed's attempted murder. Of course, Aohed knew of their scheming and thwarted them easily. Fearing the *Creator's* wrath after their failure, both Carodon and Hysth fled for their lives, leaving Aohed's realm, and each creating their own separate realm to rule. Left alone to his lonely sanctuary, Hysth's resentment toward Aohed, Carodon, and his own imprudence slowly took bloom. He is single-minded, and to this day lives solely to create disarray among the other gods. He is indiscriminate in his warring, be it god of light, or a god of darkness."

Amaria lifted her hand to her chin as she listened. Her expression was blank, giving nothing for the priest to dissect.

"Let me say this, milady," Ishvar continued. "Like most powerful deities, Hysth's followers are fanatical, and they will die for their master with no reservations. Hysth gives power to those who serve him. He is influential, angry, and extremely patient; a dangerous combination. Unlike other dark gods, he is not consumed with madness. He is merely embittered for his own mistakes, and bides his time to bring down the others."

"Does Hysth openly war? Will he create armies?" Amaria asked.

Ishvar tapped his temples, his countenance displayed obvious discomfort. "He will do whatever suits him, be it spiritual, or physical, war. Of all the dark gods, he is perhaps the most dangerous, if only because of his diverse methods."

Amaria hadn't moved. She sat like a statue, ruminating over what had been told to her.

"You are bothered." Ishvar commented.

A sardonic smile slipped across the woman's face. "I have a dilemma."

The cleric inclined his head. "A dilemma? If it involves the *Corrupter*, then perhaps you should explain this dilemma of yours."

"Would that I could, holiness." Her green eyes fell to the unresponsive wood of the desk. "It is a burden I must bear alone."

"So you say, milady, but beneath your facade, you cry for help."

Amaria remained still. She looked up to meet the eyes of the cleric. "Let me ask you one more question, holiness."

"Of course."

"If someone were suffering mentally, so much so that even the easiest of decisions became arduous and puzzling, would Aohed cure them from such internal torment? What if this same person also had a darkness within them that they wanted no part of. Would Aohed heal all this from someone who wished it gone?"

Ishvar leaned back in his chair. The conversation had certainly taken an interesting twist, and the priest thought for long moments before making some attempt to answer. "Certainly, Aohed would rid such defects from a suffering soul. But, it is not so easy." He suddenly fixed his sight upon Amaria, holding them tight. "This 'person' must take the first steps."

"What steps are those, holiness?"

"I sense the conflict within you, milady." The cleric's words were piercing as he removed all subtleties from the conversation. "You are not well. I felt this from the beginning of our conversation on the walkway. Know this, milady, Aohed cannot help you until you make an effort to help yourself."

Amaria mirrored the priest's gaze. "And how do I help myself?"

"You must start the slow path to salvation. Make a donation to the god of the gods, a pledge that will start you in the right direction. Then Aohed can begin his union with you, a union that will, in time, be your deliverance."

The woman shot from her chair, her face red with outrage and disgust. "*Coin!* Yes, is there not always some price to be paid for help from the gods! I can see where Aohed's priorities truly rest upon. Know this, *holiness*, I am one soul that will not be duped into giving up every last bit of coin I own so that you may furnish a wine cellar in your temple. A fine salvation from such a generous god," she spat.

In controlled ire, Amaria spun on her heel and plowed through the exit door. Silently, Ishvar watched her go, then stared sullenly at the door for many minutes, trying to recall how the conversation had turned sour so quickly. With mixed expressions of concern and sadness, he returned to his paperwork.

"Mistress Eversvale, you have a visitor who awaits you downstairs in the lobby."

Amaria viewed the servant girl servant, Janea, indifferently. "Who is it?"

The girl tautly shook her head, "I do not know him, milady, but he is someone of importance. He arrived in a bedecked carriage and is accompanied by two guards."

"Tell him I will appear shortly."

"Yes, Mistress." The servant hustled away from Amaria's room and closed the door. Since returning from the temple early in the morning, she had yet to leave her room at The Cardinal and the Jay. She planed to spend the remaining hours relaxing and reading some cultural parchments which she had procured from a merchant the previous day. When the servant came knocking on her door, it had startled her, for dusk was nearing and she hadn't expected visitors. Moving to the wall, Amaria snatched her sword belt and clasped it around her waist, atop the flaxen bodice that dropped past her hips. Then, moving to the water drum, she cupped the fluid in her hands and splashed her face several times, as if attempting to reawaken her senses. Pulling her hair back, she tied it with a piece of blue fabric, then exited the room.

Halfway down the stairs a voice called to her. "Amaria Eversvale, even on such short notice, you are quite the vision."

She found Senastas Baranor smiling at her. The councilman was dressed for casual wear, but his red and black embroidered vest and perfectly tailored leggings proved far more elaborate than any commoner could ever afford. His hair was neatly fretted and combed. A few feet behind him loomed two armed soldiers, their helmed heads swiveling attentively in all directions of the modest inn. The men, with bearing and finery that surpassed the ordinary footsoldier, were obviously Senastas' personal guards. She was happy to note that Thavas was nowhere to be seen.

Amaria graciously returned his smile as she reached the landing. "This is a surprise," she said.

The councilman twisted his mouth in a strange expression, "Yes, well, I apologize for such an unexpected visit. I would have sent a messenger beforehand, but my decision to ride here was quite impulsive on my part, and there was little time to pre-warn you. If this is not a convenient time, I can come later."

From several feet away, Amaria could smell the unusual fragrance that the councilman had applied upon himself. The scent was rich and sweet, but not overbearing. When she reached his side, it was no stronger than it was from a short distance. Tilting her head, she said, "No, it is fine. What is this about?"

Ignoring the last question, the councilman stated, "You really should stay at the council hall, milady. This inn is," he looked about, a hint of displeasure on his face, "adequate, but no place for you. You would be well cared for at the council hall, I am certain."

"The offer is appreciated, Councilman, but this place suits my needs just fine."

"At least let me pay your lodging fees. Gerald, pay the innkeeper a tenday advance."

One of the guards aimed a step toward the main counter. Amaria quickly blocked his way. "That is unnecessary," she announced. "I have no difficulties financially."

The guard looked anxiously at Senastas. "Amaria," the councilman pleaded. "I understand you can afford it. That is not the issue. My offer is a matter of etiquette. If you will not let me accommodate you, then I will not leave this room until I have paid your stay."

Amaria was in no mood to argue such a trivial point. Flapping a hand in exasperation, she proffered, "Very well, do as you wish. But, I claim no debt to this."

Senastas seemed pleased. "Excellent. Now, with that out of the way, I wish to take you on a carriage ride."

"A carriage ride?" Amaria burst into laughter. "Are you courting me, Councilman?"

Senastas' face turned flame red at the question. Although her words were made in jest, the councilman wondered if a faint implication lay buried beneath the outer facade. It took a moment to overcome his sudden embarrassment. When he did, he chuckled at himself. "If only I could, milady. I am afraid I would do you no justice, for it is the man who should protect his lady, not the other way around."

"Do not slander yourself because you do not wield a weapon, Councilman. A man with your insight and acumen is far more impressive than some drunkard waving about a sword."

Senastas gave a self-conscious grin, "Yes, I suppose. Shall we be off, then? I shan't keep you long."

The night was rearing its vanity as Senastas led Amaria outside the poorly ventilated inn and into the refreshing open air. The councilman's bodyguards followed close at hand, watching the shadows warily. A closed carriage sat along the cobbled road, the russet geldings stock-still as they waited patiently. Senastas opened the door for Amaria as the guards took to the standing platforms that flanked the coach. Amaria entered with a courteous nod, followed by Senastas. A momentary scrape, a shortened spark, and a candle was lit. The interior of the curtained carriage flickered with a golden glow.

The coachman prodded the horses, and the carriage lurched into motion. Amaria could feel, as much as hear, the bleating of hinges and the rattle of the ironbound wheels. It had a soothing effect, and she closed her eyes momentarily to give the sensation a few more seconds.

At first, only silence pervaded within the coach, both of them unable to find constructive words. Amaria didn't mind the silence. Due to the rattling of the horses' progress, the common nightlife of the city seemed to have faded away. It almost felt as if they were riding along a secluded country road, away from the chaos and tumult that was Valgamin. If only that were true, she mused.

The candlelight danced while she gazed upon Senastas. The man was rather handsome, as she noted before, but in a far different way than she was accustomed to. She had spent her life as a soldier surrounded by men on a constant basis. Most of these men, soldiers themselves, were of the rugged sort, hard and vigorous. Even her husband, a charmer though he was, fit the mold of the tough, resilient fighter. Perhaps that was why she found his death so unfathomable. Senastas displayed a different kind of handsome. His facial features were soft, his eyes deep, perceptive, yet sympathetic. It felt as if he desperately wished to see the good in everything, yet all too often was dismayed; the calamity of youth, for certain.

"Are you still going to help us?" the councilman asked, throwing Amaria out of her reflections.

The woman closed one eye, peering speculatively at the man. "Before I answer that question, I have one for you, Councilman."

"Please, milady, call me by my name. Formalities grow stale as dry wind in the world of courts and magistrates."

Amaria half-smirked. "Fair enough. May I ask a question?"

"Certainly."

"How much do you trust Thavas?"

The query did not seem to surprise Senastas. He calmly drummed his fingers as he answered, "Thavas can seem a bit, how should I say, shrewd. There has always been an air of vagueness to the man. Still, I can say without doubt that he can be relied upon, for he is one of my advisors after all. If I did not trust him, I would not keep him around. He has been a tremendous help during my short-lived governance in the council."

"He is not all that he seems, I fear. You would do well to keep a close eye on him." How badly she wanted to tell him the truth! For his own safety, the councilman deserved to know of Thavas' treachery. But, she would say nothing. Her fears of Ephram held her tongue. She had yet to place all the puzzle pieces together, and though she was loathe to wait, she would do so until her choices became clear.

The carriage came to a sudden halt. Amaria turned a wary eye on Senastas, but the councilman simply smiled. "Step outside with me, milady," he said.

As Amaria exited the coach, she discovered that they had stopped near a rich, open grassland flanked by a thick grove of trees on one end and a sparkling pond on the other. Even in the darkness, the thin blades of grass shown green as they reached skyward. She realized that they had ridden outside the confines of the city. The pale grey of the city gates were almost invisible in the near distance, but their stark silhouette blocked the stars beyond.

"Valgamin is not known for its eye-catching scenery or location," Senastas said, gazing admiringly at the landscape. "Though not spectacular, this place is tranquil and restorative. It is my favorite spot." Stepping off the cart path and onto the grass, he mentioned, "I have servants cut this regularly to keep it passable. I even fish those waters on occasion, though the fish are but small. I throw them back, for they are not worth the time to cook."

Amaria followed the councilman, listening to the man's reverie. It was a calming place, she admitted. The maddening bustle of Valgamin was absent, and the cool autumn air massaged her lungs. Looking at Senastas through the dimmed light of the lantern held by one of his guards, it seemed that even the lines of worry that plagued his young face had disappeared.

"It is good to have a place like this," she said.

"Every man should," he added, "if only to cast ones doubts and fears into the endless sky and leave them behind." Senastas paused before including, "Of course, mine seem to reappear every time I reenter the city. But, the short respite is well worth it."

The two walked through the even grassy plain in a sort of retrospective silence. It was something that Amaria hadn't done for a very long time. She could hear the footsteps of the two guards walking behind them, but, she paid them little attention. The silver moon, a half-circle on this night, was almost directly above and seemed to cast its glow with more luster than was common.

"You never answered my question."

Amaria drew her thoughts back to the councilman. "Your question?"

Stenastas' eyes were directed forward as he spoke. "Are you still going to help us?"

She waited a long time before speaking. Her voice, emotionless, answered, "I will kill this wizard for you."

"Very good," Senastas smiled, "for I do not think it could be done without you."

Amaria lifted her hand, palm outward. "I am not finished, Councilman. When this is done, I shall possess no more responsibility over what takes place in Valgamin. Ephram is evil, certainly. But, there are other evils in this city, evils that might pose a greater threat, though you have yet to detect them."

"What evils do you speak of, milady? How do you know of them?" A sudden urgency filled his voice.

"When I learn enough to tell you, I will. For now, even I am baffled."

Senastas stroked his hands together. "You speak like it is some kind of riddle."

"If it is a riddle, then it has succeeded in confusing me. Fear not, Senastas, I will inform you when I understand myself."

They continued their stroll, their shoulders not quite touching as they walked side-by-side. The grass rustled gently with each of their steps. After a bit, Senastas came to a stop. "It grows late, and I have a busy day tomorrow." They reversed their direction, pointing their gait to the carriage. Drawing near, the councilman asked, "What drives you, Amaria Eversvale?"

The woman stopped in her tracks. She fixed Senastas with a curious stare. "What do you mean?"

"What makes you get up in the morning? What leads you to the decisions you make? What are your world intentions?"

Time passed as Amaria considered the question, turning it over in her mind. Not so long ago, the answer would have been effortless. She had lived to take her revenge upon the fortress that had taken her family, and then later, her husband. She ultimately succeeded in her quest, but to the ends, it only grieved her worse. Now what? What was left of her life? With a shrug and the shake of her head, she answered, "Perhaps to right the wrongs of my life. Although, each passing day I find it harder to believe such a feat can be accomplished."

Senastas gazed at her perceptively, his expression erudite and somber all the same. "Your face is the collage of a thousand different emotions, Amaria Eversvale. I see them clearly. You hold bitterness, anger, hatred, disdain. You are filled with skepticism and disbelief. And yet, all the same, I see a genuine love and desire for the good of our world. You seek a world of justice."

"There is no justice in this world, Councilman." It was bitterness that exuded from her voice.

"Perhaps you seek the wrong kind of justice," Senastas said, just as they arrived at the carriage. The coachman greeted them with a wave of his hand and moved to open the coach door.

Amaria considered the councilman's words. All her life, her vision of justice had been to bear vengeance upon those who wronged her. *Is that not justice?* Those who cause unwarranted anguish upon the innocent deserve to reap that same anguish upon themselves. It is the way of the world. What can Senastas possibly mean with such words?

"I did enjoy our time together," the councilman mentioned, interrupting Amaria's musings. "I wonder if another time we…"

Senastas' words were cut short by a high-pitched whistle, ending only as the arrow pierced his unprotected body.

Six

An explosion of activity occurred around the carriage as Councilman Baranor fell to his backside, the shaft of an arrow protruding from his stomach. His eyes glazed in shock, peering at the wooden rod that had burrowed into his body like a determined worm.

Amaria was at his side in an instant, her mouth a perpetual cadence of furious curses. She inspected the wound as she pointed toward the grove and shouted, "It came from the woods."

One of Senastas' bodyguards shot forward in a sprint, doggedly seeking the offender. He quickly disappeared in the veil of night, and Amaria returned her attentions on the gravely wounded councilman. Blood ran down the sides of his abdomen on to the dirt of the cart path. Although conscious, he was so absolute was his astonishment that he made not a sound. Amaria gingerly tested the firmness of the arrow lodged in the wound. It was taut. An expert archer had fired the arrow. The shot made especially impressive due to the late hour, with only the moon and minimal starlight to guide him.

"Godsbedamned!" she muttered. "We've got to get him to the healers now! Help me lift him carefully." The other guard took the councilman's legs as Amaria gingerly raised his torso. Senastas groaned in displeasure as they slid him into the coach, his body writhing painfully.

Just then, a piercing cry sounded off from the woods. Amaria gave the coachman a hard look. The voice of a one-time captain issued forth. "Get him to the healers! Waste no time! Worry not for his comfort inside the coach. He'll not make it if you go slowly." Turning to the guard, she commanded, "Do not pull free the arrow. Stay with him and talk assuringly. *Keep him awake!*"

"Yes, milady!" Concern draped the face of the bodyguard.

"I am going to check on your friend. Go now!" Amaria ran in the same direction as the previous guard. Behind her, she heard the coach lurch into motion. Senastas was in bad shape, but she had seen men survive worse wounds. Regardless, it was out of her hands now, and she had to force it from her mind if she was to locate his would-be assassin. Moving with exceptional speed, unhindered by her armor, she soon found herself in the dark confines of the tree grove. A faint whimper came from up ahead, followed by silence. She slowed, moving carefully through wide boles as she labored to scout her pitch-black surroundings.

The snap of a twig caused her to pause. Amaria stepped warily through the undergrowth, which led shortly to a small clearing. Squinting hard in the darkness, she could barely make out the profile of a body on the ground. Drawing near, she discovered it to be Senastas' bodyguard. An arrow protruded from his side, and his throat had been slashed. Checking his sword, she found no blood upon it. Unfortunate, she thought, for a blood trail would make her pursuit so much the easier.

"I don't think he is going to make it, lass."

Amaria glanced up from the body, and directly into the sharpened point of a cocked arrow. The bowman was no more than ten feet away, wearing all black, a small blade around his waist. A second man, in identical clothes, stood a few feet to the right, sword at the ready.

"Who sent you?" Amaria demanded.

The man with the bow chuckled sardonically. "Come now, lass, have you a less obvious question? I wouldn't freely give that knowledge even to save my life."

Amaria's eyes went cruel. "Your oath will be put to the test, my murderous friend."

The man laughed again, harder this time. "Are you questioning my aim? Did you not see the arrow I put into the councilman! I dare say my best shot ever, being dark and all. No archer hits him square in the stomach from such blind distance."

"You will rot in the hells!"

"Bah! Let us get on with this." The man shook his head

slowly. "Killing women is not my favorite pastime, but you came looking for it, and I cannot very well let you live."

"I am going to slay you both." Amaria stated, her voice emotionless.

"Yes," the man said, "that would be something."

With stunning quickness, Amaria dropped to a knee and spun just as the man released his string. She heard him swear when he realized he had missed her. Amaria's blade was freed from it casing, but instead of going after the bowman, she directed her assault upon the second man. Her spinning sword whirled beneath his ill-prepared guard, cutting his abdomen clean though. The man barely had time to grunt as he fell.

The bowman released a string of curses as he frantically tried to ready another arrow. Amaria bull-rushed him, kicking his sternum and sending him reeling backwards. The man lost grip of his bow, letting the weapon tumble to the soft earth.

"Godsdamn woman!" he screamed. "You move like a ghost!" He pulled loose his sword and regarded his enemy through trembling brows.

Amaria held off, not forcing her attack, letting the panic seep into her foe. "Tell me who sent you," she said with as much calm as her anger would allow.

"I have already told you! Not even to save my life. Only in death can I escape his darkness."

"Perhaps after enough torture, you will change your mind." Amaria took one threatening step forward.

The man laughed again. Amaria saw him raise his sword, and she prepared to counter it, realizing too late his true intent. With one smooth stroke, she watched him cut his own throat. His body went limp, and he dropped to the ground, lifeless within seconds.

A deathly silence covered the wooded grove. Amaria stood still, exasperated, staring as his blood soiled the earth below.

Despite the brilliance of midday, the bedchamber of the sickhouse was all gloom. The curtains of the lone window had been dropped, allowing only minimal sunlight within, and the lamps dimmed. Although a small ventilation shaft in the wall allowed air to circulate within the room, there remained a staleness that seemed ever present.

The men inside exuded fatigue, their faces draped with tiredness and concern over the councilman who rested upon the bed. Amaria herself was no less weary, for she had not slept throughout the night. After her skirmish with the two assassins, she had walked the short distance back to the city gates. At first, seeing her bloodied sword and disheveled appearance, the guards refused to let her through. It took some convincing on her part for them to recognize that she had aided the councilman. Ultimately, they taxied her directly to the sickhouse where Senastas lay. By the time she arrived, the healers had done all they could, and Senastas was sleeping soundly.

As the night wore on, visitors came and went, their expressions distraught and confounded. It was obvious that the young councilman was well respected, for all who arrived seemed hesitant to leave, fearing they might never see him again. When morning reared light to the world, a squad of footmen retrieved the bodies of the guard and two assassins from the previous night. Amaria sent word for Ornan to join her at his earliest convenience, and each of the other councilmen had made an appearance, all of them openly upset over the circumstances.

At present, a handful of people filled the chamber, including Ornan, Thavas, and Senastas' bodyguard from the previous night. Second Councilman Veran Marticis had made his second appearance, sitting silently upon a chair, staring at the motionless body of the injured Senastas. The young councilman was naked, save for the bandages wrapped around his waist and a small towel to cover his manhood. The healers had mentioned that the lining of his stomach had been punctured, and blood loss was severe. But, in their words, he seemed "resilient," and they liked his chances. Of course, they then finished with a more pessimistic, "One never knows with injuries such as these. He could heal completely, or he could die within hours." Since, the councilman had awaken only once from his heavy slumber, saying only a few garbled words before losing consciousness again.

Ornan had been silent since his arrival, but he stayed close to Amaria, as if protecting her from the assassins she had already killed the night before. His russet eyes never wavered, nor did he complain of missing a day's work to spend it in the sickhouse over someone he'd only met briefly. His possessed a powerful loyalty to Amaria, though he concealed it beneath a level demeanor.

"The city guard has already started their investigation." Veran Marticis announced, trying to tame the level of anxiety inside the room.

Amaria shrugged. "They'll find nothing, Councilman. The only two men who could tell us anything are both dead."

Veran only nodded a response, his mouth curled in a cheerless scowl.

"Thavas, take a walk with me." Amaria spoke, altering her attention to the steward.

Thavas, on the opposite side of the councilman's bed, looked at her with muted trepidation. His words were slow coming. "Right now?"

"Yes, now. I have some questions that need answering."

Thavas nodded. "Of course, milady." He circled the bed to where Amaria waited for him.

When Ornan also moved to Amaria, the woman waved him off. "Stay here, Ornan. We will be back soon." The Radamite nodded, though he was obviously displeased.

Amaria and Thavas exited the bedchamber and proceeded down the austere hallways of the sickhouse. The building was a dreary place, filled by the occasional wretched moan of those struggling to hold life, their strength zapped by the cries of those waiting to die. The stench alone was maddening, reminding Amaria all too much of a mortuary. She gave a silent prayer that her final days not be spent lying on an infirmary bed.

"Something bothers me, Thavas Iimon." Amaria was still wearing the same outfit from the night before, her ivory hair disordered. She wondered if her face looked as tired as her body felt.

"What would that be, milady?"

Amaria halted her progress and turned to lock her stare upon Thavas. "Nobody could have followed our carriage last night. Their pursuit would have simply been too obvious. We left the city, after all, and even the guards at the gate mentioned that no other persons had exited the gates afterwards."

"What are you getting at?"

"Whoever planned to kill Senastas already *knew* where he was going. They were set up in those woods, waiting to take him down. Last night, Senastas himself said that the choice to call upon me was impulsive." The woman darkened her jewel-like green eyes. "So tell me, Thavas Iimon, how could anyone have known where he was going, save for his closest advisors?"

Thavas stared at her, as if seeing her for the very first time. "You have been through quite an ordeal, Mistress Eversvale. Perhaps you are not thinking clearly."

Amaria flushed in anger. The complacency on Thavas' face infuriated her, and confused her all the same. After the battle with Ephram, he had pleaded like a pathetic child for her grace in not exposing his connection with Wyur to Senastas. Now, his face burned in defiance, almost goading her to say something she might regret. Damned if she would ever understand the man! "I tire of these verbal games, Thavas," she spat. "It is all I can do not to tear your lungs from your chest."

"And then who becomes the murderer?" Thavas smiled arrogantly. "All threats aside, I did not order any assassins to kill Senastas."

"Pardon me if I find that hard to believe."

Thavas shook his head sadly, as if pitying her. "It is but a drop of Hysth's power to perceive such things. It is the *Corrupter* who holds blame for this attack. I do not know why he seeks the deaths of the councilmen, but he has succeeded in killing one, and perhaps a second. We must destroy him soon."

"What happens afterwards?" Amaria snarled. "When Wyur's primary rival has been eliminated from Valgamin, what plans have you prepared for *your* god?"

The steward had not backed down amid a venerable glare

from Amaria. He stood face to face with the Knight of the Dove, giving no quarter and showing no weakness. The tension between them intensified, almost radiating about the hall. With a crooked smile, Thavas said, "That bridge is to be crossed when we arrive."

Amaria opened her mouth in retort when a familiar voice interrupted her. "Shera, Senastas has awaken." It was Ornan. "Come speak to him."

Both Amaria and Thavas abandoned their confrontation and sped to the room of the councilman. They found Senastas lying with his head resting on the same feather pillow as before, but he was awake. Councilman Veran Marticis was at his side, his thin hands holding the man's upper arm as he whispered softly. Senastas nodded once, then twised his neck enough to witness Amaria and Thavas through drooping eyelids.

"Ah, lovely Amaria," the words scratched past his lips, "Veran tells me that you stayed in this room beside me all night."

Inwardly, Amaria felt a tinge of satisfaction knowing that he had given no immediate greeting to Thavas. "I have, Councilman, as has your personal guard," she pointed to the bodyguard who stood motionless in the corner of the room. The man looked terribly aggrieved, as if he had failed utterly in his job. "He acted quickly in bringing you here."

Senastas nearly chuckled, but his face twisted in pain and he released a flurry of coughs. Veran wiped the weakened man's mouth with a wet rag and gave him a comforting pat on the arm. When the fit had passed, Senastas returned his attention upon the woman. "I told you to call me by my name, Mistress Eversvale. And furthermore, I seem to recall it was you who took charge when the arrow was fixed in my gut."

"Only out of necessity, Coun , Senastas. I am sorry to say your other guard died during efforts to seize your attackers."

"Yes, I have been told. Abram was a fine soldier and not easily replaced." The councilman closed his eyes for a moment, discomfort clearly evident in his skin texture. With great effort, he added, "And yet, you managed to kill them both. Your value seems to have no end. You are quite remarkable. Should I ever walk away from this forsaken room, I hope you are still in Valgamin."

Amaria didn't know if Senastas fully meant what he was saying, or if he was delirious from his weakened state. Either way, his last statement felt odd to her. Was it a modest romantic gesture? Perhaps just a statement of appreciation made by a man who was reeling from a significant wound? She might have asked him, but his head lolled to the side and he slipped back into a heavy slumber.

"You look tired yourself, milady." Veran commented with genuine concern. "You have done more than enough for us. The council will forever be in your debt. Why do you not go and get some sleep for yourself."

Amaria threw a glance at Ornan, and the Radamite nodded in concurrence with Veran. She *was* tired, and for the moment there was nothing else to accomplish by staying in the sickhouse. Sleep would serve her well, and even thinking of the cot in her room at The Cardinal and the Jay made her legs wobbly. "Yes, I think I will do that," she announced.

"What do you wish me to do, shera?" Ornan asked, sidling next to her.

She looked at her friend, gratitude forming upon the smile of her lips. "Thank you for coming, Ornan. You need not stay here any longer."

"I will walk you back to your room," he said, leaving no liberty of debate.

Amaria gave a fatigued nod, and then moved toward the room's exit. Thavas' voice rose from the silence, forcing her to pause momentarily. "Yes, o' Knight of the Dove, just as Senastas said; your value holds no end. You will hear from me soon, and we shall continue our hunt." His words were sinister whisperings that curled like talons inside her head.

"I wonder who the hunted will be, Thavas Iimon?" she grunted, stepping beyond the door and leaving a dark faced steward trailing her with his eyes.

Seven

The cold, basalt walls were a harsh, remorseless black. They rose upward fifteen feet, connecting at the top in a semi-circle to form a kind of bizarre archway. Beneath this arch stood a single woman, her body clothed in a drab shirt and low-hanging breeches. She squinted heavily in the darkness to examine the underground rock that encircled her body.

Amaria Eversvale, the emerald of her eyes overcome by the gloom, scanned the barriers along her flanks. The shadowy walls were smooth and daintily illuminated by a sourceless crimson glow, which cast a sinister, unholy radiance about the corridor. Looking closely, she perceived delicate etchings along the basalt that trailed inconspicuously in patterns. The symbols appeared to dance in the baleful light, but they were mysterious and indecipherable.

Though slightly warped, the ground was passable, and Amaria commenced careful steps further into the subterranean passage. A brimstone-like fluid sloshed within tiny pools where the earth had broken away, and she took extra caution to avoid them. Without a torch, Amaria found there was enough light cast by the red glow to allow her a few feet of vision and nothing more, leaving an eternal murk of sheer darkness beyond, eager to devour her.

The windless air was sharp and rancid, and Amaria wrinkled her nose with each breath. Even in the unnatural silence, her ears were soaked with a subliminal, mournful wail, as if the very ground was spiteful of her presence. Amaria wished to the gods that her sword was available to her. Regrettably, her hands could only twitch nervously while she continued along her enigmatic path. Her features, unmoving brow and lips, seemed to be chiseled from very stone that surrounded her. Even without her weapon, she remained on guard, prepared to defend herself at a moments notice. Pausing a moment, she wiped beads of sweat that had dribbled their way past her brow and down her cheeks and nose.

The unearthly glow intensified, growing brighter and brighter until she was forced to shut her eyes to repel the searing luminance. The very earth shook momentarily, and her legs buckled in an effort to stay afoot. Then the tremors ended, the light faded away, and Amaria cast about.

She was no longer inside a corridor, but rather amid a circular, tomb-like enclosure. The walls remained the same black stone, but running in vertical columns along them were horrific totems of unspeakably monstrous faces. The flaming sconces that lined the chamber highlighted the ghastly visages. Amid the glimmering shadow and light, the faces seemed almost alive. In the center of the room, cut from a single piece of obsidian rock, was a throne, elevated to loom over those standing on the ground. The great chair was adorned with studs of red marble that eerily reflected the torchlight like the piercing irises of some mythical beast. Amaria stared at the throne in fascination when a shape began to coalesce within it.

At first, it appeared to be some kind of growing shadow, like an inkblot that lengthened as it spread across paper. Then the shadow took form; arms, legs, and finally, a head. Features developed, and soon, where before there was only an empty throne, sat a man dressed in black and red, calmly regarding Amaria with interest.

"Welcome, Knight of the Dove. It is so rare that I entertain visitors."

The man looked young, perhaps in his early thirties, with pale, creaseless skin that was accentuated by black hair cut short at the temples. His face had no prominent features save for his eyes, which were as black as the throne he sat upon. When Amaria did not respond, he tilted his head slightly and gestured with an arm.

"I chose to take the appearance of someone more conducive to your own. While it is no match to your beauty, I hope you can look upon me without retching in disgust." His voice was harsh and yawning, like two massive boulders grating upon each other.

"What is this place?" the woman asked, scrutinizing the sallow figure. He radiated pure malevolence, and she felt it leach upon her with adroit purpose, making her skin crawl. Yet, he merely smiled hospitably, his bearing noncommittal.

Stepping down from the throne, he extended to his full height. He loomed a solid head higher than Amaria, his red and black robes like a wraith striving to swallow her. Presenting an extensive bow, his vision never wavered from hers. "You stand in Hysoroian, the realm of Hysth, *my* realm." He traced his finger slowly along the edges of the throne. "To those who strive to thwart me, I am known as the *Corrupter*. To those who serve me, I am the *Shaper*."

This man with the pallid skin, a crooked grin across his pasty features, was *Hysth*! Though it seemed implausible, she knew, without a doubt, it was true. And yet, the panic she expected to suffer, standing before a god of darkness, remained absent. She felt no fear, only a misguided agitation. "I am dreaming," she stated dryly.

Hysth shrugged. "In a way, yes. Your body lies sleeping upon your cot. I cannot harm you physically, milady, even if I wished it. But, your mind is here, and you will not forget what I have to say."

"Then speak your mind, Hysth, and let me return whence I came."

The tall man sighed, shaking his head slightly. "Milady, there are things you do not know. Things about the world - things about yourself. You have yet to understand the importance you hold over the entire physical realm. You must learn exactly what you are."

Amaria scoffed. "You waste my time, *Corrupter*. I already know the demons that plague me, and I am certain you can perceive the struggle I have forced upon myself. I seek answers, not the source of my struggles, as you recited."

"Yes, I know your struggles." The discordant voice of Hysth echoed off the walls, jarring her ears. "If you remember, it was me that you called upon, among others, to empower you when you besieged Erdoth Fortress. I granted you strength and skill that even the greatest of warriors cannot fathom."

"The greatest error of my life," Amaria remorsed. "Those demons have yet to release me from their ravenous grip. I would rather have died."

"I can help free you of those demons, Knight of the Dove." No inflection of slyness underscored Hysth's voice. He spoke plainly, thoughtfully.

"Then why don't you offer me the answers I seek? Tell me who I am, what I can do to be free."

The ashen lips of Hysth curled into a frown. "Unfortunately, I cannot give you these answers directly. At least, not now."

Amaria laughed derisively. "Then, as I said, you waste my time. Release me from this forsaken place and taunt me no more."

"Hear me out." The robed appearance of Hysth climbed back upon the throne. He settled in comfortably and raised his fingers to his chin. "What you seek cannot be learned in an instant. In time, I can answer all your questions, but you must be willing to listen."

"I am listening!" Amaria shouted. "It seems you have nothing important to say."

"No, Knight of the Dove, the words I speak hold much importance. Think of it like untying a gigantic knot. Pulling free one thread will not loosen the entire cluster. Rather, it merely allows you to pull free a second thread, which then must be loosened to reach the third thread. Eventually, the entire knot will be undone, but only taking each step one at a time. The answers you seek lay hidden within a massive knot, Amaria Eversvale, and they can only be found after you have loosened each thread."

The woman considered this. Gods, how she tired of the cryptic nonsense that had suddenly become a part of her life! She could feel his slow, methodic beguile lure her toward him. Hysth held a sort of dark appeal, a charm that enticed and appalled all the same. But, did he have merit to his words? Could she trust a god known as the *Corrupter?*

"There is no risk for you, Amaria," Hysth continued, gazing down upon her from his throne. "The price I ask is a simple one."

"The price," Amaria scornfully mimicked. "Always, there is a price. And what price must I pay, *Corrupter?*"

Hysth smiled, his perfect white teeth displayed prominently past the concealment of his lips. "Remove Thavas Iimon. Kill him. It is nothing difficult for you. You would be doing us both a favor. He plays you for a fool, Amaria, feeding you with schemes and lies, not to mention becoming a thorn to my plans."

"Who is Thavas Iimon, beyond what I already know of him?"

The god of corruption snarled, his face showing dark creases above and below the brow. "He was once called Agmon," he spat, "a minion of Wyur who has dedicated himself to destroying Ephram, my high priest. The weasel has methodically followed Ephram for nearly twenty years, hounding but rarely confronting him. He is powerful, much more than he has shown you, though not so strong as to defeat Ephram. That is why he has sought your services, Knight of the Dove, filling you with his deceit. If you follow through with your own promise, in the end, he will betray you. It is strange though, for Ephram feels some strange, unexplainable pity toward the man. Even when I command my high priest to destroy him, he always gives Agmon a chance to flee." The god almost smiled for an instant. "Ephram has his own unique qualities, some of which are quite irritating, but he has doubled the amount of followers in my service since he has become high priest. Still, I will not suffer Agmon's, or Wyur's, meddling any longer."

"Why did Thavas appear so weak in my first confrontation with Ephram?"

Hysth shrugged. "Perhaps he thought you would defeat Ephram on your own, and he wished to hide his power. He is stronger."

Amaria shook her head, the wheels turning in her mind. "So you are asking me to betray and murder Thavas?" She paused, then added, "It is a sinister game you gods play."

"Indeed, it is, milady. And it always will be."

"Why should I trust you? How can I be certain that you will keep your word? Was it not you who betrayed Aohed?"

The dark pupils of Hysth flickered, and an unrepressed anger shown across the pallid face of the god for the briefest of moments. An instant later, it subsided. Hysth blinked once, then straightened his back and answered, "That was a long time ago, Knight of the Dove. It has no bearing over our current circumstance."

"I kill Thavas, and you will tell me all the answers I seek? That is the agreement?"

The god gave a slow nod. "That is the agreement."

"One more question, *Corrupter.*"

"Go on."

Amaria stepped in front of the great chair, her neck bent upward to square Hysth with an icy gaze. "Who ordered the assassination of Senastas?"

"Is it not obvious to you? The same man who had the First Councilman killed is responsible."

"Thavas Iimon," Amaria stated.

"Yes. Done in hopes to blame me, and generate your anger in my direction. He must die, Knight of the Dove. Now go. I have other matters to oversee."

Amaria was suddenly thrown backward, her hind side slamming upon the cold stone of the ground. She felt the earth break, and then she was falling beyond, thrashing helplessly as light and darkness coiled in discordant patterns across her eyes. She was overcome, her mind wrenched asunder. With a final gasp, she slipped away, drifting aimlessly on a rippling sea of nonexistence . . .

When she awoke, Amaria was in her room. Sweat huddled in tiny pools along her breasts, shoulders, and back. She sat up from her cot, gathering her senses. The menacing presence of Hysth had vanished from her mind, and her head swayed as she gained balance and stood. Skulking to her window, she noted that the dipping crest of the sun, throwing weak strands of purple and orange across the expanse of sky, fought to stave off the approaching dusk, which was only minutes away.

Thinking back, it was hard to believe that only this morning she had been in the sickhouse, frazzled and exhausted, watching over a gravely injured Senastas. Returning to her room, she'd collapsed upon her cot, not waking until just now. The whole episode of the previous night; the walk with Senastas, the arrow that had driven into his stomach, the fight with the two assassins, it seemed like weeks ago.

A peculiar sense of loneliness consumed her. She needed to speak with someone, if only to forget her uncertainty. Damn that Hysth if he wasn't persuasive! No wonder he was called the *Corrupter*. But, the woman was no fool, and she understood that he could be trusted no more than Thavas. The torrent of lies came from both sides, and her choices would have to be made with careful precision. She needed to speak with someone who she *could* trust, someone who wouldn't put her on her guard every single moment.

Her desire was to see Senastas. The young councilman always had the right words to cleanse the doubts that festered within her soul. Sadly, he lay in the sickhouse, probably sleeping as he should be. Ornan would be finished working at the warehouse, even with the additional time he had undoubtedly accrued to make up for missed work this morning. But, she hated calling on him twice in the same day. As a captain, she had learned to never abuse the loyalty of her followers, lest their respect lessen. She wasn't about to do that to Ornan, who had become as loyal a friend as she could ever hope for in a rogue city like Valgamin.

Perhaps a simple stroll on her horse would suffice.

Stripping off her clothes, she splashed her body using the water basin. It wouldn't clean her thoroughly, but she was in no mood for a full bath. After drying herself, she donned braise leggings and a loose fitting olive shawl that revealed her lithe body and womanly curves slightly more than was common. She concluded by wrapping her sword belt around her waist.

As she entered the foyer of the Cardinal and the Jay, the servant Janea greeted her. "Hello Mistress. Are you going out this night?" The girl smiled prettily, her red hair bouncing off her shoulders.

"Yes, Janea. Tell the stable boy to ready my horse."

"Certainly, Mistress."

Amaria watched the servant girl hustle out the door, noting, not for the first time, how attractive she was. If she kept a good head on her shoulders, she would make a man very happy one day. The girl was certainly ready for a man, which she never wavered from telling Amaria, in her youthful manner, at every opportunity.

Scooting to the counter, Amaria called to the innkeeper. The short, rotund man turned from some parchment he was writing upon and grinned at her.

"I have an errand to run. I am not sure how late I will return," she said.

The older innkeeper nodded in affirmation. "Use the side entrance when you come back, if it pleases you, milady. The front door will be locked up, but your key will work on the side door."

"Very well."

Amaria moved away from the counter and past the exit, stepping into the welcoming air of dusk. Sharp gusts of wind immediately battered her, tousling her ivory hair in all directions. The stable boy was coming around the corner of the building, leading a reluctant horse that neighed irritably in the raging wind. When the stallion noticed Amaria, it calmed instantly. The woman neared it and patted its neck fondly as she looked it over.

"You have cared for him well." She placed a gold scepter in the boy's hand, much to his delight. "I will return him late, so worry not. I can place him to the stable myself."

"Yes, milady."

Amaria mounted the horse, and suddenly felt at home. The last time she had ridden him was upon her arrival in Valgamin, and since, had only visited him twice. She mentally scolded herself for her neglect as she spurred him forward. It felt natural to have the muscular animal under her legs, his long strides and clomping hooves music to her ears. The gale of wind continued to hound her, but the strong horse pushed on without so much as a whimper.

As she rode, she again fell back into a wrestling match with her own emotions. She began to wonder exactly what she was doing in this city. Had her choices benefited her, or harmed her even worse? Amaria's temper was constantly on the verge of exploding, and sometimes it seemed she actually searched for an excuse to set it free. A sudden desire to leave Valgamin gripped her. She wanted to escape this, to leave the knotted mess behind. All she had to do was turn her horse toward the gate and forever leave the muddle that had ensnarled her. But she didn't. Something kept her going forward, further into the throng of the city. She had made a promise, she reminded herself, an oath, and that was something even Amaria wouldn't recant upon. If she no longer had her promises, what was left?

The sharp wind swept callously among the streets, cold and harsh even for mid-autumn. Yet, that didn't seem to hinder the nightlife of Valgamin. The unsavory crowd dotted the street corners and alleys, all manner of entertainment and dubious activities at their disposal. Amaria observed the mass gathering with little interest, ignoring the vulgar catcalls and propositions. Then something pricked her curiosity. A gaming hall appeared along one of the streets. It wasn't the first one she had passed, but it was the first one she had taken the time to notice. A tiny establishment, the hall was a thatch building with a large wooden signpost that read in scrawled marks: The Gentle Dagger. Inside, she could hear the hoots and hollers of gamblers, and it willed her to go inside.

Amaria stabled her stallion at a run-down, disheveled animal lodge that edged the building. After threatening the stable-keeper with unbearable suffering, she felt confident her horse would be cared for, and she marched unbothered for the entrance.

The hinges on the single-paneled door creaked as she forced it open. In the time it took to achieve two full steps, every head inside was pointed her direction. The cozy, smoke filled room was dimly lit. Hanging lanterns swung from the ceiling, giving just enough light for three round tables and two long tables. The long tables were used for dice, a game that Amaria had no inkling to play. A game of chance, dice involved no true skill. Luck was not something she deemed herself bursting with, and she wasn't about to wager her coin on pure chance alone. The round tables secured her attention. The men huddled around the circular board were playing quads, a game consisting of dagger-length wooden sticks, each colored with one of four hues; red, blue, green, or black. Every stick had white paint marks upon it, denoting a unique value for each piece. The objective was to deal, trade, and plot your sticks upon the board in a manner that gave you the highest value. Quads was a complicated game that required much skill and was painfully addicting to those who had a flavor for gambling money with their intelligence.

For most of her life, Amaria hadn't the taste for wagers and betting. But, her late husband Royce, a gambling shark, had gotten her interested in quads, and though she never reached his skill level, she was a formidable player.

"May I join?" she asked a heavy-set bald headed man who sat at a table with one empty seat.

Five men at the playing board and a number of casual onlookers glared at her with a droll blend of amusement and antipathy. She coolly ignored their derision and kept her eyes firmly upon the wrinkled sockets of the bald man.

He scrutinized her body, pausing at the breasts that showed enticingly beneath her shawl. After several moments, he lifted his vision to meet hers. "This is not the place for a lady," he said, gruffly.

Amaria's face was cold stone. "Is it concern that stays you, or fear for your wounded pride when I take your last copper?"

A stunned hush filled the room. Seconds passed as every gambler wondered with tense fascination how the man would respond to such a clear insult. Suddenly, the bald man laughed, his voice ringing loud about the hall. "Good then, take a seat, milady. We shall see how far your mouth can truly take you."

For two hours, Amaria battled wits with five hounds. She made a good showing, keeping her coin stack well supplemented and simultaneously earning the respect of her opponents, especially when they learned her identity. Although she often had to draw their eyes upward from beneath her neck, she enjoyed reminiscing of her days as a captain in the Illidor army, and they seemed eager listeners. As the night wore on, six players became four, but the Knight of the Dove was not quite finished. One player in particular, a minor noble named Darthon, had not found the humor, or the tolerance, for a woman at the table. His mood had increasingly deteriorated with each victory she scored, but Amaria found his sulking as added incentive to thoroughly defeat him.

"Fifty-six," she said after a particularly intriguing duel, unable to withhold the rare smile that formed across her lips. A series of grumbles ensued from the other players as they withdrew their sticks from the center area. Amaria gathered the pile of silver crowns and added them to her own.

"You certainly have proven that a sword is not the only thing you are capable of wielding," the bald man said. He was a local trader named Johan, boisterous, with a flavor for innocent jesting.

"My talents often surprise even myself," she answered.

Johan's narrowed brows swept over the woman, appraising her. "There are other talents of yours I am certain I'd enjoy as well, milady. But I fear you'd cut me through just for asking."

"Your fears have merit," Amaria muttered, returning to her sticks. Johan laughed loudly, doing the same.

Several matches elapsed with Amaria continuing her good fortune. At one point, she realized she might actually be enjoying herself. Somehow, she had forgotten about the dilemma that plagued her mind, and was simply having a good time gambling against the common-folk. It reminded her of the years she'd spent in the Illidor army, hobnobbing with other soldiers. Nothing worried her back then. She was a skilled soldier, in love, and the world had endless potential. So young and naïve she was! Unbeknownst to her, fate was biding its time until the day it could destroy her. Now her life was the opposite; solitary moments of joy within an inferno of sorrow and regret. She had paid for such anguish with the blood of others, but it was her own blood that should have been spilt. She had turned hard as steel; emotionless and uncaring. It was a sad existence, and until she discovered the path to spiritual freedom, she would be forever damned.

After winning one contest with particularly high stakes, the middle-aged noble, Darthon, cursed aloud, anger apparent upon his red face. "Such luck, even for a lady, is undeserved. Perhaps all your skills are merely stokes of luck."

Amaria exploded from her seat. Reaching over, she lifted the noble from his chair by the collar of his doublet. The man was larger than her, but he wilted under the aberrant strength her body somehow contained.

"Tell me, good sir," she shouted into his face, "is this luck as well?" With reckless force, she tossed the man's body like a doll. He went crashing through the adjacent gaming table, scattering people, sticks, and silver pieces in all directions. Every person in the room gazed at Amaria in morbid shock. Sure, the man had insulted her, but it was nothing more than a resentful jab, something which happened all too often on the gaming table. He had not threatened her, and certainly did not warrant physical harm.

Johan was out of his seat and next to Amaria as quickly as his rotund body could carry him. "Gods, woman! What are you doing?"

Breathing heavily, Amaria stared at the wreck she had instigated. The table was destroyed; the players crawling about the ground gathering up coins they believed were theirs. Turning away, she wordlessly scooped up half the winnings from her stack – the rest she would leave to pay for the damages she had caused – and moved to the exit.

"You have a temper straight from the hells!" Johan called to her.

Amaria didn't respond. She kicked open the door and left, the embers of anger still burning within.

Eight

Amaria waited.

The skies had opened its wrath upon the land, resulting in a gale of a rainstorm. Dull grey had consumed the world, the dense cloud cover thwarting any hopes of sunlight escaping past the opaque haze that pressed like mush against the city. Much of the populace had not even emerged from their homes on this day, and those that did scurried about like rats fleeing a predator while the fierce downpour splattered unrelenting upon the cobbled streets. Most went about their business in silence, but those who did speak had their voices drowned out by the constant thudding of the raindrops. Amaria watched them glumly beneath the lackluster protection of a small, leaky canopy linked to a carpenter's business; the building located only a few city streets from the council hall.

The air smelled of moisture coupled with the chill of mid-autumn. Amaria tugged the mantle of her armor over her arms as she swore under her breath.

Damn him for making me wait!

It had been two days since her gambling episode at The Gentle Dagger and subsequent outburst. Gods above, where had such a volatile temper emerged from? She was spiraling; the extremities of her psyche becoming more obvious, and it worried her. All her life, she had been quick to annoyance, but never did she explode so suddenly over such an insignificant matter. Was it the frustration mounting within her, her inner turmoil finding a way to extend beyond the confines of the personal hell that she lived everyday? If so, she needed to find a way to control such forceful emotions, and quickly. Irrational outbursts led to a quick death, and though dying wasn't much worse than living in her mind, it wasn't going to happen in Valgamin. There were still scores to settle.

Last night, Thavas had sent a message to her room asking that she meet him in this exact location, at this exact time. Here she was, just as he requested, only Thavas had yet to appear. No doubt it was completely intentional on his part, and Amaria's hatred for the man grew with each additional second she lingered under the wooded shelter.

Purposely, she altered her thoughts, bringing them back to Senastas Baranor. The young councilman had occupied her mind repeatedly over the past few days. The woman understood what that might possibly mean, and she wasn't particularly pleased about it. She had already loved once. Her companionship with Royce, and consequent marriage, was powerful and compelling. Their affection for each other had been as fierce as their nights of lovemaking, their bond so intense that, at the time, it seemed unbreakable. The day she found Royce beaten, bloodied, and dead, she truly believed that her capacity to love had been severed completely. Was she wrong? Now, less than a full year afterwards, she could sense the budding of those old feelings, aimed at a young councilman named Senastas. It made her none too happy. A romantic relationship was the last thing she wished for, or even had the time to dawdle upon. Were she capable of ignoring these infant sentiments, she would do so without blinking an eye. Unfortunately, as her adopted father, Meran, once told her, the heart cares little for circumstance.

But, were these feelings the same? The young councilman couldn't have been more opposite than her deceased husband. Royce was a warrior, a hunter, at home with a bow in his hand, a sword at his waist, and a mare beneath his thighs. He was devilishly handsome and a roguish, flirting charmer who exuded the essence of mannish virility. And yet, she thought with a touch of sadness, his loyalty to her was absolute.

Senastas was attractive, but imagining him with a sword was laughable. The councilman's weapon was his introspective nature. She wondered if his intelligence knew no bounds, for he seemed to mentally absorb everything he witnessed, and his perception of the world and his own role within it was something that Amaria had never encountered before.

Was she truly developing feelings for Senastas, or was it mere pity due to his agonizingly dogged sense of duty to Valgamin? She admired an honorable man, and the councilman certainly had a fully supply. But, in this case, her admiration could be clouding her judgment. Hopefully, she wouldn't have to find out. She needed to leave Valgamin and escape this undesired situation, but she couldn't until she had fulfilled her promise and eliminated Ephram Yâramesh.

The sloshing sound of soaked boots on wet cobble caused Amaria to snap to attention. She instinctively slinked back against the darkest part of the shelter and gripped the hilt of her sheathed blade. The footsteps drew nearer, and then Thavas emerged from the rounded corner of the building and strode under the canopy. The man was sopping wet, his sleeveless grey robe flopping heavily as he moved near to her. Water ran down his face and carried across the bridge of his nose, until it fell in drops from the tip. Thavas wiped water from his eyes and regarded Amaria with a ludicrously blank stare.

"You are late." Her voice held little empathy.

"How is your sword arm, milady?" Thavas inquired.

She gave him a wry look, her right middle finger tapping the dove-fashioned pommel of her sword. "My sword arm is always fine."

Thavas offered a satisfied nod. "Ephram is still in the city. I have located his whereabouts, and I wish to delay his execution no longer."

"How did you find him?" she asked.

The man looked away. "That is a question for later."

Amaria snorted. Thavas always avoided giving straight answers, and more often then not, the answers he did give were outright lies. He was bred for deception, and there was no irony in his service with Wyur. Like Ephram, he cared for nothing save to further the dark ambitions of his god. Amaria would find distinct satisfaction when she killed him, more so than even Ephram.

To those ends, she had made up her mind. After she defeated

Ephram, she would exact the same punishment upon Thavas. They both were going to die by her hand, and Valgamin would be better for it. She wasn't sure who held responsibility for the death of the First Councilman, or the attempted assassination of Senastas, but it was one of the two. If they both died, her problems were solved, and she could leave this damned city and continue her exile somewhere else. Perhaps she could travel south, or southwest to Ornan's home kingdom of Radam.

"Shall we be off then, Knight of the Dove?"

Amaria broke free of her reverie, her face laden with scorn. "Can I expect a better showing from you this time around?"

Thavas' fox-like features contorted into a grin. "Of course," he said. "He merely caught me by surprise last time. I have spent the night preparing myself. This time, it is I who will surprise."

And who will you be surprising?, she wanted to say, though she bit her tongue. She assumed that Thavas would try to kill her after they, *if* they, succeeded in besting Ephram. She wouldn't be caught off guard, and truly, she was hoping he would try. It would make his death easier on her already tormented conscious. "Lead the way," she affirmed.

Thavas started into the heavy pall, Amaria following behind. In full armor, she was forced to exert considerable effort to stay with the willowy steward, who moved far easier in his robes, even drenched as they were. The storm gave no quarter, the droplets raining with such ferocity that even her vision was affected. For a brief moment, she felt concern as Thavas rapidly weaved from street to street. Anxiously, she spared a glance behind her, squinting past the water that slithered down her face, into the grey of the storm. Catching sight of what she had hoped to see, a sigh of relief escaped her lips, though not loud enough for Thavas to notice. Ornan was still following them. It was fleeting, but she had caught a glimpse of his nimble form disappear behind a building, one block behind them. Her confidence renewed. With her friend watching her back and keeping a hidden eye on Thavas, she was guarded from the tricks the steward might attempt.

Several streets later, Thavas led her beneath the awning of a storefront and came to a halt as the thunderheads boomed above. His breathed quickly, leaning against the shop and wiping away hair that clung to his forehead and cheeks. "We draw close. Let us catch our breath for a moment. We will have to move more cautiously. Ephram has guards about."

"Where is he?" she asked. She felt twice as heavy in her rain soaked armor, though she wasn't concerned, as once her blade was freed from its casing, very little impeded her skill.

"There is a large building up ahead." The steward pointed a finger into the rainstorm. "It is a rundown, modified warehouse. Ephram has temporarily set up his offices there. I'm not sure how others haven't noticed his presence, but it does not surprise me. Ephram is full of ploys and illusions."

Kneeling, Amaria adjusted one of her boots. "What of these guards? Where have they come from? There were no guards during our first confrontation with the wizard."

"He was not expecting trouble, then. Since our encounter, he has taken strides to ensure his welfare, and the mission he pursues. Many other servants of Hysth have been called." The steward paused, reflecting on his words. "It will be more difficult this time around."

The woman shook her head. "Was it not difficult enough the first time?"

"Our battle with Ephram will be no different if we eliminate the guards beforehand."

"Please tell me these guards aren't more wizards. I've had my fill of sorcery." Amaria stood again, this time adjusting the armor that covered her torso. She was glad she hadn't taken her bow along. Firing arrows would have been useless in this weather and the added equipment would have only weighed her down further.

Thavas stepped to the edge of the awning, squinting into the misty film as if he were gauging what direction they would travel. "I have yet to discover any other priests. I believe the guards are simple knights in service of Hysth, though undoubtedly formidable."

"I've killed a few swordsmen in my day," Amaria remarked,

impassively. For a second time, she gazed into the storm, looking for any indication of Ornan nearby. She saw nothing, though she knew he watched them. If there were guards about, the Radamite would probably have to do some fighting of his own. She hoped he was able to handle himself. With the short-lived scrape of steel, her sword was unsheathed. "We must deal with the guards swiftly. Ephram should have as little time as necessary to prepare for us."

Thavas nodded grimly. Reaching into his robes, he pulled loose his short blade. The weapon was nothing special, but Amaria had an inkling that there was much more to Thavas' prowess than a simple blade. The steward gripped the handle tightly in his left hand and commenced their progress again, back within the anarchy of the rainstorm.

The pair casually circled several storefronts and fell into a wide avenue. They cantered down the street, their flickering eyes ingesting every detail around them. Standing under a canopy along the right side of the avenue were two men. At first impression, they appeared to be city guards simply keeping dry amid the downpour. Amaria knew better, and she suspected Thavas did as well. The men wore a combination of darkened scale and leather armor, with studs across the shoulders, arms, and chest. No helmets graced their faces, but swords hung innocently at their waists, and she noted that their sword hands held the pommels tightly as they viewed the newcomers intently.

The men stepped from the canopy, and one called to them. "Ho, there! A word with you!"

Amaria and Thavas made no response, but continued their gait. The two soldiers quickened their pace, and as they neared twenty feet, Thavas halted. Extending his free hand, he muttered a hushed syllable, and a series of yellow-green darts burst forth. The projectiles pummeled one of the soldiers in his face and chest, and the man fell to his knees screaming as his hands covered his head. Not wasting time, Amaria engaged the second guard. The fledgling soldier had the opportunity for one swing before she disarmed him and drove her weapon through his sternum. The man soundlessly dropped to the rain soaked ground, his blood mixing with the churning water.

The other swordsman was still kneeling in agony. Thavas stood several feet away, mercilessly watching the poor man's slow death. Acid, Amaria realized. The man's armor covering his chest had been eaten away, and his torso and face were falling apart. Though she felt no pity herself, Amaria had no desire to continue watching the gruesome spectacle. She stepped over to the unfortunate victim, who still garbled pathetically as the acid consumed him. "Give my regards to Hysth," she muttered callously before decapitating him.

The battle had been brief and decisive, but Amaria looked at Thavas with burning anger. "You damned driveling fool! Save your magical energies for Ephram! I can kill these swordsmen with ease." She paused to shake her head aggressively. "And that screaming won't help us surprise anyone!"

The robed man shrugged. "My apologies. I tend to act rashly when men are bearing down upon me with murderous intent."

"It's a wonder you are still alive." Turning her back, she moved onward toward their destination. There was no sense in arguing with the man, for he obviously cared little of her input. *Why did I agree to do this?*, she wondered for the millionth time.

Thavas quickly caught up, falling into step at her side. The rain continued to pound them, but neither seemed to notice. Without pointing, the steward abruptly said, "Up there. That is the building."

Even through the storm, Amaria could see the structure where Thavas claimed Ephram had holed up within. It was a wide, single-storied stone edifice. Four guardsmen lounged near the entrance, beneath the protection of a covering, watching the rain with disinterest. Closer, another pair of sentries walked the street, but they soon stopped when they noticed the approach of Amaria and Thavas. All of them were dressed in similar fashion, darkened armor with studs. Amaria wondered if they had heard the screaming of their comrade through the gale.

The two closest sentries raised their hands and called them to halt. Amaria, acting as if she hadn't heard the command, scooted toward one of them, and in the blink an eye, her sword was buried deep in the man's gut. Guilt almost seized her, but she quickly shoved it away. During her days serving under the Illidor army, she would have scorned the idea of killing an opponent before he was given the opportunity to draw arms. It was considered heavily unethical to attack an unprepared foe. But, much had changed since then. The personal walls built over the last year had prevented her from caring.

Pulling free her weapon amid the man's death throes, she wasted no time assaulting the second. In the background, she could hear the guards at the entrance cry out in alarm and rush toward them. Amaria made quick work of her next foe, slicing open his neck, before turning her attention to the oncoming force. Three guards approached from the entrance, which meant one had gone inside to warn Ephram. Additionally, from around the side of the building, two more sentries had come running at the cries of their comrades.

That gave Amaria and Thavas five opponents.

In response, the steward began tracing several lines in the air. Amaria almost admonished him about using his magic against simple swordsmen, but she quickly abandoned the idea, deciding that it was useless to argue with the mulish servant of Wyur. When Thavas had finished his gestures, the lines in the air suddenly glowed to life, making a pattern that resembled a fisherman's net, or perhaps a spider's web. With the flick of his wrist, the lines shot forward, spreading out larger and encompassing three of the guards. The surprised men crashed to the ground and toppled on top one another, stuck in some kind of magical netting.

"A novice spell. It will hold for less than a minute," Thavas stated.

"Long enough," the woman answered. Her stark white locks of hair had turned several shades of grey in the heavy rain. Running a quick hand over her face, she wiped the strands from her eyes and prepared to battle the two skirmishers still moving freely. The pair of men slowed as they reached her, spreading in opposite directions. She sized them up only briefly before going on the offensive. The swordsman she assaulted proved more skilled than the others, parrying her twice before his partner joined the duel from her blindside. Amaria felt the man's approach, and instead of falling away to get a clear view of both opponents, she dropped to one knee and whirled her sword around, slicing through the newcomer's calf. As the man screamed in shock and pain, she was already on her feet again, dueling the first guard. Throughout their clash, she grew increasingly impressed with his ability. The swordsman continually blocked her thrusts, but found himself fully on the defensive, unable to launch an attack of his own.

Amaria realized her foe was beginning to feel overmatched. He stepped backward, looking for any hope in a fight where none was available. The duel resembled a wolf hunting a turtle, for even though the turtle has its shell to hide within, it's only a matter of time before the wolf works the reptile free and feasts upon the flesh. Ultimately, Amaria's sword would feast upon the flesh of her opponent. After several seconds, she finally snuck past his defenses, wounding the man numerous times before finishing him off. At the same instant, Thavas executed the guard with the wounded leg by slitted his throat.

The magical net holding the three remaining guards was dissolving. Amaria ran to them, sword primed, and ruthlessly slaughtered their subdued bodies while they frantically strove to free themselves from their trap. Gurgled cries died in the downpour, and when it was over, the rain washed away the blood of seven more bodies.

Amaria, catching her breath, paused to examine herself. She bore no wounds. Thavas, who had put some distance between himself and much of the skirmish, drew close.

"It is quite a spectacle to watch you, Knight of the Dove."

There was no amusement in Amaria's expression. Motioning to the bodies that lay lifeless on the ground, she uttered, "Why don't you ask the guards if they feel the same."

Thavas laughed, though how he had the gull to do so was beyond Amaria. "They are dead, Amaria. I cannot ask them anything."

In no mood for humor, the woman pointed at the entrance to

the makeshift warehouse. "Ephram awaits."

"Indeed," Thavas said.

The pair sauntered toward the open door, now completely unmanned. Sighing, Amaria steeled herself for what might be her greatest battle yet; the arch-priest of Hysth.

A cold, unnerving silence imbued the interior of the building. "No welcoming party," Amaria remarked at the empty room.

The large, high-ceilinged chamber, an anteroom of sorts, was well lit by sconces along the walls, and several bland wooden tables and chairs lay scattered about the room. Little ornamentation covered jagged walls, but someone had gone to the effort of carving several figurines which sat intermittently atop the tables. The tiny miniatures resembled various unrealistic monsters that, more than likely, were meant to resemble Hysth. Many of the chairs were drawn back from the table, an obvious sign of recent use, as if the occupants suddenly had more important matters to attend, and hadn't the time to push their chairs back in.

Thavas spat on the floor and quietly cursed. "Ephram will greet us in the next room."

Amaria let her eyes move to the large oaken double-doors that displayed themselves in the back of the anteroom. They were closed, and she could hear no sounds beyond, but she knew Thavas was right; Ephram waited for them.

Turning to the steward, she said, "Get your best magic ready. If you disappear like last time, I will kill you myself."

"Worry not, milady. I have a few surprises for Ephram."

Amaria chided him, "Why don't you surprise me by actually making yourself useful."

She didn't give the steward time to counter her verbal jab, for she sidled to the double-doors. Bracing herself, she reached up and pulled the iron handle. The heavy doors opened with a deep, resonate scraping sound. Sword primed and teeth clenched, Amaria stepped inside with Thavas on her heels.

As both were expecting, Ephram was present, sitting comfortably in a chair behind one of his work desks. No evidence of stress graced his elderly features, and there seemed to be a slight grin hiding beneath his colossal beard. On pure instinct, Amaria quickly digested every detail of the chamber. It was huge, far larger than the anteroom, obviously filling the remaining space of the building. Other than the arch-priest, she counted six more dark-clad guards, spaced at intervals along the walls, their weapons drawn and their focus upon the intruders. The rear area was cluttered with Ephram's possessions; his desk, bookshelves, and tables held strange experimental equipment. The mess that littered his furniture made it quite clear he was not a man who strived to keep things orderly. The remaining section was sparsely bedecked, sporting the occasional divan or lounge chair.

She drew her focus to the wizard himself. He was exactly as she remembered him; long white beard, wide-brimmed hat, and robes of black and crimson. Thick, unkempt brows hovered over eyes that presented a bizarre mixture of outward derangement and deep-rooted wisdom.

"Agmon, you 'ol sop!" the wizard shouted. It was unclear to Amaria whether he was upset or amused. Regardless, he clearly didn't see Thavas as a genuine threat. "You are one stubborn horse's ass!"

"It ends this time," the steward responded.

The wizard's grin slightly upturned. "Yes, I suppose it does. Hysth has no more patience for you." Grunting, he rose from his chair and extended an arm. His polished staff, impressive in its full length, appeared in his bony hand. "I must admit, I will miss our verbal sparring."

Amaria watched the wizard with keen awareness. She couldn't explain it, but her level of anxiety was far greater standing before Ephram this time around. Her nerves were nearly spiraling out of control, and the woman held tight to maintain her composure. The wizard seemed to sense her tension, and he viewed her curiously.

"I see you have brought the lady with you again, Agmon," Ephram said. "You have quite the dilemma, Knight of the Dove. I urge you to consider Hysth's words. A poor choice would prove costly, and I would mourn the loss of such potential. Those were not average swordsmen you slaughtered, milady. Do not throw such talent away."

Had she a suitable retort, Amaria would have bit her tongue, regardless. Her concentration stayed upon the nearby sentries and the staff that Ephram clutched in his hands. She hadn't the time for psychological warfare. Twisting her mouth, she whispered to Thavas, "How quickly can you eliminate the guards? I can hold the wizard for a short time, but I'll need help."

The steward's gaze did not waver from Ephram, but he replied under his breath, "I have just the solution." Without pausing, he raised his arms upward and subtly beckoned. Only Amaria, standing directly next to him, could distinguish the chant beneath the steward's breath. "Great Wyur, send your servants to aid me."

The incantation was peculiar and Amaria backed away from the steward, not knowing who, or what, to expect. In the back of her mind, she heard Ephram curse across the room, but her attention fell upon the four swirling pillars of smoke that had appeared alongside Thavas. The tiny pockets soon evaporated, leaving four figures in their wake. The figures were grotesque, like hairless, disfigured humans. Their skin was a sickly basalt color, with misshapen bubbles forming in random areas across their unsightly bodies. Some of the bubbles, mostly near the joints, had burst like ripe fruit, releasing a thick lime-colored puss that oozed slowly over coarse skin. Their eyes looked like orbs of solid black glass that immediately turned to Thavas for direction. From the short distance away, Amaria's nostrils burned from their stench.

"Kill the black-clad swordsmen!" Thavas commanded the hideous fiends, his voice emitting full authority.

Without hesitation, the figures began to move. Their bulky frames, though slightly hunched over, scuttled with unexpected quickness on twisted legs. Their claw-like hands gripped menacing spiked clubs.

"What kind of foul beasts have you summoned?" Amaria

shouted to Thavas, her face bent in revulsion. The monsters reeked of evil, and she found herself questioning whether it was right to fight alongside them. Ultimately, she disregarded her doubts, knowing that her plan was to kill them both anyway.

"They are but minor minions of Wyur, from his home plane. I haven't the authority to summon servants of greater power, but they should keep the sentries busy while we deal with Ephram." Thavas swung his focus to his archenemy.

Across the chamber, Ephram slammed his staff against his desk, shattering a section of the wood. Several papers flipped into the air before settling randomly on the stone floor. "You make a foolish choice, Knight of the Dove. To ally with Wyur is to damn yourself. The *Deceiver* is a pathetic excuse for a god, and soon the upstart will be destroyed completely. All the established gods have grown tired of his incessant meddling, and if Hysth doesn't crush him, another will."

Amaria shook her head. "You are mistaken, wizard. I do not ally myself with Wyur. I am here to kill you, with or without Thavas' aid."

Around them, the guards and Wyur's minions had already begun to clash. Ephram, his thick brows aimed at Amaria, didn't seem to notice. "I am days away from establishing a new temple dedicated to Hysth, right here in Valgamin. Your intrusion is only an annoyance. The *Shaper's* influence will spread within this city." The wizard halted, scrutinizing the woman, "It is a shame I must kill you, so near to discovering the full scope of your talents."

Before Amaria could answer, Thavas extended his hand and muttered a word. Yellow-green darts emerged from his hand and streaked across the room toward Ephram. An instant before the projectiles could pummel the wizard, they dissolved in the air, leaving no trace of their existence behind.

Ephram's madcap eyes widened, and he chortled wildly. "Do you truly believe you can match abilities with me, Agmon? Indeed, you are foolish, servant of Wyur, and your crude magic is laughable. Observe what true power is."

The wizard lifted his staff high in the air. The demonic

figurine at its pinnacle began to glow a dark crimson as Ephram chanted a phrase which Amaria couldn't decipher. An inhuman hum resounded about the room as the staff shined brighter, and the woman realized that whatever spell the wizard was casting, it was of a grand nature. She heard Thavas screaming to her, but the eerie drone that continued to increase in volume obscured his voice. Turning, she looked his way. The steward persisted yelling at her. Unable to grasp the man's words, she focused on his mouth, concentrating on the subtle movements of his lips. It took a moment, but then she understood. *You must stop his casting!*

Mind reeling, she dropped a hand to her boot and reached for her dagger. Her fingers wrapped around the tiny hilt, but she had time for nothing else. A series of fireballs, cataclysmic in their fury, exploded across the chamber. Amaria dove to the ground and crawled to one of the tables that rested nearby, flipping the top end to face Ephram, hoping that it would shield her from the mad wizard's ire. A virtual inferno engulfed the room, sending waves of heat in all directions. The chamber turned the color of saffron amid the flames, and smoke rose to the ceiling. Amaria pressed her face against the cold stone floor in a futile attempt to find some relief within the incalescence. All around her, the inhuman screams of Wyur's minions and the screams of the guards resounded off the walls, with Ephram's mad cackle rising above it all.

He's killing his own men!, she thought, a sick feeling rising inside her stomach.

It was never more clear to Amaria than at that moment. To serve Hysth was sheer madness! Ephram's guards, men willing to put their lives on the line to serve him, were simply being burned alive for no reason save for Ephram to display his power, a tactic of pure arrogance. Amaria could feel her rage escalate. Sword still in hand, she took the chance of lifting her head and inspecting the room. As quickly as they had come, the flames began to die out, but the carnage wrought by their fury had been calamitous. She was able to identify several charred bodies in the devastation, tiny pockles of fire still burning upon their dead, black flesh. The woman wondered if Thavas had survived. Peeking over the crest of the turned table, she looked for Ephram. The wizard, carrying his staff like a walking stick, was calmly stepping forward into the core of the swirling smoke, viewing his work with smug satisfaction.

Amaria ducked back behind the table and waited for the wizard to draw close. She would take him by surprise and, with any luck, gain a quick kill. It might be her only chance to defeat him, for the arch-priest was a powerful mage indeed. Seconds later, she could hear his sandals upon the floor. With a deep breath, and a cavalier prayer to nobody in particular, she leapt from her hiding spot with sword arching savagely.

The elder mage showed remarkable quickness for an aging man, his ironshod staff blocking the woman's death blow, then deflecting two subsequent attacks. Putting space between himself and his aggressor, he casually studied the woman.

"I enjoyed our little duel the last time, Knight of the Dove." Ephram's appearance went feral as he grinned, "Perhaps we can make this one even greater. A battle for the history books, as they say."

"How can you destroy your own men?" Amaria spat the question.

The wizard shrugged noncommittally. "They were in the way. This fight is between you, me, and that damnable Agmon," he looked around warily as if searching for the steward, "wherever he's gone off to."

Amaria attacked again, feigning low and swinging high. Ephram just barely brought his staff up in time to keep himself alive, but he instantly retaliated, thrusting the butt-end of his staff low, toward the thigh of Amaria. The woman parried the blow easily and again the two were at a standstill.

Six dancing lights, like tiny flames of a candle, came whirling from the fringe of the room. They battered the wizard in succession, extinguishing upon contact, but causing Ephram to curse in pain and anger as he tried to back away. "Agmon, you goat's ass!" he screamed. The lights had left several marks upon the wizard's face and robes where they had struck and burned.

"You're going to wish you died from the fire!"

The smoke had almost entirely dispersed from the room, and Thavas abruptly walked into view, his robes scorched badly on the left side and his left hand and face seared from the previous fiery onslaught. Remarkably, however, he seemed to have suffered no serious damage. With sword gone, he was already mouthing another incantation as he neared.

"Hold!" shouted Ephram, pointing at Thavas.

As Thavas seemed primed to deliver whatever spell he was preparing, his body froze like a statue, as if time suddenly went still for the servant of Wyur. His arms stretched wide and his mouth was agape, but he made no movements. Ephram chuckled haughtily at his immobile enemy, enjoying his clearly superior ability.

Amaria, taking full advantage of the wizard's momentary distraction, pushed her assault. She pressed hard, and Ephram drew back on his heels in a desperate attempt to fend her malicious strikes. In a brilliant move, her sword dove past the defenses of Ephram, plunging into his side just below the ribs. The older man screamed loudly and dropped to the ground. Amaria prepared to finish him off, but the wizard slammed his staff upon the floor and cried out some cryptic phrase that made little sense. Six whirling giant swords appeared next to Ephram, and Amaria quickly backed away to avoid getting sliced in two.

The wizard lay on the ground for several seconds before lifting his body, amid much grunting. He was pressing his forearm against the side where Amaria had struck him, and blood seeped through the black of his robes. The massive, magical blades swirled around him in circular patterns, keeping Amaria at bay. The bearded man glanced at his injury and shook his head dolefully. "This is my reward for showing you mercy the last time we battled. You know, woman, it has been many years since I have been truly wounded in battle. Agmon is like a small bird, vainly pecking away. But you, milady, have a killer's ferocity. I give you one last opportunity. Let us stop the ridiculous fight and join together. If you wish, we can even climb those mountains and confront Wyur himself in his little refuge. You can rid the world of the *Deceiver!* Think of it!"

Amaria hardly listened to the wizard's words. The time for negotiation had long since ended. Instead, she was timing the magical blades, measuring her chances for an opening to get past and strike at her foe.

Ephram noticed her obvious lack of interest in his offer. Raising his voice louder, he said, "Bah! You have chosen the wrong side, Knight of the Dove. But, for you, one last little bit of knowledge. I have a unit of soldiers waiting for my signal. If you continue your assault, I will unleash them upon the citizens of the city. They will mercilessly slaughter all who cross their path." Ephram watched Amaria closely, trying to gauge her reaction. "Will you let all those innocents die simply because of some pointless quest to kill me? What will you truly achieve?"

"You willingly let your own men burn. You have no right to live." Amaria kept judging the whirling blades as she spoke.

"In your eyes," said Ephram, "perhaps I don't. But, you cannot fathom the reward for serving Hysth. If you did, you would not mourn their losses."

"Your words are cold and bitter, Ephram," Thavas' voice rang out. Apparently, the spell that was holding him in place had run its course, for the steward was once again coming forward, yelling angrily. "You may be more powerful than me, but you are fearful, and you are beginning to understand that your defeat is simply a matter of time."

"Attack me again, and I unleash my denizens upon the city," Ephram threatened.

Thavas lifted a palm. The very air swirled, and then a vaporous haze began to form around the area where Ephram stood. The sickly green fog quickly engulfed the wizard, but his curses were clear as day. "Fools! You have damned this city!" A strange sound, like the howling of an angry hawk, came from his direction. "I have signaled my men. They are free to wreak their havoc." In a fit of coughing, the wizard shifted away from the poisonous haze, but that also meant he left the safety of his shield of blades.

Amaria was on him instantly. The two clashed again, both

fighting with their own lives at stake. Behind her, she heard Thavas' voice.

"I have nearly exhausted my magical energies."

"Then find a weapon," she answered.

The woman was growing confident. She could feel Ephram tire, and soon her blade would again sneak past his staff. Diving forward, she thrust her weapon for the arch-priest's chest. As Ephram brought across his pole to deflect it, a burst of electricity carried from his staff, through her sword, and into her body. To Amaria, it felt as if a thousand brutal tremors shook her. Senseless, she fell, her body still shuddering from the devastating blast.

Ephram stood over her, his unruly smile even larger than normal. "There are many tricks at my disposal, Knight of the Dove. This is just one of many. Perhaps you do not realize just how invincible I am. A shame."

Amaria was still undergoing massive waves of pain. Her vision blurred, her fingers went numb, and she didn't even know for certain if she still held her sword. The wizard loomed over her like death itself, his gaunt hands extended. Godsdamned, she couldn't move! Where in the hells was Thavas? Had the fool abandoned her?

"Goodbye, Knight of the Dove." Ephram's words were cold.

The tip of the sword that emerged from the wizard's stomach not only surprised Amaria, but judging from the utter amazement evident on Ephram's face, the arch-priest was wholly astounded. Like some kind of snake, the blade then disappeared back through his body. Ephram, his movements abruptly sluggish, turned his shoulders around, getting a clear look at the person behind him. Upon seeing his killer, his mouth opened as if he were about to speak, but only blood dribbled forth. A moment later, he was sprawled upon the stone floor, lifeless.

Ornan, his weapon covered with the blood of the former arch-priest of Hysth, gave the dead man no consideration. Without so much as a hint of superiority in his eyes, he dropped to Amaria's side and asked, "Are you okay, shera?"

The shockwaves of pain had begun to recede, and Amaria

started to regain feeling in her limbs. Still, she was quite sore, and she groaned loudly, grasping the Radamite's shoulder to sit up. "I am fine, Ornan. Thanks." She paused, and then wondered aloud, "Where is Thavas?"

Both swung their heads and found the steward standing near the exit, viewing Amaria and Ornan with upturned lips. "The deed is done! Victory, at last! You have my valued gratitude. But now, I have other matters to attend. Farewell, Amaria Eversvale." The man dashed out the door, leaving a fuming Amaria in his wake.

"Damn that Thavas!" she swore, shaking the cobwebs from her head. A string of shrill whistles carried from outside the building, followed by screams and shouting. Turning to Ornan, Amaria said, "Ephram's men are still outside. We must go!"

Ornan helped her stand, and the duo hustled toward the exit, Amaria still recovering from her bout with Ephram's magic. When they reached the street, two details immediately struck the woman. Firstly, the storm had let up. Although the sun hadn't yet found a channel through the opaque grey mass hanging in the sky, at least the wind and rain had subsided, giving some semblance of normalcy to the weather. The second thing she noticed was the handful of black-clad swordsmen milling about the area. These men were identical to the sentries she had battled earlier, and they busied themselves hounding terrified citizens whom happened to cross their path. Fortunately, fewer soldiers existed than Ephram had made her believe, but even a handful was too many. A few city-guards currently engaged them.

"Ornan, go help the city guards. I would go with you, but I still have business with Thavas."

The Radamite gave her a quick look of acknowledgement before leaving her side in a sprint. Amaria watched him for only a second before pivoting in the opposite direction. She was confident in Ornan's skill and did not worry for him, for her own focus was directed elsewhere. Like the true coward he was, Thavas had fled, and Amaria strived to catch him before he escaped. In the back of her mind, she had a good inkling of where he was going. The sickhouse. She hadn't a clue what the steward planned once he got there, but her gut informed her that the lying Thavas would somehow involve Senastas.

While her body overcame the last remnants of pain and she regained full capacity of her facilities, Amaria ran down the streets of Valgamin. One blackguard tried to confront her, but she made quick work of him, driving the edge of her sword into his jaw. She didn't even witness the man fall, for she was already past him. The sickhouse was a good five-minute lope from her current position, and the woman was determined to cut that down at least a full minute. She speculated about Thavas, pondering whether he also ran, or if he somehow had a mount waiting for him upon his departure. For a brief moment she considered shedding her heavy armor to gain speed, but she decided against it, believing that the cumbersome attire would probably be needed if a fight awaited her.

Although no one dared question her, the woman garnered several stares from pedestrians as she raced down the walkways and streets. The frivolous gawking didn't bother her, and she was thankful they kept their mouths shut, for she hadn't the time to answer some bystander's pointless curiosity. Her muscles ached in protest, yet she pushed herself onward. Heart pounding, the only sound she could distinguish was her own boots upon the cobble.

Eventually, the sickhouse appeared ahead. A healer, standing at the entrance, gave her a questioning look as she approached. Amaria paused to catch her breath, then beseeched, "I am here to see Councilman Senastas Baranor. It is urgent."

The healer regarded her coolly. A young man, in his early thirties, with jet-black hair and tapering eyelids. "Why the urgency, milady?"

Swearing under her breath, she abruptly shoved her way past the stunned man and entered the building, hustling with abandon down the hallway. There was no time to explain her business, and she could always apologize later. For the moment, her only concern was Senastas' safety. When she arrived at the councilman's room, she noted that the door had been left slightly open. Nerves primed, she did not hesitate. Surging through, she burst inside and found herself in the exact circumstance she had feared the most.

Senastas stood at the far end of the room, gazing at Amaria in a muffled combination of fear, confusion, and excitement. Just behind him, pointing the tip of his sword directly at the base of Senatas' naked throat, was Thavas. Upon seeing Amaria, the steward smiled.

"Shut the door behind you if you please, milady."

Amaria's expression was one of pure abhorrence, but hesitantly, she complied. Then the three of them were alone. "You are pitiable!" she sneered. "Leave the councilman out of this."

The steward guffawed, his visage clearly showing pleasure in the situation. "You did so well, Knight of the Dove. I could never have defeated Ephram alone."

"Godsdamn you, Thavas! You trait—" Senastas' ravings were cut short when Thavas yanked hard on the concilman's hair and pressed the blade harder to his throat.

"What do you intend to do?" Amaria asked with harsh, calculating eyes.

The point of Thavas' sword moved slightly. Amaria could see the councilman inhale as the blade lightly punctured his skin, causing a small stream of blood to fall down his neck and onto his tunic. Merely a scratch, but the steward had made his point.

"I am no fool, Knight of the Dove," the former steward said. "I knew you would try to kill me afterwards. Your misguided quest for redemption makes you predictable."

The tension in the room had grown sharp. Senastas remained silent, but he was agonizingly aware of what transpired. He held as still as possible while the sharpened edge was pressed against him, waiting for the verbal contest between Amaria and Thavas to conclude.

"It was you who killed the other councilman," Amaria openly accused. "How? How did you make one commit suicide?"

Shaking his head, Thavas answered, "So effortless, really. I used the most effective way to destroy a man's life without harming him physically. I paid a harlot to seduce him. You see,

Amaria, even the strong-minded have their weaknesses. Councilman Barrowswynd carried the affair for two weeks before I approached him. Naturally, I informed him of my knowledge of his uncouth, illicit doings, and then I offered him a choice. Either he take his own life, or I send the proof of his affair to his family," the man grinned evilly, "and I had *much* proof. Fortunately, the man proved spineless, choosing death over humiliation. Shameful, really."

Senastas showed disgust on his face. Without moving, he verbalized his loathing. "By the gods, Thavas! Why? What reason did you have to kill him? What wrongs had he committed on you?"

"A simple distraction was all I needed, and he was perfect. While you and the rest of the council were mourning his loss, I had ample opportunity to setup my network of spies, and I performed it right under your pitiful noses. Even I could never have predicted how flawless the plan would work. You even suspected me, Amaria, and still I succeeded."

There was stunned silence. Both Amaria and Senastas were boiling in anger, but they found themselves speechless in their astonishment. Amaria tightened the grip on her sword, though she didn't move. Finally speaking, her words were soft, but her tone was venomous. "You sent the assassin to kill Senastas, did you not? I should have killed you afterwards."

A dark smile formed on the servant of Wyur. "Yes, the assassins. They were prisoners, you know, tortured sufficiently to understand that failure was unacceptable. You know a god is powerful when he can place fear of that kind into a man. The fool killed himself rather than face Wyur with his failures. Of course, even in the afterlife, Wyur will pursue them." The steward's eyes bore jagged holes through Amaria as he spoke. Narrowing his eyelids, he snarled darkly; a sinister expression of deceit. "You were just a pawn, Amaria, in a game played by gods. You have lost, Hysth has lost, and Wyur has reaped great victory. I have retained enough magic for one last spell. It is one that I intentionally reserved for this very moment. Goodbye, Knight of the Dove."

The steward began to mutter phrases under his breath. For a few seconds, all was still. Just before he finished, he drove his sword deep into the neck of the councilman.

Then Thavas vanished.

Senastas emitted a stunted cry of pain before he collapsed.

"Gods no!" Amaria screamed, surprised by her own burst of emotion. She leapt over the resting bed and knelt at the councilman's side. Senastas was already glassy-eyed and hazy. His life drained at a rapid pace while blood spilled all over the wood-tiled floor of the sickhouse. She settled her arms beneath him, and the young man gazed up at her. A sadness draped over his tender eyes, his mouth cracked open in a hopeless effort to speak. Almost void of words herself, Amaria could only manage a single phrase, "I'm sorry."

Then Senastas was no more.

The room was silent for a period of time. Amaria had given up the notion of chasing Thavas. He had clearly used some kind of teleportation spell, and she hadn't any idea where it had taken him. Instead, she quietly held the lifeless body of Senastas Baranor, trying to push away the sentiment that was gripping her heart.

The door burst open and a male healer, middle-aged with greying hair, wearing white robes, stepped into the room. "I heard a scream! What has " When he saw the body of Senastas, he nearly tripped over his own feet. Recovering, he leaned back into the hall and cried out, "Fetch the city-guards immediately! Waste no time!"

At once, the healer returned. White robes shuffling behind him, he eyed the scene skeptically, first observing the councilman's body, then shifting over to scrutinize Amaria's bloodstained sword.

Interlude

The monolith loomed like a giant arm clawing at the heavens. Far too thin to serve as a useful tower, the circular pillar rose several stories into the air, completely hollow inside. The stonework, some kind of ancient limestone, visibly showed age with its fading color, but the blocks remained undamaged and held firm.

Agmon Lionor, formerly Thavas Iimon of Valgamin, stood within the great edifice, recovering from the teleportation he had just undergone. His head swam for several minutes, but the grogginess ultimately receded. Leaning against the rounded base, he gazed at the hundreds of runes etched into the floor. It was those runes, through use of his teleportation spell that had allowed him to travel atop Urak's Edge in only a few heartbeats time, completely bypassing the daunting trek that would have taken days, if not weeks. And of course, the runes also helped him escape Amaria Eversvale. As Agmon began to feel like himself again, he wondered just how furious the woman would be. With luck, she would be blamed for the murder of Senastas, though even if she weren't, it mattered little, for Ephram was dead and the gateway now open for Wyur to move within Valgamin.

Agmon shifted to the single door and pushed it open, taking a deep breath before stepping into the frigid air. He stood atop one of the highest peaks in the entire mountain range, and the single robe he wore did little to fend off the sweeping wind that thrust him off balance. The snow had deepened since his last visit, and due to the drastic high altitude, Agmon found himself breathing rapidly to adjust.

Strangely, the tower had been a mystery to even Wyur. The primordial stone column was already present when the *Deceiver* searched for a location to create his shrine, and the god immediately found a purpose for the structure, making it the root foundation for traveling in and out of the mountains.

Not tarrying in place, the servant of Wyur scanned the area and located the small church-like keep that stood firmly on a rise in the distance. The keep was named *Wyurnescia*, meaning 'the last refuge of Wyur.' The *Deceiver* himself had established the shrine as his paramount temple of worship. Although Wyur's churches had now spread to other parts of the world, *Wyurnescia* was the foundation. Most apprentices were sent to this location to develop their beliefs and skills, just as Agmon had, back in his days as a humble initiate.

Agmon nearly slipped on two separate occasions as he hastened toward the keep. Ten minutes later, limbs shivering, he reached a neglected iron gate and thrust it open. The rusty hinges squealed irritably, and Agmon caught himself wondering why Wyur, for all his power and might, couldn't keep better care of such nuances like the old gate. Beyond was a paved walkway of rounded stones that led to the set of granite stairs. At the crest of the stairs, near the entrance, a priest of Wyur stood causal watch. The man was garbed in a thick grey overcoat with hood pulled firmly over his face.

As Agmon ascended the stairway, the priest threw back his hood and grinned. "Agmon! Welcome back! How fares your assignment?"

"Favorable, Jarkis," he replied, trying to hold back his excitement. He patted the man on the shoulder. "I shall give you more details soon, but I believe I should report to Urosish first."

The other priest nodded and replaced his hood. "Certainly. I look forward to it. It is good to see you again."

Agmon stepped up to the ten feet high double doors, forged of blackened metal and inlaid with multi-colored jewels that were patterned into religious symbols of Wyur. Pulling them open, he walked into a large, semicircular chamber tiled in marble. Two statues stood on each end, both depicting a handsome faced man with amiable features and arms spread wide. The images were serene, and Agmon spared a moment to appreciate the fortune that Wyur had blessed upon him.

More priests lingered inside the chamber, and Agmon greeted them all before moving toward another set of doors. Soon, he was stepping down a wide hallway flanked by several rooms on each side. He hadn't bothered asking where Urosish was, for he already knew. The high priest would be waiting for him at the very end of the corridor. Agmon tried to hold his composure, but found it difficult. His mission had been such an absolute success that he was barely capable of maintaining the calm demeanor that was expected of every servant inside *Wyurnescia's* walls. When he reached the entrance to the hallowed sanctum, he halted, for only Urosish was free to traverse further of his own wish. No guard stood watch, but Agmon knew it was unsuitable for him to barge in without invitation. Only the high priest could enter the Sanctuary of Wyur uninvited, and Agmon, a servant of transitional status, would be forced to linger at the door until Urosish found time to call him forward.

When the rich, sonorous bellow of Urosish's unmistakable voice beckoned him, he mentally gathered his wits and slowly entered. The sanctuary was surreal. Although Agmon had visited the sacred chamber twice before, each time was like the first. Streams of sunlight flickered through a myriad of stained glass windows, lighting the room with a variety of colors. Upon the domed ceiling, an extravagantly patterned fresco depicted a conquering Wyur forcing his brethren to bow at his knees. Four long, walnut benches, lined in parallel rows, faced the front of the room where the altar stood.

The altar itself, lying upon a wide dais adorned with arcane sigils, was fashioned of a black marble-like material and seemed to absorb the dappling light from the windows. The image itself depicted a squatting figurine of Wyur, arms cradled and holding a bowl filled with sloshing dark fluid.

The regal pose of Urosish stood next to the alter. Like Agmon, the high priest also wore robes of grey, but his were of superior quality, draping his body like an elegant performer stepping onto a grand stage. His once black hair slowly turned white and his crown thinned, causing the high priest to comb his shoulder length hair backwards in effort to hide the blemish. In his fifties,

Urosish still possessed a sparkle within his eyes, his wrinkled face ever vibrant and full of life. Viewing Agmon with deep consideration, the high priest commented, "You have been in a fight."

Agmon suddenly realized that he still bore the signs, and wounds, of his battle with Ephram. The left side of his clothing and skin remained singed, and doubtless his face looked haggard and dirty. Strangely, it felt as if the skirmish had taken place days ago, making it difficult to believe that in truth, he dueled Ephram just this morning. "Yes, Holy One," the servant replied, "it was my final contest with Ephram Yâramesh."

An eyebrow raised on Urosish's wizened face. "Indeed? And the outcome?"

"Hysth's arch-priest is dead, Holy One. I watched him die with my own eyes."

At first, the high priest was silent, letting the revelation slowly sink in. He calmly located a stool to sit upon and mouthed, "Remarkable. How long has it been since you first volunteered for this?"

"Almost twenty years, Holy One." Agmon bit his lip, trying to preserve his humility. Until now, the true impact of his success had not gripped him fully, but seeing the surprise on the high priest's face, he began to realize how significant his accomplishment truly was.

Urosish suddenly smiled at Agmon. *Smiled!* He had never before done such a thing in the servant's presence! "If there was ever a perfect example of what determination can achieve, Agmon, you have become it. Tell me, how did you accomplish this feat where so many before you could not?"

"Not alone," Agmon answered truthfully. "I acquired the aid of Amaria Eversvale, convincing her that Ephram was evil. She proved quite the match for the great wizard, and together we destroyed him."

Urosish grunted. "The Knight of the Dove. Yes, no doubt she gave the old wizard fits." Urosish massaged his hairless chin and pondered the wondrous news. "Have you left any loose ends? It would be unfortunate if others lay blame on Wyur for any trouble that has been caused."

"In order to work freely, I found it necessary to *remove* two council members in Valgamin. It is my hope that neither death can be tracked to me. In fact, I made a special effort to entrap Amaria Eversvale so that she would be blamed for one of the murders. Even so, I have a minor worry. She witnessed me kill the second councilman, and the woman had taken heart to him. I expect she wants me quite dead."

"That could be a problem," the high priest said.

"Perhaps, but I have my doubts. If she is charged with his murder, then she'll be executed, and our worries are over. If not, she still has no knowledge where I have gone, and she couldn't possibly find us up here."

Urosish pursed his lips. "Never take a threat too lightly, Agmon. Of all people, you should know this. If the tales of this woman's deeds hold any truth, then she shan't be underestimated."

"What do you suggest, Holy One?"

"The first action will be to bolster our defenses. *Wyurnescia* is no fortress, and if Amaria comes seeking vengeance. We best be ready."

Agmon couldn't even imagine the idea of Amaria scaling the great mountain range to seek him. His body shivered involuntarily. "How could she find us up here, Holy One? Urak's Edge is enormous. It would be easier to find a dagger in a sea of swords."

"Are you willing to take the chance, Agmon?" the high priest countered. "No, if she comes, we will be prepared. Besides, I have often wished for an opportunity to unleash the xrogosh."

The servant thought about the great beast that lurked beneath the keep, a captive to Urosish. He'd never witnessed the monstrosity first hand, but the tidbits of information he'd learned about it made his mind recoil in disgust. Although he loved and revered Wyur, Agmon sometimes wondered why the god allowed such grotesque monsters to represent him. It was one of those things he preferred not to dwell upon.

"I also believe," Urosish continued, "that we should send

someone back to Valgamin, just to see what happens with this Knight of the Dove."

Agmon's heart sank. He had undertaken an amazing feat, but had no desire to return to the vicinity of a woman who probably wished him dead more than any other living soul. Still, he was a servant of Wyur, and the *Deceiver* demanded loyalty. What better way to show his loyalty than to volunteer? Sometimes personal sacrifices must be made when dedicating your services to any cause, much less a powerful deity. Loudly clearing his throat, Agmon offered, "I am willing to return, Holy One, if that is your wish."

To his surprise, the high priest shook his head. "No, Agmon. You have accomplished your goal. If anyone has earned some respite, it is you. Relax and enjoy it, for soon, Wyur will require your services once again."

Relief swelled within Agmon. Showing excessive gratitude, he bowed and said, "Thank you, Holy One."

Urosish nodded his acceptance to the gesture and added, "Once you have sufficiently cleaned up and rested, we will discuss your advancement. Until then, you are dismissed."

Agmon's jaw nearly dropped. *Advancement!* Despite his success, he had not expected such an honor. Elevating one's stature within the workforce of the *Deceiver* was rare and, more often than not, a result of abilities rather than accomplishments. Agmon was nothing more than a lowly magician. In truth, he was not even considered a priest, for he had never served or trained in the ways of clerical duties. He was merely a servant, one who had dedicated his life to aiding Wyur's ambitions. As far as he'd ever witnessed, only priests rose in rank, and the announcement utterly shocked him.

By the time Agmon stopped his ponderings of self-worth, he was already ambling down the hall toward his own quarters. In his haste to leave Valgamin, Agmon had abandoned the possessions he'd owned while serving as a steward to Senastas. It was of no consequence, however, as Agmon left nothing behind which would incriminate himself, or Wyur. In fact, the servant had intentionally kept his properties to the bare minimum. Any objects liable to associate him to Wyur were always stored on his body, and all other valuables were left here in *Wyurnescia*.

Now that he was home again, a great sense of liberation filled him. For nearly twenty years he was consumed with a sole obsession and purpose. With it suddenly over, it felt as if his own life had been regained. He was back within the company of friends and the safety of *Wyurnescia*. The world seemed limitless with possibilities, and Agmon would seize them.

A smile crept onto the servant's face.

PART II

Aruk's Edge

Nine

When the murk that had been Amaria's vision gained focus, there was a fleeting moment of optimism. Then she remembered where she was, and all the brightness of her world perished.

For the third straight day since her arrest by the city guard, she found herself locked inside a dank prison cell, her wrists chained above her head against the cold granite wall. Her weapons and armor had been stripped, and the only effort made by her captors to maintain her modesty had been a torn, loose hanging tunic that barely concealed her torso and womanhood. Her disheveled hair fell in knotted strands past her armpits, the ivory tresses darkened with filth. Just beyond the bars, an oil lamp burned brightly, exposing the woman's current state with lustrous radiance. The woman's humiliation had been thorough and complete.

Upon her arrest, she hadn't fought back. So shaken by the appalling turn of events, she could think of nothing save her own misfortune. Senastas was dead, and just like Royce, he had died at the hands of her enemy. For three days she glumly pondered such a fate, eventually concluding that her treasure was sorrow, her triumph desolation. She drank from her misery, letting the mental toxin force her to a painless submission. With her headstrong defiance severed, her death sentence would become nothing but a merciful escape.

At one point, she considered calling upon the dark gods, allowing their ominous power to consume her again so she might escape her captivity and bring wrath upon the people who had imprisoned her for a crime she was not only innocent of, but had attempted to prevent. A part of her loved Senastas, and to be arrested for his murder was an affront to her pride.

If any pride remained.

In the end, she realized that whatever vengeance gained would be hollow at best, and wrongful as well. The remaining councilmen had no facts, save the healer's description of what he witnessed upon arriving at the scene. All evidence pointed to her, and for that, she couldn't blame them for believing in her guilt. If anyone, it was Thavas who should inflame her ire. The servant of Wyur had outwitted her, *bested* her! She pictured his laughing face, his smug features ridiculing her, and her resentment for the man escalated. If, somehow, she escaped confinement, she would not rest until she hunted him down and cut the grinning lips from his face, chivalry be damned!

In a perpetual state of sorrow, her mind wandered discursively until another face came to mind. Ornan! What had happened to him? Although he'd proven incredibly useful, she hoped the Radamite would find a way to steer clear of her current situation. She didn't want Ornan imprisoned as well. He had already done all he could.

Two guards stepped into view, gazing at Amaria through the thick iron rails that served to cage her. Since her imprisonment, guards had paced by at regular intervals, often offering words that were less than pleasant. Most either cursed her for killing the highly respected Senastas or heckled her for sexual favors. Amaria easily tuned them out, never altering the impassive look upon her face. Sadly, it didn't seem to dissuade them, but at least they didn't get the pleasure of scoring a reaction.

Currently, the two footmen stared at her pretentiously. Both men wore helms, hiding much of their faces and shadowing their eyes. "We need more prisoners like this," one of them cackled. "She's far easier on the eyes. I wouldn't mind an hour in there with her." The guard chortled at his own remark, the condescending laughter reverberating off the walls of the prison.

"How honorable you are, to mock a woman chained to a wall."

The words had been flung from Amaria's mouth before she'd been able to stop them. She scolded herself immediately. She hadn't intended to respond, but impulsive won over.

"So, the whore has a tongue." The footman hacked a wad of spit across the cell. The sticky ichor just missed her left hip, lapping the wall beside her with a popping sound. "Careful that I do not cut it from your mouth. You are nothing but a deceitful murderer."

"Am I?" Amaria lifted her vision from the floor and placed them upon the guard. Her pupils darkened as they bore down upon him. "Listen well, soldier. Every man I have ever slain has been in the midst of battle. If that is murder, than I am guilty many times over. But, know this, I did not kill Senastas."

"Lies!" the man called, walking away and biding his partner to follow.

The other guard remained in place, his body unmoving as he viewed Amaria for a lengthy period of time. The woman returned his stare, her face remaining impassive but her mind probing for an indication of the thoughts that churned beneath the man's steel helmet. When at last he turned to leave, she called to him.

"Halt, soldier."

Almost instinctively, the man paused at the words. With an air of total disbelief, he swiveled his shoulders and once again inspected her. Chained and caged as she was, the woman was in no position to give orders, yet her voice exuded total authority. It was very clear that she had once been in command of many men.

"Remove your helmet."

Amaria watched the guard lift the helm over his head, revealing a youthful face framed by short black hair. His thin lips were closed and unwrinkled. Astonishment took Amaria. How young this man looked! He couldn't have been more than twenty winters. His youthful features gave the impression of someone receptive, not yet hardened and set in his ways.

Placidly regarding the young sentry, she asked, "What is your name?"

"Jerris." The footman showed no apprehension or anxiety while speaking to the prisoner.

"Do you think I am guilty, Jerris?" Through the bars, Amaria studied him closely. She didn't know why, but she felt a strange impulse to converse with the man on the other side.

The young solider did not respond immediately. He stood

with helmet in one hand and spear in the other, choosing his words carefully. When an answer came did come forth, a certain fervor spilled from his mouth. "I met Councilman Senastas once, milady. I was standing watch along the city gates at night, not yet three full weeks into my service as a guardsman. That night, his carriage comes rolling up. I had heard he was an amiable fellow, but even so, I was nervous in his presence. I know not where he was headed that night, but he spent an hour talking with me, ensuring that my job as a watchman was suitable. He'd never met me before, yet he spoke to me like a friend. If indeed you killed him, milady, then you deserve nothing less than to lay upon the flaming coals of hell and burn."

Amaria was caught wordless. She hadn't expected such harshness from the young guard, and when she finally built some semblance of a retort, Jerris was already speaking again.

"Yet, I wonder if you truly are to blame. I do not see the guilt in you. Instead, you seem . . . sad."

Lowering her eyes, Amaria confessed, "I tried to prevent his murder, Jerris. I failed him, and myself. It seems the pattern of my life."

Jerris stepped to the bars, his features sincere. "If you are innocent, milady, then Aohed's mercy will see fit that you are freed."

The woman lifted narrowed lids. "The gods have no mercy, young Jerris."

The man opened his mouth to answer, then halted. With a solemn shake of his youthful face he turned and walked away, leaving Amaria alone to her tortured thoughts. As she watched him disappear behind the wall, a small flicker of hope unexpectedly rose within her.

The veneer of the annulose chamber sparkled. Constructed of cerulean marble, the sheen from the floor plating shown so spotless that Amaria could almost view her own reflection within its flawless facade. Murals dappled the rounded walls, exquisitely painted, but once the woman inspected the scenes depicted inside the gaudy images, her suspicions rose immediately. They were ghastly pictures overflowing with mayhem, torture, and killing.

"Welcome again, Knight of the Dove."

She spun around and discovered a pale-faced man in black and red robes regarding her. "Hysth!" she spat venomously.

The man smiled. His eyes seemed to suck the light from the room. "Ah, you recognize me. Then no introductions are in order." Gesturing to her waist, he added, "Notice that I allowed you your sword this time."

Amaria looked down and found her sword belt around her waist. She was dressed in her plate armor, cloak and all, and with that knowledge she relaxed ever so slightly. Her hand dropped to the nickel pommel of her blade. "What is it you wish, *Corrupter*? Are you seeking reparation for the slaying of Ephram?"

Hysth's mouth widened at the accusation, then he laughed a sinister laugh. "Reparation? Ha! I think you overestimated Ephram's use. A hundred priests chomped at the bit to replace him, all of them fully capable." The god shook his head. "No, it was a mild setback at worst, and one that will quickly be rectified. Besides, had I wished to duel you, this is hardly the place for it."

"Then why have you summoned me?"

"Because I still have need of you, Knight of the Dove. You might have failed me once, but I have a tendency to believe that you aren't one to concede to failure." Hysth waved his hand as if wishing to change the subject. "But before we get into the bore of details, let me show you a few things. I felt obligated to present a more appeasing setting this time, rather than the dank tunnels far beneath my citadel. We are actually standing in my personal palace, and very few visitors have stepped foot in here. Even fewer had lived afterwards." The god gave a devious, self-basking grin.

Amaria furrowed her brow, derisively. "Am I supposed to feel honored?"

"You may feel whatever you wish, milady. It is of no consequence. But please, indulge me for a moment, will you? Walk with me."

The ashen-faced god stepped to a doorway and bade Amaria to follow. Reluctantly, she complied, and soon they were outdoors, standing on a small balcony that overlooked a great sprawling city. She immediately wrinkled her nose as a waft of fetid, sulfurous air burned her nostrils. Her eyes broadened as she gaped upon a world conceivable only in her nightmares.

Hysth waved a hand outward. "This is Xerinus, the capital city of Hysoroian. When I first created this world, it was but a few buildings. Now, it reaches beyond the horizon."

Indeed, the black basalt buildings of the metropolis extended past the woman's vision, a virtual carpet of various dwellings that continued in all directions. She wondered just how far it stretched, and where all the inhabitants had come from. Up above, the sky cast a constant reddish hue over the populace, and Amaria could find no evidence of sun or stars. The temperature was warm enough to reach the point of becoming uncomfortable, with no breeze to speak of. Peering down at the streets below, she witnessed all sorts and manner of creatures. Some appeared to be large demons, complete with bat-like wings and multiple horns upon their heads. Others were truly alien in appearance; creatures so bizarre that even her imagination couldn't have conceived them. Spattered among the populace were humans, though there seemed to be no cohesiveness in their advent. Some were hauled roughly in chains, obviously slaves, while others sauntered freely, unsympathetic to their captive brethren. It swiftly became apparent to Amaria that, in this unforgiving place, individuals worried only for themselves. In one section of the city, several wooden stakes had been fixed into the ground along the street. A man was tethered to one of the stakes, and a horned fiend had just set him afire. The unfortunate victim thrashed and screamed in agony while the beast stood back and watched him vesicate, a sickening smile of pleasure draped across the demon's dog-like maw. Most shocking to the woman was that others passed by the torturous scene and hardly noticed, as if something like this happened all the time!

"How can you allow such ruthless acts?" she asked in sickened awe, "All is chaos."

The *Corrupter* shrugged. "What you witness may seem unruly to you, milady, but there is order amid the brutality. It is the order of survival. Those that are strong, survive. Those that are weak, well . . ." he motioned to the flaming pyre. The victim had ceased his cries, and now his charred remains lingered motionless. The corpse still smoldered within a pocket of smoke, but the demon had lost interest and leisurely departed the scene. "It may seem gruesome to you, but you are from the physical realm, and there are vast differences from that place and the abyssal realms."

Even Amaria, who had born the slaughter of several hundred men by her own hand, averted her eyes from the grisly scene. Placing them on Hysth, she inquired, "And what of Ephram?"

The god twisted his head slightly at the question, then snickered. "Ah yes, my former arch-priest. He is here in Xerinus. I placed him in the firm care of some especially cruel slavers. He shan't be enjoying himself for some time."

"How can you do that?" Amaria gawked. "He was a faithful priest. You once told me that many new followers had joined your cause under his leadership. Why would you cast him away like that? Is there no loyalty in service to you?"

"Milady, a god does not grow powerful by tolerating failure." When Amaria only stared at him in disgust, he added with a hint of clemency, "Perhaps, only because of your *touching* concern, I will free him after a few years and let him live whatever life he can manage in Xerinus. It is far better than I have given others."

Amaria turned around and leaned against the rail of the balcony, facing the doorway. "I have seen enough of this hell you call a city. Reveal what you wish to say so that I may leave."

"Yes, of course." Hysth ran his thumb and forefinger along his chin, his lids creased in thought. "I am going to help you achieve something that we both desire."

"And what, pray tell, could be something we both desire?"

The god laughed aloud. "Is it not obvious? The blood of Thavas Iimon upon your sword."

The woman shook her head. "We have already discussed this,

Corrupter. That bargain was severed by my failure."

"I did not bring you here to bargain with, Knight of the Dove. I simply wish to give you the information you require to kill Thavas. It is what you want, and it is what I require. I'll give you nothing else."

Just then, a shadow flashed over both of them. Amaria strained her neck upward and witnessed an enormous bird-like creature flying overhead. It circled above them, a black silhouette roving the windless air amid a burning scope of crimson. The monster resembled a crocodile with leathery wings, only five times larger, and with longer limbs. Intense, burning red eyes scanned the area below. Abruptly, the airborne creature shot downward like an arrow, accompanied by an unholy shriek that made Amaria wince in startlement. Down below, the woman could see people scramble off the streets in a maddened haste to escape the piercing teeth that protruded from overlarge jowls. Unfortunately, the flying terror had already established a mark. One of the horned fiends, a beast who bore similar resemblance to the demon that had earlier burned the man alive, proved too slow in its effort to flee. The sweeping monster consumed the fiend's torso with its first bite, then took to the sky with the thrashing remains locked in its mouth. In the span of a few heartbeats, it was nothing but a tiny speck on the far horizon.

Hysth chuckled as he watched the creature disappear. "It is a fascinating place, is it not?"

"Fascinating is the not word that comes to mind. Evil reigns here." The woman visibly frowned as she watched the teeming masses return to the streets and carry about their business as if nothing had happened.

"Don't I know it," the god answered, his voice dripping with arrogance. "Hardship breeds strength, milady. If ever I need an army, there is no question in my mind that I have the resources to build the most powerful army ever formed."

That was not something Amaria wanted to think about. Truthfully, the thought terrified her. The monsters that inhabited this abyssal hell would run amok in her world, slaughtering innocents without remorse. Fortunately, they would need the means to travel there. She hoped that such a method was impossible, and that Hysth was merely trying to intimidate her. In that respect, he was doing a fine job.

"Let us return to the topic at hand, Knight of the Dove," the *Corrupter* continued. "I am going to help you locate Thavas. Hopefully, this time you'll follow through and kill him."

"Perhaps you aren't aware that I am awaiting the block for the murder of Councilman Baranor. Your information will do me no good when my head is in a bag."

The god dismissed the comment with a wave of his hand. "I am not concerned with that. Nor should you be. In your design, it was never meant for you to die by the axe of some dim-witted executioner."

"My design?" Amaria fired back. "What abstruse nonesense do you throw at me?"

Hysth lifted his pallid hand, palm outward. "Pardons, milady. I said more than I should have. Just know that there are other concerns that should occupy your mind."

The Knight of the Dove ran a hand through her hair, trying to drive away the frustration brewing inside. Perfectly coifed, the ivory locks slid like silk between her fingers. Just another benefit of this dreamlike state of unreality, she mused. But something was nagged her - *What did he mean by my 'design?'* Surely, she wasn't a creation of Hysth! If that were the case, wouldn't she have known by now? The possibility made her sick. She'd almost rather kiss the block than live with the knowledge that the Corrupter had created her. On the other hand, it was possible that even Hysth didn't know what he was talking about. Frustrated, she pushed the questions from her mind. It did her no good to dwell on them now, for as the *Corrupter* said, there were other concerns.

Rubbing her temples, she muttered, "Give me the information I need to know. I grow weary of this."

"Then I shall make this quick." Reaching into the folds of his robes, Hysth pulled free a small leaflet of parchment. He handed the paper to Amaria and said, "Wyur's temple is located high in Urak's Edge. That is where Thavas now stays. This map will aid you as you trek through the mountains in your search. Without it, the chances of you finding the temple are virtually impossible."

Dumbfounded, Amaria nearly threw the leaflet into air. "Do you take me for a fool? How in the hells am I supposed to use this? I am dreaming, remember! I cannot take it back with me."

"Just hold it in your hand when I send you back. I think you'll be surprised."

Amaria studied the map. The marks and locations were clearly scribed, but she was unfamiliar with the territory, and she realized that she would probably have to hire an experienced guide to direct her when she climbed the great mountain range.

"Are you ready then, milady?" Hysth asked.

She wasn't sure. A large part of her did not covet the idea of accepting help from the *Corrupter*. Most of her problems in life had stemmed from that very thing; calling to the dark gods for assistance. If anything, she should have learned from such a colossal error of judgment. However, the mental image of Thavas resting comfortably in a bed provoked her vengeful appetite. Her sword thirsted for his blood, and she wanted nothing more than to have her weapon drink from it and see his carcass fed to the vultures.

"A last request, *Corrupter*. Before I go, show me your true appearance. I wish to see what you look like, so that I may know what demon I conspire with and not this stale façade you gallivant within for my benefit."

"A rare display of curiosity from you, milady? I am surprised." Hysth lowered his head and seemed to consider the request. When he spoke, his words were slow and drawn out. "Apologies, but I must decline. The mere sight of me might drive you to madness, Knight of the Dove. Keep in mind I am an ancient deity, made from substances not of your world, or mine. Even my own subjects," he waved a hand outward, toward the city, "have never seen my true appearance. I wear many faces.

Amaria nodded. She had hoped that by seeing Hysth's true form, she would be so utterly appalled she would recant on her deal, thus avoiding the torment of knowing once again she had garnered help from forces of darkness. Somewhere inside her, she had the heavy suspicion she was making a terrible mistake. Even so, Thavas must die for what he did to Senastas.

"Then send me back," the woman said.

Hysth grinned amiably. "Certainly. I recommend that you hold onto the map tightly."

A searing pain exploded upside Amaria's head, as if the broad side of a hammer had clouted her. Her vision blurred and she reeled helplessly, arms outstretched, trying to grasp hold of anything to steady her disorientation. Falling to her knees, she cried out, but no sound was made. Another blast of pain knocked her fully to the ground. Her surroundings wavered, then blacked out entirely as she writhed in agony while the world around her disappeared.

Ten

The clanging rattle of iron on iron woke Amaria, returning her to reality. In a languid stupor, it took several seconds before she gained sufficient strength to lift her head. Blurred vision slowly came to focus, and she discovered a jailer busily unlocking the bars to her cell. Behind him, two guards patiently waited as the jailer, a bearded fellow with slits for eyes, finally wrenched free the latch and threw open the door.

"Ah, the woman is awake," the warden grumbled, his voice humorless. "She had slept a full day." He stepped to the chains that held her arms and worked the cuffs around her wrists.

"What is happening?" Amaria asked weakly, still combating her lethargy.

"The council has requested your presence. We are to escort you there," one of the guards spoke.

Amaria, waking in slow progression, registered what had been said. Had she really been asleep a full day? It didn't feel like she'd slept that long, though she supposed it was possible, especially considering her dream-like visit with Hysth. Perhaps time, in her world, had passed in quicker succession then it had while she spoke with the *Corrupter.* Whatever the reason, she didn't care, for now she was meeting the council. What did those damn politicians want from her? She nearly asked that very question aloud, but the guard who had just spoken proved quicker with the tongue.

"Councilman Marticis was right. You'll need a change of clothes, I'm afraid. This rag won't do."

The jailer eventually finished unlocking her cuffs, though she noticed he had spent far more time viewing her lower body extremities then was necessary. Had it happened under normal circumstances, she would have seriously considered poking out the man's tiny eyes. But, at the moment, she was too disoriented to care. Her arms, finally free of their bonds, dropped flaccidly to her sides. Several days of hanging had made her muscles and joints extremely tender and sore, and when the two guards grabbed hold of each arm, she made no effort to resist.

The sentries brought her to a stairwell and led her upward. At first, she tried to memorize the exact path they took out of the dungeon, hoping she could use the knowledge to escape at a later time. She quickly abandoned such a notion. The course they followed seemed roundabout, and she found it difficult keeping track of what floor they walked on, much less what direction they traversed. She did notice that each new hall was more astutely decorated than its predecessor. After ten minutes of continuous marching and stair climbing, they arrived at an open doorway. Without a single word of forewarning, a guard shoved her roughly inside. The room was absolutely bare save for a small rack of clothing in the far corner. No windows lined the walls, and only a small burning lantern by the entrance gave light.

The guard who seemed the duo's official speaker pointed a pudgy finger at the clothing stand and callously stated, "Choose an outfit and put it on."

"Not with you staring at me," she shot back.

The sentry seemed amused by this. Shaking his head, he offered, "This is not something we have time to haggle about. Murderers aren't given many privileges in this place. We'll not leave you alone."

Amaria wanted to scream that she hadn't killed Senastas, but such a gesture was pointless. The man obviously didn't care. Still, she wasn't going to concede on the other subject so easily. "Listen, soldier," she affirmed a most serious manner, "I will not remove my clothes while you gape at me like a drunken boor. I have plenty of time on my hands and can wait all day, if necessary."

"Perhaps we should change you ourselves," the guard threatened with a slight sneer.

"You are welcome to try. I will enjoy killing you."

There wasn't a single ounce of jest in her expression, and both guards answered her boldness with momentary silence. As the standoff grew increasingly rigid, the sentry abruptly swiveled his body around and directed his comrade to do the same. "Fine. You may change behind our backs. Do it quickly, though, and try nothing. You may have noticed, we are armed, and you are not."

Satisfied, Amaria viewed the garments. All of them were hideous; a mishmash of the poorly hemmed, simple castoffs, or outfits so old that they were considered terribly out of fashion by present day's standards. After careful evaluation, the woman selected a brown, long-sleeved tunic that was so loosely fitted and lengthy it hung like a robe. To complement it, she selected an olive pair of wide trousers which she rolled up at the ankles so walking was possible. As a whole, the entire assortment was laughably unflattering, but to Amaria, it felt nice to wear real clothes as opposed to the thin piece of cloth she'd worn in the prison cell.

"I am ready."

The guards almost looked surprised that she hadn't attacked them with their backs turned. To Amaria's relief, and she wasn't certain why she even cared, they hardly noticed her newly assembled clothes. Little time was wasted as they once again commenced their purposeful indirect route to whatever place they took her. Amaria tried not to speculate what might happen. Since her imprisonment, she had found it easier to just let things transpire without her control. Was that a good thing? Was she actually gaining better dominion over her own impulses? Or, perhaps it was merely a troubling sign that she had simply given up.

Minutes later, Amaria stood face-to-face with a set of closed double-doors. The guard banged his fist upon the thick wooded portal, and it cracked open an instant later. A head, displaying the weathered attrition of middle age, peeked out.

"We have brought the lady, just as instructed," the lead sentry asserted.

"Bring her in," the man answered, pulling the door fully open.

Amaria followed her captors into a spacious, well-lighted rectangular chamber. It was, without question, one of the more heavily decorated rooms in all of Valgamin. Perfectly centered, a finely wrought square table built of pressed and matted mahogany was supported by elegantly mosaicked plates of marble that ran parallel across the floor. Atop the table reared a thin, miniature stone sculpture of a scepter embedded in rock. Arced chairs surrounded the central piece of furniture, most of them occupied. Several tapestries and wall paintings lined the enclosure, and the single window sported azure-colored glass and displayed extravagant silk curtains.

It didn't take long to realize this was a meeting chamber for the high-elected officials of the city. Amaria instantly pinpointed the exact vacant chairs that should have been occupied by the First and Third Councilmen, were both not dead. The remainder of the council shown present, as well as a smattering of highborn magistrates backed by their retainers. A plethora of quills and parchments littered the table, though most were unused. Everyone in the room focused directly upon her. She steeled herself and made every effort to appear unaffected by their shameless stares.

Letting her own vision wander, she weighed any escape options lest the need arise. Then, she spotted an additional attendee that had almost escaped her notice the first time. Sitting inconspicuously in one corner, his elbows resting on the table and his narrow, delicate chin resting in his hands, lounged the cleric she had met from the temple of Aohed. Ishvar Aronis, she recalled his name as. Dressed in the habit of his priestly order, robes of sheer white fastened by strakes of sky blue, he calmly waited. The presence of clergy caused Amaria concern. Was a priest required for a sentence of execution? This hardly seemed the place for a trial. But then again, Valgamin had no sovereign laws of an overruling kingdom to adhere to. They could dole out their punishment however they saw fit, and swift punishment usually meant the block for undesired criminals.

Veran Marticis, dour eyed and sullen, stood from his chair. He appeared even older than when last she'd seen him. Deep creases traced his pale cheeks, and his needle-like greying hair looked brittle and unhealthy. No doubt the recent deaths of two councilmen had taken a heavy toll upon the aging man. "You are dismissed," he said to both guards.

As the sentries exited the room, Amaria's vision fell upon the pair of long swords that hung crossed on the rear wall, their shining blades reflecting the lamp light of the meeting chamber. How easy it would be to seize one and harvest her anger upon the defenseless aristocrats that deemed her guilty of a crime she hadn't committed! Of course, with her arms as sore as they were, she might not be able to even hold the sword upright.

"Mistress Eversvale, please, sit." Veran motioned to an empty chair directly in front of her. Soundlessly, she complied, though she found the high-backed piece of furniture uncomfortable while so many watched her every move. Even as she settled into her rightful place, their cold scrutiny did not cease. A grim face marked each attendant of the gathering, and an agonizing silence imbued the chamber. Was it the scornful silence of her already passed judgment?

Veran Marticus had returned to his seat, and Amaria noticed that the councilman seemed to have difficulty looking at her directly. Yet, it was he who spoke again. "Milady," he stammered between heavy breaths, "tell us what occurred the morning of Councilman Baranor's death."

The directness of the question surprised her. She had expected them to tiptoe around any convincing details, like any true politician, so as to arrive at the desired conclusion without ever establishing its base. Pulling her soiled hair behind her back, Amaria dived into yet another tale of tragedy that would leave her unending regret. She left out no truths, made no effort to sugarcoat details as she presented the story as best she could remember. Her audience remained in utter silence as she described her battle with Ephram, including how Ornan had come to her rescue and run the wizard through from behind. When she explained the moment Thavas murdered Senastas, she included her own lament over how she might have been able to prevent it. She added Thavas' admission to killing the First Councilman, Jonathon Barrowswynd, and explained how he achieved it. Upon conclusion, she could feel her own heartbeat against her chest as she revisited all those feelings of frustration and anger once more.

It was Tyris Andor, the Fourth Councilman, who spoke next. Today, the man held a long-stemmed tobacco pipe in his left hand, the tiny glow of burning sliced leaves barely visible within the overpowering light from the oil lamps. "Though I did not know him personally, Thavas Iimon had shown himself to be a valuable, hardworking steward. Do you have any way to prove that Thavas Iimon was, or is, a follower of Wyur?"

Amaria glumly shook her head. "I have no physical evidence, if that is what you ask."

Tyris puffed on his pipe for a few seconds, filling the room with the sweet fragrance of tabac spirits, then turned to Veran and lifted a curious eyebrow. Veran remained stoic, giving nothing so much as a nod in response. The eldest councilman quietly cleared his throat and commented, "Thavas has not been seen since the night before that incident."

"That is because he has fled," she responded.

"And why, Mistress Eversvale, should we believe that? It seems far more likely that you would have killed him as well. For all we know, his corpse is rotting away in some hidden ally." The speaker was a magistrate whom Amaria didn't recognize. He was middle age, dressed in all lace and cuffs. Although his words were accusing, there lacked sharpness to his tone, as if he merely wished to probe her for the right answer.

"There is a refuge high in Urak's Edge, a temple of sorts, where servants of Wyur conspire. It is there that I believe Thavas has escaped to." Amaria kept her voice even and factual. She figured that the less she fidgeted and ebbed her voice, the more her words would be accepted.

Veran rubbed a troubled face with his palm. The dark rings around his eyes spoke of a man who hadn't slept well in days, perhaps weeks. Gesturing to a retainer, the councilman whispered something in his ear. The servant quickly scurried out of the room, and Veran returned his interest to Amaria. "A temple in the mountains, you say? That sounds quite outlandish. How could you know such a thing?"

How indeed?, thought Amaria. That was the first question she would have difficulty answering. Ephram had mentioned it on separate occasions, and of course, Hysth had told her plainly. But, Amaria wasn't about to tell the court that the *Corrupter* had instructed her with such information. News of that sort wouldn't be received well. Rather than lying, however, she presented only half the truth.

"Before he was killed, Ephram had spoken several times of Wyur's refuge in Urak's Edge. Thavas never denied it."

Tyris lowered the pipe from his mouth and asked, "Do you know where this 'refuge' is? Urak's Edge covers an enormous area, and is quite hazardous. One does not walk blindly up those rocky steppes."

The woman shook her head. "I could not pinpoint an exact location. But, I am confident I will find it."

Again, momentary silence settled into the room. Every member of the court seemed to be weighing her words. Her assertions were hardly believable, but she had a convincing manner that caused the council to hold back their accusations. Amidst the silence, the servant reentered the room, bearing a flask of water. He wordlessly handed the container to Veran, who drank the clear fluid without shame. When he finished, he wiped his upper lip and placed the glass upon the table. "That is better," he muttered, half to himself. Casting an unreadable look toward her, he said, "Milady, it seems the gods favor you."

Now *that* was an unforseen declaration. Amaria hadn't felt the favor of the gods since her self-destruction at Erdoth Fortress. Inclining her head slightly, she asked in a lilting voice, "How so?"

"A healer at the sickhouse claims to have seen someone hastening down the hall, a man fitting Thavas' description, right about the time Senastas was murdered."

Amaria responded with a mere nod, as if the information did not surprise her.

"But there is more," Veran added. "Having witnessed no sign of Thavas for the last six days, we decided to empty his quarters of any belongings so that we might use the room for another."

Veran craned his body, allowing himself to reach into one of his pockets. He withdrew a small round medal and held it up for all to see. "*This* is what we found."

Nonchalantly, the councilman slid the token across the table. It skittered toward Amaria, and the woman effortlessly grasped it. Promptly, she inspected the metal trinket. Twice as large as a normal coin, it was perfectly circular, with smooth edges rimmed in gold. The remainder of the piece was forged of some odd, durable obsidian. Etched inside the center was the image of a face, half covered by a macabre mask, the other half depicting the stoic visage of a handsome man. Amaria didn't recognize the symbol. Brows furrowed, she peered at Veran, her face a question mark. "What is this?"

"That is what we wondered, at first." Veran answered. "We elected to bring our query to the temple, and it was Brother Aronis who welcomed us." The elder councilman turned to view the unassuming priest in the corner.

Ishvar offered a half-smile before he spoke, "That is the symbol of Wyur, the *Deceiver*, dark god of lies and false prophesies. His sole purpose is to cause havoc and dissent among the other gods. He reeks evil. Whoever owns that . . ." he paused, his serene face altering into disgust as he searched for the correct word, "*piece of garbage* should be sought out and dealt with. This is not something to be taken lightly, friends. The *Deceiver* knows nothing of remorse. He is a detriment to our society."

"I must note, however," Veran added, "that when Thavas first disappeared, we searched his entire room inside and out. Nothing was discovered. Not until last night, when we returned to empty out his chamber, did we find this little object lying in plain view, as if casually tossed in the corner."

"Someone must have placed it in his room," one of the nameless magistrates exclaimed.

Veran shook his head. "That does not seem likely. With Thavas missing, we posted a guard at his doors during all hours so the council would be instantly notified of his return. The guards that held watch reported nothing, and there had been no tampering of the room's single window. The only explanation that makes sense, however unlikely it may be, is that the token went unnoticed the first time."

Amaria had a better explanation, though she had no intention of expressing it aloud. Hysth! She wasn't certain how, but apparently, the *Corrupter* managed to place that coin in Thavas' room. It must be! Such knowledge troubled her, for she hadn't expected the dark god would have the capacity to manipulate objects in the physical world. It appeared Hysth held more power than she anticipated.

"So Thavas truly was a servant of the *Deceiver*?" a noble in attendance asked.

"It would seem that way." Tyris Andor answered. The Fourth Councilman leaned back in his chair and mindlessly tapped his pipe on the table. His face was a droll mixture of incredulous pity and satire.

Furtive glances were thrown across the room, various expressions of disbelief or frustration. Even Veran, who desperately tried to remain composed amid the silent tumult, seemed ready to fall apart at the seams. His steady countenance belied the exasperation of what occurred over the past several days. Amaria worried that the fellow could only handle so much more before he fell physically ill.

"So how are you proposing we handle this situation, Councilman?" the same noble inquired, an unnecessary edge to his voice.

"I was hoping that perhaps Lady Eversvale might assist us in that decision," Veran answered, albeit weakly.

The nobleman's eyes expanded, stabs of incredulity cast from his pin-like irises. "Absurd! You are letting the one who is under trial make motions of action? What madness is this? There is no evidence that she is innocent! That coin proves nothing!"

"The intent of this assembly was never to cast judgment, Lars. You were fully aware of that." It was Tyris who spoke, coming to the aid of his beleaguered colleague. The man's disposition was a far cry from that of his older friend. On appearance alone, he looked less affected by the tragic events that had recently taken place, though his façade bore the air of genuine concern, coupled with a trace of curiosity.

Lars, the nobleman, seemed on the verge of a retort. His lips quivered as he momentarily hesitated, then suddenly withdrew his glare of defiance and looked away.

Veran emptied the remaining contents of his drink, letting the cool liquid ease some of the burning stress that mounted. "Look, gentlemen, we all have our doubts over who possesses guilt and innocence. The bottom line is that we cannot know for certain." The councilman turned to the priest. "Brother Aronis, I would very much welcome your wisdom."

The priest nodded and placed calculating eyes upon Amaria, as if visually dissecting her soul. "I have met Lady Eversvale once before. She had come to Aohed's temple seeking solace for some matters that weighed heavily upon her heart. She asked questions regarding the dark god Hysth, which at the time, I found very peculiar. Only now, after hearing her story, does it make sense to me." He paused, throwing one final, prolonged glance at Amaria before turning to view the council. "To anyone who looks closely at this woman, it is quite clear that she is conflicted, battling some kind of inner chaos. I find it painful to even gaze upon her, and I cannot boldly claim she is incapable of murder. However, something leads me to believe she is not a liar. She might hide certain truths from us, yes, but I do not see someone who would speak boldfaced lies. If she claims that this servant of Wyur killed our beloved councilman, then I believe her."

"So now it is the clergy that determines guilt and innocence in Valgamin?" Lars spat, glowering at Ishvar.

"And what would you have us do, Lars? Take to her to the block right now and place her head upon the ramparts?"

Veran's words were surprisingly harsh, as if a portion of his anguish had ruptured from his mouth and splattered upon the nobleman. Lars shrunk in his chair, his vision falling to the table and his mouth closed.

The Second Councilman frowned, ashamed of his own outburst. "Mistress Eversvale, even if we are to accept your innocence, that still leaves us yet another issue. The knowledge of a temple dedicated to Wyur somewhere in the mountains concerns me, and I believe both of us have a score to settle with Thavas Iimon."

The Knight of the Dove gave Veran a wry smile. "You can be assured I am not finished with Thavas."

"And you still believe you can locate this place?"

"I do," she answered bluntly. In truth, she didn't know how she would, but she recalled her meeting with Hysth.

"Urak's Edge is a veritable death trap, Mistress Eversvale," Tyris interjected. The man had a clandestine smirk across his lips, challenging Amaria and eagerly anticipating a response. "Not only will the coming winter be brutal, but there are beasts and other rumored monsters that dwell high up in those peaks. Methinks you cannot survive alone."

The woman crooked her head at the other councilman. "I have yet to be foiled by an obstacle, Councilman, and I have crossed more than my share."

Tyris laughed aloud. "Such avowals could only come from the Knight of the Dove!"

Veran lifted a palm, and Tyris quickly restrained his cackle. The eldest councilman shook his head in refusal. "All of us are aware of your past achievements, milady. None here would rebuke their grand enormity. But, in proper conscious, I simply cannot allow you to trek that path alone. You will be accompanied by a small retinue of soldiers."

Before anyone else could convey surprise at Veran's revelation, Lars shot from his chair with the quickness of a cat leaping upon its prey. The nobleman's face was nine shades of red, pulsating veins along his forehead. "Have you lost all reason, Councilman? First, we deem her innocent without proper grounds, and now you offer her the services of *our* military? What next? Shall we present her as Third Councilman so that she may govern the position of the man she murdered?"

"That is quite enough, Lars!" Veran fired back, his voice sharp as an axe and launched from a man too strained to cope with a blathering nobleman who hadn't the rank, or status, to dispute the current head of council. "You will return to your seat and say no more, or I shall summon the guards to escort you from this meeting. Think hard before you choose!"

The glower from Lars bordered rebellion. Veran, to his credit, gave no ground, and two pairs of eyes issued silent threats for what seemed a thousand heartbeats. Just as Veran prepared to command his retainer to retrieve the guards, Lars slowly descended back into his chair. All in all, it was quite a display from both ends, and Amaria could sense the discomfort from every soul who sat within the chamber.

Veran slowly drew his vision around the table, meeting every attendant. "The matter is no longer under debate. The council has decided that Amaria Eversvale, the Knight of the Dove, will be released to pursue Thavas Iimon, the former steward of the late Senastas Baranor. A company of twenty well-trained soldiers from Valgamin's city guard will supplement her. These men will serve as additional protection during a trek through a dangerous region, as well as give witness that this woman carries out her expedition. It is my hope that once justice is served, there will be closure to these unfortunate, and sorrowful, incidents. If there are any final objections, you may bring them forth at this time." The elder councilman squared Lars with morose scrutiny, practically goading the noble to speak up. When it became obvious that Lars had fully retreated from the squabble, a smirk almost appeared on Veran's face. "Then it is settled. Tyris and Amaria, if you would be so kind as to stay a moment longer, the rest of you are dismissed."

The scraping of chairs upon the plated floor resounded in concurrence as the attendants disassembled from the chamber. Amaria watched the priest, Ishvar, stand from his chair and gather his papers. He was an ascetic figure; his skin pallid and his frame stooped ever so slightly, both a result from years of sitting at a desk buried in his studies. Try as she might, the woman could not discern the man's feelings. The cleric's mouth was but a sliver across his face, his visage portraying nothing to hint whatever thoughts lie beneath. Thus, it surprised her when, as he stepped past the woman on his way to the exit, he briefly glanced her way and his mouth faintly upturned.

Then he was gone with the others.

Only Veran and Tyris, along with their personal servants, remained in the room. Both men were in deep contemplation.

"How many do you think agreed with our verdict?" Veran asked Tyris. The rest of the assembly gone, the elder councilman withdrew his air of authority and headstrong countenance. Now, he simply reverted to an old man who needed a full days sleep.

"I'd guess about half," Tyris answered. "None of the others had the courage to openly defy you, especially with the strain the council has undergone of late. Doubtless they'll be gossiping like lonely midwives by the time they are on the streets though, forming opinions of your sanity and hoping to manipulate the circumstance to their own advantage. Knavery is their way, as you well know. But do not forget, old friend, that you have your loyal followers as well. You've been good to many, and some of those men will back you to the last. It may surprise you, but there are actually some benefits to being a good, upstanding fellow."

Both men talked openly, obviously unconcerned that Amaria could hear every word.

Veran nodded, the loose strands of his reedy hair leaning awkwardly in several directions. "And what of you? Do you agree?"

Tyris snuffed out his pipe and placed it upon the table with a sigh. "You already know my feelings toward priests." Amaria caught a flutter of disgust cross the councilman's face. "But that notwithstanding, I respect your judgment. You are a wise man, Veran, and if you feel this is the right move, then I relegate any qualms I have regarding the woman's honesty."

"I hope such wisdom turns prolific. Mistress Eversvale," Veran said, transferring his attention to Amaria, "you'll be pleased to know that all of your possessions have been kept secure, as well as your room at The Cardinal and the Jay. I had considered having someone polish your sword and armor, but thought better of it, deciding you are probably particular of such things. In a moment, my servant will escort you to your clothes and armor."

Amaria cast a fleeting look at the servant, who stood against the wall with his hands behind his back. The wiry fellow stared straight ahead as if deaf and blind, though she knew he listened to every word with overabundant interest.

"I have planned for the expedition to depart in four days," continued Veran. "It would have been ideal to wait longer, giving you ample time to recover from your weakened prison state, but the weather grows colder every day and those mountains are unforgiving. After my servant directs you to your belongings, return to your room at the inn and get some rest. Tomorrow I will summon you, and we can discuss any requests you have for the journey. Do you understand all this?"

The woman nodded compliantly.

"Very good. I have faith that you will prove me the wise man that Tyris claims me to be. Understand this, Mistress Eversvale, you will be watched during the next few days. Any attempt to flee will confirm your guilt."

"I understand, Councilman. The thought of fleeing will not cross my mind. My sword thirsts for Thavas' blood."

Veran signaled his retainer, and the gaunt man quickly stepped forward. "Escort Amaria to her possessions."

"Yes, milord."

Amaria was sped through several halls until pointed to a small closet. The woman nearly clamored for joy when she witnessed her armor resting comfortably in the corner of the tiny room. Like seeing an old friend, she mused. She dismissed the servant and hastened to her belongings. With a critical eye, she inspected every piece of equipment closely. Gods be praised, nothing had been tampered with! Every portion of her platemail was accounted for, and her sword still displayed dried blood from the conflict several days ago.

Next, she reached into her pack, feeling for the spare coin she always kept there. Her hand brushed upon a piece of parchment. Curious, she thought, trying to remember when she had placed paper inside her pack. Pulling the sheet loose, she unruffled it, and nearly dropped it to the floor when she realized what it was.

In delicate black ink, the subtle markings and lines of a map were inscribed upon the ashen piece of parchment. It was a map of Urak's Edge, the location of Wyur's temple clearly marked. Rapt in a mixture of shock and horror, she could only stare dumbfounded at the drawing for several seconds.

Then she understood. She had formed a new ally, one as black and callous as the feathers of a raven. Hysth had strung her like a puppet, clutching the strings and luring her to his bidding. She was dismayed, for it seemed she would never separate herself from the evil that clung like a shadow to her very soul.

"Gods above," she whispered, tears of anger and frustration forming within the corner of her eyes, stinging as she held them back. "It would have been better *had* they put me on the block." Attempting to push away her inescapable disconsolate outlook, a foreboding sense of impeding doom descended upon her.

And she openly wept.

Eleven

It was a colorless and chill morning. Amaria endured the drab arrival of daylight while she watched the procession before her with tempered rigidness, like that of a briery old captain whose wars numbered in the hundreds. A company of soldiers, along with several retainers, prepared mounts and loaded a supply cart. She observed their labors, overcome by a sense of newness as memories of her days serving the Illidor army came flooding back. She pined for the exploits of her old regiment, winning battles and reaping honors. Back then, Amaria Eversvale was a champion, a respected leader who administered commands with cool precision and complete authority. The title 'Knight of the Dove' meant something, and she carried it with pride and privilege.

Now, she carried it like a curse.

Twenty soldiers would be under her leadership, and though a far cry from the hundreds she often fronted in Illidor, she was energized and eager to be off. She monitored them with keen interest. They shouted and hollered at each other, a lively bunch who, by all appearances, looked charged for the journey. For that, she thanked Aohed, for she initially worried these men would respond unkindly to joining her in a venture through Urak's Edge. To her surprise, most had enthusiastically accepted. Guard duty, it seemed, was the model of unbearable tedium, and the men jumped at a chance to tackle a mission of extreme importance. The only true obstacle proved convincing the men that Amaria was innocent of murder. It hadn't come easy, but once accomplished, she had established twenty skilled warriors ready to travel with the famed Knight of the Dove.

"Quite a display, shera."

Amaria turned to her side, where Ornan stood. Unused to the cooler northern weather, the Radamite had several sheets of thick cloth wrapped around his body, covering the leather garb worn beneath. With sword belt wrapped around his waist, and raven black hair pulled tight behind his head, the man viewed the preparations with slight indifference. As usual, his only interest consisted of keeping Amaria from danger. The woman was at an absolute loss to explain the man's fierce loyalty to her. She tried to reason it out, to think of some rationale which caused his overprotective manner. Her usual guess, that being of a sexual nature, didn't seem to apply. Though he obviously enjoyed the pleasures of a woman — which she discovered first hand one day when visiting him unannounced and finding him 'entertaining' a female guest — his attraction to her was not based on sexuality. She found the whole premise quite odd, but was grateful all the same. Ornan had saved her on more than one occasion already.

"Are you certain you want to come along?" she asked Ornan, her breath floating in the air like white mist. The Radamite had taken leave of work so he could attend the convoy. "It will be dangerous."

"I would have it no other way, shera."

Amaria nodded, her thick mane of ivory hair tumbling loosely about her face. She had only asked out of courtesy, for she already knew the answer.

From the gathering of soldiers, one broke away and approached the two of them. Amaria didn't recognize the man until he removed his helmet. "Mistress Eversvale," the young soldier offered as he neared.

"Jerris! You are looking hale on this dreary morn," Amaria responded, an uncommon cheerfulness to her tone. A mix of amusement and satire possessed her face as she gazed upon the young prison guard whom she'd met while locked in her cell.

The youthful man peered at her with pale blue eyes. "My superior, Captain Gortesso, said you had specifically requested me for this expedition."

"I did."

"Why?"

Amaria opened her palms and tapered her eyelids, acting as if she couldn't understand the question. "Why not?"

Jerris' face contorted and wrinkled. "Milady, these other men are heavily trained men-at-arms! Skilled swordsmen and the like. They are the very best the Valgamin militia has to offer. I am nothing but a common prison guard. The extent of my battle experience derives from sparring duels during training sessions. I fear I will be useless, and you will be disappointed."

Amaria engulfed the young lad with a penetrating gaze of emerald and spoke like a true captain. "You are strong and carry a spear, yes? The standard you wear upon your surcoat is the same as the others, is it not?" The woman shook her head brusquely. "No, you are no different. You only have yet to prove yourself in battle, for in my mind, you have already proven yourself trustworthy. A soldier to be trusted is valuable indeed."

The look upon Jerris' face was amusing. He seemed uncertain whether to be flattered or troubled by her words. Offering a half-smile, he sputtered, "Yes, milady," before turning on his heel and sauntering away.

"Are you going to protect him?" Ornan asked, visually following the soldier's departure.

"I'll keep an eye on him, no more," she replied. "He'll surprise himself before this is over, my friend." She had never seen the young man fight, and secretly she realized that she would pay closer attention to him than she might the others; at least initially. Something about his nature had inspired her to request him. He was a thoughtful lad, introspective and sensible. She was gaining an appreciation for men who used their minds before their sword arms, for there never seemed enough.

One hour later, a contingent of mounted soldiers and one large supply wagon departed the cobbled streets of Valgamin and embarked upon the rutted path that led northeast toward the mining settlement of Yhull, nestled in the foothills of Urak's Edge. In uniform, her squad was nearly identical, wearing rust-colored, long sleeved surcoats over chainmail. The veneer flapped restlessly amid the inconsistent gusts of late autumn that swept in low from the eastern peaks, pummeling them with a bitter forewarning of the coming winter. Only their headgear differed. While most donned single-piece steel helms, some wore none at all. One man, looking as if he rode to some tournament of chivalry, sported a basinet with visor tilted up. All were in a jovial mood, boasting and bantering to each other, sparing no insults and receiving them doubly. Even the clouds, churning above like some strange atmospheric shield thwarting the sun from infiltrating the world, could not dampen their spirits.

The wagon, rumbling and clattering as it jolted along, hauled their provisions; foodstuffs, wools, extra weapons, and other supplies. The soldiers rode strong, healthy beasts, though Amaria's white stallion was the finest of them all. Even the great warhorses could not measure up, and the woman had renewed pride in her magnificent charger.

Amaria sent two men half-a-league ahead as scouts. Though she expected no resistance along the jarring, disused path that led to Yhull, scouting was common military practice. There were some procedures that she was an absolute martinet for.

Indeed, their way seemed clear of danger. The steady beating of hooves had a therapeutic effect, and Amaria fell into a peaceful trance as the column of soldiers forced their way further along the crude dirt road. She cleared her mind of concerns that battered at her, and absorbed the unpolluted air of the countryside. Yhull would be a full day's march and the woman intended to enjoy it without dwelling over the follies of her life. She imagined herself five years younger, still rising up the ranks of the Illidor army, prepared for any challenge that might bar her path. Invincible, the Knight of the Dove, the champion that would thwart the evils of the world with her blade alone.

"I see tranquility in your face, shera."

Ornan had wrenched her from her reverie, but she merrily smiled at him nonetheless. The Radamite rode at her flank, astride an old draft mare that was a far cry from the powerful destriers hauling the Valgamin retinue. Still, the aging beast kept pace and Ornan didn't appear bothered by the obvious disparity of his animal.

"My friend, I wonder if my true place is back in Illidor, performing what I had trained half my life to do. I miss fronting an army."

"They would take you back in a heartbeat," Ornan responded, pulling loose the wineskin he had procured for the trip. "Of that I am certain."

Her companion took several swallows of the fluid, then offered his container to Amaria. She declined with a subtle shake of her head. "Why, then, is it so hard to return?"

"Most people find it difficult to face their failures, shera. Sadly, I believe you are the only one who sees your past as a failure. Almost certainly you are regarded as a hero back home."

"Undeservingly," she whispered irritably.

"By the blood of Gesh, how long will you do this to yourself?" Ornan's normally quiet tone had suddenly been replaced by a terseness rarely heard from the Radamite. He locked his hazel eyes upon her own. "Such self loathing thoughts will never heal you. Do you not understand this? Surely you must tire of it?"

The Knight of the Dove, mouth agape and wordless, stared at her companion. He spoke the truth, she knew; a truth she could not remedy. She hated herself ever since the day she found Royce dead, discovered his body mutilated by the hands of her enemy. Her fault, she told herself, and from that moment on, she deemed herself a failure. Ornan did not pity her, for instead, he sought to drag her free from the resignation that consumed her. Her admiration for the man's friendship increased. "My apologies, friend. It has become such habit to me. I often find it difficult to break. Perhaps our task ahead will commence a rehabilitation of sorts."

The Radamite stroked his twin-braided goatee, contemplating her words. "Yes," he nodded, "perhaps it will. Let us make the most of it then."

As another sharp gust assaulted the traveling legion, Amaria shivered and pulled her mantel over her arms, tying the edges of the cloth to her wrists to keep it wrapped about her body. "This cold *already*," she whispered under her breath, wondering just how frigid the air would grow once they climbed the mountains. It wasn't a pleasant thought, but at least they had taken appropriate preparations, loading several extra furs into the wagon for emergency purposes. The way it looked, every last fur would be used by the time this expedition was over.

Along the east, Urak's Edge maintained its ceaseless wall of black peaks, stretching to the sky and gifting the troupe no horizon in that direction. Amaria tried to estimate how long it would take to scour those crags in search of the temple. Unfortunately, she was no expert of mountainous terrain, and thus, there was no accurate assessment forthwith. She recalled the map hidden safely within her pack, the map given to her by Hysth. Thus far, she hadn't shown it to anyone, Ornan included. Circumstance would force her eventually, but the mere sight of the cursed parchment made her despondent, reminding her all too much of recent failures and foul arrangements.

By midafternoon, the clouds detached in certain areas to allow pockets of blue sky to materialize amid the grey curtain. The winds grew sporadic, and the overall weather more tolerable. In route, the company chanced upon a small pool that floated lazily alongside the road, its clear waters bristling. Seizing an opportunity for drink and rest, Amaria called the expedition to a halt. She quickly dismounted and stretched tired legs before walking her mount to the pool. The stallion happily lapped up the cold water while other horses joined him on both sides. Reaching inside her saddlebags, Amaria removed a waterskin and quenched her own thirst.

Using her backhand to wipe the escaping droplets of water from her chin, she studied the men around her. Many had their backs to Amaria, their chainmail unlatched and opened as they heeded nature's call on the opposite side of the path. The woman felt a similar need, but for her, it wasn't so easy as leaning along the edge of the road. She scanned the area and happily noted several trees and bushes that would provide sufficient cover as she took care of her unpleasant business. Directing Ornan to watch her mount, she disappeared within a thicket of bushes a hundred or so yards from the main body of her unit. Several minutes later, upon her return, a soldier approached her.

"Milady, we are roughly five hours from Yhull. We should arrive shortly after dusk." The man had the lithe body of an archer, but his face was haggard and course, complete with two scars and a crooked nose. Sun-scorched, rough-hewn features made his age indeterminable.

"Very good, Seth. Make certain everyone has properly fed and watered their horses. I do not plan on stopping again."

Seth nodded in conformation. "Yes, milady. I will see to it."

Amaria dismissed the soldier, and the man skirted to his assignment. She had designated Seth as her second in command, which simply meant he carried out all the tasks she hadn't the time, or desire for. Before joining the Valgamin guard, the man had served the Hjord army — a small kingdom far to the northwest — for twenty years as an archer and swordsman. A veteran of many campaigns, he understood the caravan routine. Though other soldiers present had fought in wars, she had been advised that Seth was the most trustworthy of the bunch.

After all the animals had been replenished and the soldiers content with their break, Amaria started them up a second time. The assemblage of horses resumed treading a path northeast, renewed vigor on the faces of the men. As Ornan silently fell in at her side, she allowed herself a sliver of optimism. One loyal companion accompanied her, and twenty trained warriors. For what seemed like an eternity, things appeared to finally be going well.

Gripping the hilt of her sword, she silently prayed they would end well.

Other than the possibility of being the most easterly established community in the whole of the world, there was little remarkable about the village of Yhull. Wedged in a low valley, like a chisel between blocks of wood, Yhull was the haven to a high percentage of miners who prospered from the untapped riches which lay hidden deep inside Urak's Edge. A friendly place, visitors came rare enough that they were earnestly welcomed each and every time, likely in hopes they would return again someday.

Dusk had suppressed the sun only a short time ago, and much of the small populace still milled about the center of town, enjoying the company of friends and clinging to the last remnants of the fleeting day. All too soon, sleep would call them, and beyond that, a world of pick-axes, wheelbarrows, and murky tunnels deep inside Urak's Edge; a droning reminder of the life they had chosen.

When a contingent of soldiers abruptly appeared, plowing their way through the dusty roads within a thicket of darkness, it came as quite a shock to the townsfolk. A myriad of faces stared at the procession, their expressions a mixture of surprise, excitement, and concern. In peaceful places such as Yhull, men-at-arms often carried grim bearings, or ill intent. Soldiers and their ilk were unpredictable and unsympathetic to the daily lives of commoners. They were trained killers, toughened men made even tougher by the company they kept and the weapons they bore. Kind words came hard to such men, for their lives revolved around wars that most people sought to avoid.

Amaria understood those trepidations, and she strode past the throng nodding amiably to each person and making every effort to appear non-threatening. She had already conveyed her expectations to her troop over their conduct. Any who managed to cause trouble would answer to a woman whose temper was almost legendary.

A man appeared up ahead, waving his arms and hustling to intercept the moving line of soldiers. Capturing Amaria's attention, the woman immediately steered her mount to greet him.

The fellow, of average height and slightly overweight, was dressed in a comely red tunic, sporting shoulder-length brown hair and stubble along his chin. The muscles on his face seemed to vaguely alter when he recognized the front rider as a female. Through a stern voice that contradicted the tension upon his face, he said, "Welcome to Yhull, milady! I am Arlomew Rowasen, acting burgher of this humble village. May I assist you and your men on this night?"

Amaria leaned down until her elbow rested upon the horse's withers. "Well met, good sir! Do not fear my men, for we are only staying the night and shall be on our way in the morn."

"Passing through?" In perplexity, the townsman crumpled his

brow. "Pardon the question, milady, but where would you be headed? There is nothing beyond this point."

"We are on special assignment from the council of Valgamin. Our task leads us up Urak's Edge." Amaria spoke with as much benevolence as she could muster. A trustworthy impression was vital if they were to obtain a guide in this tiny place to direct them into the mountains.

With furrowed brow, the burgher regarded her words. Lifting his shoulders, he proffered, "Far be it from me to withhold Valgamin's affairs, but your lodging concerns me. Old Mert uses his cottage as a hostel when visitors find their way here without proper lodging, but I'm afraid he has only two rooms. He couldn't possibly serve all of you."

"All we need is a roof over which to lay our bedrolls, good sir. There are twenty-two of us. The common room of someone's abode would work splendidly, if someone is willing to allow us use for the night. We will pay handsomely and cause no trouble."

The man needled his fingers across the front of his tunic, deep in thought. Then his eyes shot open in revelation, as if someone had slammed a lantern across the back of his head. "The festhall has a foyer large enough. Let us go speak with the owner."

One half-hour later, twenty-two bedrolls were spread across the lobby of the local tavern. Amaria, using funds granted her by the Valgamin council for just this purpose, had paid well enough to convince the proprietor, a young man who had recently taken over for his aging father, to close early. In order to appease the disgruntled patrons, Amaria purchased them a drink on their way out.

With that business out of the way, Amaria wasted no time undertaking the task of securing a guide. Half of her troop already slept soundly while the remaining men elected to fraternize with each other, or more preferably, the attractive local women. Several of the lasses were all aflutter over the sudden presence of so many strapping, healthy men-at-arms. Amaria gave it little thought. It was their own lives, and she would not interfere, nor had she leashed her men in any way regarding intimate relations with willing ladies. She had, however, told them that rape of any sort would be dealt with by the business end of her sword.

After several inquires, the woman acquired the services of a staunch-bred rapscallion named Peran. The man hunted regularly in the mountains and throughout their discussion had proven himself knowledgeable over certain landmarks and the terrain. In fact, he seemed quite eager to help, at first. His enthusiasm waned when Amaria described how high the company intended to climb. It took plenty of coin to persuade him, but the deed was ultimately accomplished.

Not until later, when speaking with Arlomew Rowasen, did she discover that Peran had also been Jonathon Barrowswynd's guide the fateful day the First Councilman flung himself from the ledge to his death. It was a harrowing omen she'd rather not have toyed with, but Peran seemed the best man for the job, and testing fate was nothing new to the Knight of the Dove.

By the time the woman retired to her bedroll, nearly all her men had embraced slumber inside the walls of the festhall. Her muscles throbbed from a full day of riding and her mind weary from additional time spent within Yhull. Removing her outer armor, she eased herself down upon the floor. Her head felt ten pounds heavier than normal, and she experienced an almost blissful feeling as she placed it upon the feather stuffed cushion knitted at the end of her bedroll. In mere seconds she had almost drifted off when a voice forced her back to reality.

"Shera, do you feel confident in tomorrow's venture?"

Ornan, his own roll placed next to hers, had withdrawn over an hour ago, though he was obviously still conscious and alert.

"By my sword, Ornan! Have you stayed awake just to insure I returned safely?"

The man's silence answered for her.

Shaking her weary head, Amaria stated, "I am confident, friend. With you eternally looming over my shoulder, what have I to fear?"

The Radamite seemed pleased by this response, for he muttered something that sounded like gratitude and said no more. In an uncommon moment of gratefulness, Amaria thanked the gods for Ornan and his undying loyalty. Though it seemed to zap the remaining strength from her body, she grinned through the darkness at her friend.

Twelve

Even at noon hour, the mist lingered waist high across the band of soldiers, making them appear like floating torsos amid a sea of roiling white. The sun had neglected to rouse from its slumber, and again the world seemed little more than layered shades of grey.

Under the advice of Peran, Amaria left the horses behind in Yhull. The terrain was simply too difficult to traverse by animals of that sort, and in the end it would only slow them down. Thus, without use of the wagon, every member of the unit crammed their small packs as full as possible with supplies, and Amaria also had a litter built to haul additional equipment. Every second hour, two men rotated to haul the carrier. It wasn't ideal, but it worked nonetheless.

The initial climb out of the low valley was strenuous, as the walls rose at steep angles around Yhull. Once they reached the summit, however, the ground leveled to a more gradual incline. Standing at the ankles of the great World's Edge, the looming barrier seemed infinite. Emptiness filled the pit of Amaria's stomach while she gazed upward into the masses of rock and plant, and higher up, to the enigmatic snow-capped peaks whose tips were veiled by the hanging clouds. How much ground those mountains covered! She couldn't fathom the chances of finding a tiny shrine hidden amid that magnitude of earth.

Scraping earlier reservations, she had given the map to Peran. The squirrelly man understood the markings and locations, but claimed he'd never been so high, and that it would be an arduous climb. "Two weeks, probably more," he had said. Even so, the challenge seemed to spark a flame in Peran's resolve. A smile graced his face when he explained the numerous dangers that would make the trek difficult. All sorts of beasts and rumored monsters prowled the ridges and forests that persisted along the many faces of the mountainous range. They would have to remain alert at all times.

A chill carried in the air, and Amaria withdrew any hope of one last heat wave before the winter season. Their breath was visible, lifting to the heavens in unison like some sort of archaic ritual. Though no one had yet donned their furs, each man wore his gauntlets and helmet, if he owned one, in efforts to keep every body part warm. Peran had a sheepskin jacket hanging across his shoulders and seemed oblivious to the midday coldness. He kept the soldiers at a constant pace, not rushing them, but maintaining a steady tempo to prevent tiring or lingering. He had spoken very little during the conception of the voyage, but occasionally he turned back to Amaria and offered an assuring nod.

At the rear of the column, two men struggled to keep up with the others. From ahead, they looked as if there were swimming upstream against the haze that eddied beneath them. Amaria swung around and shouted, "Let's move back there! We'll leave you behind if we must!" She felt no pity for them. Last night, the laggers stayed awake with their newly gained female companions well into the morning, only now paying a brutal price. Scaling a mountain and womanizing apparently didn't mix well, and she frowned at their poor judgment.

Ornan, his old boots scraping against the rocks, walked up ahead to join Peran. Amaria watched her friend exchange whispered phrases for a few minutes. Then, Ornan fell back and rejoined Amaria.

"What did you speak about, friend?" she asked.

"I asked him how soon we would begin to cross paths with the beasts of this place."

When he offered nothing more, Amaria prodded him irritably, "And?"

"He says we are already beyond the safe point."

"Isn't that a nice bit of news," the woman snorted. "No matter, the danger will threaten us eventually."

Peran brought them to a halt at the boundary of a large forest. When he reached the edge, he turned back to Amaria and called,

"Milady, through these trees is a more direct route. The going is difficult, but it will save time. We lose at least a day if we go 'round it."

Amaria did not hesitate. "Lead on."

"Yes, milady." Peran plunged into the first row of trees, followed by Amaria and Ornan. The scent of pine and sapling pervaded amid the copse, and the woman paused to take several deep breaths of the sweet aroma. The soil itself grew soft, sagging slightly beneath the heavy boots of the soldiers as they hoofed across the ground in their ungainly fashion. The area came alive with muted sounds of wildlife, a symphony of buzzing and chirping from things that felt secure within their leafy cover. No paths had been cut, no trails to follow. The company forced their way like pioneers in a land that knew nothing of them.

And such an untamed land it was! Even within the bitter chill, several types of wildlife and flora, kinds that she'd never seen before, deemed this area home. Amaria felt like an intruder, raiding a world that found no joy in her presence. This wonderful place was not meant for the thoughtless rape of man, the unrelenting way in which they compel the very ground to its knees in order to own it, to form a society fitting of their own needs. Though she enjoyed the purity of the area, it saddened her to know they must travel this way and disrupt such a natural setting.

"Milady, how soon would you like to set up camp?"

The ligular guide scooted over to stand near Amaria, waiting an answer. The woman slowly returned to the present state of affairs, rolling the question in her mind. "Dusk will be fine. Perhaps we should stop a moment and let the men eat?"

"That would be wise, milady. It will be some four hours before sunset, and your men have not eaten more than tidbits since breakfast."

The woman assembled the company and instructed them to rest and appease their hunger. Weary from the ever-ascending hike, she heard not a single protest. They quickly found places to sit among the high-branched trees, delving into their pack for their foodstuffs. It was fresh rations they ate on this day, things such as newly picked fruits and unsalted meats, foods that would rot and turn rancid if not consumed within a few days. The salted provisions, beef and hardened produce, would be eaten last, when nothing else remained.

Amaria pulled free her bow, laid it to the side, and dropped to the ground atop a host of dried pine needles that scattered as she landed. She leaned against a tall evergreen and reached into her rucksack. Withdrawing an apple, she assaulted the fruit aggressively, tearing apart a large portion on the first bite. Ornan found a seat next to her and did likewise.

Peran remained standing, watching the woman with temperance. "Do you have hunters in this group, milady?" the guide asked.

"We have three or four talented archers among us," she answered, already grasping where the conversation was headed.

Peran nodded in approval. "That is good. Your provisions will not last you this whole climb. You'll need to hunt for game if you wish to keep your packs full."

"Understood, Peran. Tomorrow we can begin. Let us enjoy this first day without the worries of finding wild animals skulking among the trees." Though not a hunter herself, Amaria had fired arrows with more accuracy than anyone else during her service in the Illidor army. With the help of more experienced hunters to locate the prey, like Peran, she was certain they'd have no trouble keeping their stomachs full.

By dusk, their progress had not yet taken them out of the woodland. Bizarre, sorrowful moans, the kinds only nightfall could bring; wolves, land sharks, and other beasts that prowled the earth under the cloak of darkness, echoed through the starlit sky as the last rays of sunlight waned and vanished. It felt as if the soldiers attended a concerto of melancholy howls, reverberating off the blackened trees which surrounded them.

The company erected a crude campsite, and a dozen or so men huddled around the comburent fire, praying that the source of those noises were not as close as they sounded. A few men held spits in their hands, frying lizards and other animals diminutive in nature. Jerris, the young prison guard, was amongst them. An unfortunate groundhog lay impaled at the end of his poker, charred and half-eaten. The young rake was doing a fine job fitting in with the more grizzled veterans, and he appeared to be enjoying himself.

Amaria, already down upon her bedroll, closed her eyes and listened to the din of her environs. Day one in the books, with no setbacks yet to speak of. It wasn't remarkable by any stretch of the imagination, but a positive start boded well. With a little luck, she could get her men to the temple unscathed. What happened then was anyone's guess. But, that lie far down the road and many days ahead. Tomorrow is what truly mattered, she thought, and hopefully another unproblematic day of hiking.

One step at a time, she reminded herself, one careful meticulous step.

The morning carried with it a shrill wind. The forested area of the mountain's base whistled as zealous gusts twisted furiously through the leaves like bolts from a crossbow, pummeling them with no regard to the early hour. The tall trees, far less dense than the jungles of the south, could only provide small bits of refuge from the unrelenting fury. Amaria had no intent to dawdle in place, and she barked at her men to wake, giving them a boot when they failed to stir. The rousing process took longer then she would have liked, but eventually they tread a path through the undergrowth at the pedestal of Aruk's Edge.

The temperature was dropping, and though not quite freezing yet, it wouldn't be long. The men grumbled while they pumped their legs, crushing twigs and dried leaves and grousing over the bitter cold. Soon they would need to don their furs, though not a single man had done so, yet. None wanted to be the first to show weakness before the others. Amaria almost scoffed at their senseless pride, but didn't, for she realized she would've done the same thing. To endure the elements was a major accomplishment among the order of soldiers. In time, she'd certainly have to *order* them to wear the furs just so they wouldn't to freeze to death.

"The sky is ominous."

Peran looked back at Amaria, the words still hanging from his lips. Indeed, there was something strange about the clouds, mottling the blueness that lay hidden behind it. Rather than drift aimlessly like most overcast skies, these clouds seemed to gently *swirl*, like a cyclone amassing above their heads. To the north, the sky was even darker, a thick shadow dangling in the heavens. The sight gave Amaria a chill.

"What do you think of it? A storm?"

The guide paused and craned his neck, viewing the pallid mural that loomed above their heads. He had very little hair on the top of his head, a matter he overcompensated with by growing long the thin black strands that grew around his ears. The padded leather gloves he wore matched color with his sheepskin attire, giving him a sort of mountain hermit appearance. "I do not know, milady? But unless it starts to break up, something will hit us."

The Knight of the Dove threw a glance at Ornan, whose grim persona equaled her own. "Well, there is little we can do about it. With luck, it will disband, for we cannot stop and turn back."

She couldn't tell if Peran was dismayed by the response or undeterred, for he merely inclined his head once and resumed his steady gait. The Radamite, however, still watched her.

"And what do you think, friend?" she asked.

Ornan pointed his gloved hand to the peaks that emerged high above them. "I think there is a man up there who has yet to feel your justice, shera."

Amaria grinned slightly. "Indeed. Well said, my friend." She slapped him heartily on the shoulder as they followed Peran further into the wastelands of Urak's Edge.

Despite the dropping temperatures, the day passed smoothly. When sunset neared, Amaria pulled the group together near a sluggish mountain stream and announced that they would make a short circle of the area in search of prey. The news did not fall unexpected among the troop, for she had already discussed it with them during the morning gathering. A smattering of trees and undergrowth, along with the slow flowing brook, surrounded them, and the woman hoped something was out there worth hunting for.

Half the men had proven at least adequate using a bow, and the others were put to use flushing out potential prey. Amaria established teams of two and instructed them to return after a short period of time, with or without a quarry. Wandering too far might get them lost, nothing short of a death sentence out here. Four soldiers remained by the campsite to give the wandering men a central location to convene.

Amaria, arrow nocked, stalked through the dry flora, mimicking the movements of Peran, who had spent years hunting along the ridges. Ornan followed them with an unmistakable air of disinterest in the hunt. His eyes were squared solely upon Peran. Amaria supposed the Radamite didn't trust their guide enough to leave her alone with him, fearing he might betray her. Entirely unwarranted, she believed, for Peran seemed an honorable man incapable of betrayal. Still, there was comfort in having a protector at her heels.

A scream shattered the serenity of the evening. The woman froze as everything around her went quiet. She listened intently, but nothing followed.

"Where did that come from?" she asked, her question cast at both men.

Her answer came as a second shriek, more urgent than the first, clearly from the lungs of a man.

"This way!" Peran yelled, surging to his right at full speed.

Amaria chased after, not looking back to see if Ornan followed. Tree trunks and branches whipped past her face as she pushed herself forward, heart racing like a metronome calibrated ten times too fast. To her left emerged another pair of soldiers running in the same direction, yelling and calling to her, but she did not heed them. She gripped her bow as if trying to crush the bent handle with her jittery palm.

Then she arrived on the scene, wiping sweat from her brows and barely able to credit what she witnessed.

"Holy gods!" someone uttered.

A gigantic lizard-like creature dominated the clearing, its scales running along its spine like an axe. Twice the size of a lion, its eyes darted back and forth in an almost mechanical pattern, viewing the collection of stunned people who stared upon it. The grotesque reptile sported a gaping maw full of razor-sharp teeth that were bloodied, dripping, and gnawing through an unfortunate soldier's abdomen. The poor soul was still alive, screaming through diluted breaths as the beast tore him to shreds. On the ground, several feet from the current conflict, another body lie. Unmoving, it was already indistinguishable as human within the mass of crimson and entrails that soiled the earth around it. Only the torn attire marked it as another of Amaria's men.

"A lyzcan." Peran whispered.

"We've got to help him!" a fellow soldier called out, his vision glued to the gruesome beast in sheer horror.

"He's beyond help," Peran answered with the staleness of someone who had seen it before. The ill-fated man in question stopped screaming and went limp, though his body still spasmed and convulsed in erratic fashion. His condition was no longer reversible.

Amaria fired an arrow that bounced harmlessly off the scaled neck of the beast. Grunting her frustration, she unsheathed her sword. "Stay back, all of you!" she called to the others as she moved nearer the lyzcan.

"You cannot face it alone, milady! It will rip you apart!"

Amaria wasn't sure who had said the words, but it mattered not. "Do as I say!" she reiterated. "Fire no arrows!"

The lyzcan caught sight of her as she cautiously stepped toward it, her blade steady in her hand. In a single motion, the monster opened its mouth wide and released the dead soldier from its jowls. The lifeless body dropped to the ground with a sickening thud. For a single heartbeat, it appraised the woman, a sort of primitive vehemence locked behind its swiveling eyes. Then it shot at her.

A front claw caught the Knight of the Dove on the crown of her head, knocking her down. It was a jarring blow delivered with incredible speed. Amaria, temporarily dazed and on her stomach, found enough presence to roll once, avoiding a second claw that had intended to pin her to the earth. She quickly found her feet and backed out of range. Touching the top of her head, she noted that the attacked had not pieced skin, for no blood ran upon her gauntlet.

She felt the battle energy, the numbing of the senses and veins of ice when one fought for ones life. She tunneled in on the creature, her blade whirling before her like a scythe cutting wheat. The lyzcan jetted forward, its teeth primed to remove her head from her shoulders. She fell to her knees and let the monstrosity's momentum carry above her, then thrust her sword up into the soft part of its neck. The monster squealed and reared back, wrenching Amaria's weapon from her hand. The lyzcan bled profusely from the wound, though it did not fall. With her blade lodged in the underside of the lyzcan's neck, Amaria suddenly found herself weaponless.

A second soldier, unable to simply observe without taking action, rushed the beast's flank and drove his own sword under the protective scales on its side. The lyzcan bellowed again and rammed the soldier with its reptilian forehead, knocking him clear of the battle. In droll irony, the soldier's sword remained in the wound, and now the beast carried two blades upon its body.

"Shera!"

Amaria swiveled her shoulders to witness Ornan lobbing his own weapon in her direction. She caught the sword by the handle and refocused on her opponent just as the lyzcan rushed again. She spun sideways, but the beast caught her across the shoulder with a huge claw. She staggered for an instant, blood seeping from beneath her pauldrons where the claw had scored flesh. As the monster attempted to snatch her within its death-like maw, she leapt forward, dropping beneath its neck a second time.

Using her free hand, she reached up and grasped the hilt of her own protruding blade, and with all her strength thrust both weapons into the same wound. The maneuver was lightening fast, and the two swords gorged deep into the giant lizard's throat.

The Knight of the Dove rolled away while the lyzcan thrashed about in pain, its piercing squeal echoing off the surrounding trees. Crimson poured freely from the dreadful wound. Falling to its side, the creature abruptly went quiet, save for heavy breaths as it gasped for air in a subtle decrescendo.

Then it was still.

Amaria calmly approached the corpse and retrieved the two swords that ran parallel in the fatal wound. The silver steel of the weapons discharged the blood that covered them, like a decanter full of red wine. The other soldier, who had sustained no serious injury, pulled free his own weapon from the beast's side.

"You've done it again, shera." Ornan announced, taking his sword.

The woman did not reply. She viewed the two broken bodies that were once men under her command. They had been wholly mauled to an unrecognizable point. A sickness twisted in her stomach, and she felt as if she were going to vomit. With concerted effort, she swallowed the bile that formed in her throat. The gruesome scene hadn't caused this, but the knowledge that two of her own had fallen before she could save them.

"Two days in, and already two gravesites," she spat angrily.

"There was nothing you could've done, shera."

Amaria wasn't listening. Scanning her men, she located Seth. Her second in command was squinting, face incredulous over the scene. "Get the shovel from the litter," she commanded, "and some rope. We will bury the men right here. Peran, is this meat edible?"

The guide quickly stepped forward. "I would believe so, milady."

"Then let's cut it up. We have two days feast at least."

Thirteen

Amaria had grown weary of the rock that shuffled and slid beneath her feet. They climbed a steep slope, the stone beneath them sprawling and loose, as if a large rock far above had shattered eons ago. The horses would never have managed this, for even the men were having the worst of it.

They were five days out of Yhull, and had exited the wooded area early the previous day. Once beyond the protection of trees, the men had quickly donned their furs against the freezing currents. The pelts already looked hideously worn and dirty, covered with dust and grime, but not a single man cared as long as it warmed them. Now, they scaled a part of the mountain that was nothing but rocky terrain. Peran admitted to never being this high, and he hadn't anticipated the precipitous incline that confronted them. At first, the group had tackled the slope by walking at an angle, but the path had narrowed between a pair of giant granite boulders that posed like monoliths at either side. They were now forced to go straight up a narrow, hazardous trench that by sight alone seemed impassable.

Amaria peered up the scree slope, viewing the stone face that seemed to stare down upon them. Behind her, a soldier set off a slide of rock with one step, and suddenly the ground itself was in motion, rumbling freely downward. The men beneath shouted and dropped to their hands and knees, grasping anything to steady their bodies and keep themselves from being dragged to their deaths. A hundred feet below the pieces came to rest in a vast array of jagged edges. Only luck alone kept the soldiers from falling, each man remaining latched to the slope and thanking the heavens they survived. Amaria watched from above the fracas, relief evident as her charges slowly rose to their feet, their steps far more careful than before.

They came beneath a high arching cliff, hanging above them

as Peran led the troop along the crest, a three-foot wide space that ended with a daunting four hundred foot drop. It felt like many nervous hours passed by the time they reached the overhang, though in truth, it was merely a dozen minutes. At the top, Amaria let the men relax and gaze out over the incredible view. The world extended for miles below, rising and falling to the whims of the great mountain. Yhull was nowhere to be found, smaller than a speck of dust within the staggering span of earth.

The blizzard hit in late afternoon, a deadly mixture of vigorous winds and snow. In minutes the world became a featureless white, the company enveloped like a child under a blanket, deadened and sightless in its fury. Confusion quickly set in, and Amaria hastily commanded them to set up the single canvas tent they carried along. An anxious time followed as the panicked men set the stakes with numbed hands into the hardened ground, but soon their diligence paid off and their protection firmly set in place. The shelter wasn't large, but twenty-one men crammed their bodies tight like sardines, finding temporary refuge from winter's wrath. They huddled together and waited.

"It's colder than a witch's tit!" one of the soldiers griped. "What do we do?"

The woman sat with her knees up against her breasts, unmoving. "Unless you want to die as an ice sickle, I suggest you wait with the rest of us. There is no moving in this."

And so, for almost two full days, they cowered under the canvas while the snows half-buried their shelter. It was an uncomfortable wait. Occasionally, someone stepped outside to hurriedly relieve themselves before diving back within. One soldier, a golden haired lad named Breke, exited for that very reason just like the others, except he never returned. A couple the men wanted to go looking for him, but Amaria refused. If one man became lost simply emptying his bladder, it was far too perilous for a search party.

Thus, seventeen warriors remained, along with Ornan and Peran. As the howling winds and lashing snow battered the canvas, Amaria wondered how many more would be lost before it was over.

The air felt like glass, cold and still in the aftermath of the snowstorm. The blizzard abated less than an hour before, and Amaria immediately prompted her men to roll up the canvas and get moving. Enough time had been wasted, and she'd have gone mad if she'd stayed under the tent much longer. They'd found Breke's body about fifty feet away, sitting in the snow, his body frozen stiff. The man's legs were tucked under his arms and his lifeless eyes were open, like windows to a soulless shell. They had buried him in the snow, for the earth had become too rigid to dig.

They trudged through three feet of white powder, avoiding the huge drifts that had manifested like great dunes of sand. The men had gone completely silent, shivering as they marched headlong into the unknown. Peran himself seemed less sure of the situation, pausing often to peer curiously into the snow covered landscape. The map was always in his hands, and every few minutes he inspected it as if to reassure himself. On two occasions Amaria had been asked where the map came from. Both times she evaded the question by mumbling something and then cunningly changing the subject.

Progress was slow, but it was progress nonetheless, and Amaria finally called them to halt under the natural shelter of an extended wall of granite. They consumed more of their meager supplies, quenching what thirst they had with the snow itself. In the corner of her eye, Amaria noticed Ornan moving away from the communion, disappearing around a boulder and into the white world beyond. Her curiosity got the better of her, and she lifted from her seat to follow his tracks. She found him sitting upon a small rock that had obviously just been brushed free of snow. Ornan's back was turned and his elbows rested on his knees. For all the world he looked like a statue, stoic and motionless.

"Are you regretting your decision?" she asked as she approached him, a tenderness to her voice that she would never use with the others.

Ornan didn't turn around to look at her. "Never, shera. The circumstance is hard, but I am meant to be here."

"Why then, are you over here, away from the rest of us? You look as if despair has fallen upon you."

Ornan turned to view her. His leaden hazel eyes shown deep and thoughtful, as if a world of knowledge and beliefs stirred behind them, never to escape their confinement and reveal themselves. "Is it not common to require some time alone, shera?"

The woman nodded, knowing the feeling all too well. "Would you like me to leave?"

"No. You are already here. You might as well keep me company, silent as it may be."

For a few minutes they viewed the altered landscape in concert, radically changed by the blizzard, and said not a word. When Amaria could no longer withstand the stillness of her companion, she spoke again. "Why do you watch over me as you do?"

Ornan reached to the ground and clutched a handful of snow. He sifted it like fine powder between his gloved fingers. "You are my closest friend, Amaria Eversvale. But that is not the reason."

The woman nearly fell to ground, staggered by the man's usage of her full name. Had he ever called her Amaria before? She couldn't remember. Brushing the thought away and collecting her thoughts, she continued, "What is the reason, then?"

"Truthfully, I do not know. It is strange, but I feel like I am meant to protect you. It is intrinsic, like the gods themselves have beckoned me to safeguard you from harm."

Amaria chuffed. "I thought such gods no longer cared for me."

"They do care, shera!" Ornan pivoted his buttocks on the rock to view her directly. "It is only that you keep pushing them away!"

She steeled herself, trying to keep from tearing up. The subject fashioned an unwanted sentiment. Damned if she would show such emotion! Averting her gaze, she shook her head, somberly. "My past experiences. My failures? What of them? The gods of light have done nothing for me."

"Haven't they?" The Radamite turned away, leaving his words to hang in the crystal air.

Amaria mentally rewound her life, harking the past like transitory flashes of clarity. She recalled her adopted father, Meran, a man whom had rescued her when those black armored knights from Erdoth Fortress slaughtered her blood family. She was lucky to have been raised by him, for he had treated her like she was the only thing in the world that mattered. And Royce. That devilish firebrand of a husband had brought so much joy and affection to her. Gods, he loved her so! The perfect couple, respected and envied by all. And of course there was Ornan, watching over her like the brother she never had, saving her life a time or two. And even with all this, she refused to acknowledge the fortunes of her life.

"Royce was murdered. My marriage snatched away like flame in water." She hadn't realized she'd murmured that last statement aloud until Ornan responded.

"Some people in this world will never know love as you knew it, shera."

"Perhaps they are better off, for they have not experienced it and know not what they miss."

The Radamite scoffed at her words, his face incredulous and showing the barest hint of indignation. "Some would take that risk, shera."

Guilt suddenly devoured Amaria, and she felt a terrible sense of abasement for her blatant reaction. So full of self-pity, she hadn't even grasped the veiled suffering that Ornan, her close friend, endured. What kind of a callous monster was she?

"Ornan," she whispered. "I am sorry, my friend. In my self-pity, I never took the time to realize your own pains. It is inexcusable. How could . . ."

A wave of Ornan's hand cut short her apology. "We need not speak of this further." He stood from the rock and rubbed warmth into his arms. "I am ready to return."

Amaria wanted to say something, *anything*, to further her apology. But, she was rendered speechless. Uneasily tilting her head once and frowning, she turned to follow her own footprints back to the others.

Two more strenuous days they heaved through snows, the frigid weather giving them no quarter for their laborious efforts. Though the winds had gone dormant, the air seemed sharp enough to freeze and shatter limbs. A fourth soldier had joined the void, dying on watch during the night. He was found stationary, his back resting on a tree trunk and his sword drawn across his lap, the cold steel stuck solid to his furs. For the first time, the men became visibly upset and anxious, throwing uneasy glances as if death's bony hand dangled over their shoulders. Clearly, the elements controlled the predicament. If one could die for no other reason than having watch duty, any of them could be next, for a sword had no affect against the cold.

To augment the problem, Amaria noticed that her troop had begun scrutinizing her figure more increasingly and without shame. No longer the typical stolen glance, they drank her in, like young men just coming to maturity. Had intimacy been so long for them that they could demean her as if they hadn't had a woman in years? She didn't wish to become more hardened and brusque than she already was. But, if any of their looks ripened into bold advances, a quick and painful example must be made.

Following their awkward discussion, a full day had passed before she felt comfortable speaking with Ornan again. Ultimately, they said nothing more of the topic, and both seemed pleased with that decision.

Somewhere along the line, the snow upon the ground had thinned out, going no deeper than a foot. It made for easier progress and lightened the mood of the traveling band. Still, within the pallid draped landscape, Amaria began to feel like they were wandering in circles, making no progress and destined to die with ice sickle's hanging from their brows. It was then that Peran came rushing up to her.

"Milady, you need to see this."

"What is it?" she asked credulously.

The guide pointed up the slope where he'd been roving. "Come, I will show you."

Amaria, with Ornan on her heels, followed the spindling figure of Peran as he shuffled around a solitary mound and led them to an area that leveled out.

"There, milady," he said, his finger aimed toward a space ten feet ahead.

She saw it immediately, for it was unmistakable. "Footprints." The word came as barely more than bated breath.

Peran grimly nodded. "Indeed. It appears someone watches us."

Fourteen

Amaria stood over the first foreign print. The trail curled around a stunted ridge and disappeared out of sight. They were clearly made by a single person, and judging from the amount of space between marks, it looked like the culprit had run from the scene. Oddly, Amaria could find no indication of how the subject initially arrived in the area, unless of course, he backtracked using the exact same prints.

"Do we follow them, Shera?" Ornan asked.

Amaria hesitated in her response. Whoever left them was either ignorant, or had placed them deliberately. "Perhaps it is their intent that we follow."

"You mean, a trap," Peran added. The guide unslung his bow and readied an arrow.

The woman shrugged. "A possibility. We must assume there is more than one man, for what are the chances that some lone hermit lives way up here?"

Peran shook his head aggressively. "Living alone at these heights would be nigh impossible, especially during the cold months."

"What should we do then? Try and go around them?" Ever since the blizzard had hit, Ornan had worn a hood over his head. The cowl hung well past his face, shadowing the features beneath. With the innumerable amounts of cloth wrapped liberally and indiscriminately about his body, he looked like some kind of beggar mystic. "That will be difficult. The clearest route looks to be straight ahead."

"I have a feeling we couldn't avoid them even if we tried. They know we're here. Of course, none of us can say if these people intend us harm or not, but we should expect the worst." In the very bowls of her stomach, Amaria had a strong feeling that nothing good would come of this. *Servants of Wyur!* It had to be! Somehow they had discovered her presence, and intended to stop her before she reached the temple. She'd expected some resistance beforehand, but with the threat so near - it unnerved her. "We follow the tracks."

"Are you certain, Shera?"

"Yes. If they intend us harm, we'll take them head on. I'll go inform the men to prepare their weapons. We will move slow and warily. Peran, fall to the back. I'll take the lead until this is over."

It took about ten minutes, but Amaria had her men organized into a jagged column where they could account for every angle and viewpoint. The archers had bowstrings pulled taught, and the swordsmen gripped their pommels in nervous anticipation. After the frightening encounter with the lyzcan, they were eager to combat something more familiar.

Amaria sidled in the lead, trying to inspect every last foot of the scenery that stretched before her. The prints wound around several knolls and reached through a small, thinning grove. The trees allowed her fledging company some cover, but it also hid well her adversaries; if that's indeed what they were. She prayed for a pointer, some trace of movement up ahead that would signify their location. Unfortunately, a combination of green and white was all she could see; undergrowth topped with snow that progressively turned rigid and icy. It crunched like dried leaves beneath her feet, and she swore when she realized how difficult sneaking would be in this climate.

Utter silence had engulfed the area, as if the very ground itself anticipated a coming battle. The tang of odor was absent. The dropping temperatures had reddened their noses and numbed their sense of smell. Risking a peak behind her, she spotted most of her men creeping warily forward, their backs arched and their weapons primed. Jerris skulked back there, his spear gripped tight in both hands. If they were ambushed, this would be the lad's first real combat experience. Fighting with your life in jeopardy tended to dull the nerves and stimulate that survivalist instinct. She hoped the young prison guard proved himself up for the challenge. Ornan, as usual, was nowhere to be found.

The Radamite always took to his own strategy during these kinds of situations. He'll probably be invisible for much of the scuffle, only to materialize and slay my would-be killer at the last moment, she mused with a silent chuckle.

A shrill sound issued forth, and Amaria recognized it immediately. The woman dove face first into the snow. The high-pitched whistle shot past, but the arrow had not been aimed at her. The pain-induced cry of one of her men disturbed the serene silence. She didn't look back to see if the arrow had killed him outright or merely injured him. "Cover!" she yelled aloud. More arrows singed the chill air, shrieking past like a flock of birds. Her battle sense took the forefront and she gave one last command. "Swordsmen, advance! Use the trees for cover! Bowmen, return fire!"

Amaria, bow in hand, caught sight of a figure half-hidden behind the bole of a great spruce. She took aim and let go the string, drilling the projectile into the man's neck. A perfect shot, and she watched the man fall with grim approval. As arrows launched from her own side, she used the opportunity to advance, plastering her back against yet another tree. The scenario reminded her of a match of Jranin; a game played upon a wooden board covered with figurines. In Jranin, two opponents maneuvered their figurines upon the slab of wood, hoping to outwit their foe and eliminate his pieces to achieve victory. It was a popular game in Illidor, and now Amaria felt she was playing a real life version. Every single tree or knoll in the battlefield was presently being utilized as some form of protection against the barrage of arrows that streaked both ways.

Somewhere in front she heard breaking snow, footsteps moving toward her, just on the opposite side of the trunk. She dropped her bow to the ground and moved her hand to the hilt of her sword. In one swift move she silently freed the blade, and following one more fortifying breath of air, leapt out to meet her attacker. The man, a foot soldier, wore a standard grey breastplate etched with a symbol familiar to the woman. The symbol was a face, half covered in a mask; the very same image that graced the token Veran had presented her with during her so-called trial. The facts presented themselves clearly; Wyur's sentries had come to stop her.

Upon seeing his enemy, the blackguard slashed hard with his sword. It was a swift attack, but not swift enough. The Knight of the Dove parried the blade sideways and spun the opposite direction, whipping her weapon in a full circle before driving it into the unprotected backside of her enemy's knee, severing the limb completely. The man dropped in a fit of agony, clutching at his wound while the snow beneath him turned red. She left him there to suffer, her attention already upon another pair of sentries coming her way. Both were helmed, their faces invisible beneath.

The two men witnessed the unnatural quickness in which she had dismantled her first foe, and they hesitated for just a split-second. Amaria wasted no time exploiting their indecision. Diving like an acrobat, she came at them with her blade wheeling. Wyur's guards stumbled to evade her furious onslaught, one falling to the ground when his feet would not move quickly enough. On his back, Amaria made easy work of him, for his own breastplate nearly pinned him immobile. She cut his throat and whirled to face the second man. He crouched guardedly. To his credit, he hadn't fled, despite standing face-to-face with a foe that had already scored two kills. He hefted a battleaxe, a powerful weapon, but overly heavy and cumbersome. It would do him no favors against her speed.

A passionate appetite, the kind that came in the midst of war, had bloomed in full splendor. That appetite was the insatiable bloodlust, the dark part of her that enjoyed launching her foes into anguished eternity. It invigorated her, made her all the more deadly. The woman became a living tool of destruction, or more darkly put, murder.

Taking a moment to view the progress of her troop, Amaria noticed that the battle was no longer being fought with arrows, but with close combat arms. The ringing sounds of steel echoed throughout the grove and men joined the brutal dance of life and death. As a whole, her men were outnumbered, but not terribly so, and she retained confidence they would overcome.

The man with the axe rushed her, swinging his weapon overhead. She blocked and counterattacked, but he parried her weak attempt. They circled each other, and then Amaria advanced. She made two attacks on his left, intentionally allowing him to block each. Then she subtly shifted, as if bringing across her sword to attack his opposite side. The blackguard, on his heels, mirrored her movements and altered the position of his axe to defend his right flank. Instead, the woman struck his left again. The steel bit deep into flesh at his bicep. He cried out and leaned over to compensate for the wound, but his movement proved sluggish. With one powerful swipe, she cut through collarbone and neck, removing his head from his torso. The body collapsed to the ground, but Amaria had already walked past, her sword still thirsting.

Much of what followed was a mere blur to her consciousness. Only brief flickers of reality reached her senses; the resonance of steel, the howls of pain, the urgent movements of those still standing and fighting. She strode about the diminutive battlefield, a merciless vessel of death, her emotions deadened as she cut down any soldiers brazen enough to step in her path. And then, finally, none were left.

The truth of the world convolved before her eyes as the lust to kill dissipated. Her wits returned and she witnessed the remnants of the skirmish. Dozens of bodies lay sprawled across the earth, most of them wearing the silver of Wyur's sentries. Blotches of crimson tainted the purity of the snows, the life it once held now released to the soil as its shell was rendered apart. The woman inspected her own health. A minor cut along her forearm and nothing more, not a single wound of even moderate harm. The barest tinge of guilt pricked her. What gods given ability had shaped her to slay so many and yet endure no significant injury? It was a question she'd asked hundreds of times, and always it went unanswered. Long ago, she came to accept her unnatural skill, embraced it even, but those thorny questions always lingered.

"Men, assemble!" she called, returning to her duties.

A pathetic group of straggling soldiers sauntered to her side, and she took a quick head count. Seven, some bearing wounds which would need tending immediately. Peran still lived, the crafty guide probably hiding through the worst of it, for which she didn't blame him; he was no soldier. Then something else struck her.

"Where is Ornan?" she asked, an edge of panic to her voice that contradicted her position as commander.

"I am here, shera."

Behind her, against the trunk of a pine, leaned the Radamite. Utterly composed, he looked as if he'd napped through the whole incident. His clothes and blade, however, were splattered with blood. The woman wondered how many spines his weapon had greeted unawares, but she did not voice her ponderings aloud. Instead, she nodded to him; a relieved tilt of her head that expressed more than she would have liked.

Viewing the carnage, Amaria counted at least two-dozen fallen enemies, probably closer to thirty. Unless some of her own fallen still lived, which was quite unlikely, she had lost nine, roughly one-third of her enemy. Not terrible losses, especially considering *they* were the ones ambushed, but it certainly could have been better. The stench of death had begun to waft about the air. "Have we killed them all?"

"No, milady," a soldier drawled through the thick accent of a southeasterner who'd been forced to learn the common tongue later in life. "A handful of them gots away. I seen them run north. You can see them footprints."

Looking past the dormant bodies, Amaria noticed the ruffled snow where the cowards had fled. "Let them go. I have a feeling we'll meet them again." Next came Amaria's least favorite part of battle. The aftermath. Collecting the dead and scouring for survivors. Fortunately, this was small-scale compared to the great wars of her past. But, that didn't make the losses any less painful. She always took a portion of responsibility for the demise of soldiers in her charge. After all, she was their commander. In this particular case, these men really hadn't a goat's notion what they fought for. They merely agreed to take part in an adventure with the legendary Knight of the Dove. Probably not one of them considered the possibility that they would never return.

The survivors went about the gruesome task of slitting the throats of any wounded minions of Wyur that lay upon the snow, saving only one for questioning. The dwindling company couldn't possibly take prisoners, and a dagger to the throat was more merciful than freezing to death in this unforgiving land. Of her own, two of the fallen were still alive, writhing in agony over critical wounds. They wouldn't last the night, Amaria knew, but she patched them as best she could and assured them they'd be fine, like any commander of true loyalty would.

"Milady, I survived."

Amaria was busy gathering supplies upon the field when the voice briefly startled her. She swiveled her shoulders to see young Jerris facing her, a drawn paleness draped over his features; the look of someone who'd killed for the first time and remorsed over it. She smiled at him. "Indeed you did. And I see that the tip of your spear is red. They say that a man's first kill will define his character more than anything else. Truthfully, Jerris, how do you feel?"

The prison guard took time responding as he pondered the question. Eyes lowered, he spoke slowly. "I am thrilled to still live. I have faced death and emerged victorious. Yet, a separate part of me mourns the loss of my innocence and the death of my victims. I have taken life, milady. Shouldn't there be sadness in that?"

Amaria patted the young man on the shoulders, a genuine act of sympathy combined with reassurance. "A man who cannot see the calamity of battle is no longer a man. I have grown too callous to this scene, and it worries me. I loathe losing the sentiments that made me who I once was, so long ago." She locked her stare upon him, her jade irises sharpening. "Hold onto that sadness, Jerris, for it will keep you from succumbing to the desolate grip of war. If you can fight again and still hold fast to the sorrow, then you have conquered the worst of what the dark gods can cast your way."

Jerris' thin lips upturned and he nodded. "Your wisdom is appreciated, milady."

"Get some rest, Jerris."

Amaria watched the young soldier amble away before drawing her vision to the sky. In the west, the sun made its final stand before the brooding orchid hue tucked it beneath the earth for another night. It seemed liked dusk came earlier with each passing day, and that meant the cold grew stronger. The troop had only enough time to set the canvas before nightfall.

When the tent stood, flapping erratically like broken wings in the emerging breeze, she commanded the survivors join her outside. They stood in a semi-circle, with the shuddering prisoner positioned in the middle. The man was in bad shape, one leg wholly useless and a spectacular sword wound just beneath the collarbone. He stared up at the procession that surrounded him, unable to maintain his dignified manner amidst a tumult of pain and fear. His hair, curly black, messily matted his face and his beard was poorly maintained. Amaria guessed he had not yet reached forty winters, for the lines of age were just beginning to form upon his face. Stepping up to him with hardened authority, her boots landed inches from his head. Kneeling, she gripped his chin and forced panic-stricken eyes to look at her own.

"How did you know we were coming?" she asked evenly.

The man only stared at her, lips quivering.

A popping sound bounded off the trees as Amaria clouted the prisoner across the cheekbone. His neck snapped back, and before he'd even recovered, she had grasped the back on his hair and pushed his torso upright while pulling his head back, leaving his neck fully exposed. A pathetic grunt issued from his crooked neck, and blood seeped from the new lesion Amaria had just caused.

"Listen well." Impossibly, her voice sounded even colder than the frigid air they breathed. "I have very little patience. I am not here to amuse myself by pushing the limits of your willpower. You will answer my questions. If not, your screams will echo through these mountains like the squall of a thousand vultures. Now, tell me, how did your men know we were coming?"

"I do not know. The " he momentarily shrieked as Amaria

yanked on his hair, then blustered, "I speak the truth, lady! I swear it! My commanding officer gave us orders to move out. Told us that our spies noticed a small force moving up the mountains. We set up the ambush. That's all I know, blood and gods, I swear!"

"How far is your temple from here? What direction?"

The man nearly sobbed. "No more than two days, straight northeast."

"How many soldiers are stationed there?" Amaria's questions came forth like a hammer on nails, emotionless and efficient.

"The temple is not a military outpost. Only a few guards patrol the grounds." He gasped for a pained breath. "But just recently, the high priest had transported fifty soldiers to the temple. Thirty-five of us were sent to ambush you."

The woman chuckled. "That leaves only a smattering of men-at-arms to protect them."

"It is the priests and wizards who will do you in, lady." The last comment was made with a subtle sneer, the last act of defiance from a dying man.

A sharp crack and the man went limp, his neck broken by one powerful tug. Amaria turned to view her men, the dead prisoner all but forgotten. Seth, the former second in command, had died in battle, and thus far she hadn't named a successor.

She spoke to her dwindling troop with all the force she could muster from her chilled vocal chords. "Someone get this godsbedamned body out of my sight. Then get some sleep. I'll take first watch tonight. Be about it now, quickly!" As they began to break up, she added, "Peran and Ornan, come with me a moment. I wish to discuss some things with you."

The men settled into the canvas tent as darkness fell over the land. It was a solemn night, the images of her dead warriors still fresh in Amaria's mind. Had the Valgamin council *any* notion of what they sent their soldiers to face? The cold proved as much a menace as the enemies they confronted, for nothing could warm their sprits, something truly needed after a bitter skirmish which left over half their force dead. A part of her wished she'd gone alone. Most likely, she wouldn't have made it this far, but at least she wouldn't have taken others to die with her. *Seven men!* That was all that remained of her Valgamin garrison. Seven godsdamn men!

"What ails you, shera?"

Ornan and their intrepid guide had followed her to stand near a collection of pines, thirty yards from the canvas. Their breath rose like plumes of white smoke amid the brittle air. For all the world, they were misplaced refugees, Peran and Amaria in ragged furs and Ornan wrapped in his countless layers of torn cloth. When she looked at them, her face seemed as frail as the greenery that struggled to survive around her.

"Give me your honest opinions. Should we move straight for the temple?"

Peran bluntly nodded. "You don't have much choice, milady. Your men cannot last much longer. If you wish to arrive at all, you need to make the shortest route possible." The guide pulled loose the map and unfolded it for all three to look upon. With a tiny slab of timber, he pointed to a location. "I believe I have figured out where we are. As the prisoner said, it shan't be longer than two days. I can graph the path out for you, milady, and you would have no trouble leading them the rest of the way."

Amaria jerked at his last statement. "Aren't you coming?"

He shook his head. "No. I am not a man of war, milady. I have led you to where you wish to go, but I do not wish to die raiding a temple high in the endless peaks of Urak's Edge."

"What will you do then?"

"I will begin my decent tomorrow morning."

The woman cast an incredulous look at Ornan, who only shrugged in response. A fragment of irritation mounted within her. What madness did he speak? She had few men the way it was. She didn't take kindly to the prospect of losing another. "You'll never survive. None here could make it all the way back down alone. Not even you. You'll either freeze to death or be eaten."

Peran seemed unconcerned. "I have ways of survival. I'll take my chances."

"Come now, think clearly!" Amaria would not give this up so

easily. "When we overtake the temple, all of us will have a place to recuperate before the long journey back down. No doubt there is a great amount of food stores up there. We'll stay as long as you wish, and make our return only when we are fit and healthy."

A derisive laugh issued from Peran's lips. "And what makes you certain you can overtake this temple? Other than yourself and Ornan, you have seven men! It is suicide, milady, even with your ability. You heard the prisoner yourself; they have priests and wizards. I want nothing to do with sorcery!"

"If sorcery frightens you, then let us do the fighting. Wait until we've driven them down."

"And if you fail? What then?" Peran appeared no more convinced than before.

Amaria cursed under her breath. "I have no intention of failing, Peran. By the gods, listen to me!" She pointed a gauntleted finger toward the canvas tent. "If those men see you walk away, what message does that send? They're fearful enough as it is *without* having the only man who can navigate these mountains leave. Above all else, I need them confident. We are so near our goal!"

The lissom man was wracked with conflict. His countenance shown anguish as Amaria's rationale worked his guilt. Putting his chin to his chest, he massaged his face using both hands. "I do not want to die up here, milady."

She clasped his shoulder; a heartening grip like a commander would give a subordinate. "You won't. I only need you to get us there. We'll handle the fighting."

There was a long silence. Peran stirred, twisting his foot in the snow. "I will sleep on it," he said at last. The man suddenly looked exhausted.

"Then sleep. We will speak of it in the morning." Amaria smiled at him as if he'd already agreed to stay. The man turned on his heel and ambled off to the tent, Amaria silently watching him.

With the guide out of earshot, Ornan drew his knowing eyes upon the woman. "You certainly have a way with persuasion, shera. But what if he does not live?"

She colored at his words, so straightforward and without bias they were. "I'll have to make certain he does."

"Yes, your intent leaves no misgivings. Though, as you well know, none can control everything that happens."

"Mountain take you, Ornan! Must you be so honest?" Her words sounded harsh, but there was no bite to them. Try as she might, she couldn't keep the satirical grin from appearing on her face.

Ornan mimicked the expression. "Honesty is one thing we *have* control over."

"So it is. Go sleep, my friend. There is more marching to be done in the morn."

The Radamite pivoted to leave, but hesitated. Once more he looked at her. "You are certain he will stay. I can read it on your face."

Amaria gave him a shrewd look, one side of her mouth curled upwards and her eyes narrowed in a sneer. She was the definition of utter confidence.

"Ornan, my friend, no man has yet turned me down."

Loneliness can be more spiteful than the worst physical pain. It was a lesson Amaria once learned, gifted to her the morning she sat upon one of the balconies of Erdoth Fortress, terribly wounded and completely alone save for the hundred black armored bodies strewn about the courtyard and within the fortress itself. On that day, in a fit of sinister rage, she'd slaughtered the unfortunate soldiers who hadn't fled. Perhaps they deserved it. Yes, they *did* deserve it! The way they'd brutalized Royce was unforgivable, and all of them had paid the price with their blood.

Vengeance alone hadn't damned her. It was *how* she'd attained such vengeance. Had she utilized her army, carried out the conquest with her men, she wouldn't be the same tormented soul of today. Too late now, for the pages of history had been written in the books. Curse her soul for refusing to wait a single night! She wanted justice right then! The dark gods, wringing their fiendish talons in eagerness, were more than willing to oblige. And thus, her ultimate success became her ultimate failure.

As Amaria dithered in the bleak chill of night, the stars hanging above her like stationary candles, she remembered that loneliness. The tent was no more than fifteen feet away, nine warm bodies dozing within, and still Amaria felt completely alone in the gelid wasteland of the mountain. It was the silence, the stark, unforgiving silence that drove a person to submission. So little wildlife lingered this high, and more often than not, the only sounds one would hear were of their own making. As Amaria sat, unmoving in the grinning darkness, she felt like the last living entity left in the world.

She planned on giving herself one more painstaking hour before waking the next unlucky soul to relieve her. She had no trouble staying awake, for the biting weather made it difficult to grow comfortable. It was the seclusion that she found unbearable. She'd much rather be in that tent, surrounded by the company of others, awake or not.

Not far away, something rustled, pulling her from her musings.

Instantly attentive, Amaria's hand unconsciously gripped the hilt of her sword. She waited, her vision darting into the impenetrable cloak of night. A heavy silence lingered, an insufferable hush that seemed almost alive. Several seconds of nothing passed while she listened, and she nearly wrote the whole episode off as her imagination. Then it sounded again, this time accompanied in intervals by the cracking of snow. Amaria leapt to her feet, motionless as a cat. *Was that movement she saw? Yes!* A mere twenty feet away, the blackness writhed, taking form. Her blade scraped from its sheath in urgency.

A figure stepped into view, emerging from the night like a spectre. The woman gaped at what she saw. An aging man, wearing only a worn tunic and trousers, paced calmly toward her. His face shown the ravages of time; deep wrinkles, crooked nose, sunken eyes. A thin layer of greying hair covered both jaw and chin, though it was nonexistent atop his pate. And yet, for his emaciated, weathered frame, he walked with the limberness of a young man.

At his approach, Amaria mustered enough wherewithal to hoist her weapon in defense, though her brain still strove to fathom how the figure appeared so casual amidst a frigid winter. He wore nothing but a thin tunic, and sandals no less!

The man held up a gaunt, skeletal arm, his palm open and facing her. "You need not raise your sword. I am no threat." His voice was soft, but filled with vitality and strength.

"If you are no threat, why do you approach in the middle of night?" The sharp end of her blade still pointed at the old man's neck.

"Is there a better time to speak with you alone?"

Amaria eyed the stranger circumspectly. He was like a farce, the image of a dream. "Why do you not freeze to death?"

The man seemed to grasp her train of thought, and he nodded with empathy. "Yes, my clothes. I should have thought of something more suitable. Do not worry, Amaria Eversvale, I am quite fine."

"Who are you? How do you know me?"

Taking two more steps in her direction, he found a suitable spot to sit, resting against a fallen branch. "I am Aohed, the *Creator* as most call me. You spoke to one of my disciples in Valgamin, if you recall."

Amaria nearly burst into scornful laughter. "Aohed! And I should believe this, I suppose. Yet, I thought you had other matters to spend your *godly* time on, rather than worry for lowly humans."

The man did not flinch at the mockery cast his way, nor did he seem offended. "It is true that I leave most affairs of the physical realm to my servants and disciples. There are many worlds that require close attention. This is just one. But you are no ordinary human, Amaria Eversvale, as you well know."

"Indeed, I am not! Not every human has everything they value torn away from them!" Her contempt had not dispersed. "The games you gods play. I hope I have entertained you!"

Sorrow consumed Aohed's face when he looked at her. His

eyes, gemlike orbs of crystal blue, appeared to possess the weight of the world within them. "You must understand there are many, many forces that seek to control you, Amaria. The gateway to power is ever alluring, and you are like that one special key to get inside. It will not be the last time you feel them tugging on your mantle."

"Can you not stop them?"

The old man scratched the whiskers on his face. "I don't expect you to understand. Things are not so simple, especially in your case."

Amaria was utterly baffled. She stammered for long moments before asking, "What am I to do then? Even now, Hysth hounds me. Twice I have been pulled into his forsaken world to indulge him."

"Yes, I know. Hysth is a shrewd one, and very dangerous. It was a poor choice of Wyur to contest him, for Hysth will never tolerate an upstart whom attempts to outwit him. The *Deceiver* will learn a steep lesson." Above them, the stars appeared to grow in number, giving the pair a virtual limelight ambiance. Aohed paused a moment to admire them, the expression on his face impossible to read. When he spoke again, he still stared upward. "Perhaps more than any of them, except myself, Hysth appreciates your value. That is why he hounds you so. Do not think for a moment that you have seen the last of him, even after you accomplish this task."

"Why have you come here, if not to tell me how bleak my future is?"

For the first time, the old man smiled. "I came to give you piece of mind."

"Piece of mind? Is that what you call this? Forgive my curtness, but telling me that I shall always be tormented by Hysth gives me no piece of mind."

"Stem your anger and listen. Do you not see, your passion is a great thing, but it is also what the dark gods prey upon. Control it." A forcefulness grew from Aohed, surprising Amaria. His humbled serenity vanished and he appeared compelling, more intense. "You agonize because you believe you are doing Hysth's bidding. Torture yourself no more! It is true that the *Corrupter* bids you to wipe out the temple, but the outcome will not benefit him other than to stroke his ego with a sense of revenge. His establishment in Valgamin was ruined by yourself, at Wyur's bidding, and now he uses you for the same purpose. But while these two gods squabble like children, you will have successfully set both of them several years behind. It is a great success for the gods of light! They bicker with each other, and more souls are saved. That, Amaria Eversvale, is your piece of mind."

Amaria pondered this. For all purposes, it made sense. She had dealt a great blow to Hysth by killing Ephram, and damned if she wasn't going to deal another blow, this time to Wyur. "What about Senstas?" she blurted suddenly. "He was too great a man to be murdered in such a fashion."

Aohed frowned, his expression mournful. "Yes, he was. As I said, there are many forces that seek to control you, and they will do whatever they can, cause whatever harm they feel necessary, to do so. Senastas was a tragic loss, but he is at peace now. Do not lament him."

"That is impossible," she retorted. "Gods above, what is so special about me? You speak as if I am the single most significant person on this world."

The old man shrugged. "Perhaps you are."

"Why? I must know."

Aohed issued a great sigh, his hands fiddling with the folds of his tunic. Any normal person's skin would have been bone white from lack of circulation. His skin shown a fleshy pink, utterly unaffected by the cold. "Soon, Amaria. It will not be long."

The woman grunted her frustration and spat upon the earth. "Why can you not tell me *now?*"

"Show patience, Knight of the Dove," he answered, avoiding the question. "I must take my leave now, but heed what I have told you. No more doubts. You are the greatest warrior this world has ever seen, and you've a keen mind when you don't lose it to your qualms."

"One more question," Amaria almost shouted, insuring she was heard before the man disappeared.

"Quickly, child."

She steeled herself. "Did you really need my coin, as the priest in Valgamin said?"

A second grin appeared on the old man's face. "Ishvar is a wonderful servant, Amaria, but even wonderful men of god can make mistakes. He was only testing your desire to join the faith, but I fear he pushed you further away."

"Answer the question, please."

"I need not your coin, Amaria Eversvale. You pay me with the kindness and faith of your heart."

The woman nodded dryly. "Kindness and faith. Not so easy a payment for some."

"Words of truth. It takes much healing for a black heart to grow warm and open. I see that yours remains closed and still you push me away."

And Aohed was gone, though his words lingered long after.

Fifteen

"What is that blue in the sky, Shera?"

Ornan craned his neck, acerbic cynicism dressing his face. Although too early in the morning for the sun to appear beyond the rising crests of the east, for the first time since her men had stepped foot upon the godsforsaken Aruk's Edge, the skies had extended a new ambiance. No longer shrouded by an opaque mass of grey clouds, the billows had broken away into roving patches of cumulus, swaths of white fabric upon a mantle of deep blue. Though the air remained bitterly cold, the winter gale was absent and the emergence of the sun proved a cheerful omen for all.

Amaria nibbled on a piece of hardtack, its taste far more akin to discarded mortar than any kind of edible substance. She watched her friend bask in the brilliance above, and smiled. The feeling was contagious, for the rest of the men also moved at a more buoyant pace than they had the previous night. But the good fortune hadn't stopped there. Peran, albeit reluctantly, yielded to Amaria's pleas and stayed with her men. All in all, it was a promising new start to what had been a miserable day the previous.

"That, my friend, is a fortuitous portent. Perhaps the sky has reconsidered and sides with us after all." The woman was all cheer this morning.

Ornan looked at her with a wry grin. "Isn't that the way with our mistress mother nature? Always switching allegiance at the last moment."

They both laughed before joining their comrades, who had finished repacking the tent and supplies. All together, they were no more than a decare. Ten souls who'd braved the worst of Urak's Edge, and lie so very close to their destination. But what, or whom, they would face at the temple still lingered in mystery.

How many wizards and priests lurked there? Amaria brushed it from her mind, knowing there would be time to scout when they drew closer. For now, another full day of marching waited for them, hopefully the last.

Sidling out of camp, Peran led them directly northeast. The sullen guide had informed her he would change their course due east near late afternoon, basing his reasoning on the knowledge that the fleeing sentries had also exited northeast. It would be assumed by the enemy that Amaria would follow their tracks to locate the temple. Thus, Peran would divert their coarse just enough to prevent a second ambush.

Moving about the untouched terrain, the thinning air began to take its toll on their stamina. Despite their raw physical endurance, breaths grew hoarse and laborious while they climbed ever upward. At regular intervals, Amaria allowed them momentary breathers, mostly to regain dwindled energy. Once, they arrived upon a crystal clear mountain stream. The top had frozen, but they broke through the ice, and the water beneath was cold and pure. All of them took turns gorging on the cleansing fluid. Their food reserves had nearly depleted, though Amaria anticipated they carried just enough hardtack and brittle biscuit to last them until they reached the shrine.

As afternoon turned to evening, Peran redirected them along a line of serrated boulders that wedged into the earth like a natural wall, and by dusk the small group had completed an uneventful day. Just after the sun melted into the west and the last vestiges of radiance clung about them like dying flames, Amaria had her men pitch the tent. Rather than crash to a dreamless slumber as most had done on previous nights, the entire body remained awake as nightfall revealed its solemn cloak. They sat in a circle, ten of them, with no fire to take solace in. It was feared, and reasonably so, that they were simply too near the enemy to risk giving away their position with flame or smoke. Thus, they sat together in cold, foreboding darkness.

On this night, they would revel in their camaraderie, for it was their last night spent together before reaching the summit of their goal. They shared old stories, jokes, and even a song or two.

What drink that remained was freely shared among the group, strengthening a bond that would be severed by steel the following day. A strange mixture of emotion gripped them; sadness, excitement, accomplishment. Of twenty-three that started this journey, only ten remained. They survived, enduring an ambuscade and an angry cold that strove to beat them down at every opportunity. Tomorrow, they would face the servants of Wyur, fighting to their deaths if need be.

But, that was tomorrow.

With Amaria's permission, one of the soldiers lit a small piece of kindling and placed it within the middle of the circle. It cast very dim light, but enough for them to see each other's faces. One last somber memory.

The biscuit Amaria chewed nearly crumbled to dust on the first bite, yet she savored each dry swallow. This, she remembered as she looked upon her men, is the greatest aspect of war. It is what she had missed so dearly these last few months. A soldier is not meant to fight solitary battles. It is the companionship, rearing your weapons for a single cause, which brings men together.

"And what will you do, shera, when this is over?"

Amaria did not look up from her pathetic meal. "I do not know. I haven't given it much thought. I'm the single-minded sort."

Ornan chuckled. "I hadn't noticed."

"What of you? Back to the warehouse, I assume, hauling crates like a glorified mule?"

The Radamite passed over what could have possibly been an insult. He knew the woman too well to take her words as anything but jest. Uncurling his legs and stretching them forward, he said. "Work is like a dagger in the back, shera. It slowly carves away our prime, leaving us old and withered." He smiled. "Like you, I try not to consider it much. I wonder, though, if it is time I return to Radam. No family remains there, but merely seeing home again might very well be all the family I need."

"Home," Amaria repeated. "Up here, home sounds nice, does

it not?"

"Most certainly. Life enjoys the mockery of our choices, for we scorn the place of our youth and travel to places we have no business being in. Then, we long for what we scorned in the first place." Ornan scratched the back of his neck, nodding as he did so. "Time has a way of healing old wounds."

"And some wounds never heal."

The Radamite shook his finger at her. "Not tonight, shera. They'll be no forlorn lamentations tonight. We shall enjoy this time. One never knows what the next day brings."

Amaria instantly broke her glower, chortling at her friend. "Agreed. Only joy tonight." Her disposition eased and for the remainder of the time, she joined her comrades in their merriment.

Late into the night the carousing lost its vigor. A deep melancholy fell over the men as they broke the circle and turned for the tent. Despite their fatigued bodies, sleep would not come easy, for all thoughts focued on the following day. A few precious hours of slumber would be a generous result.

Jerris took watch when all others had piled under the canvas. The young lad admitted he was far too tense to gain sleep, and had offered to take the first of two watch slots. When all voices died away and stillness took hold, Amaria circled the camp one last time, kneeling next to the young prison guard as she joined him. He sprawled against a rock, blowing into his hands to combat to cold.

"Are you well, Jerris?"

He looked up at her with liquid, youthful eyes. "Well enough. I'd be lying if I said I did not fear tomorrow."

"Fear?" Amaria guffawed. "Of course you fear! You wouldn't be human if you didn't. I'll offer you a little secret, Jerris. All of us hold some fear."

"All except you, milady."

"My nerves are just as human as yours, and my fears just as strong. It is true, I do not worry so much for myself any longer. But I have other worries, such as Ornan, you, and the rest of those men in that tent. I have already failed thirteen soldiers."

She paused and noticed, by his expression, that Jerris needed more encouragement than she offered. Inhaling and exhaling slowly, she added, "We are all nervous, Jerris, even the enemy. You will do fine tomorrow. Take solace in the fact that you have already survived one skirmish."

Jerris acknowledged her with the barest tilt of his head, though he said nothing.

Standing, Amaria patted him on the shoulder. "Wake one of us when you are ready to hand over the watch. Good night."

She sauntered away, her footpaths steady and direct. Jerris watched her go. "Good night, milady," he answered through a clearly troubled face.

The snow drifted with a certain tranquility, like white feathers from the heavens, yet the morning was the warmest they had encountered in the whole of their journey. Just as the previous day, very little wind carried across the mountain, the air fresh and serene and welcoming them with cheerful ambiance. Up above, a thin layer of cloud only partially obscured the deep blueness of the atmosphere.

The peak they traversed upon did not ascend to a point, but rather rounded out, its crest leveling and stretching in length for a good league. One hour into their march, they found themselves at the eastern most edge of the summit, the mountain falling away no more than fifty feet from where they stood. Beyond, the elevation dropped rapidly, caused by a succession of jagged cliffs and shelves of granite. Descending the mountain in that direction would be difficult, if not entirely impossible. Just beyond those sharp ridges, masking any hope of a horizon, lolled an eerie, swirling white mist that rose up from miles below. The haze was incredibly thick and literally impossible to see within. Like all those barroom tales, it was as if the world itself simply ended.

A part of Amaria goaded her to scale down the side of the mountain, to enter that shifting mist and truly discover what lie beyond. What would she find? What chaos veiled itself within that pallid shield? The thought stimulated her, but common sense hastily won over. Her task would be fulfilled before she would entertain any such crazed notions.

Peran declared they were three to four hours from reaching the temple, which meant a noontime arrival. That would allow Amaria to spend an extra hour or two scouting the area and formulating a strategy. Of course, not much of a plan could be established with only ten bodies to work with. Even so, ten was more favorable than one.

They advanced cautiously. The time for impatience had ended, for they already braved the weather. Now, they must brave their enemies, and that required unwearied vigilance.

The baying of a horse, not so far away, caused the party to freeze in mid-step.

"Riders!" Amaria hissed. "Down!"

At once, everyone dropped heavily to the ground and pressed themselves against the snow as much as their armored bodies would allow. Immediately after, a pair of mounted men appeared from the backside of a small hillock, less than a hundred feet away. Amaria's men, hoping to go unseen amid the expanse of white, were still as stone while the men drew near. Suddenly, even the delicate brume that took to the air with each of their nervous breaths seemed painfully noticeable.

Horses laboring uncomfortably through the snows, the riders drew close. Sprawled as flat as her body would allow, Amaria gazed upon the interlopers. They were scouts of Wyur in reconnaissance, of that she was certain. Their armor matched that of the soldiers who had ambushed them, and they gazed about with furrowed brows and an observant bearing. For a brief second, Amaria considered attacking them, but retracted the thought instantly. Other riders could be near. She decided there would be a better opportunity to make their presence known.

Inside fifty feet they came, and Amaria was certain they'd be spotted. The dull thudding of hooves on the frozen earth never felt so close, and she instinctively closed her mouth and held her breath in response. Yet strangely, just as they rode by, their attentions seemed inexplicably pulled elsewhere. Their heads turned in the opposite direction when they drew nearest, and after an immeasurable amount of tense moments, they rode past. Amaria watched them depart, her cold eyes visually damning them while she made a silent prayer to the gods of luck. Relieved to have gone unnoticed, it still meant that there would be no surprise attack, for their enemy clearly expected them.

The remainder of the morning excursion, a steady trudge north through protesting snows and delicate air, proved uneventful. As the great orb of light reached its climax in the sky, kindling the sparse flora and casting a brilliant shine upon the covered ground, a tall stone plinth came into view in the near distance. It was no normal tower, for it was threadlike and narrow, like someone had lodged a gigantic javelin into the earth which reached several dozen feet into the air. Amaria halted the men and beckoned Peran and Ornan to follow her. The three proceeded forward to inspect the structure, and soon realized it was no ordinary lookout post. It couldn't have been more than forty handspans in circumference, hardly enough room to fit two men inside, and yet it reached far into the sky like a beacon amongst a white backdrop, dark and grave.

"Move with care. I see two men standing guard," Ornan whispered.

They crawled into a position behind a tree-covered mound, giving them clear view of two sentries who held post at the base of the structure. They appeared tired and inattentive, causing the woman to inwardly grin. Behind them, upon the tower itself, Amaria could see a single door.

Barely a speck upon a great rise, the temple itself sat in the distance to the north. Far enough that no one would see them assail the sentries.

"I don't see other wandering soldiers nearby. If we take them quickly, our enemies will be none the wiser.

"Arrows, shera?"

Amaria nodded and gingerly unslung her bow. "Peran, you have a decent shot. Aim for the one on the left and fire on my signal."

In seconds, both had their bowstrings taut against their ear, and at Amaria's call, they let loose. With pure efficiency, the arrows struck home. Amaria's target was drilled mercilessly in the neck, killing him instantly and splattering an array of red mist onto the building he protected. The other guard was hit in the collar, just above his breastplate. As the poor man staggered and tried to make sense of the situation, Amaria put a second arrow into his jaw, finishing him off.

The trio scurried over the drift and up to their victims. Ornan wasted little time dragging the bodies to a partially hidden area and stacking them. "Shall I bury them in the snow, shera?"

Amaria hadn't heard the question. She gazed at the monument, transfixed by its appearance. "What do you make of this?" she gaped aloud.

Peran stepped up and gingerly touched the dark stone. It was smooth as silk. "Limestone I believe, though I've never seen anything like it. Ancient, perhaps, or otherworldly. Look at the construction! Perfectly round and symmetrical, not a single blemish. I can't imagine any human hands creating this."

Amaria agreed. From top to bottom, it shown perfectly. No evidence of brick and mortar, or assembly; as if some god had fashioned it elsewhere and situated it on this spot like a grim tombstone. "The door," she said, moving forward. Built of timber, the door was battered and weather worn, a far departure from the remainder of the structure and an unsightly blemish. Someone had built it far more recently.

With each man behind a shoulder, Amaria released the latch and pulled it open. Hinges groaned but gave little resistance, and she gazed freely within. "Gods almighty," someone whispered behind her. Inside, little space was available. If all three of them attempted to fit within, they would be pressed against each other like galley slaves. Something entirely different, however, shocked them most. Tiny blue runes, etched by hand, covered almost every inch of the stone floor, clear marks of sorcery. For one long minute, none dared take a step inside, content to simply stare in wonder.

Amaria snapped out of the dreamlike paralysis first. "Peran, retrieve the others and bring them here."

"Yes, milady." Technically, Peran wasn't under the authority of Amaria, but the woman had such firmness and clout in her words that few disobeyed. The guide hustled off to the south without another word.

Neither Amaria nor Ornan watched him leave. They still viewed the strangely shaped signa that carpeted the tiny chamber. "What do you make of it, Ornan?"

"I am no fan of magic, shera."

She grunted in response. "They are here for a reason, and considering that this place was guarded by Wyur's sentries, it is unquestionably here for the *Deceiver's* purposes."

Ever curious, the Radamite knelt close to the entrance and tentatively stretched out his hand, touching the first rune. Nothing happened. He withdrew his hand and looked up at Amaria. "Perhaps it is not so important. Why only two guards?"

The woman gave his comment considerable thought, then countered, "Two guards could easily be intentional, so as to make it appear insignificant." She shook her head. "I don't like it. I've got a feeling we need to do something."

"And what do you intend, shera? Have you knowledge in the scripts of the arcane?"

Well, she *had used* magic before, on that fateful night her world turned upside down, but those magics had been gifted to her by the dark gods, through sheer force of her own will. Gazing upon the floor, she understood nothing about these runes. "No," she answered. "I wonder if we could disrupt them somehow? Notice that they all touch one another. Do not magical runes use the energy of their adjoining runes to gather in strength? What would happen if we scrawled upon them?"

Ornan looked at her as if she had just suggested he eat his own sword. "You are going to meddle with those things?" He stood and took three steps backward. "Methinks you play with fire, shera."

Amaria threw him a devious look. "That often seems to be my method. Help me find a sharp rock."

"There are no rocks around here, shera. Here, take my dagger. It is dull and near worthless as it is. It needs replacing." He tossed her the small weapon, and she caught it by the leather wrapped handle. Tapping the point, she noticed that the blade did not draw blood. Indeed, it was dull, but not so much that she couldn't scratch up the floor of the great monument.

Ornan appeared to back further away as Amaria knelt near the entrance and reached forward, dagger in hand. Steeling herself with whatever fears she might have, she plunged the blade downward upon a rune, scratching with as much muscle as she could muster. At first, nothing seemed to happen. Suddenly, there was a *pop* and a blue spark flung upward into the air while another rode up the dagger and into her hand, shocking her. Startled, Amaria threw herself backward into the snow. The stone floor of the tower continued to crackle and cast sparks for another minute before dying out. Flexing her hand after the mild shock, she glanced at Ornan. The Radamite could only shake his head, wordlessly.

"Well," Amaria stuttered, "it didn't seem to like that much. I'm going to try again." She gripped the dagger tight and returned to her place at the entrance.

"Shera! I…"

She stopped him with a wave of her hand. "I'll be fine, Ornan. Quiet now." Aiming at the very same signa, she began to scrabble over it, mixing nonspecific white nicks and scrapes within the delicate azure rune structures. Once again, the ground began to sputter and hiss with energy, but Amaria endeavored despite the slight tremors that writhed up her arm. Soon the entire floor came alive with electricity, bursting with noise and heat. The woman tasted warmth seep into her mouth. She was biting her lip, but she ignored it and scrawled on, moving to other runes. The full interior sizzled, alight with bolts of sorcerous power, a pulsating argent. It became unbearable, and as blue tongues of fire licked her face and body, Amaria bailed, flinging her bulk outside for a second time.

From the apparent safety outside, both watched the glowing inferno in wonderment. It brightened, growing so brilliant that Amaria and Ornan covered their faces and turned away. And then it vanished. Just like that; no great explosion or blast of lightning, just a barren darkness.

Unable to withhold their natural inquisitiveness, they rushed to the entrance and peered within. "I do not believe it," Ornan gasped.

Save for several jagged scrape marks, the remains of Amaria's efforts with the dagger, the floor was completely bare. Of the mystic runes that literally draped every inch, not a single trace, as if they never existed.

"How did you know, shera?" the Radamite asked in disbelief.

The woman shrugged and handed the small blade back to her friend. "A hunch, though sometimes I believe my hunches are not truly my own. Regardless, it's something less to hold concern over."

Soon after, Peran led the remnants of the band down to join them. When the guide noticed the shining blue signa missing, he questioned Amaria, but the woman dismissed him with a vague answer that left him unsatisfied.

Amaria quickly gathered the troop together in a line. Pacing before them, authority exuding from her pores, she spoke. "If you look to the north, in the distance, you can see our final goal. *That*, my friends, is what you have come all this way for. Have you endured only to fail at the end?" A series of refusals issued from the mouths of the soldiers. Amaria smiled at them. "That is good. If you wish to hold any chance of survival, you will heed my every command to the finest detail. We will approach slowly, and as we near it, we will stop often. I wish to scout the surroundings and formulate a strategy. Remain with me until I say otherwise, and make no noise!" At that, she paused and met the hard gaze of every man. "You are good men. Let us go."

A half-score of soldiers commenced the final approach of what would become a mighty triumph.

Or a glorious failure.

The ensuing clash was foretold and planned by Urosish, the high priest of *Wyurnescia*. For him, the only possible outcome was victory, a glorious success for the *Deceiver*. Yet, neither Amaria nor Urosish were aware that the course of the skirmish had already been greatly altered, and Urosish's greatest maneuver eliminated.

Upon conception, the high priest's plan had seemed flawless. Minimize the temple's forces, thereby making the assault look simple and effortless. Not until Amaria had made her initial charge would he shift the final piece upon the gaming board. A full hundred and fifty elite warriors awaited the summons of Urosish from halfway across the world, preparing themselves within a different temple of Wyur. When they received Urosish's magical message, they would travel by pairs to the ancient monolith, transporting themselves in a matter of seconds from thousands of miles away. Then, in a cohesive advance, they would crush the paltry contingent led by the Knight of the Dove from behind, slaughtering each of them by sheer force. The high priest had laughed when he envisioned his scheme.

But even the most cunning of plans can go awry.

Unbeknownst to him, Amaria had destroyed the runes of travel which had been etched into the floor of the monument. Those same runes had taken Urosish a solid year of unremitting study and preparation before he became skilled enough to inscribe them. And now, they were detached, ruined. As the soldiers would hear his summons, they would transport from their own end, unaware of their severed destination. Two by two, one hundred and fifty soldiers would be torn asunder within the void, their mutilated bodies to rot in some dimensional limbo. None of those waiting their turn could possibly know what had happened to their predecessors, and thus they would continue to send off, until every last one no longer existed.

So it was that one of the most influential skirmishes of the eastern world, and one virtually unknown to the common populace, would be carried out by only a handful of souls.

Sixteen

A stream of deadly projectiles shot forth toward the western flank of the shrine, surprising the sentries who manned the wing. Amaria had placed her remaining three competent archers, Peran among them, inside a concealed half-bunker, and they fired at will upon the men-at-arms. It was a simple strategy, but one she hoped would suffice. As their arrows instituted mild disorder, she'd rush the remaining force from their own hidden position just south of the keep, hitting them while their attention was diverted.

Earlier, the woman counted about twenty sentries prowling the temple grounds, with a handful of priests mixed in, draped and shuffling in their somber grey robes. She had no inkling of the clergy's power, if indeed they had any, but she wouldn't invite trouble. All of them would be killed; no prisoners taken.

"We should go now!" An urgent voice said from behind her, a soldier.

"Not yet!" she snapped. Two of Wyur's guards lay writhing upon the snowy earth, arrows jetting from their bodies. The remainder had gathered their wits and taken cover, while other wandering guards heeded the shouts of alarm. Now the full force gathered in preparation to rush the archers. If Amaria waited too long, all three of them were as good as dead, but if she charged too soon, she wouldn't catch the enemy by surprise.

"Now!" she ordered. Her regiment burst from a thicket of bramble like several giant spears hurled from ballista. Clearly faster, Amaria quickly put space between herself and the rest of her men. Without turning around, she screamed to them, "Run, godsdamn you!"

Her archers still fired, more out of fear than anything else while the sentries moved to rush them. By chance, one turned and caught sight of Amaria. A stunted cry of panic, like a croak from a dying frog, warned his comrades. In unison, the others pivoted to witness the Knight of the Dove's seven-man horde plunge into them like a woodcutter's axe. Then, it was steel on steel, a cacophony of chime and peal. Bestial grunts issued from the men as their innate instinct to subsist overtook all other sensibilities.

Amaria felled her first foe with one stroke, the poor man's weapon never raised before his lifeless body crumpled to the snow. Her second combatant was not so easily taken, however. A huge man, six and a half feet tall with bulk to match, tamed a massive greatsword in his hands. The giant grinned wildly as he swung the weapon. They parried twice, and Amaria felt impatience brew inside her. She needed to cut her foes down quickly to even the odds, but this man made a work of it. Blocking away the din of the battle engaged around her, she curbed her edginess and refocused.

The man laughed, displaying large gaps between yellowed teeth. His greatsword arched menacingly for her neck. She ducked and twisted, bringing her blade upward into a gap of armor along his ribs. Her combatant hollered angrily, and with stunning mobility, kicked her in the head. Her neck snapped backward and she toppled away. The woman felt like a boulder had hammered her. Mind swimming, she almost didn't notice his sword lunging for her. At the last instant, and against the will of her own aching skull, she rolled to the side. The sword missed her, its deathblow splaying the snow beneath.

Amaria was no longer of conscious mind. Like the others around her, instinct took the forefront, and her immense knowledge of swordplay came freely without cognizant thought. Still on her back, she lashed out with her weapon, catching the brute on the forearm of his sword hand. The limb didn't sever, but the cut was deep and the man pulled away as he cursed his wound. Too late did he realize that his sword remained lodged in the snow. He reached for it, but Amaria was already on her feet, her sword plowing savagely into his temple, splitting his skull in a cascade of gore.

Wiping blood from her face and refusing to feel the effects of her pounding head, she noticed that the robed priests had fled to the temple entrance. Only the men-at-arms remained to fight. Thus far, it looked an even contest. Knifing her way through the throng, she cut down two enemies from behind, including one who had been dueling with Ornan. Grabbing the Radamite aggressively by the shoulder with one arm, she used the other to point to the temple gate. "With me!" she yelled over the noise of the scuffling. "Let us confront the cowardly priests."

"Only us?" he asked.

She nodded in affirmation. "The rest are fine. They'll follow when they can. Come!" She yanked him away from the mass of bodies and directed him toward the dismal looking iron gate which blocked the pathway to the temple entrance. The swinging door was unlatched and she shoved it aside roughly, stepping onto the stone walkway that led to the veranda stairs. A small gathering of priests, their faces all hidden behind cowls, cowered along the deck. For a moment, she wondered if the fools would simply stand there while she cut them down like overgrown grass.

Six pillars of smoke suddenly materialized, the vapor spiraling like a lethargic, virid funnel.

She had witnessed something similar once before, and the pit of her stomach twisted as she observed the disfigured shapes emerge from their murky summons. One of those damn clerics, or someone from inside the shrine, had beckoned these horrific beasts from whatever hell they called home. She recalled the time Thavas had performed a similar trick during their battle with Hysth's arch-priest, Ephram. She also remembered Ephram burning them to ashes, and it bolstered her optimism. These ghastly beings could die, just like people.

The morbid figures ambled like mindless corpses toward her and Ornan, their dark grey hairless skin bubbling and oozing. Spiked clubs dragged along the ground, held by clawed hands.

The first to confront Amaria grinned a sickly grin. Upon it, only a single black eye leered with demonic hatred, the other a mess of green and black puss which drained from an empty socket. Amaria lunged for a killing blow, but a flick of the monster's wrist and his club knocked her sword careening to the side. She used her momentum to spin completely around and slashed the beast deeply along the ribs. A deluge of obsidian fluid erupted from the wound, but the monster never faltered. It swung its own club savagely at the woman. Amaria dodged the clumsy overhead swing, then rammed the point of her sword through its torso. The minion of Wyur dropped to its knees and growled, a beastly growl like that of a wolf, before it fell and was still.

Two more of the monsters already closed in. Amaria lashed out, trying to keep them at bay while those menacing spiked clubs loomed above her head, threatening to cave in her skull. She managed to block the first attack, but as she did so, the second beast belted her across the shoulder, denting her pauldrons and piercing skin where the spikes had found unprotected crevices in her armor. Then claws grasped her neck at the peak of her spine, squeezing with uncommon strength. The sharp, nail-like fingers dug deep, forcing her to wince from the pain. Without thought, she twisted and squirmed free, then shouldered the lumbering body away. Her neck throbbed and her shoulder bled, but her injuries appeared relatively minor. Stepping backwards, she forced both foes into her line of vision.

They shuffled toward her, their faces masks of death. Amaria tightened the grip on her hilt, mentally calculating her tactics. Then, one of them inexplicable crashed to the ground. On its head dressed a gaping wound of fluid, sordid and black as ink. Behind the beast, one of her own soldiers pulled free his sullied sword. The man must have followed them, for which she was immediately grateful. Offering a hasty gesture of gratitude, she turned her attention to the second monster. Having only a single foe to worry about, it proved easy toil, and she left the moaning inhuman shape without legs and half a face.

One look at Ornan made it clear that he'd collected his own share of victims. Along the left side of his face, three long intermittent gashes traveled from his temple to the base of his jaw; no doubt the work of the nasty claw-like fingers. Blood drained from them, bestowing her friend a macabre half-crimson mask. His right arm also bled from some unidentifiable wound, but he had punished the transgressors, for at his feet rested two crumpled shapes; the remains of those grisly monsters.

Casting about, Amaria immediately realized that the cowering priests had fled for a second time, entering the confines of the temple and shutting the doors in their wake. As if a pair of locked doors would stop her, she mused dryly.

The battle on the grounds had also come to an end. A score of bodies littered the snowy earth, most clad in the silver-crested armor of Wyur, but three of the dead were her own. What remained, four battered and bloodied men-at-arms, along with Peran, joined Amaria and Ornan at the top of the veranda stairs. *Gods*, thought Amaria, *three more men lost*. She wondered how many wizards like Thavas prowled inside. How could this motley band of seven do anything against such magic?

Tall double-doors of blackened metal patterned with all sorts of jewels stood before the group, the last barrier before the sanctimony of the temple.

"I won't be going inside, milady," Peran said, perceiving the woman's train of thought. His bow held firm in one hand, a hatchet in the other. "I am no soldier of close combat."

Amaria viewed the man with discernment. He looked as if he'd marched through some sort of natural disaster. She wondered if he had ever killed another man before. True, he was a hunter. But, killing animals for food was far different than slaying men in cold blood. Though a fine survivalist, Peran hadn't a warrior's mentality. She needed every man she could muster to sack the temple, but she wouldn't send a good man like Peran to his death for her own selfish purposes. Her reply was calm and grateful. "I understand, friend. You've done more than I could have asked. Wait here and protect yourself. You shall be retrieved after we are victorious."

The guide offered a half-smile of thanks and slinked out of the way. Amaria swiveled her concentration upon the remainder of her pitiful band. She brought forth her commanding voice. "There will be magic inside. I cannot say how powerful, so heed this; the way to combat magic is to strike quickly. Standing idly gives wizards time to cast their spells. Hit them swiftly and move to the next man. The last thing a godsbedamned wizard wants is a struggle with arms. Like you, I am no follower of the arcane, so regard my words; waste no time counting, just cut them down! When these doors open, abandon your wariness and begin the slaughter."

Tired, dubious looks cast about, but when Amaria stepped to the entrance, they readied themselves. An ominous *click* sounded off as she turned the handle. Surprisingly, the priests hadn't locked the doors, obviously submitted to the fact that they couldn't keep the attackers from entering. Amaria flung the portal open and rushed into the dimness beyond. Ornan followed on her heels, and then came the rest of her soldiers, all of them a bundle of nerves.

She emerged into a spacious, heavily decorated marble floored chamber. However, the woman gave little mind to anything save the men in grey robes. Some scuttled about like rats fleeing a threatening snake, while others who retained a backbone, held their ground in defiance, gripping whatever makeshift weapon they could muster or invoking some minor cantrip in their defense.

The initial stages were nothing short of butchery. Like fanatical hellhounds, Amaria's unit stormed into the narthex, and the bodies dropped in droves, piling like a mass execution. As the defenders realized the futility of their stand, they fell back, escaping through any of the several doors which dotted the walls of the foyer. The Knight of Dove mindlessly pursued a screaming group that sprinted in vain to avoid her unruing wrath. Cries of fear, or the dying, echoed through the halls, and Amaria's only thoughts were to add to the growing crescendo.

Entering a separate hallway in pursuit, a bolt of white light suddenly flashed from the other end. Like a missile, it battered the woman in her left hip, spinning her to the floor. Sparing not a moment of recuperation, she climbed to her feet while her wounded joint ached in protest. The corridor had all but cleared out except for two figures standing at the other end. Though adorned no differently than the fleeing clerics, Amaria knew these robed men were wizards, not simple priests. They stood calmly, studying her with interest before removing their hoods.

The shorter of the two, a shapely woman with curled brown hair pushed behind her head, held a stern countenance and no submission. Amaria gave her little regard, for the second wizard demanded her loathsome affections. She immediately forgot her injured hip, and a fiery hatred reinvigorated her as she sighted Thavas. He looked the same as before - his face astute and cunning, giving nothing to the unobservant eye, but speaking volumes to those intended. He did not smile at Amaria, showed no emotion of any sort except the barest tinge of recognition.

"You are a persistent whore, Knight of the Dove." His words drifted across the hallway in a deliberate, gradual state.

Amaria flashed him a devilish grin. "I do believe that is fear I see on your face, dear Thavas Iimon. You seem far less confident than when you knifed Senastas and fled." Her voice rose. "You godsdamn coward! Your fear is well warranted, for you will be dead in minutes."

"How?" the man shot back. "How did you convince the council of your innocence? Impossible! What trickery set you free?"

"Though I enjoy watching you squirm, I have no desire to waste my time in debate. Start praying for your soul, Thavas, for I shall be merciless to your body!"

The Knight of the Dove came at them recklessly. The female wizard threw a second bolt, but Amaria dove to the floor and the magical projectile flew harmlessly over her head. Then she was running again. The lady mage frantically attempted to cast another spell, but Amaria's sword met her next. Her eyes widened for a brief moment, then she withered and slid off the blade, landing gently upon the smooth floor.

Thavas backed further away. His face already reeked of death; any hope of survival lost forever when Amaria, the inexorable Knight of the Dove, had reached the temple gates.

"I helped you defeat Ephram!" he blustered, like a fool begging to be spared.

Amaria advanced on him, her face cold as the stone walls. "Are you going to die groveling for your life? Gods man, get up and fight!" It reminded her of the time she killed Harash, the Lord of Erdoth Fortress. He had also pled for his life after she bested him in battle. There was no more cowardly way to die.

Tears rolled down Thavas' face. *Tears!* He continued to back away until the end of the hall prevented him from going further. "I spent almost twenty years hunting Ephram! Half my life! The high priest awarded me Master Wizard of *Wyurnescia* for my achievement. Please, do not take this away!" The man could barely speak he shook so much. "What do you wish for?"

She stepped within three feet of Thavas, bearing down upon him with the combined furies of all the layers of the abyss. How pitiful he was! The bastard wouldn't even fight! "And this is how the Master Wizard of the temple dies? How fitting." She drove her blade through his stomach. The man gurgled wretchedly for a moment, uselessly grasped at the steel weapon which pinned him to the wall, then slumped over and was still.

Amaria placed her boot upon his chest and freed her sword, glumly watching him collapse to the ground. A strange sentiment filled her. Agmon Lionor, known to her as Thavas Iimon, was dead, and though Senastas couldn't be returned to the living, she had dolled a fitting punishment to his murderer. She wiped the blood from her sword upon his habit and gave him not another thought.

The grueling sounds of close range combat still resounded elsewhere in the building. The wing she stood within had been vacated, only the bodies she felled serving as her company. They sprawled in several graceless angles across the stone flooring, their clothes and skin matted in the stanch crimson flow of their own blood. The image reminded her of the childhood stories her adopted father, Meran, would tell her on occasion. These were tales of fierce monsters who would lay siege to unsuspecting villages, slaughtering the people and leaving them dead where they lay; scores of innocents arranged awkwardly upon the deserted dusty roads. Meran's tales always included a hero who would defeat the beasts and avenge their evil. Even as a small girl, Amaria had pictured herself as that hero.

And yet, in an odd twist, it almost seemed like she was the monster. Perhaps the souls of all those dead bodies would attest to just that. She didn't care. However they spun their viewpoints, Wyur had harmed her *first!* Amaria Eversvale was not a tolerant person, and Wyur would soon know that better than anyone.

She followed the trail of the dead back into the narthex. A grim calm had fallen upon the great open hall, for the fighting had moved away from this area. Scanning the bodies, she caught a man lolling slightly, his face a mask of agony. A younger cleric of Wyur, she realized, half of his grey garb matted and sticky in scarlet. A quick visual examination did not reveal the exact location of his wound, but she guessed a sword puncture along the side of his stomach, perhaps his kidney. If the latter, even she could sympathize. Few wounds were more excruciating than that of a kidney.

In a total state of calmness, she knelt next to the lad. "Are you in pain?"

It really wasn't a question so much as an attempt to get the writhing man to speak. A single rasping moan and he swayed enough to look at her. His face shown bone white, like a ghost.

"Yes," he managed to utter.

The woman nodded. "Your injury is fatal. You will die. Of course, in your current state, it will doubtless take a full day before you pass on, and there will be much pain during that time." A sheer, bold-faced lie. He'd die within the hour, but she needed him to believe otherwise. "I can end it for you quickly and painlessly, but you must answer my questions. Do you understand?" She spoke as a mother would do a son.

The grimacing man managed a nod.

"Good. I wish to know where the high priest of this place is?"

A weakened hand lifted, pointed to a set of doors opposite the entrance. "Beyond those doors," he labored aloud, "follow the hall to the very end. The sanctuary is there. He waits." A line of blood, like red wine, dribbled down the corner of his mouth.

"Who is the high priest?"

The man shuttered and groaned, but still found words to

answer. "Urosish."

"Is he powerful? Does he wield magic?"

It was feeble and anemic, but the cleric affirmed her with a shaking incline of his neck.

Amaria stopped herself before she cursed aloud. Not that long ago, she would never have believed so much magic existed. Now, it seemed like half the world was a spellcaster of some type.

Without an ounce of warning, she cut the cleric's throat, killing the poor lad in an instant. The woman stood and viewed the assigned double doors circumspectly. They were still closed. Had the priests and wizards intentionally drawn her unit away? With a brush of her finger, she unfastened the latch and impelled the oaken slabs exposed. Beyond lie another hallway, this one wider and longer, flanked by rooms on each side; some closed off, others laid bare. Three hanging oil lamps lit the corridor just enough to create a pleasant mix of muted luminance, surreal and peaceful. At the far end stood a solitary door, like a lone sentinel with its wide girth and ornamental engravings.

Amaria advanced cautiously. At any instant, she expected guards to pour from one of the darkened rooms and assault her. It never happened. She reached the entrance to the sanctuary without a single whit of resistance. Naturally, her suspicions rose. Had the cleric been truthful? It was said that a dying man always spoke the truth, especially if they suffered. She had felt no deception in his words, for he could only think of the pain and his approaching death. No, the sanctum was most definitely beyond this door, and the high priest waited. Following several calm and focused breaths, she braced herself, sword at the ready, and plunged through.

The sanctuary presented a chilling, yet blissful aura. Stained glass windows absorbed the sunlight and cast about the chamber a throng of roving saffron. Above, the ceiling curved into a dome, portraying a rather daunting illustration of Wyur forcing the other gods into submission; a gorgeous rendition, but disturbing all the same. Simplistic wooden benches lined the room, aimed at the centerpiece of the sanctuary; the alter. Fashioned out of what looked to be a single giant slab of black stone, the image presented a rather handsome interpretation of Wyur, kneeling with folded limbs and supporting a wide basin. Amaria didn't wish to guess what manner of fluid swilled lazily inside. The alter rested upon a pulpit with engraved runes similar to those Amaria had witnessed upon the floor of the monolith.

On first impressions, one could say that the sanctuary was a breathtaking example of fastidious workmanship and nurturing care. Yet, a heavy ambience pervaded, a forbidden sentiment that unnerved her, like she were suddenly beneath a giant looking glass to which disapproving eyes scorned her. Clearly, she was not welcome, not only by its retainers, but by the deity it was designed to worship.

The chamber wasn't empty. Positioned along the walls stood those damnable grey-robed men; eight in all. And situated upon the podium in the front, stately and imperial, a middle-aged man regarded her, undoubtedly the high priest. His attire, though still colored with the same identical grey as the others, was spectacularly expensive and reeked of opulence. He viewed her with a colorless, hardened stare, showing composed interest, though judging by the vein that throbbed from his temple like a blue worm, Amaria didn't doubt the pure infuriation that boiled within.

"You have certainly proven yourself to be no fluke, Knight of the Dove." His voice was resonant, powerful. "Nothing shows honor like slaying dozens to avenge the death of one man," he mocked.

Amaria endeavored to ignore him, concentrating on her next move.

Again, the high priest spoke. "I am Urosish, high priest of Wyur, and residing vicar of *Wyurnescia*, the temple which you defile. You have committed an act of unpardonable heresy in the eyes of the *Deceiver*. He has willed that your punishment be severe."

A terrible smile grew across Amaria's face. "I have defiled your church?" She craned her neck at an upward angle, and a wad of spit issued from her mouth. The world seemed to freeze as every man present watched the ichor arch across the room and splatter against the alter, landing directly upon the face of the graven image of Wyur."

Uroshish turned the color of fire. "Bitch! You infernal unholy whoremaiden!" he spat, barely able to form words amidst his rage. "You dare despoil Wyur's image! Kill her now!"

Amaria didn't wait to see what fantastic spells the surrounding wizards could toss her way. She went at the nearest one, an unfortunate fellow in the midst of casting when she removed his head with one blow. Alas, seven more remained, and they invoked magic with deadly intent. Amaria caught sight of yellow darts coming her way, and she bent her torso just enough to avoid them. They splashed against the wall, burning holes in the deeply stained wood. She recalled the acid spell that Thavas had conjured and the horrifying damage it had done to Hysth's guard, and she silently thanked the gods for her nimbleness.

Magical projectiles and bolts of light seemed to fly toward her like a veritable hailstorm. Through total concentration and skill she evaded most, cutting down a second victim in the process. A strange grinding noise began to echo in her ears, though she hadn't time to investigate. Something sharp stabbed into her shoulder blade from behind, knocking her to her knees. She reared up and fought on, ignoring whatever damage she'd incurred. The third wizard froze in fear when she whirled his direction. He never made a sound, even when his blood soiled her blade.

In a bizarre moment of clarity, Amaria noticed that the barrage of spells went suddenly absent. Her entire left arm ran crimson, but she cared not what the extent of the injury was, for she suddenly understood why the wizards had stopped their casting. Looming in the center of the sanctum, swaying gently as it inspected its new environs, stood the most demonic, ghoulish construct she had ever laid eyes upon.

Over ten feet tall, the closest natural beast Amaria could compare it to was a warped version of a mantis. It bore the same color and carried a similar wedge-shaped head. Its mouth was an ovular cavity with two curled pincers on the ends, and two fulvous, annular eyes sparkled and seemed to notice everything all at once. But this thing had legs like that of a human, only larger! Its gaunt, rigid torso carried long arms that sharpened into points.

The remaining wizards, save for Uroshish, who watched discreetly from a dark corner, were massacred like rats in a fit of confused hysteria; for they never even defended themselves. Whatever this atrocity was, whomever it faced, it had one sole purpose; to kill. The fiend lumbered toward her, dislodging and smashing the benches like straw, all the while emitting an insect-like click-clack sound. When the monster thrust an arm at her, Amaria ducked beneath and lifted her sword into the huge limb. The maneuver would have cut through a human's arm, but it merely crafted a slight gash upon the stiffened crust-like covering of the demon. No fluid drained from the tiny lesion, and the beast angrily battered the side of her head like a club to a piece of fruit. The woman lurched across the floor, all limbs and hair. Free of her hand, her sword careened against a wall.

Dizziness swept over her, blackening her vision and pounding her head. She swayed when she attempted to gain her feet and tumbled over a broken piece of bench, landing hard amid the shattered debris of wood. The fiend never hesitated, coursing toward her with all the grace of a hulking giant inside a tiny room. Amaria had no time for respite. She forced herself upright and unsteadily searched for her sword, now hidden somewhere amid the wreckage.

The mantis-like creature had reached her again. Weaponless, she dodged the savage thrust of its sharpened arms and tried to put distance between her and the fiend by skirting to the other corner of the sanctum. As she turned to run, she felt a twinge, like a pulled muscle in her back. It was no pulled muscle, however. The demon's second thrust scored true, plunging through the right side of her lower back, alongside the spine.

The pain came moments later, and Amaria collapsed to her knees, weakening by the heartbeat. She tried to crawl away, but she could hear that awful vibrating sound emanating from the monster directly behind her.

Something bludgeoned her across the head. It felt like her

brain exploded. Her eyesight drifted, and then she knew no more.

An endless sea of shadow.

Nothing could accurately describe the emptiness that encased Amaria when her senses returned. It seemed she floated in eternal darkness. There was some kind of solidity beneath her, steadying her, but when she looked down, she saw nothing but drifting darkness coiled ceaselessly below. Either she had gone utterly mad, or some kind of invisible ground prevented her from a downward helix. She pressed her hand against it. It felt smooth and cold, like a marble floor underground.

Amaria sat up and instantly noticed she bore no wounds, her flesh hale and unblemished. Gazing about, she quickly discovered there was very little to see, as if she loomed far above the world, the night sky embracing her with a pall of obscurity. Some ambient, sourceless light gave just enough illumination for her to see for miles if she wished, and yet she suffered an impression of blindness. There was literally *nothing* around her. Had she been mistakenly cast into some empty void for all eternity? She hesitated to stand, fearing that the hidden ground would cease to support her and she would fall eternally.

"You have the look of unease, milady."

Amaria swung her shoulders aft and found a man standing only a few feet away. She recognized him instantly. *Aohed!* He looked exactly the same as before.

Like her, his feet pushed against nothing but black expanse. He took another step closer, his manner unconcerned over the apparent invisible floor. When they made eye contact, he smiled.

"I had contemplated bringing you here. Quite the quarrel I had with myself, in fact. My logical reasoning had warned against it. It told me that the world was better off with you dead." The old man chuckled briefly. "It is not always easy to follow one's logical reasoning, even when you're a god."

"What am I doing here?" Amaria asked. "Is this my place in the afterlife?"

The old man shook his head. She could have sworn his eyes

laughed at her. "No, Knight of the Dove, this is not your place in the afterlife. Just so you know, you aren't dead, at least not yet. I've called you here to help you."

Amaria threw an exasperated arm in the air. "How will you do that? I have already been defeated."

"You haven't been defeated, Amaria, and your help comes as a simple reminder. You have an entire source of power within you that you have yet to exploit in this battle. Release that power. Use the theurgy that courses through your veins. You have used it before, at Erdoth Fortress, if you remember. With it, you will defeat that demon Urosish has constructed."

"Theurgy?" She furrowed her brow and spat, "You mean magic! Bah! Do you not remember? The dark gods gave me such magic, and only because I called upon them. I have no wish to exercise their services again."

Aohed bit his lip, thinking. "I hesitate to call it magic, milady, for I don't speak of common tricks or illusions. What you have is more of an innate strength gifted to you since birth. The dark gods didn't give it to you at Erdoth, they merely fueled it, kindled its flames, so to speak."

The woman shook her head, confounded. "What are you saying? I can summon power akin to that of a wizard?"

"It is a gift, Amaria Eversvale, but not one to take advantage of. The theurgy runs *through* you, is a part of you. When you apply it, a part of your essence is used up. Overuse, and you'll wither like dried fruit. In this instance, however, I believe it is essential if you wish to survive."

Amaria spun the information in her mind. She had always known something was different, special, about her, for it had been too obvious to overlook. But the arcane? She hadn't spent a single day under the tutelage of a mage in all her life. "What kind of person I am to hold such power? Tell me who I am."

The figure sighed and rubbed his chin. The lines of age and the frail body did nothing to hide the vast knowledge that sparkled in those timeless eyes. At last, he offered a tapered smile, though no cheer shown within. "I suppose it is time you are told. This has carried on long enough. Listen carefully, though, for you haven't much time."

His voice turned very soft.

"You are not a natural creation, as you may have guessed. You were birthed by a human, but your conception is far more complicated," Aohed paused, then glumly added, "and rather unfortunate. You see, you are the brainchild of a united plot envisioned by the dark gods. In secrecy, they pooled the greatest of their powers into a seed which they planted in an unsuspecting commoner. You were to be their tool to wreck havoc upon the physical realm, diminish the numbers of those who serve of the gods of light, and to disseminate general chaos. They wished to use the destruction you caused to assert their own foothold as the role of saviors to a crumbling world. Most likely, they never even considered the fact that they'd still have each other to contend with after you completed your task."

"So, I am evil." It was spoken like a statement of fact.

"No. Well, to be more exact, yes and no. By mere chance, one of my lesser brethren discovered their baleful scheming and revealed it to me. We had little time to waste, for their dark seed had already been sowed in the human female. You contained so much power, even in the womb, that we couldn't destroy you. In a hastily arranged meeting, we came to the only conclusion we saw possible. We infused you with our own powers as well. It was all we could do to counter the dark gods. Thus, upon your birth, you were bestowed a fearsome sundry of potency from all the gods. Nothing like you has ever existed in this world, and such as it is, you have become a sort of 'personal battleground' between the deities. They have, and will continue to, manipulate you for their own means."

Silence engulfed Amaria. She sat like a statue, her chest's rhythmic breaths the only sign of life while she absorbed the shattering knowledge Aohed imparted upon her. It was too much to handle at once. She felt like an overfilled waterskin, the fluid spilling over the neck.

"Think on this, Amaria," Aohed added. "The death of your real parents was no action of happenstance. Nor the tragedy of Royce. The dark gods were playing their game, developing your darker nature in hopes of bending it to their will. You are a dangerous soul, made even more dangerous by the fact that good and sinister forces have such interest in you. Do you think that Hysth will let you be, after Urosish is dead? He will not. You will be hounded, your strings pulled, until the day your wasted body is lowered beneath the earth."

"Then I am better off dead!" she shouted with abrupt ferocity. "Why do you give me advice to succeed?"

The old man showed no reaction to her starting outburst. "Because you still have a conscious. Make no mistake, lady, you are mortal. A part of you is still human, birthed by a mortal mother. You are like a woman balancing upon a fence. The thin width of the picket is your own will, but on either side looms the will of those who strive to control you. To maintain your balance is difficult, but possible. Bear in mind, there is good in you as well. Although I regretted your initial existence, a part of me is reluctant to let you go."

And with that, the life Amaria Eversvale once knew vanished forever. Her outlook, her beliefs, rendered asunder and all that remained was the foreboding knowledge that she would never be free of her tormentors. Her life, her existence, would be a constant struggle to retain sanity.

Then something else sparked within her, stubbornness. She had always been intractable to an extent, but now the element swelled, as if rising up to meet the challenge. Many things in the world Amaria hadn't control over, but she could hold fast to her stubborn nature with fervor unlike the world had ever seen. Perhaps that would be her sanity.

The old man watched her closely, gauging her subtle response. In time, he said, "Had we time to discuss the philosophical ramifications of what I have told you, I would be more than willing. However, a friend of yours is dying at this moment to save your life. You must return."

Realization hit her, and she leapt to her feet. "Ornan! Send me back, Aohed!"

"Farwell, milady." The aging man wavered and grew insubstantial, as if reality itself could not hold him. He blinked, then disappeared altogether. Her own head throbbed glaringly, and it felt like a sharp stick poked her back. Shutting her eyes fretfully, she attempted to alleviate the suffering that wracked her. She was overcome with a sensation of freefalling, her limbs flailing uncontrollably as she plummeted to a melancholy bottomless pit.

When her eyes reopened, the amber hues of *Wyurnescia's* sanctum greeted her with contempt.

The scene coalesced around her like parts of a dream stitched together forming a whole. Amaria sprawled clumsily among the wreckage of the sanctuary, face down. Her head still labored and gnawing pain seized her back with every subtle movement. After considerable effort she managed to push up on her elbows and view the scene around her.

Demolition. The interior of the once hollowed chamber was now nothing short of ruin. Every last bench had been rendered to kindling, the idol upon the dais fallen and cracked in half, and even the windows shattered. A part of her found illicit pleasure in the devastation, but there was no time for such gratification. A solitary figure, warring like a man possessed, stood against the menacing demon. Ornan, and he did not look well. His body, half his face, was drenched in crimson. Amaria could see clearly one gaping wound in his stomach, the hole crusted with black. His left arm seemed useless, hanging loosely at this side. He feigned and dodged to avoid the deadly limbs of the creature, but he slowed.

Immediately, she forgot her own pain. Overcome with urgency, she jumped to her feet and swiftly located her sword. Her fingers curled around the hilt with a sensation reminiscent of reuniting with an old friend, and she charged the lumbering fiend.

The creature noticed her movement, but only after she had hurdled into the air and plunged her sword into its exoskeleton-like chest. The triangular head squealed, and Amaria pulled free her blade, intent on a second strike. A sweep of its lumbering arm, and the monster batted her into the ground. She slammed hard into the debris-laden floor, and cried out as every nerve reignited in agony.

Ornan retreated into a corner, his face pale as a spectre. Back against the wall, the man slid to a sitting position, his chin barely held upright.

Enduring her discomfort, Amaria gritted her teeth and held fast her wits. The fiend already cleaved a path toward her, showing no ill effects from her savage sword thrust. She threw a glance at Ornan, catching sight of her loyal friend in a ravaged state.

As the creature drove its limb in spear-like fashion to impale her, she rolled to her right, avoiding the sharpened tip, and sprung upwards. Hilt in both hands, she swung with every scrap of strength that remained. Sparks of magical blue light enveloped her sword as it swept into the monster. With an inexplicable bright, radiant flash, the blade cleaved a path through the demon's neck. The bulbous eyes immediately lost their luster, and its head dropped away from its body as the giant figure crumbled to the ground, dead.

The sudden kill surprised even Amaria, and she gaped at the lifeless fiend in ominous silence for several seconds before remembering Ornan. The Radamite was near motionless in the corner, looking for all the world like someone had covered him in red and black paint. Arms limp, only his face maintained a glimmer of life. She ran to his side in moments.

"Ornan, my friend, look at me." The woman took his chin and held it up so she could gaze at him directly.

Her friend offered a weak smile. "I am glad to see you alive, shera." His voice sounded harsh and gritty. "I thought I had failed after the beast battered you unconscious."

She returned his grin. "You have never, nor will you ever, fail me. Hold and I'll get you healed up."

Ornan's smiled faded. He motioned to the gaping black mess of a wound in his stomach and ever so slightly shook his head. No words were needed to express the meaning.

"Godsdamnit, Ornan! After all this, you die?"

Strenuously, the Radamite lifted his right arm to Amaria. The woman took it in her own and held fast. "Shera, apparently you are not the only one with whom the gods use. I have fulfilled my purpose. You have lived, and with that knowledge I die. Thank you for your friendship, for it has meant everything to me."

She wanted to scream at him, though she wasn't sure why. Perhaps, to thank him for his emotional stability and unfathomable loyalty? Perhaps, to curse him for leaving her now, rendering her alone once again? She did neither. Instead, she held his hand tightly until his lids dropped and he breathed his last. She offered no tears, made no cries of mourning, for such gestures gave no comfort. It seemed another chapter of her sorrow was complete, another loss of a great friend layered to her conscious. A part of her expected such a conclusion, despite her angst and resistance. *How many more will die in my lifetime?*, she wondered. *Will I have no friends at all?*

"What have you done? You have destroyed the original shrine of the great Wyur! I curse your fallen friend, and I curse you for your debasement of a holy relic!" Urosish had appeared from some dark corner of the room, his robes flowing as he stepped over the wreckage of his home and place of worship. A strange mixture of unremitting hatred and awful realization ignited his face. His eyes reeked of the same look of death that had been on Thavas' face just before she killed him. "How can you justify this act of heresy?" he barked, voice cracking as he did so.

Amaria calmly stood and faced the high priest. He would die, she knew, for there was no other way to draw an ending to this gruesome event. "How can you justify the evils you have waged upon Valgamin? The dead councilmen? Look at you! Even now, you shake before me, like a groveling beggar! Do I inspire such fear from the great high priest of Wyur?" She spat and shook her head, scornfully. "You are a pathetic dog! The world will breathe freely with you gone from it."

"Die, unholy whore!" Urosish screamed, lifting his arm.

The Knight of the Dove rushed her foe. Blue light flashed from the high priest's hand, and she became aware of something pounding her chest. A wave of heat and pain consumed her, but even then, she did not halt her momentum. As she neared

Urosish, his face spasmed while he frantically attempted to conjure another spell, despite his fear. As the last syllable of his chant nearly escaped his lips, a terrible agony gripped him, and his voice failed.

Her sword tasted him, scourging his chest and prying through his backbone, pinning the unfortunate man against the wall. As the world he knew disappeared in that instant, he gave no last words, no final pronouncement to his god. He simply died, like any mortal of inconsequence.

For Amaria, it didn't feel like the cataclysmic finale of a great war, but rather one of dry mercy. No sense of accomplishment, no exuberance, or feeling of restored honor followed. Nor did she feel failure. It seemed she had no emotion at all. The outcome was decided, and nothing more. Still, the knowledge imparted by Aohed of who she was, *what* she was, remained strong. No longer would she stumble through life as an unknowing pawn.

The corpse of Urosish slid casually from her blade, collapsing to the ground with an uninspired, lifeless thud. Her emerald eyes glazed cold as she viewed his dead body, no remorse within her. While the pain of her wounds slowly writhed their way to the forefront of her thoughts, something made her believe that the trials of her existence had only begun.

Seventeen

The winter day was harsh. A bitter, frigid wind swept over the crest of the great mountain, taking pleasure as it pummeled anything which had not found shelter. A drab sky of grey dulled the world, offering no hope to the antagonistic scene, no joy to the colorless landscape.

Amaria sat upon the outer steps of the desecrated temple. Despite her wounds, she endured the fierce gusts that flung her ivory hair in all directions like white flame. She needed the fresh air, for the interior of that damnable building disheartened her, the very atmosphere dreary and unwelcome.

Behind, the door grinded open, and footsteps followed. She turned to see Peran immediately pull his jacket tightly around his body as he encountered the merciless wind. With him, two more men stepped outside, the final remnant of soldiers whom accompanied her to this place, for the rest found death amid a pursuit they knew little of. Was she to blame? Who could say? It was not their fight. Yet, Veran had been adamant that she not go alone, conscripting the contingent of Valgamin militia to accompany her. In the end, they had slain Thavas and the others, but how much triumph can be said of an outcome where nearly everyone dies, including her most loyal friend?

For five days they rested within the walls of *Wyurnescia*, healing their wounds and gathering strength for a difficult hike back down Urak's Edge. During that time, they had buried the dead of Valgamin, and burned the dead of Wyur.

"How are you feeling, milady?"

Jerris, the young prison guard turned grizzled warrior within two weeks time, sat beside her along the steps. He had shown much resourcefulness during the scrum inside the temple, and she felt proud of him for it. The other Valgamin soldier, a man named Kaoere, was a classic brawler. His wounds proved far more severe than Jerris', and Amaria had initially suspected he wouldn't survive the first night after the skirmish. The man was stubborn, however, and after she'd sewn together two of his more grievous injuries, including a nasty laceration on his neck, he was clearly improving.

Peran had spoken little since the battle. Amaria wondered how many men he had struck with his arrows, and the impact it had doled upon him mentally. He suffered no injuries, but his face demonstrated an indescribable anguish. The squirrelly escort would never be the same after this episode, and Amaria suffered guilt for forcing it upon him.

"I heal," Amaria answered Jerris, staring straight ahead into the wintry air.

The young man grunted a response. "Yes, we heal what can be healed. But, the memories of this place will never mend."

Amaria turned to look upon Jerris, his youthful face showing newly gained knowledge. "A friend once told me that in time, memories heal if you give them the chance." She shrugged. "I know not if that is true, for I have yet to let my own memories heal."

Silence held them for many heartbeats, and then a different voice spoke. "We should leave this place soon." Peran looked at her, his face tired for no reason. "Two more nights of recuperation, and then I depart for Yhull. I yearn for my home."

She nodded. "We will follow. You have done everything I've asked and more. I hope the loot recovered from this place shall keep you from forced work ever again."

"It is not work I worry about, milady. It is what I have seen that haunts me."

Amaria had no words to make things better, so she said nothing. The woman simply wished to let this episode of her life drift away, to disappear amid the cyclone that was, and is, her tortured life. For now, she basked in momentary serenity, and she understood that such moments would be rare for the remainder of her life. With Jerris next to her, the woman sat quietly and let the bracing wind wash her face.

Epilogue

"Milord, pardon the intrusion, but word has been sent from the gates that the soldiers whom accompanied Mistress Eversvale have returned."

Veran nearly dropped the quill in his hand. "Returned? Are you certain?"

The servant nodded. "Quite, milord."

The councilman rose to his feet. "Have them escorted to the main stables. Prepare several attendants to see to the needs of the exhausted soldiers. And summon Councilman Andor as well. Quickly now, go."

"Yes, milord."

The servant hustled away, leaving Veran alone in his office. *I wonder what news they bring?* A boyish excitement filled the man as he gathered his linen jacket and dressed it over his doublet. With nothing else to bring, he exited his study and urgently paced down the bare corridors of the council hall. In the late hour, few others ran errands, but Veran greeted them all as he passed by. Two sets of stairs, and then he went beyond the front doors, standing at the dais to the hall entrance.

An hour ago, the chill of darkness had suppressed the melancholy colors of winter. Snow glittered in the air, exceedingly visible near the great oil lamps that surrounded the large building. Veran pulled his hood about his face and skulked forward into the night, heading for the large stables maintained strictly for use by the council and its retainers. The worst of the winter storms had yet to arrive from the mountains, but the nobleman still mumbled irritably to himself about the weather. Ever since relocating to Valgamin twenty years ago, it was the cold he hated most. In Jorusio, the place of his birth, far to the south, he had come to tolerate the fiercely humid summers, and truly enjoyed the coolness of the colder seasons. But, in

Valgamin, he would never accept the stark, unforgiving winters and the obtrusiveness of the snows.

Though only a walk of two minutes, the canopy of the stables didn't come soon enough. Islanar, the stablemaster, awaited him. The sturdy, muscular man wore sleeveless leathers, and Veran pondered how he did not freeze to his death.

"Milord, I have cleared the main circle for our soldiers. All other mounts have been placed in stalls."

Veran nodded as he reached the overhang, his buckled boots stepping in filth and grime. "Very good. We should be expecting twenty horses, all of them tired and hungry."

"Food has been prepared, Councilman," Islanar affirmed.

Veran nodded and noticed the arrival of a dozen or so servants, all prepared to ease the burden of the returning men-at-arms. Ignoring them, he focused on the road. His seams were bursting in anticipation to witness their return, to hear their tale of a triumphant journey through the heart of Urak's Edge. After an indefinite period of lingering, a familiar voice interrupted his anxious musings.

"How is it that the two most prolific men in Valgamin stand shivering in the middle of night?"

The councilman looked upon a grinning Tyris. "It is rare indeed," he replied, "when the winter is the last thing on my mind, even as I stand amidst its wrath."

"Careful, my friend, for it will grow jealous of your inattention and grow even colder this year."

The elder councilman chuckled briefly before returning his focus upon the road, while Tyris commenced barking orders to the attendants. The sheer blackness seemed lifeless, until the resonance of several hoofbeats caused Veran to dart his eyes frantically into the speckled gloom. Then a procession became visible. First, there appeared four armed cavalry escorts. Behind them, emerging in slow increments, a column of horses.

In unison, the two councilmen cast glances at each other.

"Merciful Gods!" sputtered Veran.

Only two men, *two men*, rode upon the other horses. They looked haggard, their gear muddy and worn. Before he knew it,

Veran was running toward them, oblivious to the biting chill. The first rider he approached, a young man, looked down upon him, a vacant stare of exhaustion across his face.

"Where are the others?" Veran asked.

"There are no others."

The soldier had neglected to address him properly, as any member of the Valgamin militia should a councilman, but Veran overlooked such carelessness, especially considering the man's current state. "What do you mean, soldier? What has happened?"

"They are dead. We are all that is left." A brief pause, and then the rider continued, "The temple was found, and the evil destroyed."

Veran almost stumbled. "The woman? Is she dead?"

A curt shake of the head. "No. Mistress Eversvale is alive. She parted ways with us at Yhull upon our return trip, taking her horse and riding overland to the northwest. She gave no explanation, and very little farewell. Much of the temple loot she left to us, for the woman took little."

The councilman could hardly fathom the soldier's words. The Knight of the Dove had left! He had anticipated a great retelling of the events in order to justify his decision to free her. It seemed that wasn't going to happen. Fixing his vision on the young soldier, he exacted, "I want to know everything that transpired."

The man opened his mouth to reply, but was interrupted by another.

"Veran, let these men rest for the night." Tyris had stepped forward. "For god's sake, look at them! Who could think clearly in such a condition? We can grill them come morning."

The elder man rubbed his temples and sighed. "Yes, of course." Casting about, he caught the eye of his retainer. "Get these men quartered in the council hall, and have them washed and cleaned."

The procession of horses was led away, and the two councilmen stood alone in the brisk night. Tyris placed a gentle hand on Veran's shoulder. "We will uncover this riddle tomorrow, my friend. You could use a little sleep yourself."

Hunching, the weight of the world seemed to once again fall upon Veran's shoulders. "Do you think we shall ever see her again, Tyris?"

The man shrugged. "If there is an enigma of this world, it is that woman. We'll not know the answer until we see that white hair of hers come striding through the city gates."

Veran nodded, solemnly.

"Come," said Tyris, "let us escape this cold. The both of us will be dead should we stand here much longer."

In chorus, two friends strode back to the council hall, leaving a path of footprints amid fine white powder in their wake.

About the Author

William A. Kooiker lives in central Virginia with his wife and daughter. <u>Knight of the Dove</u> is his second novel and third published work. His previous work includes the critically acclaimed novel <u>Tower of Ruin</u>. Visit him at:
http://www.williamkooiker.com

Discover other fine Kerlak publications at:

http://www.kerlak.com

Printed in the United States
100175LV00003B/196-204/A